The Forgotten Gods

KATIE CROSS

KCW

List Of Alaysian Words

Amicala—Friend of the mortals.

Beelae—Family dinner, normally with gods and demigods. A formal event, with high attire, that typically lasts six to eight hours, extending through seven different courses of food. Entertainment is often provided.

Bua—No.

Giuseppeglacidonium—Gio's full name.

Hatata lu Centray—Home of the bearers (Mothers).

Hatata lu Konzones—Kitchen, or home of the chef.

Hatata lu Monilary—Demigod home.

Ibarbelonbabellasaan—The Room of Great Power.

Monilay Rostina—Demigod castle.

Monilay mal—Bad demigod.

Nonnatusnevillatoputatazo—Island of the Amulets.

Rostina lu Lune—Castle in the sky.

Rostina—Castle, also a shortened version of *Rostina lu Lune*.

Sangessa—Allegiance. A deal made between a mortal and a demigod, where the demigod agrees to care for the mortal with magic and basic needs while the mortal is loyal to that demigod for the rest of their life.

Seema—Fruit native to Alaysia, with seeds and edible rind inside. Grows on a bush along the sand.

Tagata—Protector, friend, that's often a family member. A tagata is assigned to a mortal or half-mortal child when they are young to help them learn about their role in Alaysia.

Tirra mora—Firm ground.

Umu—Ground-growing Alaysian fruit with juice inside.

God Magic Amulets

IGNIS
> Luppentonisa
> Samthanruadanosa
> Handuinolomolokaya

GELAS
> Kibbukonialamonta
> Nicomedianthekus

VENTIS
> Oceanusorilianno

To Mike Thompson.
An epic metaphorical throat-puncher.
The world's best Trivia Master.
My eternal friend.

Love ya, ya filthy #(@#%(!)(@#$*

Introduction

THE FORGOTTEN GODS takes place about a week or so after RISE OF THE DEMIGODS ends.

There are some novellas that I've released in between these two novels to help broaden your picture of Alaysia and Alkarra.

Of particular interest to you might be DEREK, the seventh novella in The Network Saga.

While Bianca is cavorting around Alaysia, Derek is in Alkarra dealing with his *own* set of issues. Both stories happen at the same time, but in the two different lands. For maximal reading enjoyment, I recommend you dive first into DEREK so you know more of what's happening in Alkarra while Bianca is in Alaysia.

There are no spoilers in DEREK.

You don't have to read it, but I highly recommend it.

You can buy it by going to www.katiecrosssbooks.com. Type DEREK into the search bar to find your copy in all formats.

It's only available on my website in all formats at katiecross books.com.

Let's just say that you won't regret it.

Derek Black is one witch that never disappoints.

—Katie

Chapter One

A splash woke me from a deep sleep.

Midnight opened in dark, silky petals over my cottage, coating the forest in shadows. A gentle breeze sifted through branches overhead, twining through a canted window. The wind danced over my skin, sharply cool. I shivered. Dulled moonlight lingered in the wood, never making it to the forest floor. Patches of snow still lingered in the deepest root wells.

Another splash.

The hair on the back of my neck straightened. There should be no gathered water in the middle of my cottage, deep in the sprawling heart of Letum Wood.

I cast a spell to amplify sound and the quiet rang too loud. My heart pounded in painful slams. Priscilla had moved out. She lived in the old building for Miss Mabel's School for Girls as she transformed it into Miss Priscilla's School for Girls.

Was the noise real?

Had I imagined it?

A drip of water followed.

My body tightened. Not my imagination, then.

Had Ava come? No. She never visited at night. How would she get here? Besides, why would she make water sounds? The sinuous remnants of a dream, perhaps? A glint hovered over my bed, flashing in the low light.

Not a dream, either.

I threw my arm out to reach for my sword, Viveet, which hung on the wall to my left. Before my fingers snatched her metal hilt, a whip wrapped my ankle. The clammy grip tightened.

I screamed.

Everything disappeared.

* * *

Icy water surrounded me.

The shocking embrace forced me to close my mouth, hold my breath. Salt water burned my eyes when I opened them to see watery darkness. My arms flapped, attempting to find *up*. The pressure on my body, the utter disorientation, sent me into a panic. I suppressed a scream to save precious air.

A quick transportation spell yielded no change.

I paused, tried again.

No movement.

The glacial water closed in like a restricting glove. A blaze burned through my chest as I held onto the air. How long could I hold my breath? Not much longer, but perhaps enough. Batting aside questions of who—or what—wanted to kill me, I renewed my efforts to orient myself.

My next step was to find the surface . . . or die trying.

Pain assaulted my eyes when I forced them open. I lifted both hands to my face and released a trickle of air. Bubbles dribbled over my fingertips, moving up. That way to the top, then.

I paddled the same direction, dizzy. The urge to release all the air inside my lungs nearly drove me to do so. With great concentration, I let go of another thin stream. Bubbles slipped free, slowly. The exhale provided a reprieve as I worked my way up, up, up.

Tingles spread through my chest. I swam harder. My head grew thick, murky as the water. Darkness closed in as the last air escaped. Horror drove me faster.

The hunger intensified.

Papa, I thought. *Papa.*

The watery whip from earlier slipped around my left wrist and yanked. I jerked, shocked from the sensation. I raced higher and higher. Too long. It was still taking too long. A bucking sensation overcame my chest—my body wanted to breathe, but I wouldn't let it.

Thoughts blurred.

Papa.

Fear ripped through me. Hot and bright and desperate to just *breathe* already.

I broke into the air.

The cord released me as I soared into the sky with a giant gasp. Equally frigid air assaulted me a second before I crashed back to the water. I recovered a single breath before a wall of water slammed into me from the left. The contact knocked me senseless. Head over feet, I tumbled through a wave.

My fractured thoughts recovered when I calmed. The frightening struggle stopped. *Something* had brought me here, then saved me at the last moment. Dare I wait to see if it would save me again?

Unlikely.

The top of the water found me on its own. I rose into the air, stole another breath, and shoved the hair out of my face. A second gasp followed, then a third. The anxiety dissipated as I gathered my bearings. A quick scan confirmed no incoming waves.

Also, no land.

Only bitter cold, sparkling sea.

Tremors wracked my body as I pulled my arms closer to my chest. My teeth clattered like old bones. Numbness spread through my fingers, toes. My cheeks hurt and eyes burned like coal. The sordid facts lay out in an obvious array now.

Nearly dead.

Dark ocean.

Midnight sky, speckled with stars.

"Prana!" I snapped. "What do you want?"

A low drawl rolled from behind me. "I should have let you drown."

I swirled around with a weak sputter. A cloud moved away from the moon. Light raced across the ocean in a rippling line, right to a shadowy figure on top of the water.

Prana hovered a few paces away, her bare feet riding on top of a circular, constantly-rolling wave. A tenebrous, emerald gown moved like seaweed around petite ankles. It pasted to her squat figure, tight as skin. Water rose to her knees, then lowered, never higher than her waist.

Her wet-appearing hair tumbled to the side as she cocked her head. Malevolent dislike contorted her features.

Beyond her, waves agitated in a circle at least forty paces high. Any attempt to swim past them would be a death wish.

"Why didn't you god magic your way to the top?" she asked.

Silently, I cursed myself. To admit to Prana that I'd forgotten would be embarrassing. God magic was still so new, so untested, that I tried to ignore it as much as possible.

"Lovely prison," I muttered instead.

She brightened into a grim smile. Her slanted, glinting eyes appeared black in this light. Moonlight gave her skin a yellowish hue.

"We have much to discuss," she said briskly. "I'd prefer to spend as little time in your presence as possible."

"Th-the feeling is m-mutual."

Frozen clumps of hair trembled around my head. My scalp prickled painfully from the sheer cold.

Prana rolled her eyes.

Deep in my stomach, a heavy tightness formed. The confrontation I'd been secretly dreading for months had finally come. All the stored words that I'd planned to say to her disappeared. The cold made it impossible to think and my near-drowning didn't make me amenable to anything.

"While it's l-lovely to see you, and I'd prefer b-being asked to tea, c-can you get it over with now?"

Prana snarled with bared teeth. A fin rose from the water behind her, skimming outside the cresting waves. I ignored it. Certainly, I didn't imagine the graze of something on the bottom of my foot, however.

"You have failed to keep your end of our bargain, witch."

"Not true."

Prana leaned forward, fists on her ample hips. "Defend yourself."

"The exact wording of m-my agreement stated that I would *try* to banish the demigods."

She hissed. Water freckled the air around her, flailing in globules.

I ignored her ire.

"That I can amply prove, considering that I stopped an uprising, collected a few amulets, and rid Alkarra of the demigod pests."

"Death of a few idiotic demigods is hardly *dealing* with the problem. More will come."

"That was the agreement. The r-responsibility for the rest of this mess you've made is on you. Our agreement is fulfilled."

Water surged over my head and shoved me down. I flailed,

forced myself to calm, and resurfaced. When I shoved the damp hair out of my eyes—my face had gone strangely numb—Prana's elegant dress smoldered in various shades of green, like an underwater coal. Her terrible majesty glowed against the dark sky. She glared down her thin nose.

The first time I met her, my annoyance had overridden my fear of Prana. With this strange glow to her skin, and the building power of magic lingering in the air, I finally understood why Sanako credited Prana as a foe worthy of fear. Desperate Prana had morphed into Livid Prana. I had reason to be afraid.

"The demigods have been tempered in Alkarra for now," Prana hissed. She'd wrestled her tone back under control. "They have not been *banished* and witches still have a problem. While I cannot revoke your magic, you also cannot give up this fight."

"I never said I would."

"We need them gone for good."

"What are you going to do?" I flung a half-frozen hand around us. "Do you plan to put up magical walls to keep the world out of Alkarra? I'd love to see that."

The same whip-like tool yanked me back to the watery depths. It held me in place until my chest burned. The drive for air built slowly. Too slowly. The desire to sleep followed, made me fuzzy. When the surface returned, I gave a pitiful gasp. Water filled my throat, my nose.

I gagged.

"Why are you going to Alaysia?" she demanded.

Water streamed over my face. I reached up, shoving the hair out of my eyes with a growl.

"Stop trying to kill me!"

"There must be a reason you're going to the land of the gods. What is it? What is your plan? Do you have an idea for keeping them out of Alkarra that this trip will satisfy? Tell me what's in that worthless, witchy head of yours."

"The god magic. I want to see if Ignis will take the magic out of me."

She snorted. "Are you a fool? God magic is easier to use than goddess magic. It's so simple that an idiot demigod could use it."

"It's not m-mine."

"And goddess magic is?"

My response halted.

Unfortunately, she had a point. I just couldn't quite grasp it through the slow-moving thoughts.

"What do you know about Deasylva?" she asked.

"N-nothing."

"Worthless ingrate," she muttered. Prana heaved a giant, dramatic sigh. Her pudgy shoulders lifted and fell with the movement. "You think you'll survive? *You* are the witch to cause such an unexpected twist in magic? By the sisters, Deasylva adores her fools. You should just stay home. Do nothing."

Her glittering gaze fixed on me. I vaguely registered the idea that she tested me. Perhaps told me *not* to do it so that I would.

Or did I imagine all of this?

My resolve to get rid of the god magic hardened, though it felt like my thoughts sifted through a narrowing tunnel. The frame of mind formed slowly. Vaguely, I registered that this wasn't good. My lips were frozen and awkward. I commanded my hand to fold into a fist, but couldn't be sure it obeyed. The violent shivers ached all the way into my ribs.

Prana mulled me over.

"I'm going. Unless," I added, unable to help myself, "you take care of your own problems . . . for once."

Prana thrust me back into the water.

When I finally came to the top again, my brain didn't work. The cold slipped into a deadened darkness.

"Consider this your warning." Prana towered over me, a shadow against darkness. "Go to Alaysia, do what you must. Fix this, obligation or not, so you don't lose your forest. I don't know what your magic will do over there. No witch has ever been to Alaysia and, like witches, magic changes. It evolves and grows. My sisters like to think we control magic, but we do not. We tame magic, we don't make it. Magic belongs to itself. We channel it, and it gives us greater purpose. God magic has the same origins, but different paths, different loyalties. You're putting yourself into a world you don't understand."

The implications of what she said rolled around my mind like pebbles. They shifted to and fro, lost in the greater machinations of a bid to survive. A distant part of my brain felt surprised by her shift in conversation.

Was she giving me advice moments after telling me *not* to go?

Confusion dissipated. I could hardly comprehend anything but keeping my head above water. Breath. Life. Vision. It required too much.

"You have been warned," Prana snapped. "Don't do anything stupid over there. Remember your forest, trust no one. Don't come back until you've chosen your side and you might make it out of there alive."

* * *

Water became a hard thud at my back.

The welcoming warmth of my cottage appeared all at once. I gasped, brought in another giant breath, and collapsed against the wooden floor. No fire crackled in the hearth. No light illuminated the space. With a spell, I started a fire. It blazed so hot it leapt out of the hearth, then settled back inside. The burst of heat drew my dazed mind out of its narrow focus.

Cold.

So cold.

Prana.

Dripping wet, I lay back and closed my eyes. Prana's words

rang through my mind. *Remember your forest, trust no one. Don't come back until you've chosen your side and you might make it out of there alive.*

I gently banged my head against the floor with frustrated misery. One thought twirled around as I dismissed Prana from my mind, eager to get warm again.

Monilay mal.

Chapter Two

My knuckles rapped softly on a wooden door, nestled in the hushed halls of Chatham Castle. It creaked open. A pair of warm eyes peered at me, then glimmered with a smile. The door opened, and I slipped in.

Marten welcomed me into the warmth of his personal apartment, a small affair along the back wall of Chatham Castle. Broad, sparkling windows overlooked a swath of Letum Wood and dark sky. Every now and then, the shadow of a flying forest dragon could be seen in the moonlight. Flames bounced around a stone hearth opposite us, washing the room in buttery light.

"Merry meet," Marten murmured, his voice a raspy rumble. He wrapped me in a comforting embrace. I sank deeper into it, relishing the heat. Despite a wool dress, pants, three pairs of socks, dried hair, and my cloak, the arctic temperature of Prana's grasp continued to hold me in its clutches. My body shivered every now and then.

Marten pulled back to study me. Lines wrinkled his forehead, lending greater depth to his expression. He put both hands on my cheeks.

"Are you sure you must do this?" he whispered.

"Yes."

Concern washed over his features. He gave a small smile, then gestured toward a divan near the fire. I lowered into it. An expansive painting of Mildred lingered over the hearth. Her stern visage, softened by curious eyes, peered out of history. Hints of Papa appeared in her jaw. The angle of her nose.

As always, she saw right into my frightened soul.

"She's a force of nature, even in death," Marten mused with a chuckle. I laughed, unable to help it.

"Definitely."

The fire beckoned me closer as I sat on the far side of the divan, closest to the flames. As always, a pot of tea steamed on a small cherry wood table. Notes of mint filled the air. Bookshelves, rugs, and a few pots of dried flowers here and there carried a homey ambience. Marten's smell, a mix of sage and leather, comforted me when he sat close.

For all the coziness, it felt bathed in echoes.

"I didn't wake you?" I asked.

His gaze flickered to the clock. 4:30 in the morning. A wry smile crossed his face as he rubbed his fingers together, holding them closer to the flames.

"Old men have a hard time sleeping."

I snorted. "It's impossible to think of *you* as old. You're timeless, Grandfather."

He hooted. "Coming from the girl that calls my only son an *old man*, I'm flattered. I was . . . up most of the night, thinking about you going to Alaysia today."

Mention of Papa subdued my initial response. Marten eyed me. I opened my mouth to speak before him, recognizing that I had a narrow window of time to change the subject. He beat me to it.

"Speaking of your father," he drawled.

I scowled.

Marten nudged my knee with his. An affectionate gesture,

but I still couldn't look at him. A sludge-like darkness enveloped me from the inside, sticky and hot. Papa was the main subject I didn't want to discuss.

"I don't want to talk about Papa."

The words curled inside me, like a defensive porcupine. There was nothing else to say, or there was so *much* to say that I couldn't.

"Tell me," he murmured.

I closed my eyes. Only a week had passed since the demigods had attempted an uprising. A week in which Scarlett and other Network leaders gradually stamped out the worst of chaos and fear.

Other Network leaders.

Not Papa.

Papa had ceded the throne to Scarlett in a shocking move, then disappeared after the fight with the demigods. Not a trace. Not a breath. Only a vague note that explained nothing and left more questions.

Now? He was adrift somewhere in Alkarra.

Rumors abounded through the *Chatham Chatterer,* which populated articles about him daily. Speculations over his death continued, but Scarlett had eased those by saying, *Our former High Priest deserves a rest. He made a decision he felt was best for the Network. Let's honor his work and press forward into more necessary changes.*

"I'm angry with Papa. Really angry."

"Yes." Marten gave a wry smile. "I can sense that."

I shot to my feet.

"Why did he leave?" I burst out, unable to contain it. "He left me without saying anything. He . . . he was ready to die that night. That's why he handed the throne to Scarlett, and he didn't even *warn* me. Grandfather, I could have been an orphan. I lost Mama. I can't . . ."

Finally free now, the ugly words stained my mood. More

putrid than ever. I'd spent the last week holding them inside, trying to make sense of how betrayed I felt.

Papa didn't owe me an explanation for everything he did, but . . . a decision of this significance? We had been a team. Ever since Mama died, we'd come together in a new way. When he left this time, the team dissolved. My trust in him crumbled, like a bridge of spun sugar.

"What makes his departure different this time?" Marten asked. "Your father has always been moving in and out of your life without telling you where he's going or what he's doing."

"This time? I'm an adult. I'm the Head of the Sisterhood. He could have trusted me. Included me in his plans. Something!"

"Maybe he didn't *because* you're an adult."

My thoughts jumbled around his observation.

What did *that* even mean?

I paced in front of the fire, hands propped on my hips. Heat from the flames curled along the floor, but I barely felt it. Amidst all the complicated emotions hid something else. A glimmer of light in the darkness, attempting uselessly to cache itself.

The pungent truth.

The unbearable fact that hurt the most.

Papa didn't trust me.

Marten shifted closer to the fire, lips puckered to the side. "He certainly surprised us all, and it's one interpretation of your father's decision. An angle that I never thought about, if I'm honest."

I blinked. "What's another interpretation of Papa's decision?"

Marten's brow rose. He lifted two hands in a gentle motion. "That your father had an entire Network on his shoulders. A Council that worked against him, and an unprecedented problem. He had no way to make everyone happy. Or, in many cases, *anyone.* After a lifetime of sacrifice and selfless service, it must have felt like a betrayal that his Network and his Council didn't believe in him when it mattered most. I believe your father needed . . . a break. History has certainly seen other leaders desire the same."

"Grandfather, he ceded the throne. He didn't ask for a vacation."

"Perhaps, he gave his Network—and himself, though he may not have realized it—a lifeline. You, of all witches, know how much your father has endured in his life. It has never truly been his own. He has always been in service to his Network."

Marten's grave words collected in my hollow heart, rattling with a shiver. I rubbed a hand over my face. While his explanation made sense, I couldn't accept it yet.

The teapot lifted, pouring into two cups with saucers. One swooped to me and hovered in place a few inches away. I accepted it as I stared into the flames. Steam rose out, twirling near my face. I ran the tip of my finger along the edge of the little plate.

Smooth, but firm.

If I pressed hard enough, would it break?

My gaze dropped.

"I think I understand."

Marten placed a hand on my shoulder. "Time and patience," he murmured. "They heal all wounds. Trust your father, for all may not be as it seems."

"I do trust him," I whispered. "So why didn't he trust me?"

The deeper, searching question wasn't lost on him. Marten regarded me with a baleful gaze before pulling me back into his arms. I sent the tea into the air with a spell and went willingly into the embrace, grateful for his strength. He had all but confirmed my churning suspicions. Papa had a bigger plan at work.

Probably dangerous and complicated. Or maybe he didn't

have a choice, and a reprieve served everyone. Papa had never liked the throne. All the newsscroll articles could be correct. The great Derek Black may have been tired of an ungrateful Network and hauled off, never to be heard from again.

Wasn't that just like Papa? Trust no one. Take the work into his own hands. Save the day. Bitterness filled my mouth like ash at the thought, followed by a sense of shame. This wasn't just about his lack of trust right now.

So many other issues lay behind Papa and me.

A lifetime of departures. An almost unfathomable gap. As a little girl, I'd accepted his role in the Network as Head of Protectors. What choice did I have? As a child, I hadn't appreciated how irritating and difficult Papa's secrecy and in-and-out had been. For years now, Papa had been a stable presence.

Which left me an uncertain mess. Like a child alone, frightened as she peered into the dark, I finally faced the decisions Papa had made throughout his life. He had done this constantly. Until now, I hadn't known that resentment lingered. Tucked away, like wraiths in the night.

With a shake of my head, I dismissed the collecting dark thoughts.

Not now.

Later.

"Baxter will arrive at my cottage with Ava soon." I cleared my throat. "We'll leave at first light."

Marten ran a hand down my hair with a forced smile. "I won't try to talk you out of this . . . wild idea. But I will caution you to be wary and patient. You'll be in a new world, alone, with no witch at your side. Your courage is admirable, but as you speak with the demigods or mortals or whomever you will encounter, I ask you to consider a bit more brevity."

A smile banished the last of my irritations with Papa. "You're telling me to calm my temper?"

"I'd say wittiness, but temper certainly applies."

I laughed. "That seems fair. I promise to be cautious."

"Thank you." Tears sparkled in his eyes as he squeezed my hand. "Come back to me, B? You are the brightest living manifestation of Mildred that I have. I could not bear to lose you both."

Chapter Three

Goat's empty pen stared at me after I returned to the cottage. Priscilla and Miss Celia had come for Goat last night. She would stay with them at the school while I was in Alaysia. Baxter had said, "This could take awhile. Gods tend to view time differently than the rest of us," with a great deal of uncertainty.

Really, no one knew what to expect from my time in Alaysia.

Ventis, god of wind, had extended a formal invitation and an offering of domicile to me, which made me his responsibility. Apparently, it provided greater protection from Ignis, but allowed Ventis to appease his curiosity about me, a living amulet.

The invitation was no easy feat, according to Baxter. To have a god agree to host a witch had never happened in Alaysia. Not to mention the fact that I'd broken—or stolen—several amulets, killed demigods, and, in general, caused an uproar to god magic.

I stood at my window with churning thoughts, my hand wrapped around a mug of cooling coffee. Amidst swirls of apprehension and dread, disbelief came in waves.

The land of the gods.

How could this be real?

A wintry day pelted the forest with miniature snowflakes and freezing fog. Viveet should have pressed against my left thigh, strapped to a special sheath that shrank her to the size of a dagger for easy storage. When I pulled her free, she returned to her regular size. The debate over whether or not to take her had waged in my head for days.

Ultimately, I didn't want anything to happen to her over there. Not with the question of goddess and god magic in the air. Viveet and the Volare were left in Leda's capable hands, for storage and safety. If I could call Viveet to me, I would do so when I needed her. In the meantime, a smaller dagger replaced Viveet for now. It sheathed on my thigh, just in case.

A shuffle of movement came from the depths of the forest. A flicker of shadow. Was someone out there? I peered to the right, but nothing moved again.

A gnome, perhaps.

The final sip of coffee bolstered my courage. I regarded the forest with an assessing eye a third time. Sometime in the night, the youngest saplings had rearranged themselves closer to my cottage, their trunks and branches braided together.

Why?

I asked, but they gave no definitive answer. Only gentle croons. Their anxiety had risen also, as if they knew what I was about to do. A rap came on my door. A flash of familiar, friendly heat rose in my blood, like someone had dumped warm water in my veins.

God magic.

Now that Baxter had arrived with an amulet, my goddess magic would be unpredictable. Spells and incantations were futile. Sometimes they worked, most of the time they didn't. I sighed, resigned to the battling magicks within, and used god magic to open the door.

"Merry meet," I called.

Baxter stepped inside, Ava at his side. Thick, black hair drifted around her shoulders, layered with dark streaks of red. Her broader nose was slightly scrunched, which pulled her eyebrows into intense slashes. Snowflakes lingered on top of her sapphire cloak, clasped at her neck.

Baxter didn't look much happier. Bags darkened the skin under his eyes, a testament to the demanding week following the rise of the demigods. Papa's disappearance—also not explained to or expected by Baxter—meant Baxter had no job or place in Alkarra. The last six days had kept him busy as he transitioned control of the Highest Witch's office to Leda and Scarlett and prepared to return to Alaysia.

He had no official reason to be in Alkarra anymore, which might explain his pained expression and melancholy mood.

"Well," I drawled, "aren't you excited to go home?"

Ava gazed away.

Baxter cleared his throat.

"*Home* will be busy and . . . unpredictable, so . . . maybe." The gloom alleviated into a brighter smile. "I am eager to see my sisters again, though. It's been three years, and I've missed many of them. Are *you* ready?"

His intentional emphasis seemed to imply that I didn't appear very ready. He was correct. I'd never be ready for something like this.

"Yes, I think so. Are you sure I shouldn't bring a change of clothes?"

"You'll blend in better if I provide them. There will be plenty," he tacked on, with the usual roguish smile that curled my toes.

On instinct, my hand reached to my hip, but Viveet wasn't there. The thought of departing Alkarra with only the clothes on my back left me feeling vulnerable. Unprepared.

"Anything?"

He shrugged. "My father will provide everything you need. As a reminder, we could be there several days before he's able to see you, so plan accordingly."

"You mentioned that."

He gave a distracted frown. "With any luck, we'll be able to meet with him before two weeks have passed."

I blinked. "So long?"

"Father is busy. We'll grab any opportunity we have to get his attention. Having you there, under his invitation, will make it easier to act fast. In the meantime, you can enjoy beautiful Alaysia." He grinned, white teeth sparkling. "I'm eager to show it to you. There are so many wonderful places."

"And remove the god magic."

His lips thinned. "It's a possibility we will definitely explore. Ignis . . ." He trailed away with a shake of his head. "Later."

A shiver traveled down my spine at his casual mention of Ignis, god of fire. Ignis' magic lived in me, which made me an amulet of god magic. Other implications might exist between me and Ignis, but *what* those could be we had no idea. My trip to Alaysia would provide as many answers as it would questions.

Considering that many of Ignis' demigod children had died in Alkarra and several amulets were lost thanks to me, going to the land of the gods painted a bleak picture. Ignis and I had a reckoning ahead of us, no doubt. I couldn't imagine the god thought highly of me.

Ava jabbed an elbow into Baxter's side.

"Returning home will also allow me to complete my mission," he added, "and set me free from Father's expectations."

"Free?" I murmured.

"My Father requires that his children who want to have an amulet complete a mission. Some half-mortals, too, like Ava. It's a coming-of-age ritual. A way to prove yourself. For demigods of

Ventis, it's a necessity. At the end of our mission, we report to the Council of the Gods. If we did well, we're given a much bigger amulet."

"That sounds great."

Baxter faltered, clearly torn between agreement and uncertainty. His teeth sank into his bottom lip. "Yes, in theory. In execution? We'll see. As long as Father holds a mission over my head, he controls me. Having that gone will help."

"Because he could say you haven't completed it yet and won't give you a better amulet?"

"Yes."

"I see."

"I don't know what my Father will ask of me by the end of my report." A tone of caution filled his voice. "Likely, he'll have a large reward and responsibilities."

"Is that a good thing?"

"I believe so."

The thought of Baxter gaining responsibilities also meant he'd be drawn back to Alaysia. For the first time, I contemplated that Baxter might not come back. My eyebrows lowered at the thought, which soured my stomach. That possibility hadn't been mentioned before, but hung in the air between us now.

As if he sensed my darkening thoughts, Baxter reached up and tucked a strand of hair behind my ears with a fond smile. My heart stirred. The light touch sent goosebumps over my arms. "Whatever you're thinking about so hard," he said quietly, "we'll figure it out."

I smiled.

He returned it.

His hand fell back to his side. Merrick rose in the back of my mind, but I pushed him firmly away. No. Merrick and I were friends. Baxter deserved a chance, and so did the quiet flurries in my stomach. Something existed between me and Baxter.

Alaysia would help me figure out just what it was.

Baxter's fingers tightened into a fist at his side. "Now that Ignis' children failed in their attempt to take Alkarra," he continued, "I've also been called to stand in front of the Council of the Gods to account for what I observed in the uprising."

"Will you be blamed?"

The fine hairs around his temple swayed when he shook his head. "No. Ignis allowed his children to attack and it had nothing to do with me. My mission was to keep an eye on Alkarra for my father and report signs of other demigods."

"You did that."

He frowned. "Yes, that will work in my favor. But keep in mind that the gods love control, Bianca. There's no telling what Father will ask of me by the end."

"That's . . . ominous."

Baxter's jaw tightened. He shrugged, then agreed with a nod. "It's Alaysia. Father will keep you safe. Ignis won't try to hurt you while you're under my father's protection."

"Why does he care?"

"Curiosity, probably." His tone turned musing. "I haven't spoken with him, so I'm not sure."

"Sounds great," I drawled.

The muscles around his jaw turned rigid, and I was struck again by a deep attraction to his bouncy curls and dark hair. Demigods had an allure. A sense of something about them that drew witches and mortals closer. Like a predator calling its prey.

Is that what drew me to Baxter now?

I doubted it.

But I didn't *know*.

"It'll work out," I said with forced lightheartedness. "You can always come back with me if your father doesn't want you to leave Alaysia. We'll find you a job in Alkarra."

He snorted. "If it doesn't work out there, how will I return?"

Oh.

Right.

Baxter relied on an amulet from Ventis in order to do magic. If Ventis took the amulet, Baxter would be stranded in Alaysia, little more than an overly-capable mortal himself.

"Thus you see the power of the gods." His arms spread, as if to say *what can I do*? "Father can take my amulet at any time and I'd have to stay in Alaysia, live under his power, for a very long time."

Transporting Baxter successfully from Alaysia to Alkarra with goddess magic would be very unlikely. While transportation magic wasn't complicated, it could be exhausting. More magical energy was required to cross longer distances, which made it unsafe. Witches had died transporting too far. Taking myself from Alaysia to Alkarra—once I'd finally been to Alaysia —would be difficult enough, if not impossible. Not to mention that goddess magic may not even work in the land of the gods.

For me to bring two of us back with such unpredictable circumstances?

Impossible.

"What if you didn't surrender the amulet?" I asked.

Ava sent me an amused glance.

He laughed, a brittle sound. "These are *gods*, Bianca. One doesn't just refuse the gods. With any luck, Father will see you right away and I can bring you back sooner, rather than later. Before any of the other gods or demigods realize you're there, preferably. A low profile would be best."

I shrugged. "I'm in no hurry, Bax."

"I know." His frown deepened. "Ignis may want to see you . . . or kill you. Are you sure this is a chance you want to take? You can politely refuse Father's invitation."

"I want to do this."

He sighed. This trip was Alkarra's only chance to get more

information. Questions abounded now more than ever and only a witch could answer the most important ones. Did goddess magic work in the land of the gods? If not, why? If so, did the magic operate the same way? Could spells and incantations cross distances?

These questions haunted me.

My limited experience with Ignis's amulet conjured up expectations of brimstone, flames, and darkness. A land of shadows, miserable mortals, demigods stalking around, and bitterness at each landscape. The real Alaysia couldn't be worse, at this rate, than what I pictured.

"The gods are cunning, Bianca." Baxter's brow lifted in warning. Hints of agitation lined his voice this morning. "You can't trust any of them, except my father. He's been attempting to protect Alkarra for years."

Protect, I thought, *or monitor himself?*

Exactly how benevolent could gods be?

My hand closed around the wooden box in my pocket. Inside it lay an amulet, obtained from a demigod during the uprising a week ago. Scarlett had quietly passed it to me in Letum Wood, in case I needed a bargaining chip, I presumed. I had no plans for using or returning the amulet while in Alaysia, except to potentially test a few of my theories.

Could gods call their amulets?

What would a god do to get their amulet back?

Baxter might think I'd enjoy a vacation in Alaysia, but I had plans for my downtime there. Big ones.

"What do gods look like, anyway?" I asked.

He shrugged. Ava yawned, head tilted back as she stared blankly at the wall. "Just like us. I don't know the details, though. I've only ever met my father."

"Really?"

"It's different over there," he said lightly, then held out a hand. "Beautiful, but different. Shall we go?"

Ava reached for my hand and I accepted. Her thin fingers crowding mine felt warm. She tightened her hold to the point of pain. Unlike goddess magic, god magic didn't require touch to transport someone, but I felt grateful for the anchor of her hand all the same.

"I'm taking us to my father's house first," Baxter said. "We'll figure it out from there."

The fire in my body brightened as I held my hand out to Baxter. He lifted his gaze to my eyes. His neck tightened, as if to steel himself.

With grim resolve, he threaded his fingers through mine. They felt warm and heavy, a reassuring press of comfort. He squeezed.

"*Monilay mal*," Ava whispered.

My cottage disappeared.

* * *

In little more than a blink, we arrived.

Sunshine blinded me when I opened my eyes. I held up an arm to block it, Baxter's fingers untangling from mine. Ava's tight grasp increased. The first thing that I saw was the glimmering ocean, a verdant band of blue all the way to the horizon.

"Sand and sky," I murmured.

Baxter's expression twisted. He closed his eyes, the breeze on his face with a bright flush.

The Alaysian sun lured me fully out of freezing Alkarra as I stepped closer to crashing waves. Sand welled up between my toes, crumbly as brown sugar. A breeze shuffled my hair. Sea foam lingered in the current, the scent sharp yet beguiling.

A beach stretched out on either side, cluttered with bushes here and there that rose to the height of my waist. Leaves sprouted at the top, with oblong, black globes weighing branches to the sand on the bottom.

"It's lovely, Baxter."

"Very," he murmured.

The weight of my wool dress, my boots, felt immediately out of place. For the first time since my encounter with Prana, I finally felt warm.

Baxter said crisply, "Not as cold here, at least."

Two demigod females appeared off to the right. They scanned the beach, spotted us, and then strode through the sand in our direction. The quiet allure that graced all demigods remained true, even here. I couldn't take my eyes off of them.

I held myself in check, Ava's words resurrected in my mind, as if she transmitted them through our touching palms.

Monilay mal.

Ava shuffled closer to her uncle, pressed to his side. Baxter put a hand on her shoulder, but braced himself.

"I sent word to my sisters before we arrived at your house," he murmured. "They've been expecting us."

Ava hissed through clenched teeth. She shuffled away from his side to put herself between me and the two approaching females. Baxter did the same.

I eyed the sisters more warily now.

"Why are you protecting me?"

"When it comes to demigods," he muttered, "one never knows. Aside from myself, Amorette and Juna are my only sisters that know you're here. The rest of them will find out eventually. With any luck, we'll keep it that way for the duration of your stay."

Reality settled with swift weight. This wasn't an oasis nestled in the folds where sea met sky.

This was Alaysia.

Amorette and Juna arrived with sparkling smiles. Baxter stiffly returned their quick embraces as they chattered in Alaysian for several minutes. While we waited for them to finish, the sun heated me. Sweat gathered over my spine and trickled down. Ava stepped back until she collided with my chest. I rested my hands on her shoulders with a squeeze.

"Relax," I murmured.

"*Monilay mal.*"

"Aren't they your aunts?"

Ava snarled.

The sister with auburn hair, cropped close to a sculpted face, smiled wide in my direction. Her coquettish blue eyes met mine, twins with the sky. Her graceful neck matched equally elegant, flowing arms. Both sisters wore dresses without sleeves, cut off at the knee, and loose around their waists. Jealousy of their freedom welled up inside me.

A heartbeat passed while she and I studied each other.

"My name is Amorette," she said in the common language of witches, which only stirred up more questions. Her arm swept over to the other female demigod. "This is Juna."

Juna's black hair, textured and thick like Ava's, reminded me of springs in an old clock. Her shoulders were broad, firm. She wore a backless blue dress that fluttered in the breeze, ending at her fingertips.

"Welcome to Alaysia." Juna's voice was rich and low, despite measured words. "Father sent us to tell you that you are welcome in his house."

"Thank you."

Both turned to Ava with distantly curious expressions. Moments passed like eternities while Ava glared at them. Her shoulders coiled up, like a cat about to strike. Her entire body turned hard as metal. Baxter placed his hand on the back of her neck. She calmed, albeit reluctantly. He murmured something in Alaysian.

Ava gazed away.

The tension ratcheted, unbearably thick. Finally, it dropped when Amorette warmly murmured, "You look like her, Ava."

Ava unwound, her face slack.

"Ava isn't ready to talk about her mother," Baxter said firmly. "Let it go."

Amorette rolled her eyes.

Juna's gaze lingered on Ava in vague disinterest before she turned back to Baxter.

"Father isn't here, but he's expectin' you at the Council of the Gods tomorrow mornin'. Plan for a full recountin'. It's likely to be all day."

Baxter nodded, seeming to expect this. When a breeze trickled by, his shoulders stiffened. He held his breath until the moving air stilled, then he let it all out with an expression of frustration. Juna sent him a knowing look.

Ava's scowl deepened.

"Easy, Baxter," Amorette murmured with amusement, her short, reddish strands warm in the hot sun. "No reason to upset Father already. Wouldn't want to lose your spot as favorite, now would you?"

With a chuckle, the two of them turned their backs. Sand clung to their ankles as they strode along the beach, toward a distant structure hidden behind scraggly trees. Baxter's jaw slowly unclenched. When I reached over to put my hand on his arm, he jerked. The skin blazed with heat from the sun. He blinked, coming out of what appeared to be deep thoughts.

A sheepish smile quickly surfaced. "Sorry," he murmured.

"Are you all right?"

"Fine."

"They seemed, ah, nice enough."

He snorted. "They are . . . until they're not. Let's go. I requested a beach house where you and Ava can stay, away from the *Rostina.*"

"*Rostina*?"

"Castle."

With a hesitant nod, he gestured to whatever structure cluttered most of the sky in the distance. "I'm sorry, but I won't know more about when you'll meet with my father until after tomorrow. He can be . . . difficult to track down."

I let my hand fall away. "It'll be fine, Baxter. I trust you."

The storm in his gaze only darkened.

"This way. We can at least get you settled."

Chapter Four

"Alaysia is an unstable collection of islands, basically. It's always changing." Baxter shoved his hands in his pockets and leaned into the loose earth with each step. "Each god has their own kingdom. Gelas, god of ice, in the north. Ventis, god of wind, in the west. Tontes, god of thunder, in the south. Ignis, god of fire, to the east."

We crossed a peninsula-like area, headed closer to the *Rostina*. The sun warmed my wool dress unbearably as we moved. I tugged at my collar, skin itchy. Despite the presence of Baxter's magic, and to assuage my growing curiosity, I sent a goddess magic spell that lifted my skirt out of the sand.

The fabric drew higher, gathering around my knees. Air ruffled past my heating skin, delightfully cool. I kept a squeal of interest inside. As quickly as it worked, the magic stopped. I frowned.

So goddess magic *did* work, though I couldn't be sure of how long it might last. Weakened power, perhaps? While Baxter continued his explanation, words running through the back of my mind, I sent another spell to stir the sand.

Nothing moved.

Baxter's amulet might have wreaked havoc on the spells, however. I mentally set that away to test again later.

Something was better than nothing.

Baxter turned, mouth half open to say something, then stopped. Ava wiped an arm across her sweaty forehead and gathered her skirt in her hands. His gaze dropped to her exposed ankles.

"Sorry." He gave a little smile. "Should have warned you about the heat. I can fix that."

In a blink, my wool dress had been replaced with something like Amorettes. Cool linen, sleeveless, to my knees. The tyrannical heat cooled. I held my arms up, allowing the wind to tickle my skin as it danced over the top.

"Much better," I sighed. "No wonder you told me not to bother with packing."

Baxter grinned and murmured, "Son of a god."

Ava twirled, arms lifted in the air. Her yellow dress fluttered around her thighs and a smile split her face, bright with relief and joy. It was the happiest I'd seen her for days.

"There's very little *tirra mora*, or firm ground, in Alaysia," Baxter continued, walking again. "When the gods were banished from Alkarra by their sisters thousands of years ago, they had to start over." His arms lifted. "This is what they did. Each kingdom is made up of a collection of islands where their mortals and demigods live. That's as basic as it gets."

The strip of sand that we'd been walking along, surrounded on three sides by the ocean, broadened. The *Rostina* he spoke of existed like a haze ahead, interrupted only by infrequent bursts of green. Trees, bushes, shrubs. Nothing permanent, like a forest. On the sea, boats skipped over the waves. Mortals, presumably, because they used long poles to propel themselves, like a bug skittering across the top.

"Little firm ground?" I murmured.

"*Very* little firm ground," Baxter repeated. "Particularly

when compared to Alkarra. The island where the god lives—like what you stand on now—is the most stable for that god. The rest are patches of sand or dirt or collected driftwood held together by magic."

Baxter jerked his head toward Ava.

"She lived on a collection of islands a few hours row from here. Those types of islands sometimes fade away. Most of them float around, kept from escaping into the sea by ropes that anchor them together in small communities, called collections."

Ava's scowl darkened, so I stuffed my dozens of questions aside.

"I see," I said lightly.

"This," Baxter murmured, "is my father's house."

As if we'd crossed an invisible line, a sprawling building opened to our view. I sucked in a sharp breath and quietly cried, "The good gods, Baxter."

"The *only* good god."

The white sand beach crawled ahead a few hundred paces, then ended on a wall of hardened, hazel stone. Swirls of light brown, umber, and white streaked through the rectangular blocks, each as tall as myself. My gaze climbed higher and higher and . . . *higher.*

The hardened chunks slid into a smooth surface, then stopped. On top stood a handful of . . . mortals? From here, their eye color wasn't visible. Sentries, perhaps? They each wore billowing black pants and tightly-fit cream shirts. No armor, though each held a spear.

"Demigods," Baxter said to my unspoken question. "No mortal is allowed a weapon at the *Rostina.* These demigods aren't my siblings. I'm the eldest of two sons, and the other is a baby."

"How many sisters?"

"Nine."

I whistled. So many sisters, I couldn't fathom.

"Another god must be visiting," he murmured. "Tontes, perhaps, based on the black pants and spears. He's always been over-the-top that way."

"The gods need protection?" I asked, amused at the thought.

"No."

He said it mildly, which left me to wonder why demigods with spears lurked outside. Hadn't Juna said that Ventis wasn't here? So why would Tontes visit? Amorette and Juna could have been lying, though I didn't understand why.

The castle itself pulled my thoughts away.

The *Rostina* soared overhead and sprawled to each side, built with layers upon layers of sand compressed to stone. Staircases wrapped around plentiful turrets, spiraling out of sight. Some ended on open doorways with no door. Others plummeted below the wall, their end invisible.

"Father calls it the *Rostina lu Lune*. *Rostina* for short."

"Home in the sky," Ava murmured.

"Appropriate," I said, "for the god of wind."

On the right side of the *Rostina*, a waterfall cascaded. It spilled over the top of the highest rampart and disappeared. At another floor, it slipped down the side in a more gentle easement. Pools spilled from one to another, like meandering lace. Eventually, the water raced toward the frothy sea.

"Your father has a waterfall?"

Baxter cracked a smile. "We're all quite proud of that. It's fresh water, and entirely maintained by magic. Father puts a great deal of effort into the *Rostina lu Lune*."

Speckles of glass windows sparkled here and there, but not often. Porticos, open areas, outdoor rooms, freckled various floors. Woven mats of thin sticks or collected driftwood topped most of the roofs of the turrets. A preliminary count yielded forty turrets, but more populated as Baxter cut to the side, revealing several other wings.

"How big is it?"

"I would guess at least ten times the size of Chatham." Baxter tilted his head musingly. "I'm not sure, though. Never seen it all."

Ava's open mouth hadn't closed yet. She gaped, eyes wide as she attempted to take it all in.

"You haven't seen it before?" I asked quietly.

She frowned, shook her head.

Lights illuminated open walkways that led deeper into the *Rostina*. The entire structure felt open, with space and dimension and light. No cold stone hallways here, I imagined, nor dark halls.

"It takes up the sky," I whispered.

A dry tone replied, "As does my Father."

Another demigod joined the two on top of the wall. Their potent stares weighed heavily on me as a fourth joined. They didn't speak, but such dark malevolence didn't require words.

Baxter's voice dropped. "Walk to the left and slightly behind me. Keep your head down. Whatever you do, don't look around and don't speak."

While I did as he instructed, I caught a glimpse of Ava. She'd already assumed such a position. I had a crawling suspicion that *this* is how most mortals acted around demigods. Baxter must want them to ignore me.

Silent, we passed in the shadow of the castle. Baxter strode so close to the outer rock wall that I trailed my fingertips along the edge. Grains of sand dribbled loose, startling me. The stone wasn't stone at all, but compressed sand. It was so tightly packed it might as well have been rock. Ventis lived in a sandcastle.

I wrestled back a giggle.

We passed one of several winding ramps that led to the top, where the four demigods stood. Heat slipped through my blood as we passed underneath, which meant they wore amulets. A call came and they moved out of sight.

Baxter's curled knuckles relaxed when we couldn't see them.

"Here," he murmured, nudging us away from the sandcastle. "It's not far from here."

We navigated into a small, lightly-wooded area. Ava jogged to keep up with Baxter's fast clip, and I hurried at his side, my calves burning from walking in so much sand.

"Can't you just take us with magic?" I asked.

He shook his head. "Too suspicious. We don't use magic the same way in Alaysia."

Shady gold-and-green-leaved trees populated the sand. Their leaves were thin and long. I reached down as we walked, scooping one up. It spanned the length of my hand, from wrist to fingertip. Bright lines of pink and yellow wove through, like capillaries. The fibrous texture cracked when I bent it in half, reminiscent of the Alaysian book Ava gave me on Luppentonisa.

Trees cluttered the sandy landscape now, which brought marginal relief. These trees had no life or intelligence. Sentient Letum Wood created a stark contrast to the dull trees here. I pressed a palm into the rough trunk of one tree, then let my fingers slip away.

No stirrings.

Heat pressed on us as we headed away from the castle. The long leaves clattered in the wind. Baxter glanced up during a particularly large gust, his teeth gritted. He flared his nostrils, muttered something, and kept going.

I didn't ask.

Once the castle lay far behind us, and only the sound of rushing water ahead, Baxter slowed. He drew in a deep breath.

"I'm sorry," he said, meeting my eyes. "I didn't realize there would be another god visiting my father. Juna should have told me. I don't know why she didn't. I didn't . . . I didn't want any other demigods to see you and know that the amulet-breaker had arrived."

"They know me on sight?"

"I don't know. They might."

Such news wasn't welcome.

"Why wouldn't Juna tell you?"

His scrunched expression indicated frustration. "I don't know."

"What would have happened if those demigods figured out who I was?" I asked.

"Only the gods know. This way." He clicked and gestured deeper into the wooded area. The hiss of the ocean sounded off to the left, and the *Rostina* lay behind us. Ava kept herself canted toward the waves, as if drawn to the water.

A few minutes later, a beach house came into view. It soared four stories high and one room wide, with only twenty or thirty paces across. Like the *Rostina*, it appeared to be made of sand. Willowy trees with broad branches and skinny leaves stood as four anchor points at each corner of the house, sprouting like umbrellas over the top. The walls were made of woven leaves, interrupted by windows, which provided almost no protection at all. Fabric fluttered inside. Room dividers, perhaps?

"It's stronger than it looks," Baxter said.

I certainly hoped so. A moderate surge of wind could topple such a structure. One would expect the god of wind to prepare sufficiently against his own power.

Ava regarded it with indifference. Like a tic, her gaze returned to the sea, just visible beyond the forest. Baxter stepped up three stairs to a square porch and went inside, through a doorless entry. I followed.

The floor was also made of compressed sand. It shuffled in grains under my toes when I stepped across. Rickety spiral stairs wound from one floor to the next in a coil. They were narrow, but sturdy. Treacherous in the dark, I'd bet.

Every space of the house lay empty. A sinewless skeleton of sand and bark, waiting for something to fill it back up again.

"You'll need some supplies." Baxter spun in a circle, but there was little to see. "Clothes. Some food. Are you thirsty?"

The room changed.

Hammocks appeared on the far side, dangling from hooks in the ceiling. Baskets, filled with food, gathered along the seams of the walls. Empty nails on the wall now held a dozen dresses in varying colors. Hats. Stockings. Sandals.

Books.

Seashell jewelry.

Crockery filled with water. Baxter pivoted, brow furrowed in concentration. My mouth watered at the succulent smell of something sweet that drifted out of a cupboard. It appeared against the back wall. The amulets on his wrist, tiny gems that glittered in a wrist guard, brightened.

Plump pillows burdened the hammock. Silky blankets followed, trailing to the ground with long threads. A gold-gilded mirror the size of the entire wall appeared next. By the time Baxter finished his single rotation of the room, every spare nook had been filled.

He gestured to the shocking display of god magic with a casual jerk of his head.

"Should be enough to keep you comfortable, but if you lack anything, let me know. Not overly elegant or spacious, but I think it'll be sufficient to stay for a few days." He rubbed the swirling, gray amulets of his wrist guard with the opposite thumb. "I haven't been using it much, so there's still plenty of power."

"Should be fine," I said wryly, still startled. A flash of a smile told me a hint of Baxter lurked inside the nervous ball of stress that emerged with each passing moment. I nodded toward his wrist. "Is there a limit to the magic?"

"To the amulets, yes. To god magic? No. The power restores over time, which is why we use it more carefully here."

Goddess magic could do amazing things, but the speed and flexibility of god magic flummoxed me every time. No spells to memorize, to botch in the delivery, or to recite and mull over. A simple intention, and abundance came to the fingertips.

"Ava?" Baxter asked. "Anything else?"

A string of Alaysian words followed from her. They conversed until she blinked, shook her head. Her eyes lingered on the sudden luxuries—were those tea cups made out of sea shells?—and then back to Baxter. He seemed to ask a question, a drawl in his tone.

She shook her head again.

Baxter turned back to me. "I'll return in a bit to check on you. For now, I need to report to my father. Should be back sometime tonight. If I can't, I'll send a message."

"All right."

"Will this be sufficient?"

"More than that." I leaned against a wall with a blithe smile. "I love it, thank you."

"If you need anything, use god magic to send me a note."

"I'm sure we'll be fine."

He plowed on, as if he hadn't heard, the words pressured. "I'll report at the Council of the Gods tomorrow, then I'll meet with Father afterward. He may know if it's possible for Ignis to remove the magic. That way, you don't ever have to meet Ignis."

"Oh, thanks."

A hand slapped the wall, and the pliable leaves gave a little shiver. "Though rickety, the beach house will be safe enough." Forced jauntiness infused his tone. "No other demigods will venture this far into my father's collection, and my sisters will know to leave you alone."

"I'm not afraid."

"If anyone tries to come here or—"

With a sigh, I used god magic to shove him against the wall. He slammed into it, then stared at me in wide-eyed surprise. I sucked in a sharp breath. I hadn't meant to do it—or perhaps I had?

God magic was a little *too* easy.

"Oh, jikes!" I hurried to his side. "Sorry, Bax. I didn't mean to hurt you. I don't think I meant to do that, either. The god magic is just . . . I'm getting used to it."

He stepped away from the wall with a chuckle, shaking out his shoulders. Ava rolled her lips together, schooling back a laugh.

"Listen, please?" I pleaded with him. "We're fine." My fingers tightened around his arm in a reassuring squeeze. "This looks comfortable and I trust you. Relax. Everything will be just fine."

The hesitation that stole over his face suggested that I probably should be more frightened by Alaysia, but I didn't retract the words. As an amulet, I likely held at least as much power as a demigod. Though I didn't really know how to use it, I could navigate me and Ava out of a sticky situation.

Baxter covered my hand with his and pressed it. "You're right. Thanks, Bianca. I just . . . I want you and Ava to be safe while you're here."

"Take your time at the *Rostina*." I waved a hand in that direction. "Ava and I will go swimming while you see your sisters and your old home."

A subtle command strengthened my tone. The unraveling side of Baxter had me far more worried than Alaysia. With him fluttering around like a nervous mother hen, I'd never be able to test my magic, observe their world, and understand our enemy better.

Not to mention dive into the eight baskets of food that had appeared over the last several minutes. Bright green, wafer-like crackers, what appeared to be seeds with a shiny coating, and three types of bread awaited my taste buds.

Ava came up next to me, fingers finding mine. I gave her a reassuring hug. She leaned close. The smell of spearmint drifted into my nose from her hair. Away from the *Rostina*, she'd calmed. Quietly, she spoke to Baxter again in Alaysian, and I hoped she encouraged him to go.

"Right." Baxter released a ragged breath and shoved a hand through his hair. "You're right. I need to talk to a few of my sisters, get an idea of what's going on with Tontes. Then I'll feel better. "

"Great. In the meantime, we'll go swimming."

Long moments passed while Baxter studied my face, which I kept schooled into easy confidence. Eventually, he gave in with a fling of his hand. "Fine. All right. I'll go."

He stopped in the doorway, hands folded behind his back. When he peered back at me through thickly-lashed eyes, I sensed a warning in his words.

"It's different here, B. This is not the time to do anything crazy, all right? No heroes."

While he jogged away, cutting through the sand behind the house, Ava's tight grip eased. She perked up.

"Swimming?"

I smiled.

"Let's do it."

* * *

Ava and I inspected each layer of the beach house. The floor was a thin slab of compressed sand housing untold luxuries.

Backless chairs, heavily padded, with elegant stitching. Shelves filled with books, papers written in Alaysian, globes of water filled with enigmatic colors of sand. Tiled pottery, mosaics, and paintings on the wall. On the top floor, a glass ceiling peeked into the branches and blue sky. I touched it, not convinced it was there, as the glass was so pristine.

With our exploration completed, we ventured outside. White sand, a crashing sea, and warmth occupied us for hours. The highest levels of the *Rostina lu Lune* peeked over the top of the wooded area that hid our beach house. Spiraling decorations of hardened sand poked out of promenades and floors, like twisted pieces of metal. A sea dragon, twisted diamond, spearheads. Every hour or so, a body strolled by at the top of the *Rostina lu Lune*, then disappeared.

Months of snowy days, blunted light, and frigid air drifted into memory, rocked by the intensity of my surroundings.

Island perfection.

"Water?" I asked Ava.

She frowned, lips puckered. "To drink?"

"Yes. Where does the freshwater come from?"

"*Monilay.*"

Ah. Of course. A demigod. No doubt Baxter left some in the beach house for us. How else would they get it? No barrel outside indicated rainwater collection, and Baxter hinted that storms didn't roll through here much anyway. If these islands were simply *sand*, then fresh water springs must not exist.

Alaysia might be beautiful, but a nefarious undertone thrummed in the corners.

Magic was survival.

"Too many *monilay.*"

Ava stood next to me, though we couldn't see another soul. Her nose scrunched toward the *Rostina*.

"Are you scared of them?" I asked.

She nodded.

"Do you think they'll hurt you?"

She shook her head, but her frown deepened.

"You're worried about me?"

Her lips compressed.

"I'll be fine, Ava."

With a scoff, she turned away. "Ventis." She flicked the word off her tongue. "He speaks in the wind. He *is* the wind. Be . . . soft."

"Be careful, you mean?"

Another nod.

I blinked, startled at the thought. Of course Ventis was in the wind. Did that mean that Prana was *in* the ocean? Such logic meant Deasylva would be *in* her forest. Thinking back to our encounter only a few hours ago—though it already felt like days—brought an easy answer.

Also, yes.

Perhaps I should be more careful about my time in the water.

I dismissed those thoughts, allowing them to fracture, as I flicked a patch of sand off the back of my arm. "Ventis can hear what we say?"

"Yes," she murmured, finger swirling. "In the wind. The gods see all."

Tiptoeing around the gods hadn't been part of my priority, but I heeded Baxter's gentle warning before he left. This situation from Ava's perspective altered reality. After eleven years of abandonment, neglect, and abuse, I couldn't fault her terror of the *monilay mal*.

But I didn't share it.

Ava tilted her head, regarding a carefully-constructed sand castle that resembled the *Rostina lu Lune,* as much as a blob of wet sand could. Pleased with her creation, she straightened and slapped her palms together to clear the sand.

Then she jumped on it.

While she desecrated her castle, I turned to the left. Changing colors grabbed my gaze. I held a breath, startled to see a handful of embers not far away. They hovered, as if waiting. Their varying sizes ranged no larger than my pinky finger nail. Dots the size of sand swirled within playful winks. The embers illuminated and darkened in turns, morphing from deep crimson to burnt orange. Several smoothed to yellow as pale as morning sunlight. The ever-shifting palette brought to mind Luppentonisa.

God magic brightened in my chest with a warm purl.

Ignis?

"Merry meet," I murmured.

The embers froze, then whisked away in an explosion of wind. For several minutes, I blinked and wondered if I'd imagined the whole thing.

Sunshine burned into my skin. The top of my dress stiffened from the salty water, nearly dry after I sprawled in the sunshine. My hair resembled braided cords as I tied it away from my face. A burning in my throat persisted.

I pushed to my feet, then stalled. A seven-figured star seashell, nestled into sand at my side, caught my eyes. Sunlight glinted off the black, glittering exterior when I pried it free with a sucking sound. Shocks of vibrant mulberry curled the softer underbelly. I held it out to Ava with a smile.

"For you."

Her lips curled.

"Thank you."

With a slap of my hand, I splashed her in a receding wave. She squealed, eyes wide. I tilted my head back and laughed. A wave of water dotted my chest and shoulders, wetting already dry spots, followed by a maniacal cackle.

We plunged back into the water, where the sea whisked away the most burning question of all: did Ignis sense me here?

Chapter Five

Darkness followed a watery sunset.

Yellow blurred into marmalade and then electric pink, like smashed raspberries smeared across the dome of the sky. The ocean reflected the palette in bright, watery sparkles. Not a cloud marred the view. We watched from the sand, wordless and wrapped in the magic of wild places.

Baxter appeared a few paces away. Wind tossed his hair as he looked around, spotted me, and moved closer with a droll smile. Lines trailed below his eyes, giving him a tired appearance. He stepped closer, hooked an arm around me, and pulled me close.

Startled by the blatant touch, I hesitated. Then I wrapped my arms around his waist and leaned against him. Smells of flower blossoms and sunshine drifted into my nose. Wind whistled past, coaxing hair out of my collar. It flapped around, whipping my cheek. Baxter held me for a moment, then leaned back.

"You all right?" he asked.

"Fine. You?"

"Busy, but in good ways."

My eyebrows lifted. Curiosity washed through me. "Oh?

Exactly what does the son of a god do when he returns home after leaving for three years?"

"Preparing for tomorrow," he murmured grimly. "It will be a long day with a lot of interrogation. And . . . other things."

Space came between us again as he turned to find Ava. Though I couldn't be sure, I had the feeling he blithely avoided explaining further by finding her. At a call from him, she glanced up, waved, and returned to perusing the sand. He shuffled back another step, and I felt his missing warmth like a lost friend.

They spoke in Alaysian before he swung back around to me.

"Tomorrow will be a long day for me. I'll send Gio, my . . . friend . . . to check on you. After the meeting, I should have a better idea of when Father can speak with you."

A gentle hesitation broke his words, then faded.

"Sounds good."

With a smile, he gently touched my face. I watched him jog into the trees, *Rostina* bound.

Ava joined my side. I put an arm around her shoulders, steering us back to the beach house. Once inside, Ava tossed something my way.

"*Seema*. Very good."

I caught a hardened disk, wide as my palm. The outside was the color of dark brown clay, and smooth. A dot at the end allowed me to peel away the hardened rind. Inside, dry seeds populated a light pink flesh. They crunched between my teeth, bitter like coffee grounds, and I coughed when they trickled into my throat.

She laughed.

Using the heels of her hands, she cracked the oblong disk all the way open, then split it in half. She used her teeth to scrape the fleshy part off. Though the seeds left a bitter flavor, it wasn't unpleasant when mixed with the too-sweet pink rind.

Ava smacked her lips and tossed the empty disk into the sand.

"Seema," she said again.

"Thanks."

Shortly after dark, Ava crawled into her hammock and fell asleep. I stood at the window and peered out. Lights from the *Rostina lu Lune* glowed, blurring the wild backdrop of stars. My thoughts roved to Baxter, then Ava's unusually quiet demeanor since we arrived. Until now, I'd known them only in my Alkarran world. I'd come to their kingdom and I didn't know what to think of their skittishness.

Time and patience, Marten had said.

I reached into my pocket, pressing the palm-sized wooden box to my hand. The amulet Scarlett had given me. What I'd do with it, I wasn't sure, but it seemed prudent to keep it hidden. I tucked it into the back corner of a sprawling trunk lined with velvet and filled with more clothes. A pair of slippers covered it.

I closed the trunk with a firm thud.

When I glanced up, a swirl of embers appeared in the doorway. They danced closer, stopping a hands-breadth away from my face. God magic brightened like swift lightning, reminding me that these were no ordinary cinders.

Somehow, I knew they'd come back.

"Merry meet again."

All air movement ceased.

The distant crash of the waves faded.

The embers scuttled back, hurrying through the room and to the door. They stopped in a twinkling pause, as if expectant. I hesitated, weighing my options. To go, or to stay? Baxter wouldn't be happy with me if I followed.

Yet I came to discover Alaysia . . .

"Do you want me to follow?"

They blazed.

With one last look at Ava, who slept soundly in her hammock, I obeyed.

The embers twirled ahead of me in a mesmerizing path.

They swirled around trees, skimmed over the sand. Playfulness infused every movement. Barefoot, I jogged through the sand to keep pace. Every step excited my god magic further, as if it drew closer to home. The cinders stopped at the beach, near a conflagration.

A driftwood pile, taller than me, loomed overhead. The size and power startled me. Flames burst from it, sparking in explosions of ash. Emerald and royal purple tones flickered from the heart of the fire. The sand firmed beneath my feet as I approached. Warmth rolled off of the blaze.

A ring of shadows created a circle of darkness just beyond the flame edge, where I stopped. My god magic became ferociously hungry, ready to devour. Illuminate. The world could irradiate under such potential. Quickly as it came, the surge disappeared. I reached a hand to my chest to stabilize the rapid patter.

A dizzying sensation preceded a familiar voice.

You are a witch of curiosity and passion to have followed me out here.

On the night I lost my magic, I heard a voice. A gravelly, angry sound. Presumably, Ignis, god of fire. The same voice I heard now, except he sounded genial. Thoughtful. He spoke to me through the god magic, because I didn't hear him with my ears. The words came from a place deep inside that I didn't control.

Marten's caution for brevity calcified in my mind.

"Ignis, I presume?"

The fire pulsed, as if I had amused him. His voice clarified, growing stronger.

You do not fear me?

"Should I?"

A wry tone followed. *You're being evasive.*

"Yes."

And honest.

I schooled back a smile. "Can you tell?"

Yes.

"When it serves my purpose, honesty is usually my preferred strategy."

A rumbling laugh shivered the flames. I shifted, uncomfortable with how *close* this all felt.

Why did you come to speak with me? You know the danger you're in, a witch in Alaysia.

"Curiosity."

About the god of fire?

"About . . . everything."

The fire drew in on itself, as if thinking. After a few moments, it returned to a blazing burn.

Forgive me for not introducing myself. I'm not used to witches coming to our lands. I am Ignis, god of fire.

"I know."

Do you?

I lifted my chin. I had no apologies to give to a god that invaded my land, attempted to take over my Network, and caused the death of witches in Alkarra. "You've spoken to me before. When I destroyed Luppentonisa."

Yes, he purred mildly. *A tragedy for a most beloved amulet.*

An inferno darted out in a sudden explosion. The magic in me cooled. I ducked away, arms over my face, but the racing firestorm calmed. Smoldering driftwood collapsed in on itself, giving way to a rise of purple sparks. The urge to have Viveet in hand overwhelmed me.

You are quiet for a young woman your age. I sense deep wisdom and pain. A thirst for . . . acceptance. Acknowledgment.

"Are you rooting through my soul?"

I am your soul.

The fire crackled. In it, I sensed that he waited for my response, but I would give none. Let him draw his own assumptions, though I trembled at the thought.

What could he *possibly* mean?

His voice curled up, startled. *You have nothing to say to that?*

"No."

Curiouser.

"Why did you bring me out here? Do you want to analyze my personality for your own benefit, or to show me my own weaknesses? If you want to play a game, I'm willing, but you have to establish the stakes."

You stymie me.

"You're not the first."

Why did you come to Alaysia?

"Ventis invited me."

A plausible excuse. His sarcastic rebuttal darkened the ambience. I let it slide. His modulating responses, so normal at times and unpredictable at others, made him feel a little too real.

Ventis loves to be a hero.

"Not sure what you've learned," I replied blithely, "but I was taught not to refuse social invitations to neighboring lands that want to invade and kill us."

So you're here to do reconnaissance?

"Something else."

Tell me.

"No, thank you."

You refuse a god?

"Yes, but I'm doing so politely."

A pause.

This is new.

I said nothing.

You have been trained for interrogation tactics. Impressively so. Your father is an interesting witch. I have long been fascinated with him, as far as witches go. Until . . . well, we don't need to bring that betrayal up. Or do we?

I pressed my lips together. Ouch. Clearly, Ignis had observational power in Alkarra, if he knew Papa. His children, perhaps?

Undoubtedly, they reported information to him. Through me, I presumed, though it lingered in the ether of questions-I-couldn't-answer-right-now. Right next to how-could-he-possibly-be-my-soul, which created a panic I dare not give power at the moment. Too frightening.

Too big.

Though tempted, I wouldn't take his bait. He goaded me in an attempt to get more information.

No, I had this.

Total control.

I didn't need to know what the god of fire thought of Papa leaving.

Of Papa's betrayal and lack of trust. Of—

"What does that mean?" I snapped. My fingers curled into my palm, forming a tight fist.

So much for holding out.

It doesn't take a god to realize your father left you yet again, Bianca. Deserted. Didn't even include you, an adult woman, in his plans. How frustrating.

My defense of him faltered into a pathetic, "He did what he felt was best."

Admirable, but misguided. Allow me to share some perspective? I see a Lady-witch who fears not being special. Your mother lived so quietly, and died so young. Meanwhile, your father lived so large. What if the same happened to you? What if you died without ever proving that you can be just like your Papa?

My heart sizzled like a burning poker stabbed it. The good gods. I hadn't endured such maniacal insight since Mabel and I shared a mind. Like he'd slit a knife down my heart, then handed it back.

"You make bold assumptions," I hissed, but couldn't force myself to leave.

Not yet.

Your Sisterhood will do an admirable job of proving your

worth, he continued conversationally, *since that is what you strive to do. Worth must be proven, right? The attachment to other witches approving who you are is . . . strength personified, don't you agree? But I expect nothing else so foolish from a witch.*

I breathed hard, and fast. His words barely parsed together into meaningful statements in my head. They made sense, but in a distant, this-isn't-real way. A haze overtook my mind, hiding the bared, exposed feeling his words gave me.

How to hide from so pure a truth? A sarcasm so slicing it cleaved to marrow.

"What are you trying to prove, god of fire?"

Nice diversion, but turning the attention back to me won't work. No matter how trained, smart, or canny you are, you're not more intelligent than me. My magic resides within you, lady-witch. You know this. What you don't *know are the implications. You stole my magic, and it connects us.*

Silence.

Then the damning truth.

That *is why you came to Alaysia.*

I struggled to recover stable mental ground. He'd knocked me back, shocked me with what he revealed. All of it, true. The deepest fears and insecurities that I'd ever known he'd just brought to life. Held them up, ripped my soul from my body and toyed with the silvery strands.

And why?

"I didn't steal your magic. *It* stole *me.*"

A pause.

What do witches call taking something that isn't yours?

His pandering tone set my teeth on edge, but it gave me a moment to gain my bearings. Scorn I could deal with. The derisive amusement behind his words only made my frustration worse, though.

"Maybe you should have controlled your amulets better," I

snapped, "then Luppentonisa wouldn't have been destroyed by a witch that had no idea god magic existed."

I sealed my lips shut.

So much for brevity.

In that, Ignis murmured, *you and I are agreed.*

The misery in his voice startled me out of my defensive frenzy. I swallowed, completely unprepared for a god to feel so . . . *similar.* Like we carried the same jagged pieces, broken free but yearning to return.

Quietly, the waves broke on the sand. Stars glimmered, wavering in the rising heat of the fire. The emerald-and-purple color entranced me, safer than the sound of his voice.

"Can you read my mind?"

The question felt entirely too vulnerable, and my voice too small when I asked, but it could not have been contained.

No. Nor would I wish to, to set you at ease. Witches are decidedly . . . elemental. I can sense your emotions and the deep wellspring that originates them, however. One might call it a soul, but it's not so nebulous.

"If the god magic is part of me, then you are as well?"

You are as great a surprise to gods as you were to witches, I would imagine.

It wasn't an answer, but I took it as confirmation. Neither of us sounded happy to be here. A lot of things lay open to unpack now, but I pushed them aside for the most important piece.

"Can you take the magic back?"

The simmering coals bloomed with a light blush, an unfolding flower sprawled along the sand.

That, he murmured silkily, *is the ultimate question, isn't it?*

"Do you hate me because of what happened?"

No.

"Not even after you lost Bram and Jote and . . ."

The names trailed away. Admitting my responsibility in their death felt a step too far for this conversation, but I couldn't help my curiosity. What remained to hide? Ignis perceived all the ugliest parts of me.

They are not your concern, but mine. So what is it like, Lady-witch? God and goddess magic within you at the same time? Can't be all that comfortable, though you are finally realizing just how powerful god magic can be.

Instinct told me not to give too much information. In a conversation such as this, Papa always skirted as close to the truth as possible without giving everything away. If Ignis wasn't deceiving me and I really *was* the first witch to become an amulet, then my experience with both magicks might be one of my only bargaining chips.

The gods would be curious.

Yet answers came at a price.

"It's . . . interesting," I murmured, paying attention to the warmth as it coiled in my blood. "The two magicks don't like each other."

Surely.

My brow lifted. "Did you want further details?"

*Oh, no. That seems overly sufficient. Not even a god could extrapolate a magic-altering event such as you stealing my magic, breaking a cherished amulet, and killing my children as interest-*ing. *Your time tonight has been appreciated.*

He had a droll tone. I had to stifle a twitch of my lips. "Well then." I spread my hands. "I'm glad we understand one another."

The fire had been slowly dimming for minutes, the bright blaze ebbing with each passing word we spoke.

Life in Alaysia is nothing like what you're used to, he murmured in a low tone of warning. *It will take some . . . open-mindedness on your part. Beware the demigods and the mortals. You will not believe it for some time, but trust me when I say that I am your only friend here.*

I scoffed.

Allow me the honor of teaching you what you could be with god magic, and I shall extend my protection and friendship.

I hesitated, mouth half open. "You want to teach me?" I finally managed.

Yes.

He offered a chance to find out the full extent of god magic. Tempting, but not important in the grander scheme.

Or was it?

"I want the magic gone, not honed."

But you want to save Alkarra?

"More than anything."

Give me a chance to show you what you could do with my magic.

"Like save Alkarra?"

Precisely.

"Forgive me if I can't trust the god who has been invading it to teach me how to save it."

There is much you don't see.

His impervious tone, nearly sterile in its alacrity, haunted me. I couldn't help but wonder *what if?*

An opportunity to teach you more is all that I ask. If you are uninterested by the time we finish, we will discuss extraction of the magic. If such a thing is possible.

The ease of god magic flittered through my mind in a beckoning call. If I could save Alkarra without having to memorize spells or worry about amulets stopping my goddess magic or . . .

No.

Down this road lay treachery.

"I haven't had great results making deals with deities. Your offer is appreciated, but I kindly refuse."

The lowering coals winked out along the edges. His voice seemed to fade with them.

Be careful, Lady-witch. Should you change your mind? I am always here.

The dying embers gave way to black, a breeze stirred the sand at my feet, and all the flames swept away, extinguishing in the air. A trail of smoke curled lazily through the charred logs, drifted toward the sky, and disappeared in a brisk wind.

I watched it go, empty inside.

Chapter Six

A tentative voice woke me from a deep sleep.

"Merry meet?"

I blinked awake, my eyes dry and tired. The hammock ropes creaked beneath my weight as I swayed. Their coarse braids dug into my back all night long, fluffy pillows notwithstanding. Hazy shadows from an early sunrise sprawled through the room. A lazy grandeur to wake up to. I stretched my arms above my head with a yawn.

Wait.

Had I dreamed about a voice or was that real?

"Ah . . . Lady-witch of Alkarra?"

My eyes flew back open. Ava shot out of her hammock in a smooth movement, teeth bared. I scrambled free, blinking out of a sleepy haze. A man stood in the doorway, regarding me with a curious, honey-colored gaze. A mortal.

Thirties, I'd guess, with a carefree brightness about him. Streaks of gray veined dark hair, though his facial structure appeared young. He stood at my height so that I looked right into his eyes. He wore no shirt, only pants. His open chest and shoulders remained tanned and bare to the sky.

Ava advanced with rapid-fire Alaysian. He appraised her with amusement, then answered. Her chin lifted, and he continued. Eventually, the conversation between them slowed.

"His name is Giuseppeglacidonium," she said. "Or Gio."

What was with Alaysia and impossibly long names? Gio turned to me with an equally luminous grin.

"Gio," I said with a returning smile. "That one I can easily manage. I'm Bianca."

"I know."

Startled, I reared back. He'd used the common tongue. "You know how to speak the common language?" I asked.

"God magic. It helps me understand and speak your language. To make you comfortable in Alaysia," he added quickly.

"It can do that?" I asked weakly.

With a quizzical tilt of his head he asked, "What can it *not* do?"

He lifted his arm in front of him, squared, like he wanted me to hang something on it. Ava leaned closer.

"It is . . ." She paused. "Ah . . . a sign of servant." She mimicked the pose. "It is a . . ."

"Gesture?"

"The *gesture* of work." Her tone dropped into annoyance. "He is . . . ah . . . willing to do things?"

"Oh, I see."

Baxter sent me a mortal? Blood prickled under my skin at the thought.

"Do you work for Baxter?" I asked.

"Yes."

Ava's eyes widened into globes. She choked. I blinked. "Baxter?" I repeated breathlessly. "He took your allegiance?"

Gio eyed me suspiciously now. "You don't like it?" he asked carefully. "Baxter is your friend, isn't he?"

In truth, I didn't know how I felt about it. The thought of

mortals having given their allegiance to Baxter was . . . strange. Why would he take the allegiance of a mortal so quickly? Gio smiled, but tension lingered beneath the stone-like quality of his eyes.

"The servitude of a mortal is often given as a gift for a demigod completing his mission." He shrugged. "Assuming all goes well at the Council of the Gods today, which no one has reason to believe will not, he will be able to take many mortals to his allegiance. It is my great honor to serve him."

"Then . . . congratulations," I said. "Thank you for your offer of help. Honestly, I shouldn't need much. Baxter gave us everything and . . . I didn't know god magic was capable of translating languages."

Goddess magic certainly can't do that, I added silently.

Gio gave a nod and a slight smile. "Very well. I am in the *Rostina* should you need anything. Baxter would like to see you tonight, but it's most likely he'll return tomorrow morning. If you need help, you know where to find me. It's my honor to have met the Lady-witch of Alkarra."

Lady-witch of Alkarra. Ignis had addressed me as Lady-witch last night, but I hadn't heard it from anyone else yet.

"The Lady-witch of Alkarra?" I inquired with some amusement.

His grin widened. "It's what they are calling you."

"They?"

"The demigods."

"All of them?"

"Those at the *Rostina* who know of your presence. So . . . yes, all of Ventis' daughters." He gave a flippant wave of his hand.

So much for secrecy, then.

"Oh."

He laughed, as if he read my mind, though an edge of something darkened his voice. "News of you is already spreading across Alaysia, much to Baxter's frustration. The Lady-witch of Alkarra will soon be sought by all demigods."

I managed a wobbly smile.

"I almost forgot." He turned to Ava and clapped both palms together. "Come with me."

With a wary glance to Ava, who shrugged, I followed him into the sand. He slipped easily through the trees, toward the crashing surf. A whistle trailed out of him as he walked. Ahead of him lay a wooden dinghy, overturned near the restless waves.

Gio motioned to the flipped boat and asked Ava something in Alaysian. She nodded. A flash of white against his cheeks betrayed a bright smile.

"She says that she can drag it into the water on her own," he said as an aside to me, "so it is for Ava to use, should she wish."

He turned to her, speaking rapidly. Her eyes grew wide, sparkling. Her chatter returned, then she flung her arms around his waist. A chuckle rolled out of him as he patted the top of her head, albeit awkwardly.

He spoke in Alkarran again, wagging a finger at her in warning. "I don't recommend you go far, of course. It will afford some protection, should it be needed, if you are not here. No mortal is complete without a dinghy to aid them." His eyes hardened. "Otherwise, we are little more than prisoners."

"Anything to protect Ava," I murmured warmly. She had already climbed on top of the boat and inspected the seam at the bottom. Her hands roved hungrily over it. She murmured to herself, full lips silent, but steady.

Gio canted his body to face the *Rostina* again. Seeing a closing window of opportunity, I hastily asked, "Before you go, can you answer a few questions?"

"About?"

"God magic."

He hesitated. "Can the questions wait for Baxter?"

"I suppose so."

Gio grimaced. "Servants aren't supposed to answer questions unless granted permission by their demigod, particularly not about god magic. Not that servants would know much about god magic, anyway."

My voice lifted in astonishment. "You can't answer questions about certain topics?"

His eyebrows lifted, and I realized it was as good an answer as I could expect. I waved toward the dinghy.

"But you can bring this?"

"This?" He nudged it with a foot. "Oh, this? It has nothing to do with you. Just Ava, remember?"

He winked, but the same tense expression haunted his gaze, as if this were all an act. A play. He, a mere moving part.

"Right. Of course." I mimicked his stiff smile, though I had no idea what he meant.

Gio stepped back, feet cutting through the sand.

"Then do you have a map of Alaysia?" I called after him.

He stopped. Blinked. Three seconds paused before he murmured, "A map?"

"Yes."

"For what purpose?"

"Ah . . . reference?"

Suspicion tapered his eyes to slits. "You plan to study this map?"

"Yes. Just to know what Alaysia looks like." I kept his steady gaze with an innocent smile. "I've never been here before and I'm curious what the land looks like."

His mouth opened, then closed. "Alaysia is not safe for you."

"I know."

"Ava can go in the dinghy if she needs it, but it's not advisable for you to travel. Baxter was clear on this."

Ava had returned at my side, her face a blank slate as his gaze flickered from mine, to hers, and back to mine.

"I understand, and have no desire to cause trouble."

"I will search for a map," he said in a hollow way that meant he had no plans to do such a thing. "Forgive me, I must be off."

He looked at Ava, but he spoke to me in Alkarran. "Hide the dinghy whenever she returns, until she needs it again. No reason to draw suspicion. Keep track of it. Oh, and Bianca?"

"Yes?"

"Don't get caught."

* * *

Ava's giggle crashed with the surf. A hand covered her mouth as she leaned back, cackling in delight.

"The sand." Tears leaked out of her eyes. "So funny."

A towering sculpture of Aldred shifted in front of her. His expression was twisted in comical disfigurement with a too-large nose, his sausage-like finger pointed in accusation. The sandy figure tripped, splattering to granules at her feet.

She pealed with laughter again.

Chuckling, I released the goddess magic that had bound the sand together. The feeling of energy leaving me ceased, and a silence settled in the aftermath. With no sand bubbling up into comical figures that chased her, Ava's hilarity faded.

She held up a finger, relief in her tone. "Another spell works," she cried. "This is good."

Mental checklists cluttered my mind. After hours of testing, all goddess magic spells seemed to work in Alaysia. The most important ones, anyway. Transporting. Invisibility. Simple spells like starting a fire or conjuring freshwater happened the way I desired. Silly incantations, like the one I'd just finished for Ava's amusement, held their power still.

Everything except summoning or transporting objects. Attempts to call for my favorite goblet or tree branches met with failure. Alkarra lay too far away, perhaps. The thought gave me a melancholy pang that I quickly dismissed.

No, this opportunity was too rife with possibility for homesickness.

Thus far, no god or demigod had descended, filled with wrath that I should bring goddess magic to this island, which might satisfy yet another question. Could Ventis sense me using goddess magic in his kingdom?

Perhaps. If he was annoyed with it, he gave no sign so far. While occupied at Baxter's mission report, I doubted he even noticed. My decision to test goddess magic now of all times had been strategic.

Yet, I'd be a fool to make any assumptions of the gods.

Only time would truly tell.

Sand warmed the backs of my legs as I settled into it, feet digging into the grainy stuff. A dress, only as long as my knees, left my calves open to a breeze. The material, thin but sturdy, ruffled in a sough of wind and cooled my sun-heated skin. My gaze lingered on the horizon. A distant storm passed by the edge in a dark smudge.

Such rampant beauty here still startled me. I hadn't expected so much . . . untamed appeal. Alaysia reminded me of Letum Wood. Bound in magic, driven by deities, and wildly frightening. Despite it all, I felt drawn to the savage heart.

Ava settled next to me, then pointed to the left.

"Home."

"That way?"

She nodded. Nothing visible lay to where she motioned.

"How long does it take to get there?"

She shrugged.

"You haven't been here before?"

"No."

"Do you miss home?"

Ava nodded again. "Yes, sometimes."

We'd stashed the dinghy out of sight of the shore, behind a tree. The trees and sand didn't do much to hide it, but god magic completed the job. How long the disguise would last, I didn't know, but I looked forward to finding out. Ticking off questions about god magic that had been haunting me gave a rare satisfaction to the visit so far, and we'd only been here a day.

"How many mortals live in Alaysia, do you think?"

Ava blinked. Her forehead ruffled in question. I tilted my head to the side to find another, simpler way to phrase the question. Would Ava know such a fact, anyway? She'd lived on her small collection alone, presumably, until she came to Alkarra.

"Lots of mortals here?" I said. "Or little?"

Gestures with my hands punctuated the question. Understanding flooded her face, then consternation.

"Ah . . ."

"You don't know?"

Sheepish, and with a hint of color in her dark cheeks, she shook her head. I smiled, silently admonishing myself to remember she was only eleven years old.

"It's all right."

A stretch of silence followed. Ava wrapped her arms around her knees. "More mortals than demigods," she finally said.

"I thought so."

She frowned. "Many mortals? I don't know."

With a hand on her arm, and a gentle squeeze, I said, "Don't worry about it."

A relieved smile followed.

My thoughts meandered to Baxter. What did he face with the gods? Did he physically see them, or did they represent themselves only as voices? Or at all? Presumably, the forest goddess Deasylva had a body—or so Sanako reported—yet had never revealed herself to me. All lay in assumption for these fickle deities.

I forced myself to set aside my concerns for Baxter. There was nothing I could do for him, anyway, though I'd be relieved when the Council of the Gods finished. Hopefully, it would yield more answers regarding the future.

Leda popped into my mind, and I smiled as I wondered what she was doing. Attempts to magick her a letter had yielded no obvious result, but perhaps she had received my short missive. Unlikely.

Reluctantly, I thought of Papa, wondered what he'd think of me here on a beach in Alaysia, testing goddess magic. Such mental meanderings slipped to Merrick. I'd never asked him about his opinion of beach life. He lived against a backdrop of rugged mountains and precipitous peaks in my mind. Quickly as those ideas came, I sent them away.

Why I didn't want to linger on him, I also wouldn't analyze.

The sudden appearance of a basket startled me out of pondering whether Gio had ulterior motives for bringing Ava a dinghy. Ava gasped and nearly jumped into my lap from sheer surprise. When nothing in the basket leaped out at us, I gave an amused chuckle, reached out, plucked a small piece of folded parchment out of the front.

Baxter's trim, cascading handwriting filled the inside.

Bianca and Ava,

Hope you're enjoying your day. Here's some lunch. Ava, please teach Bianca about our local food, as I know she's eager to enjoy all of Alaysia.

For what it's worth, the fruapu is my favorite.

All is fine here.

—Baxter

A sigh escaped me.

"He's so thoughtful," I murmured, then read a simplified version of the note to Ava. She'd already scrambled closer, extricating and uprooting different types of fruit, what appeared to be a bread-like stick, and light yellow eggs.

"Alaysian food," she crooned, then tossed an egg toward me. I caught it, the small thing half the size of my thumb and smooth on the outside. "Very good."

I hopped to my feet, then held out a hand to Ava. She accepted without question, already chomping on a chunk of something soft, cluttered with a salt-like purple layer on the top.

"Well," I cried, "let's take this back to the house and wash it down with some fresh water. I'm thirsty, and we have lots of time to spare."

Chapter Seven

An indigo, sinewy, paper-like structure hovered in the early-morning air.

I straightened from where I sat just outside the beach house watching the sunrise, to regard the little box with deepening curiosity. The calm morning soothed me as thoroughly as the rushing waves, particularly in such a halcyon world, unbroken by other sounds.

A gift, undoubtedly. Alaysian Baxter seemed to love them.

The package was square, a little thicker than my hand, and tied with a silky ribbon. A smile stole across my face as I gently accepted it, not surprised when it felt featherlight. Not far away, Ava snored in her hammock, tucked into a ball at the bottom.

When I touched the top, it fell open.

My breath caught.

Inside lay a lovely broach. Opaque pearls collected against a golden backdrop, sprawling out like the branches of a tree. More robust pearls formed a trunk that spread into stalk-like roots of glimmering gold.

A note lay beneath.

Bianca,

Forgive me for not returning last night. Father kept me at the Rostina after my report. There are a few responsibilities I hold today, but I shall return to the beach house this evening to eat dinner with you.

Go nowhere else, please.

Father has said he hopes to meet with you later this week, and eagerly anticipates your conversation. I'll have more updates when I return.

Also, please look outside. I hoped to bring a bit of home to you.

Miss you.

—Baxter

PS—There are many beautiful things in Alaysia. This one made me think of you.

A strange dimness of light behind the beach house propelled me out of the sand. I'd also been half-heartedly perusing a book I found on the far shelf. Alkarran. A warbling love story that Camille would have swooned over. I hadn't comprehended much of it.

Questions about Ignis and our conversation floated through my mind with too much force to allow me to focus. No sign of Ignis had reappeared . . .

. . . and why not?

Frustrated, I set the book aside and padded through the

house, over to the back window, broach in hand, to see what Baxter meant. I caught a gasp.

Letum Wood lay outside.

I set the broach and box aside, climbed out the window, and tipped my head back. A familiar canopy stretched overhead, blocking the growing Alaysian sun. Dense forest. Thick branches. Mossy undertones. Vines dropped here and there. Baxter could have taken a slice out of Letum Wood and brought it to me. My heart warmed with the kind gesture.

I reached out, touching a nearby root well, but my fingers went through the air. I curled them back in, tucking them against my palm.

It wasn't real.

An illusion, though a talented one. He'd conjured up a piece of home. Seeing it brought me comfort, despite a hollow feeling. Without the whispers of the trees, was the forest anything at all?

Yes.

But not the same.

A smile broke across my face anyway. The broach I didn't care much for, but the attempt to make me feel at home warmed me. I wandered the illusion for several minutes. It extended around the beach house, but not much farther. When I stepped far enough out, it disappeared into beach and bush and sky. For now, a bit of home wrapped this strange new world.

I quietly slipped back inside, feeling lighter than I had since we arrived. A prickle of god magic flared. A welcome reassurance that the amulet remained hidden in the trunk in the corner.

Ava yawned when I showed her the broach—she oohed over it—and then I tucked it aside. Perhaps there'd be a reason to wear it at some point.

Heat sweltered outside despite the early morning light, and the air felt like a wrung-out rag. With god magic, I conjured two sweating glasses of ice-cold water. One hovered near Ava. She eyed it, then me, and accepted with a nod. After drinking until the cool water slaked my thirst, I set it aside.

"Ava," I drawled. "Can you tell me why Gio brought a dinghy to you yesterday? Who would hurt you?"

"*Monilay mal.*"

"But a demigod could easily overcome a dinghy."

"Not if I leave."

"Before they come, you mean?"

Ava swished her water around her cup with a frown, then nodded. The pinch of her lips told me I wouldn't get much more out of her. My uneasy intuition meant there was likely more to it. Nuance I might not understand as an Alkarran, perhaps. Ava's collection was at least far enough away that I couldn't see it on the horizon. Though I had no experience on the ocean, I imagined it would be hours by boat, at the very closest.

"Gio," she said slowly, wrapping her lips around the world. "He is . . . he is a . . . he is *amicala*. A . . . ah . . . witness? No. A mortal who knows . . . things."

The last word rolled off her lips with an uncomfortable grimace. She sucked on her teeth. In the gesture, I saw a world of uncertainty.

Guilt.

What had he said to her?

"Is it good that Gio is *amicala*?" I asked.

Ava chewed on that question, clearly attempting to line up what Alkarran words she knew. She had been stumbling between languages for months now. Her progress had been impressive, but frustrating.

A whisper preceded a swirl of cinders that Ava didn't appear to notice. Visible only to me, perhaps? They disappeared as quickly as they came. In their wake, Ignis spoke.

Together, we can do anything.

The reminder sent a thrill of god magic energy through my veins. It swirled back to life, brightened by Ignis' presence.

Intent, he murmured. *Everything in god magic is built around true desire and intention. God magic, when you control it by trust and experience, has no end to its power. You may converse in Alaysian as easily as you wish, only will it to be so.*

I pulled in a breath. What did I have to lose from an attempt to execute god magic? Nothing.

Hadn't I come here for this purpose?

Without responding to him, I turned my focus to Ava. On how much easier her life would be with a better understanding of the Alkarran language. Conversation flowing between us. Deep discussions, should I need them. An utter lack of fear or stress around communication.

Heat issued, escaping me in a swirl out of my skin.

"Gio is an *amicala*," Ava said, oblivious to my internal force. "So he's a friend to us. We need friends here if we're going to stay safe, especially you."

I blinked.

Had she just—

Her eyes snapped wide open. A hand flew to her throat. She turned to me, eyes ringed in white.

"Can I speak in Alkarran?" she squeaked.

I grinned. "Sounds like it!"

Again, Ignis murmured, *I remind you that together, we can do anything.*

I scowled at the embers, though I didn't know why I should be upset with him. He'd significantly made my life here easier with this single use of god magic. Ava as well. The cinders streamed in through one window and out the next in a reddish flow.

Alarm filled her voice. "What happened?" she asked.

"I'm sorry," I cried. "I didn't mean to use god magic on you without permission, it just . . . it happened. I'm still not really sure about the line between intent and action. Like Gio, I wanted you to be able to speak."

No confused stare or request to slow my speech down came. Ava blinked, expression rendered totally blank.

"Ava?"

She nodded absently, then rubbed a hand over her throat. Her stomach growled audibly, but she didn't seem to notice.

"Does it hurt?" I whispered.

"No."

"Do you want me to try to take it back?"

She shook her head more sharply. "No. I . . . I need to get used to it."

"Are you upset?"

Her brow furrowed. "No, this will be easier. So much easier. It's . . . strange. I'm not used to you using the same magic that—"

She broke off. Her troubled gaze didn't quite meet mine. She stiffened when I sat next to her, then relaxed.

"I'm sorry, Ava. I need to learn how to control and use the god magic, I suppose, if I'm going to be here. I'm trying. It's just . . . it is strange."

"Thank you." Her fingers fidgeted with her skirt. "I'm happy. It's a good gift."

Silence thickened the air between us, without burden this time. Relief that she'd forgiven me made me weak.

"Can we trust Gio?" I ventured tentatively.

"Yes. Yesterday, he said that we must take care of each other, and I told him I wanted to go back to my collection of islands to check on my birds. Some of them might have gotten away before Bram set the hedges on fire. They might be looking for me. He brought a dinghy for me to use and . . . to keep me safe in case a demigod comes. That's all."

Full, confident sentences from Ava took a little getting used to, but she was right—speaking so simply would be much better, even at the mental cost of doing magic *to* her. Her animosity for Alaysia, at times outright hostility, led me to think of Baxter. What if her agitation was poorly-concealed eagerness to get somewhere else?

Namely, to her birds.

"Is there any mortal in your collection that you want to see?"

"Daemon. He was my . . . friend? Maybe. I don't know. He talked to Tama and no one talked to Tama. I want to go see him. We could go in the boat, since Gio brought it."

Getting off of this island held great appeal, if only to help me understand Alaysia, Ava, and Baxter better. Not to mention get more information on the watery world that threatened Alkarra. I needed all the facts I could find.

Desperation called through her eyes. With both of her parents dead, Daemon might be her only connection to her old life. How well I understood the need to see, experience, and taste those memories one last time.

Then, they could be shelved away for good.

"Sure," I said with a shrug. "Baxter will return this evening, and Ventis hasn't given us a firm time to meet with him yet, so let's go!"

Ava brightened. "Really?"

"Really. Where is your collection?"

Her gaiety soured. "A couple of hours row from here."

"That's fine."

"Truly?" She cut me a suspicious glance. "Can you take us with magic?"

A welling of anxiety rose within me at the question. Transportation spells required knowledge of where one transported in order to arrive safely. Certainly, some witches circumvented that—like Papa, for example—and we knew that transportation magic worked here, but I couldn't feel comfortable with attempting to take two of us somewhere unknown. It wouldn't be safe for so many reasons.

What if I harmed both of us? Became lost, confused?

Landed right back in Prana's domain?

The rules and edges of life blurred in Alaysia. What belonged to the gods, and what belonged to Prana? Not knowing the boundaries led me to caution, particularly with magical use.

"It is dangerous and far," Ava continued in a murmur, as if speaking to herself. She tilted her head back, hand lifted up. "The weather is good. We don't have to worry about storms."

"Do you know how to navigate there?"

"Enough."

My eyes widened. "Enough? What does that mean?"

She grinned. "We have ways, Bianca. Can you trust me?"

I softened, further set at ease by how easy our conversation had become. "Of course."

"Baxter told you not to go anywhere in his note."

I shrugged. "We'll just god magic back if we need to. You're worth the chance. Besides, it's not that far from the *Rostina* if we can row, and he won't be back for several hours, anyway. I'd love to try goddess magic in the dinghy, just to make sure it works there, too."

Ava softened. "Daemon is . . . not always a very safe mortal. He hates the demigods very much, so Shara put him in our small collection, away from everyone."

"Shara didn't just kill him?"

She shrugged.

I gestured out to the sea, eager to see more of this world. "Let's get started. Sounds like we have an adventure ahead of us."

* * *

Sea water slapped the hull of the boat.

The moment we launched from the shore, Ava's face had become the picture of concentration. Her brows pulled together, forming tight angles around her sloping forehead. Her lips pressed shut, as if she was determined not to speak. Sunlight burst from the sky, a brilliant promise of another beautiful day.

The muscles in my arms pulled taut as I leaned back on the oar. Ava fell into rowing like a natural, her legs pressed forward, body tight as she heaved back. A bundle of something smelly rolled in between our feet below the board where we sat, which stretched across the boat. Blood-tinged and stained brown, I could only assume it was dead fish.

After a few minutes, we'd created a rhythm. The physical release was a welcome reprieve for the impatient goddess magic in my body.

"Can I use god magic to get us there faster?" I asked.

She shrugged. Uncertainty showed in the ruffles of her forehead now. Her teeth worried her bottom lip as she gazed around, already seeming lost.

"And you know where to go?" I asked.

Ava hesitated, then shook her head.

"No?" I screeched.

"Well, maybe," she said firmly.

I opened my mouth to speak, but closed it again. Despite her uncertainty, she seemed determined to continue. We fell back into silence. The unease of heading into an endless vista of water crept over me. Comforted by the truth that I had two magicks at my disposal to get us out of any trouble and no amulets to wreak havoc out here, I pressed on.

Ava cracked the gentle quiet.

"The mermaids will take us to my collection." She released her oar and rubbed her palms on her skirt. The oar jerked around a bit before she grabbed it again. Water splashed on my cheek as an unhappy wave shuffled by, scooping water into the bottom of the dinghy.

"We're going to the mermaids?"

Ava nodded.

I had a feeling, based on Ava's growing consternation, that we were about to approach said mermaids.

Ava pulled the oar out of the water, then indicated I should do the same with mine. For several seconds, we rocked in the middle of the sea. I twisted back, attempting to find the *Rostina*. It loomed in the distance, now a vague speck. Being this far out in the sea, surrounded only by water, made my stomach tilt.

I suppressed a shudder, recalling Prana's violent wake up call only a day ago. The cold clutches of her deep water were a nasty reminder of the sea goddess' power. A splash and a flash of brilliant color drew my gaze to the front of the dinghy. Ava tensed, but kept her hands on the oar. Her gaze remained straight ahead.

"We are not afraid," Ava murmured. "You cannot be afraid."

You cannot be afraid.

As if such a statement didn't make the mermaids even more terrifying.

I ignored the building tension in the air and drew in a steady, slow breath. Not afraid, indeed. My heart calmed as the glinting color closed in.

Reddish brown, perhaps?

Hints of electric orange existed in the kaleidoscope of disappearing colors, lost to the deep sea.

"Say nothing," Ava murmured.

I tightened my hold on the oar. No problem there.

A face appeared in the water ahead of the boat, then vanished. The unexpected sight made a fist out of my stomach. Jikes, but these mermaids knew how to stall. Ava reached down, fiddling with the canvas netting on the outside of the package Gio left.

The face appeared again, on my side this time. Drawn to the movement, I glanced over.

Through the water, hints of light pink came into view. Like a blush of strawberries in wavering water. Flaxen hair spiraled around a mostly-human face, billowing through the sea. The mermaid stared at me. The eyes were strange to peer into. The irises matched their skin, only a darker hue of pink. Two closed slits sat where a nose would be on a witch or mortal.

Below the mermaid, graceful arms and a full chest disappeared into darker scales and deeper water. Yellowish-pink scales glittered along their shoulders and down the trunk, all the way to a glimmering fin that appeared in snatches. It would be at least as tall as me, though the body structure seemed delicate, like a bird. A hint of a translucent, webbed fin whipped back and forth.

In a word, they were exquisite.

An equally curious stare narrowed on me. I returned the look. If god magic could allow Ava to speak the common Alkarran language, could it help me communicate with mermaids?

The mermaid departed.

Ava peered over her side, where the mermaid swam close to the top of the water. This time, the mermaid bared sharp incisor fangs.

"Jikes," I muttered.

The mermaid didn't break the surface, but only barely. Ava ignored the apparent hostility. Sometime in my study of the mermaid, Ava had opened up the package that Gio left. A rancid odor turned my stomach.

The pert almost-nose breached the top, opened the two slits, drew in air, then retreated as the slits closed. Eyes dilated, turning near-black.

Ava locked in a stare with the mermaid. She straightened, reached into the slimy pile of fish guts, and paused.

The mermaid snarled impatiently.

Ava dangled the fish guts in the air, visible from where the mermaid darted back and forth. The mermaid curled her upper lip in a motion like a hissing cat and faded into the dark sea.

Ava let out a long breath, dropped the fish guts, and reached for her oar. She gripped it, slimy guts notwithstanding. I scrambled to do the same. The sickly smell emanated from her hand, but I had a feeling Ava didn't want to clean her hand in the water with the mermaid hovering close.

"Mermaids communicate through thoughts," Ava murmured. "Images. They put them into your mind. This mermaid said that they will take us to my collection in exchange for more of the food."

"That's good?"

She nodded once.

Ava threw a coiled rope into the water. The line dropped out of sight, apparently attached somewhere in the front. We remained slack on the ocean for a few moments before the boat gave a violent jerk. I grabbed the side with one hand, the oar with the other, and barely kept from tumbling into the ocean.

Ava shook her head with an annoyed mutter at the less-than-gentle start, but seemed far less tense as we cut through the splashing waves. The sun crept higher in the distance, spilling yellow diamonds onto the surface of the water as it illuminated the world.

The dinghy cut through the waves, moving faster than we could have ever rowed, and toward a new, unknown place.

Chapter Eight

We cut through sapphire water while the sun bore down in gentle persuasion, drying the occasional splash from cresting waves. The heat burned my skin as the sun climbed higher in a perfect sky.

The mermaid held an impressive speed for such a lithe figure. Ornery waves smoothed out into azure ribbons as we moved away from Ventis' kingdom. I couldn't help my admiration for the savage beauty of Prana's world.

Terrifying as it might be.

Islands popped up here and there, hidden in the distance. None with a daunting *Rostina*. Once, Ava pointed out another dinghy. A mortal rowed it by themselves, near an island encompassed in a glance.

When we slowed, a smudge on the horizon indicated a fire ahead. Ava's grip on the oar tightened as the dinghy shuddered to a stop. Silence baked around us. We rocked up and down in the waves. Ava grabbed the stinky chum and threw the whole thing overboard. It splattered with a giant *plop*.

"Don't look," she said quickly. "There are too many mermaids."

Curiosity almost drove me to peek into the clear waters, but considering the size of that mermaid's incisors, I decided against it.

My gaze trained on the horizon as Ava gripped her oar and began to row. Splashing, and an occasional, distant shriek, issued from behind. Mermaids, undoubtedly, feasting. I shuddered, grateful to leave them behind.

Within a few turns, Ava and I synced our strokes. She held up a hand for me to pause, then she dug harder into the water on her side, to turn the dingy.

We started toward an almost-barren horizon, except for the smoke. Ava directed us as we rowed. Nothing but endless water and sky could be seen. We were far from amulets, demigods, mortals, and soon from the mermaids, but even farther from Alkarra.

My stomach growled against the fresh exertion, but the pull of muscle and sinew took my mind away from worries over mermaids. Water churned into white caps and deep troughs. No wind agitated the sea, but something else seemed to.

Ava's solemn mood hovered over the small boat as an island came into view. My arms ached. My thirst intensified. Ava licked her lips again, but still wouldn't meet my eyes.

"Thirsty?" I asked.

She hesitated, then nodded. I used god magic to hand her a leather pouch of water, which she quickly drank. One appeared for me, the water cool and slightly sweet. It refilled as I drank, and I felt grateful for the simplicity of it.

With another thought, I sent the pouch back to the beach house. The simple commands gave me confidence with a magic I hadn't used all that frequently. Now, with Ignis' reminder from earlier ringing in my mind, I didn't want to *stop* using it.

Ava had paused our rowing, whether for a break or hesitation, I couldn't tell. She squinted at me. With a wave of her hand toward my face, she said, "Change your eyes and your hair." She touched the corner of her eye with her finger. "Like mine. You need to look like a mortal."

A simple transformation spell quickly yielded a result that met Ava's approval, but I stopped the magic, then redid it with god magic. No reason to draw attention with goddess magic, just in case. Besides, we'd just proven that goddess magic worked on the water, too. Another check off my list.

"Better the second time." She punctuated it with a firm nod. "You look like a mortal, not a witch or a demigod. It will be safer this way."

She gripped the oar and set her jaw.

"Now," she whispered. "You'll meet *my* mortals."

* * *

The dinghy jerked to a stop on a small sandbar.

"My collection is a floating one," Ava murmured quietly. "There is no anchor below it. It moves, connected with other floating islands by ropes so we don't get too far from each other and drift into the kingdom of a different god."

"I see."

She cut me a glance that told me, in no uncertain terms, that I *didn't* see. Not yet, anyway.

"Why floating islands?" I asked, mimicking her quiet voice.

Her nostrils flared. "The gods keep the power for themselves. They won't waste it on the comfort of mortals."

"Instead of building better islands," I murmured, "Ventis is creating his *Rostina*."

The burning rage in her eyes told me I'd hit the mark.

My arms burned in the delightful way that followed challenging work as I straightened, grateful to shuck thoughts of Ventis aside.

Ava climbed out of the boat first, scanning the view. Her feet sank into a dark-sanded beach dotted with marshes, weeds, and black rocks. The pristine white sand from Ventis's domain looked like ground pearls in comparison to this dirty field. The mangy surface dropped into water, then faded to gloom. A vast void of life teemed somewhere beneath.

How did this small of an island stay together?

Alaysia defied all logic.

This particular island wasn't much bigger than Papa's apartment in Chatham Castle. Well, Papa's *former* apartment, as it wasn't his anymore. Setting aside the flare of annoyance that rose with the thought, I turned my attention to studying this claustrophobically-small space. Tiny islands existed beyond it. Most of them held the same amorphous shape, mere blobs of sand at the surface of the sea.

Pointy bushes and a few thick-trunked trees towered overhead, the leaves twice as wide as my body and just as tall. Each tree had a rope that stretched all the way to another one, desperate bandages keeping a body together. Rounded globes grew in the middle of the tree, halfway up, like a skirt. One of them fell as we splashed out of the waves. The globe broke open, spurting glaucous liquid into the sand.

Ava held out a hand, motioning for me to stay behind her. I missed Viveet's immediate protection. In all likelihood, she would have worked here. Not knowing for certain, however, risked too much. At least for now. These mortals had no ability when pitted against my magic—I wouldn't scare them with a sword.

Ava's young voice rippled across the quiet island.

"Daemon?"

Only the hush of the waves answered.

Across the way, the skeleton of a hut drew my gaze. Made of stitched-together leaves propped against the trees, it provided a paltry escape from the sun. Belongings scattered here and there. Bowls carved from shells, cups from twisted leaves. A hammock stretched between two of the thicker trees, braided from a seaweed-like plant.

Nothing concrete existed here. No structures. No wood. The mortals must live out of their watercrafts, scraping by in a routine existence tied up in the agonizing hunt for food and drinkable water.

The source of the oily black smoke became apparent as we wandered farther up the beach. The top part of Daemon's island crackled with fire. Flames chewed through the thick leaves in the sand, belching a noxious smoke. A smell similar to sulfur lingered like a haze.

Embers lifted from the pile to twirl around me. I glared at them.

They retreated.

Yet again, Ava gave no indication of noticing them.

An ominous feeling swept through me as Ava turned back to the water, hand shielding her eyes. She skimmed the distant horizon.

"Where is Daemon? He should be back by now. He built the fire before he went fishing. The smoke brings him back, but this is too late in the morning."

Anxiety stained her voice. A reminder of her youth. In all her depths of experience, I forgot she was still a child.

Ava frowned, hands held up in question.

"And where is his place?" she murmured. "He had a shelter made from collected driftwood. It took him years to collect enough. He kept giving the pieces away to the families."

A vague wave of her hand indicated the trees, where the hammock stretched. Couldn't have been big, wherever the structure went. I eyed the burning pile, but saw no sign of wood. Only the bubbling leaves, excreting a thick substance as they smoldered.

"I'm sure he'll be back," I murmured.

Ava called to the closest island in Alaysian words. A mortal male looked up from a dinghy. He couldn't have been older than my age. A baby was strapped to his thin chest as he bent over a net. Under Ava's call, he stood straighter, then waved out to the sea. As if he called Daemon back with the gesture, a boat appeared near the horizon.

Ava whirled around, saw the vessel, and visibly relaxed.

"There he is."

Silent, as if in honor of so solemn a place, we watched Daemon row in. An intent gaze in a broad face appeared first, riding on wide shoulders and a thin body. When he was close enough to see his amber eyes, a smile illuminated his face. He rowed onto the sand with a final burst of strength.

"Ava!"

"When he approaches, don't touch him," Ava hurriedly said. "Mortals don't like to be touched by those whom we don't know. If he offers his palms, then you may reciprocate, but only if he offers."

At that moment, Daemon's dinghy hit the sand, skidded, and nearly tipped him out sideways. Small, willowy traps cluttered the bottom of his boat, shifting from the impact. Nets. Ropes. Dead fish, their buggy eyes peering out. Three of them were longer than my leg.

"Ava!" He leapt to his feet, his legs long. "Ava!

Ava raced over. She flung herself into his arms. His barrel-neck and big shoulders swamped her. When he set her down, she stepped back and lifted both hands. Daemon laughed with incredulous disbelief. They pressed their palms together. Both hesitated, then he slung his arms around her and lifted her into another embrace.

They chattered in Alaysian, so fast I could barely make out more than a blur of sound. I stepped back, self-conscious while witnessing such a happy reunion. There wasn't far to go before I splashed into the water.

You used my power, Lady-witch.

I swallowed.

Jikes, did Ignis know?

What a stupid thought. Of course he did.

You thought I wouldn't notice earlier?

"I never said that."

You never need to. Try it again. Use god magic to understand the Alaysian language.

The taunt had more temptation than I expected.

"It's not my conversation to eavesdrop in on, nor have I been invited to it. Some of us have manners."

A sound I assumed to be a derisive snort followed. *Hide behind your excuses a different time, when the fate of Alkarra doesn't rest on your ability to be the greatest weapon your land has ever known. You learn from me or . . . all of your beloved witches die. It's simple arithmetic.*

My fingers tightened into a fist until the nails dug into my palm, orienting me back into the moment.

The greatest weapon? What was he talking about?

A living amulet.

You read minds? I thought. He replied with such speed—so much ferocity—that the following sweep of heat stole my breath.

I never said that.

"And yet . . ." I murmured.

Predictability is a powerful tool, he murmured. *To that end, however, our connection is greater than you think.*

With that discomfiting thought, I shook my head. "No," I ground out, more comfortable hearing my voice than attempting to send structured thoughts. "I don't have Ava's permission to listen into their conversation. She wouldn't know that I could overhear, and that wouldn't be fair. She's reuniting with, for better or worse, her only family member."

Genuine inquiry lined his voice when he asked, *Do you not*

protect yourself first? What if she's speaking something against you to him?

"Is she?"

His voice preened. *No.*

I smirked.

The fire blazed.

Would you like me to translate?

"No need."

Is your trust in her so great?

"Yes."

For minutes, Daemon stood at the edge of the surf, water crashing around his ankles as they spoke. Eventually, he turned his wide, honey-colored eyes on me. I met his powerful gaze. Wisdom, depth, and wariness looked back. He spoke to Ava as he regarded me.

With a tilt of his chin my direction, they turned and started this way.

I will protect you if you will not protect yourself.

"Do I really need to fear him?"

In Alaysia, you should fear everyone.

Sand clung to Ava's feet and calves as she worked her way over. A cautious expression, hidden behind delight, lurked in her eyes. I kept my hands at my side, her warning a ripple in my mind.

Daemon apprised me from a few paces away. Ava joined at my side, standing slightly in front of me. She spoke quickly, but not hurried. The more she stated, the deeper Daemon's curiosity seemed to grow.

Only a few chattering replies came from his lips.

Finally, he grunted.

The low noise in his throat reminded me so much of Ava I almost laughed. He turned back to his dinghy.

Ava relaxed.

"He accepts you on his island. I'll tell you more later. We

were just catching up." She shot me a sharp glance. "Or do you already know that?"

"I didn't use magic to understand you," I said lightly.

Contrition appeared in her eyes like a flash. She gestured toward his boat, and I followed to help unload. Lines of strung fish flopped over the side and onto a leaf as tall as me. Some of them were tied together, while others were caught with traps. Several fish twitched at the bottom of the skiff in a low skim of collected water. The beach smelled like fish by the time the small vessel lay empty.

Daemon grabbed a thick stem at the top of the laden leaf. Muscles in his arms tightened as he hauled the catch up the beach, toward the hammock. Ava and I trailed behind. Once there, Ava asked him something with a gesture between the trees, which I assumed meant his previous house.

While they chattered, I drifted to the fire to give Ava room to recapture her old life.

Also, though loathe to admit it, I wanted to speak with Ignis again. Understand his rapacity, his words.

When the fate of Alkarra doesn't rest on your ability to be the greatest weapon your land has ever known, he had said.

My curiosity followed.

Charred leaves smoldered under a thinning line of smoke. Years of experience must have helped Daemon know how long he could fish before the burning leaves stopped emitting the smoggy vapors. A telltale glow of heat lurked amongst curled cinders along the sand, the black ash a strange contrast to the darker grains. Glittering shards stuck out here and there, flashing against the sunlight.

These mortals are planning a rebellion, Ignis said, bemused.

My head jerked up. "What?"

Not Ava, but the others.

"Does she know?"

She will soon, I imagine.

"How do you know?"

I'm a god, Lady-witch.

His clearly-offended reply didn't answer the question, but I decided not to push it.

"Are you going to stop it?"

Just because I know doesn't mean Ventis knows. If Ventis has a rebellion on his hands, that's his problem.

I glanced casually over my shoulder. No, it was also Ava's problem. She clearly held a deep affection for this place, dark memories or not. Daemon gestured wildly with his hands, swinging them around. Despite his animation, he spoke quietly.

Meanwhile, movement stirred on the other islands. Mortals stepped out of shade made by leaves and climbed into similar dinghys. Most of them were bare-chested, wearing as little clothing as possible. A woman peered at me as she held a suckling child, not a stitch of clothing above her waist. Her light hair unfurled, waving around the backs of her knees.

My attention returned to Ava.

"What will happen to all of them if Ventis finds out about the rebellion?" I asked quietly.

They will die, as all mortals do when insurrection occurs.

"Why?"

In a world such as Alaysia, we cannot afford revolution.

"Is your magic so frail?"

In some ways, yes, he said easily. *There is much more to it than that, however.*

God magic hadn't shown much frailty to me, but I let that pass for now. More profound mysteries lurked than that.

Be warned, lady-Witch, he growled. *If you are not careful to hide who—and what—you are, these mortals will attempt to pull you into their cause. I advise against this on grounds of physical and political safety. It's not allowed for witches to stir up trouble here in the land of the gods, as I'm sure you're aware. Tell Ava not*

*to mention your magical abilities to them. She has not thus far, but
. . . one never knows.*

"I'm surprised you care."

I will not have you harmed.

His possessive tone startled me.

"How could I stop Ava from telling them?"

Are you not mine?

His words set my heart racing. The insinuation had more to
do with magic, surely, but undertones lined it.

"No," I immediately countered.

A low chuckle followed.

"In Alkarra," I whispered fiercely, "we don't force magic on
others."

A beat of silence preceded his reply.

That, he murmured silkily, *is not entirely true, is it?*

A memory surfaced from my mind, as if coming through
fog. Papa's office, when Bram and I fought with god magic. The
curses and spells I used to bind Jote and the other demigods
replayed through my mind in rapid speed. The veritas potion we
forced them to swallow. A reminder of this morning, when I
used god magic to help Ava speak Alkarran more clearly.

My stomach twisted.

"Fair," I whispered hoarsely, a bitter taste in my mouth.

*You may flatter yourself that things in Alaysia are so much
worse than Alkarra,* Ignis said with a hint of annoyance, *but there
is much you don't understand, Lady-witch. Living in one world
closes your mind. You don't see the entire world clearly from Alkarra. How could you when you've had no contrast? Here, I give you a
chance to* really *understand. To know and do what no other witch
in Alkarra could do.*

Hunger burned deep inside at his words, resurrected with an
undulation of god magic and heat. It swarmed me with a thirst
and desire I had never been able to satisfy. The one that longed
to prove myself.

Unable to stop, I asked in a tremulous voice, "And what is it that no other witch in Alkarra could do?"

Save the land of the witches from the god that intends to scourge it, raze life from the land, and take it for himself.

"Tontes?"

Indeed.

"What about you, Ventis, and Gelas?"

We have no such plans to bother our sisters, yet require a united front to stop our eldest brother. Tontes is the strongest of all of us. With you at our side, we can stop him from invading Alkarra.

"Without me?"

Prospects would be, how do you say it? Bleak.

I scoffed. "Says the god that sent his children to attempt an uprising?"

Who said, he murmured, *that I sent them?*

"You didn't send them?"

Like you, my children tend to have an independent streak.

My thoughts scattered, startled by such a revelation.

One of the mortals finished swimming his way over. His ribs jutted out as he waded out of the ocean, up the beach. Astonishment filled his amber gaze when his eyes clapped on Ava. She beamed as they pressed their palms together. A woman clambered out of a boat and raced to her. She collapsed to her knees in the sand and yanked Ava into her too-thin arms.

Daemon's voice boomed, calling others to his island. Responses followed, carrying the news of Ava and fresh fish further down the rows of haphazard land. Ten amassing mortals stood in a semicircle around Daemon, gazing at his catch for the day.

"Where do they get fresh water?" I asked. The departure from our previous topic gave me a respite to breathe and my thoughts to roll out.

From the demigod of their collection. In a perfect world, they should. Doesn't mean their demigod is good at fulfilling. Then again, this is Ventis' kingdom, not mine. Some of us care for our mortals.

"Ventis doesn't?"

What proof do you have?

"Baxter said . . . that is . . ."

He claimed that his father is a good god? A Lei-li god? Ignis scoffed. *Baxter is a fool.*

"He's my friend."

My opinion stands.

"I trust that fool with my life."

Sometimes, trust isn't enough, Lady-witch.

His mild, unaffected tone set my teeth on edge. Did nothing faze him? Ava whirled around, looking for me. I held up a hand to draw her gaze. When she saw me, she relaxed. I smiled to set her at ease, and she turned back to her friends.

A feeling like nesting bees took residence in my stomach as I watched her. My thoughts trailed away from Ava and back to Ignis' warning.

Mortal rebellion.

Tontes.

Saving Alkarra.

"Why should I believe you?"

You don't trust me.

His reply drawled like a question.

"Did you expect me to?"

No, but I have hope that you will.

Weary of the back-and-forth, I quietly asked, "What do you want from me, Ignis?"

Time.

"Time?"

Two weeks is all that I ask. A short time, which provides a chance to show you the abilities of god magic. To explore what you can do as a living amulet of god magic. If you can do half of what I imagine is possible, then winning against Tontes is guaranteed.

I paused, soaking that in. When I said nothing, he continued.

Of course, he drawled, *such would require time here in Alaysia. You and I would work together with the magic, learn what it can do. How we can save Alkarra together.*

"You want me to stay in Alaysia, learn how to use god magic, and potentially become a weapon to save Alkarra?" I asked breathlessly.

Could gods go mad?

You already are a weapon. I want you to be a powerful one.

"And if I say no?"

An image of Letum Wood burnt to the ground flashed through my mind. Ebony clouds broiled overhead. Vicious drums of thunder broke the air, and the ground shivered from the force of it.

Will you say no to everything?

I fell into silence.

* * *

God magic returned us—and the small boat—back to the beach house after an hour or so of Ava speaking to her friends. She flittered from mortal to mortal, half-giddy. No manulele birds made themselves known, but I caught her glancing at the sky often.

At the beach house, Ava fell into a stupor of thought. I meandered the trinkets Baxter had left behind, my thoughts tangled in the conversation with Ignis. Neither of us seemed hungry as we fell into contemplative silence, though another basket had been delivered.

The familiar cut of Baxter's shoulders approached through

the sand, swift and certain, later that evening. I straightened from where I sat on the steps, lost in the dazzling sunset.

"Baxter?"

His gaze slipped up to mine with a little smile. Relief flowed through me. In the back of my mind lurked the fear that something terrible had gone awry for my friend.

That's what he was, right?

My sort-of friend-sort-of-love-interest.

A dizzying array of emotions bubbled up as he approached. Concern. Consternation. Relief. Delight. Attraction, certainly. Between it all lay a chasm of uncertainty. With so many unanswered questions about his world, and his position in it, I couldn't access clarity around what I truly felt. He approached the stairs with a broad grin. Hints of his usual verve delighted me.

"Merry meet," he murmured.

He wrapped his arms around me, pulled me close. His linen shirt smelled like a fresh breeze. I drew in a deep breath, relieved to latch onto something familiar. Warmth radiated from him in untold comfort.

"Hey," I said.

He pulled away, fingertips on my cheek. "You're all right?"

"Fine."

"I'm sorry I'm just returning. I wanted to return sooner, but reunions are plentiful and business swift in Father's *Rostina*."

Ava materialized at my side like a ghost. She leaned against the other side of the doorway. Her skeptical study of Baxter set me on edge until I saw what claimed her focus.

Around his neck dangled a massive bauble.

Like most god magic amulets, it glowed from within, emitting an obnoxious luminance. Silvery hints of gray and white streaked through, like swirling fog. It was square, set against the same blunted metal as Luppentonisa.

I sucked in a breath.

Ava gaped.

Baxter stuffed it into his shirt with a flicker of annoyance and cleared his throat.

"Is that your new amulet?" I asked.

"Yes. The report of my mission was a success, as expected. Father has given me his most powerful amulet, Oceanuso-rilianno."

Ava waited, eyes wide, expression fragile as glass. She dropped her gaze, scuffed her toe along the floor. He studied her for several moments, clearly concerned by her silence. When he reached out, touched her jaw to lift her eyes, she flinched away.

"Are you all right, Ava?"

Throat taut, she nodded. Her eyes didn't meet his.

"Something you want to talk about?" he asked.

She shook her head.

He looked at me in silent inquiry.

Later, I mouthed.

Baxter nudged her shoulder, but she withdrew farther into the house. He pressed his lips into a thin line. "Can I talk to Bianca on the beach, alone? You and I can chat more when I return."

She shrugged.

Ava's brow pulled low as I followed Baxter out of the house and into the sand. When I glanced back with a reassuring smile, she stared at me like a lost puppy. Did I imagine that her eyes returned to Baxter's back, right where the amulet sat on the other side of his chest?

She disappeared inside with a growl.

* * *

A storm budded in the distant sky as we approached the beach. Flattened cloud disks stretched wide, then billowed up like a top hat. The daunting thunderhead left little question as to who would win in an all-out battle between the god of wind and the god of thunder. A weak wind scuttled by, frail in comparison.

At the water's edge, Baxter stopped, turned, and pulled me into his arms. His blunt affection startled me, particularly the way his touch lingered like a burn. His fingertips slid down my arm, heating the sensitive skin inside. They stopped at my hand, trapped my palm against his, and his firm, slender fingers threaded through mine.

He stepped back to study my eyes, no hesitation in his own.

"Can I?" he asked. "I want to hold your hand."

Son of a god was right. Who else had such unwavering confidence? I nodded, a tickle of warmth in my belly.

He smiled.

Holding his hand wasn't unpleasant, nor unwelcome. In such a strange new world, I craved the familiar. Thoughts of Merrick surfaced. Memories of his thicker chest, more confident hold, but I pressed them back. No. Not here. No Merrick or ghosts or protective fathers or Network interests to cloud judgment. In Alaysia, I'd discover the truth about how I felt regarding both men.

I owed Baxter that much.

"So," I drawled more boldly away from Ava's obvious discomfort. "How did the Council of the Gods go? That amulet is . . . huge."

"Fine. The report required the entire day at the Heart of Alaysia which is always an . . . unpleasant place. Father did most of the questioning. Ignis had a few clarifications. Tontes mostly wanted more detailed information about Alkarra and how witches live, but I didn't give it. He spent half of the day trying different ways to heckle information out of me."

"What about Gelas?"

"Quiet, as usual. Gelas rarely speaks. Tontes grumbles in the background and seems to never *stop* having something to say."

A span of silence followed while I absorbed the nuances.

"New amulet, though," I said to break the fragile skein of uncertainty in the air. "With greater power, too, and placement in your father's world. Impressive accomplishment, Bax. Successfully free of your mission means what for you now?"

His low chuckle was more ironic than amused. "For once, it's nice not to be the one asking questions about how things work in your world."

I grinned.

He tugged me into the surf. We strolled along the edge, white foam tickling my toes. A distant roll of thunder drew my mind back to the gods and the barrage of questions I held inside. The fact that he avoided my query of what it meant to be free of his mission—and I didn't know how to bring it back—stymied me.

Ignis surfacing in my mind certainly didn't help.

A blind fool, he whispered.

I scowled him out of my head again.

Baxter stopped. Wind rustled his hair as it skated past. "I dodged your question because I'm not sure how to answer. It's good that I'm free of my mission, but . . . I have a feeling that Father means to tie me here through obligation. He also gave to me . . ." Baxter swallowed, " . . . several collections and mortals willing to be allegiant."

He shook his head, then ran a hand over his face. I blinked, torn between a glacial sense of horror and whether I should congratulate him.

"Oh," I said.

"Things are tenuous right now. Father is upset with me because of my affection for witches and is keeping me busy. Presumably, to stop me from returning to Alkarra."

"You told him that you want to go back?"

Baxter shrugged, agony in his eyes. "I don't know, to be honest. Yes, I'd love to return to Alkarra, but I have missed home. It's good to see my sisters again, and fall into the position

I've wanted for years. Most powerful amulet, a place at the *Rostina*."

Understanding washed through me. "He's keeping you busy to keep you away from *me*, isn't he?"

"And Ava." He let out a punctuated breath. "He feels that I'm . . . too fond of both of you."

"Jikes."

Baxter frowned, deeply troubled. His fingers tightened around mine.

"The problem," he murmured, "is that Father has a point. There's much good I can do here. I've also been granted the honor of living in the *Rostina*, which comes only after a successful mission. He's given me the equivalent of Chatham Castle. An entire wing—the best wing. Plus, the amulet. I have been my father's only son for a while, until recently, which means . . . things."

"Like what?"

"More responsibility, mostly." His thoughtful gaze tapered, thick eyelashes hiding a contemplative mien. "Father will expect me to be a *tagata* to the newest son, a baby only a few months old. Teach him how to represent Ventis. My sisters can do it, of course, but Father believes that sons should learn from other sons."

Ventis, I realized, was one player that I had underestimated. Wily, old god. He had Baxter on a firm leash now. Powerful amulet. A home within *his* home.

"This is complicated, Baxter. I'm sorry."

I reached up, putting my hand against his cheek. The touch felt natural, only slightly irresolute. The lines in his forehead smoothed away. He reached up with his other hand, covering mine.

"There is good I can do here, Bianca. I can't deny that. Father has given me *many* collections to care for. Mortals that aren't getting what they need. Some aren't even receiving fresh water. I could save lives without requiring allegiance, because I don't care about power or standing. That could change . . . almost everything for so many."

"But?"

"But Alkarra. *You.*"

The sense that Ventis already tugged Baxter away from my home land felt like a river current. It would thread through the most difficult passages, intent on a single destination. For Baxter, there was no fighting such a force.

How could he?

More importantly, *should* he?

"I understand, Bax."

Determination filled his stony gaze. "I'm not saying I'm never going to return to Alkarra, but I owe the mortals a chance, at least. Father has asked that I try for two weeks. That's it. It's so little time."

Alarm tripled through me.

Two weeks?

How very familiar.

"Two weeks?" I murmured. Not a coincidence that Ventis requested the same timeframe as Ignis, by any means, but certainly odd. What it meant, I didn't know.

Yet.

Ventis has his own lessons to impart, Lady-witch.

I swallowed back my discomfort and annoyance. Having Ignis in my ear—or was he? How did he know *everything*?—sent a tremor of rage through me.

Leave me alone.

Silence replied.

"I can find a solution to Father's animosity toward my feelings for you," Baxter continued, oblivious to my thoughts. "That doesn't concern me. He only needs to meet you and he'll like you. I believe that the right things always happen eventually. I believe in . . ."

He trailed away, searching my eyes. In the unstated words, I heard ghosts. Echoes of vulnerability. For all his confidence as the son of a god, Baxter had his fears too. This was just the first time I'd encountered them.

"Not all of you are *monilay mal* then?" I quipped, buying a moment to recover. My heart raced as I dropped my hand from his.

He cracked a wry smile.

"We all have it in us."

"Two weeks is fine. You owe it to your father and yourself."

"That doesn't mean you have to stay two weeks." He put a hand on my waist and pulled me a little closer. "Once Father meets with you, I will return you to Alkarra, if you wish. Though I'd rather you stay, of course," he tacked on with a charming, boyish smile.

I responded in kind.

"We'll deal with that when it happens," I said. "No need to rush it."

With a broken smile, he nodded. Reluctantly, I stepped back a little to give us space.

"You should know about a new . . . development."

He perked up, no doubt alerted by my tone. "What development?"

"I, ah . . . can hear Ignis. All the time." I rolled my eyes. "He speaks with me in my head. He can probably hear this right now, in fact. Not sure if that's a good thing or a bad thing, to be honest."

Baxter frowned. "Ignis?"

I nodded.

Shock darkened his face, then faded to concern. His lips parted, then pressed. He shifted, and I wondered if he realized he'd drawn me even closer to him.

"What does Ignis say?" he asked carefully.

"What doesn't he say?" I muttered, expecting a snarky

comment from the god of fire at any moment. "Mostly, he tries to convince me that god magic is more powerful than goddess magic. We've only really spoken twice, though he seems to be everywhere."

"Be careful."

"I will." I put a hand on his arm to reassure the aggravation of his light eyes. "He has no interest in harming me. To the contrary, he strikes me as . . . protective. I just wanted you to know."

"Thank you."

We strolled back to the beach house, one of his arms wrapped around my shoulders. Unspoken sentences cluttered the air, burdened by what I'd just revealed. Baxter's troubled frown gave me pause, but I dismissed the irrational concerns that followed. If Ignis posed a real problem, then I'd let Baxter know right away.

For now . . . I had things to explore. More than ever.

The opportunity to test my feelings for Baxter was a welcome experience here in Alaysia, but, pitted against all he faced, it ended up a woefully inadequate one. Like a candle against the sun. Until this moment, I hadn't realized how little I knew him. His birthday. His age. His plans for the future. Did he like one food more than another? Prefer the beach over the forest?

One disastrous decision from Ventis could remove Baxter's magic forever.

Yet, you hold your power forever, Lady-witch.

Ignis' second unwelcome intrusion—which grew more irritating by the moment—felt like a crater in my chest. I stopped. Baxter blinked out of heavy thoughts, slowing a pace ahead. He glanced back in silent question.

"Does your father actually plan to speak with me?" I asked. "Or is this just some great ruse meant to lure you back to Alaysia?"

A startled look, followed by a dark one, crossed his features. He dismissed it with a snort that rang hollow.

"Not a ruse. He's . . . busy. He's used to the world operating in the way which he commands it. Father is . . . well, like all gods, selfish."

Baxter looked down the beach as he continued, hands in his pockets now. We returned in silence. Distance spanned us with every return step. A welling space that stretched from my heart to his.

"Do you want to come inside for a few minutes and eat?" I asked. "It could be like old times, at my cottage. You've provided more than enough food."

Baxter hesitated, clearly torn, before he shook his head. "I would like that, of course. I had planned to," he added, with feeling. "But I need to return and discuss things with Shara. I've inherited her mess, and I mean to make her answer for her negligence to the collections under her care. Father plans to meet with both of us as soon as I return, and it wouldn't be wise to make him wait."

"Very noble of you," I murmured with a smile.

Baxter grinned widely, a reassuring return to my friend. With a wink, he departed into the sound of rioting surf, a silhouette against the ebbing storm.

A fool, Ignis murmured with finality, *for what he doesn't see.*

Chapter Nine

I stared at the beginning of a letter for several moments.

Dear Leda,

With a groan, I tilted my head back and used god magic to erase the words.

What to say?

Clouds crowded the far horizon with their monstrous, black bulk. Distant rolls of thunder issued every now and then. Baxter's lifeless version of Letum Wood had disappeared at some point in the night. Without the ghost of Letum Wood outside my door, Alaysia suffocated me less. Despite plenty to think about, my mind wandered most to Ignis.

You already are a weapon. I want you to be a powerful one, he had said.

Still, I couldn't see what he meant.

"What if I don't want to be a weapon?" I muttered.

Well, too late for that.

With a shove, I pushed the letter away.

Ava shuffled through the trees, holding onto ribbon-like plants that curled around her forearm. Their thin lengths flattened to the width of my pinky nail. She plucked them from trunks, where they pasted themselves to the bark with a tacky substance, then followed each strand to its end. Ten cluttered the sand in wrapped, organized circles for her to use later, presumably.

Embers circled in tight spirals in front of my face.

Hide.

I straightened. "What?"

Now!

With god magic, I brought Ava inside. Still burdened with plants, she yelped when I slapped a hand over her mouth, put a finger over my lips, and pointed out the window. Eyes wide, she sucked in a breath, saw my expression, and nodded once.

The magic awoke in my chest, slowly at first, which meant that another amulet had arrived. More than one, if the spikes in power meant anything.

Go back outside, but on the other side of the beach house, at least fifty paces away. Remain invisible. They're closing in. If they see you, they will take you to Tontes kingdom.

And do what? I screeched in my head.

Nothing pleasant, I assure you.

Who are they? I thought back.

The sons of Tontes.

"Monilay mal," I murmured to Ava.

Her eyes widened.

With god magic, I obeyed his command and took Ava and myself outside, beyond the house. When we landed in the sand, we remained invisible. My heart galloped. I'd effectively done two separate things with god magic—the equivalent of transporting, and doing so invisibly. Without the burden of incantations and power that goddess magic had required, it had been shockingly simple.

Trees surrounded us now. We gazed at the back of the beach house. My hand on Ava's shoulder nudged her to sit in the sand.

Can you show them to me? I asked Ignis.

I'm so glad you asked.

Four shimmering forms, like clear liquid, appeared a few paces from the front door. With shuffling, silent steps, they closed in. Demigods, for certain. Four of them. Male, from the broad shoulders and long arms.

The magic jumped, sizzling.

What do they want? I asked.

You.

Are they speaking to each other? I can't hear them.

Find out for yourself, he said with mild amusement. *You are mine, are you not?*

God magic can do that?

It can do all things.

Instead of casting a listening incantation toward a particular place, the god magic honed in on the individual demigods right away. A rustle of clothes. The shift of sand. Breaths, steady and even.

Jikes, but it was easy.

The creak of a hammock, followed by a groaning stair, preceded utter silence. Finally, a voice from the top floor spoke. Guttural. Harsh. In a thought, god magic helped me understand the Alaysian words.

"Not here," the male voice said.

What felt like several eternities later, they stomped down the stairs. The magic hiding them slipped away. Shadows collected in the trees, where two of them conversed. A third gazed around. The fourth strode around the outside of the house, searching. As he walked, he kicked the ground. Checking for hidden bodies, I'd bet.

A demigod with reddish hair and plentiful freckles stepped

away from the house. His cold, emerald eyes tracked every inch of the area.

His name is Neel. He's a lech, like his father. Tends to feint right, and loves to be dramatic. In a fight, I'd keep it straight-forward.

Neel paused, head canted back. He sniffed the air. Muscles rippled in the falling daylight as he turned to face our direction. I willed Ava not to squeak or breathe.

His eyes seemed to lock on mine.

He stared.

I held my breath, heart flopping in my throat.

Neel's gaze continued on, body swiveling. He stacked hands on his hips, and growled a command to the others. The other three demigods joined him, muttering about wasted time.

"We'll come back," Neel muttered. "She can't stay away forever. Both will need sleep."

All four of them disappeared.

Easy, Ignis murmured in warning. *Go nowhere.*

My whirling-hot blood didn't abate, so I used god magic to lock Ava into place so she wouldn't move. The demigods remained invisible, probably to draw me out. Forcing magic on her gave me no pleasure. Until I knew that the demigods left, however, I would take no risks.

Tell her without speaking the words. God magic, Bianca, has no limits. I look forward to the day you fully accept this.

An uncomfortable sensation followed his words.

No limits?

Impossible.

Yet, I tried anyway.

Don't make a sound, I said to Ava through the magic. I intended it to drop into her mind, like a thought in my voice. *The sons of Tontes are still here. I can feel their amulets.*

Tension ebbed a little when I released her from the locked position. Both of us remained invisible.

Ages seemed to pass. Darkness began to settle with a dimming sunset. Every now and then, a skiff of sand skated by. A distant crack of twig or branch broke the air. I thought of warning Baxter, but wasn't sure what I'd interrupt. If Ignis and I had this under control, did I need to tell Baxter?

Finally, the strength of god magic faded.

Then a little more.

What must have been an hour or two later, the god magic returned to sleep. The dormant emptiness thrummed like a wild thing.

You are safe.

I set Ava free.

She appeared, wide-eyed. She hurried into my arms and held me tight. My fingers cut through her hair in an attempt to soothe both of us.

"I'm sorry that I used magic on you without explaining. Ignis told me about them and I acted right away."

Ava pulled away, trouble in her gaze.

"Ignis?"

Ah. Forgot. She didn't know everything. A hand pressed to my chest, where I felt god magic the deepest.

"Ignis can speak with me. He warned me about the demigods."

Her lips pulled down. Eventually, she nodded. I would have given anything to peek into her mind. What questions did she harbor there?

I put a hand on her shoulder.

"Let's go back inside and get something to eat. I'll send a message to Baxter. We'll decide what to do after that."

With a relieved nod, Ava followed me inside.

* * *

"I'll stay the night."

Baxter declared it with fury in his voice. He paced in the sand, kicking up granules around his ankles. Darkness lay on the world in a broad coat. Stars sparkled, so thickly clustered they appeared in white clumps.

"I would appreciate that," I said.

He stopped to regard me. The tension in his expression bled away. With a sigh, he lowered onto the step next to me. Ava sat inside, pretending to look at a book, though she hadn't turned a page in minutes. A shallow bowl of burning sand stood on the table, casting bouncing shadows on the walls.

"I'm sorry, Bianca."

"Gio said that your sisters had been talking about me," I murmured. "That word had already started to spread about me being here. Do you think the sons of Tontes came because of them?"

A sharp exhalation answered. "I had hoped . . ." he trailed away. "Yes, Gio is right. He usually is. For being a mortal, he's shockingly well-informed regarding Alaysia. Regardless, I've already reported this to my father. My sisters will not be allowed to speak of you now."

"Too late for that," I muttered.

Baxter's scowl deepened.

"What would your Father do, anyway? Armed guards? I haven't seen any sort of military force here."

"There is none."

"From what Ignis said, it sounds like Ventis, Gelas, and Ignis are a little . . . frightened by Tontes."

"Father would do the right thing, I hope," he muttered.

I reached over, leaned my head on Baxter's shoulder and closed my eyes. In truth, I felt better with him here, though I wasn't sure I needed him to be safe. Ignis had saved us, not Baxter. What could an amulet-dependent demigod do that a god could not?

These thoughts I kept to myself.

Long after Baxter and Ava had fallen to sleep, I lay in the hammock and stared at the ceiling. Ava had finally calmed enough to rest, though she jerked awake often. My thoughts roiled, like the thunderstorm that retreated with the sons of Tontes.

How will I keep us safe through the night? I asked the plaintive question into the void, yet knew Ignis would hear.

I watch, always.

Despite myself, relief swept through me. Could I trust Ignis? No. In this aspect, however, I couldn't help myself. The rope of my hammock creaked as it swayed in a twining current from the open window. A lonely sound.

"I thought it would be your demigods to try to attack me first," I whispered.

Seeking revenge, perhaps?

"Yes."

A pause, then, *They want to, yes.*

"What's stopping them?"

Me.

"Why?"

Do you really require an answer?

I frowned, confounded by the question, which alluded that I shouldn't require an answer. Was something obvious that I didn't see? Probably so many things. A shiver slipped through my skin, lifting the hairs.

"Yes."

Because we could be great together, Lady-witch of Alkarra.

"Is that why you want to teach me?"

Yes. And, despite my reputation, I don't desire the destruction of Alkarra. Tontes? He craves the land and wants it back. Today, we proved fairly well suited to work together, and you are a fast learner. There is much worth exploring.

I hated the fact that I was considering his offer—again. Dangling at the front of my mind was Alkarra. My forest. My friends. All the witches that lay back there. I'd come to Alaysia to get rid of the god magic.

Now, I wondered if that wasn't a foolish quest after all.

If Ignis was correct and I *was* a weapon that could save my land, wasn't I obligated to learn more? Most importantly, if not me, then who? No one, because no other witch—or demigod, for that matter—had become a living amulet before.

"What do you get out of it if I agree to learn with you?" I asked.

Better standing with my sisters, for one, he said musingly. *Most importantly? We save Alkarra, which means we also save Alaysia.*

A shiver rushed through me at his ominous tone.

"I wanted the god magic out of me."

That option is still available to you at any time.

He spoke lightly, as if treading over eggshells.

"I'll do it," I murmured. "You can teach me more about god magic. But there's no agreement to fight with you. This is your opportunity to show me how to save Alkarra."

With me at your side.

My nostrils flared as I sighed. "We're not friends, Ignis."

An assumption that seemed fairly clear. Again, I only ask for two weeks.

"It would take that long?"

To understand a power and depth beyond time and all knowledge? Forgive me. I believed you to be far more intelligent than such a comment.

"Fine," I muttered. "Two weeks."

Tomorrow, then.

Shadows danced outside, where waves roared. Stars bustled overhead. The lullaby of the sea ushered me into sleep.

I dreamed of thunder.

Chapter Ten

A jeweled case sparkled in the sunlight.

Gems of sapphire, magenta, and silver sparkled across the top. Their faceted edges, bumpy like lined rocks, held beguiling depths. I studied them with a disinterested eye and fought a yawn.

"Are all gods this flashy?" I asked.

Ignis conjured an image of an Eastern Network witch wearing a flamboyant dress. Spears jutted from the bodice, and layers of skirts ballooned from her tiny waist. Not a soul would step too close, or be impaled. Glimmering jewels dripped from her hair, arms, and sides.

I rolled my eyes.

"Touché."

Rings littered the inside of the jeweled case, mostly gold. The bottom was clearly false, likely hiding a secret compartment, but I couldn't tell how to access it.

"What," I murmured to the case, eyes narrowed, "are you hiding?"

Ah, you do have the power of observation.

"Don't be insulting."

Are you pleased with the gems?

"Is this a gift?"

No.

"It's pretty but I don't care much for it."

Witches aren't immune to beautiful things?

"Depends on your definition of beautiful."

I felt his eyes roll.

Turn this to sand, he barked.

I obeyed with a thought. The lovely piece dissipated in my fingers, trailing to the ground in skittering granules.

Now, turn it into something else.

Another easy command. The sand returned to my palm and clumped together. A miniature version of a ferocious, lazy forest lion that populated Letum Wood formed. It snarled, coughed a few grains of sand, and settled into my palm with a yawn.

"Goddess magic can do this too," I sang while the tiny forest lion groomed itself. In truth, I didn't know the incantation to conjure this *exact* animal so easily. Surely, something similar existed in the annals of literature at the Great Library of Burke.

Forgive me for attempting to show you a modicum of your own power, he muttered. *Since you understand the lack of limits around god magic already. What do you need me for?*

"Don't be so hard on yourself," I replied. "I didn't know god magic could translate languages."

You can conjure your greatest dreams with my power.

A tower of baubles, necklaces, and broaches piled high on the table in front of me. Landslides of diamonds scattered the top, near where I stood. I eyed them. In a command, each diamond turned into a basket of *seema*. The hardened fruit piled on the table, which groaned under the burden.

A moment later, the *seema* disappeared, sent to Ava's collection.

"Jewels are not my greatest dream," I murmured.

Interesting.

I set the forest lion down to prowl across the table. "We don't know each other at all, Ignis. Let's not pretend otherwise."

Untrue. An annoyed tone overtook him. *The point is that god magic can do anything and everything.*

"Not everything," I murmured, thinking of Letum Wood. The vibrancy of the soul in the trees. Power in the roots. God magic couldn't recreate the spirit of something so alive. My heart gave a sad lurch.

A blazing blue gem appeared next to the lion. It pawed at the rolling, glimmering stone like a toy. I tilted my head. Had *I* conjured that, or did Ignis? From the depths of my subconscious, perhaps.

"Can I use god magic to find other amulets?"

Explain your question.

"Could I use god magic to find Nicomedianthekus, for example?"

Silence.

My curiosity over the lost Gelas amulet—that I pretended to have found to draw demigods into a pub called the Golden Guinea Hen during the demigod attack months ago—had never been satisfied. It swirled back to life now.

You know of the lost amulet of Gelas?

"I'm not a totally hopeless cause."

Debatable, and no. One cannot call amulets. It's part of their protection, or they would constantly be stolen.

"Not even the gods can call their own amulets?"

His voice strained. *No.*

"So god magic really can't do *everything* then."

Though he said nothing, I sensed irritation. The lion batted the gem off the table. I reached over, snatched it before it fell, and returned it to the top. The lion sighed, set its head on top, and closed its tiny eyes.

A mewl of sound from Ava brought me out of the conversation. With a flick, I scattered the sand lion and whirled around.

"Can I go to my collection?"

Ava stood a few paces away, an oar in hand. Sunlight sparkled outside, heating the interior of the house with summer-like intensity. Determination hardened her features as she tilted her chin up. No doubt, it rankled her to ask.

"Sure."

She blinked. "You don't mind?"

I shrugged. "Why not? Don't you want to see your manulele birds?"

All defensiveness softened in a moment. "Yes! Oh, yes, please."

"Would you like me to send you?"

Her eyes widened. "Will you?"

"If you wish."

Ava's arms locked around me in a tight hug. She squeezed, then danced back a step, eyes bright.

"Thank you, thank you!"

With a laugh, I waved a hand. "Go have fun at your collection. I'll be here."

With the god of fire, I added silently.

A momentary storm passed through her eyes, but faded back into excitement. She blew me a kiss while I used god magic to send her back to Daemon's island. In the emptiness after she left, a squeamish thought startled me.

Would Daemon pull Ava into their supposed rebellion if I wasn't there to stop him?

Was it safe?

Dismissing those concerns—Ava had lived there all her life except for a few months in Alkarra—I spun around.

The empty beach house stared back.

More gifts had arrived from Baxter this morning, over a

lavish breakfast. Soon, the beach house wouldn't hold more. Shells filled with neat, square pastries, coated in powdered sugar, had been a delicious start to the day.

A gray-blue gown with a note pinned to it that said, *This is your best color* lay against the far wall. I opted for the sleeveless, white dress that stopped at my knees. Delicate animal figurines carved from some kind of rough shell, only the size of my thumbnail, lay on a table, abandoned by Ava.

Embers intercepted my path across the room to attempt another letter to Leda.

Now that you're alone, Ignis drawled, *I have something to show you.*

The cinders spun in a vortex, their heat a glimmering brush on my skin, before cavorting outside.

With a sigh, I followed.

The twirling firebrands stopped at the sea, where a bright flash of green drew my gaze. Something lay in the sand, flopping around. I headed toward it, then stopped halfway there with a gasp.

A mermaid.

Servants of Prana and vile minions, if you want to know.

"You are so pretentious."

He didn't deign to respond.

The mermaid thrashed, twenty paces from the water. They clearly didn't have the energy to return to the ocean, though their head turned that way. Wet, rope-like hair gathered sand, dropping past broad shoulders. Gills opened and closed along a long neck, decorated with lime-colored scales. They swept across collarbones, down powerful arms. If standing, this mermaid would be shorter than me.

"The mermaid is dying."

The mermaid whipped around, eyes wide, and stared at me. The edges of the jaw and cheeks, near the ears, had begun to turn translucent. Eyelids blinked. The nostril slits in its lovely face, like a porcelain doll, wheezed open and closed. Underneath the baking sun, they turned limp.

"Why is the mermaid just lying here?" I murmured.

One never knows. It will likely kill you if you save it.

I opened my mouth to respond, then shut it. Were mermaids really that vengeful? Recalling the way Prana nearly drowned me, I figured they might be. If I had to serve her, I'd be cantankerous too.

"Then why did you bring me here?"

To show you how powerfully god magic works with emotion. You tend to be drawn to things that need saving, so I thought this could conjure some of your usual sentiment to draw on.

"Maybe you need some saving, too," I muttered, unnerved again by the insights into my soul he so casually shared.

Your witch humor eludes me.

"Just my witty banter."

I dropped to my knee, drawn back to the surf. Ignis hadn't been wrong. The mermaid's plight did evoke a sense of concern. The tail twitched in a half-hearted movement. Webbing trailed along the side of a fin, up to the waist, where it encircled shining scales. The fingers, five of them with a thumb, splayed out, also webbed.

How had the mermaid marooned itself here?

We weren't far from the beach house. Had they been trying to spy on us? As a servant of Prana?

Also very likely.

I inched closer.

"So what do you want me to do?"

Save it with god magic, and pay attention to the play of emotion on your power. I would like to see what occurs.

Sensing a trap, I hesitated. "This is as much an experiment for you as it is for me, I assume?"

Yes.

His lack of understanding about my status as a living amulet gave little reassurance. Nothing for it, however. The mermaid thrashed. With a hiss, their pointed teeth bared in warning. Too much closer and they might bite me. What happened when mermaids sank their teeth into something?

I didn't want to find out.

With god magic, I lifted the mermaid off the beach. While airborne, they struggled, squealing deep in their throat, as they elevated off the sand. A rush of compassion and a desire for greater speed overtook me. At the same moment, the magic quickened like a too-fast heartbeat. The mermaid disappeared.

I held my breath, shocked.

"Where did they go?" I asked.

A head bobbed to the surface of the waves. At first, I saw only viridian hair, then queer eyes peered above the water, narrowed.

"Oh."

The mermaid slipped below the surface, leaving an uninterrupted, azure skyline.

Your compassion, though misplaced, enhanced your ability to do god magic. That is the lesson here.

"Misplaced? The mermaid was dying."

It's a sea cretin.

"You're a god cretin."

The immature sling brought a blush to my cheeks. Not my best reply, but I couldn't help myself. A choked silence followed. When Ignis didn't break it—I hoped for at least *some* introspection on his part—I took matters into my own hands.

"As a god, your profound lack of respect for life is disconcerting," I muttered to try to salvage myself. "A life is a life. Some of us only have one."

A pause.

You challenge me?

"Someone needs to."

You have taken it upon yourself to be that someone?

"Do you speak to anyone else but me?"

No.

Startled, I reared back. "Really?"

I'd rather not harp on it, thank you.

"Just a question, Ignis. If it's true, then it sounds . . . lonely. Do you ever appear to the mortals?"

No.

"Why not?"

Do you reveal yourself to the worms in the soil?

"Not a fair comparison," I muttered.

I have never revealed myself to a mortal unless necessity requires it. Rarely to a demigod. Only when I must in order to have children to carry my legacy.

"Do the gods have children in the . . . um . . . usual way?"

Another blush warmed my face, but I ignored it.

He laughed, a low sound.

Indeed. Few mortal females are granted the privilege, and they are usually highly respected. For my part, I prefer one partner at a time, though it's not often feasible. So many mortals require more demigods to take care of them with magic.

"So you prefer to have one partner?"

Yes.

"Word on the street in Alkarra says you have hundreds of children," I quipped lightly. "You must have kept her very busy."

Currently, he murmured, aloof, *I have no partners. In recent past, I had several. They have all gone to the lives after this one.*

"Do you miss them?"

One of them, more than you could ever comprehend. The rest were an easy farewell.

A pause. I contemplated his revelation, struck by the idea of Ignis being . . . a romantic. Curiosity over this mortal woman followed. What kind of a mortal would captivate a god like Ignis?

You are amused by this?

"More curious."

The rumor that I have hundreds of children?

"Yes?"

It's false.

The idea shocked me. Despite never having met him, I'd built up a very specific picture of Ignis in my head. Reality went against every bit of it. Ignis didn't measure up at all against the god I'd built up in my head. I wasn't sure how to handle the disparity.

My throat dried out, requiring me to clear it before I could ask, "How false?"

Extremely.

"But Baxter . . ."

A fool.

Not sure how to reply, I fell silent.

You think that you shouldn't trust me. Eventually, I hope that you will.

My nostrils flared. "Can you stay out of my head, please? I'd like the luxury of my own thoughts."

Again, I am not in your head. The magic binds us and allows me to understand you more deeply than anyone could possibly fathom.

"I don't like that."

I'm quite aware.

I held up two hands. "This whole god-thing is new to me, you know."

There are questions I seek to answer as well.

An ominous feeling crept over me.

"Oh?"

The night of the demigod uprising in Alkarra, you successfully used god magic, though it was beyond your capability without practice. I believe this is because your heightened emotions gave you a better chance to win, though I haven't confirmed that yet.

"So god magic has a greater advantage when I'm afraid, is what you're saying?"

I'm delighted you see the correlation.

"Bleak, isn't it?"

Survival often is. I desire to test this as we gain greater understanding together. Remember this as you find your way back out.

"Back out of where?"

I advise you not to make yourself known. Where you are about to go, I cannot follow.

I whirled around. "Where am I going?"

Keep in mind that you can heal yourself at any moment.

"The good gods, what does—"

Good luck, Lady-witch.

Magic swept me away.

* * *

A broad tunnel surrounded me.

I crouched, invisible, and gained my bearings. The sense that Ignis had just dropped me into the middle of a fight didn't fade, though no enemy presented itself. Perhaps, like a true lech, he'd simply felt embarrassed after revealing himself so thoroughly. I snorted at the thought of him with a female partner.

Who would tolerate such a scoundrel?

After several moments of quiet, my racing heart calmed.

Where was I, anyway?

My head tipped back. A ceiling soared hundreds of paces away. Time-darkened sandstone, nearly black, loomed in the darkness. I blinked.

Are you testing me? I asked.

Ignis remained silent. I shouldn't have been surprised that he'd abandon me here—wherever this was—but a part of me was. Correlations to Papa leaving came with a little too much clarity. Had I done something to spur others to drop me so thoroughly, or did happenstance dictate such terms?

With a shake of my head, I brought myself fully into the moment.

No one else lingered here.

Shallow bowls, wide as I was tall, flanked either side of the tunnel. White-and-gray flames danced over what appeared to be a bed of sand—burning sand. No scent of char issued, but a sharp stench permeated the air, like cedar. Atop the flaming sand lay piles of driftwood tied by fabric. Lazy smoke drifted higher.

To my left, a dim light. The entrance, perhaps. To the right, a glimmering . . . something.

The strange fire illuminated the way to the right. Curiosity pushed me closer. I reached to my side, but Viveet wasn't there. A quick glance confirmed that there was nothing else—not even a stick—that could be used as a weapon here.

Doors passed by on either side as I crept by, created with amalgamations of driftwood or hardened sand or leaves. A door of foggy glass passed by on my left. Another, half open, peeked into a room full of tiny shelves. Chunks of coral organized in a rainbow pattern crowded the cubbies, bleeding orange-yellow-aqua-coral-white. Glass jars, tinted rose, cluttered around a window that overlooked the sea.

Alaysian script, carved in the sand outside the door, hinted at what lay inside.

Room of Curiosities.

I pressed on.

The tunnel narrowed, ending in a shiny wall. At my back, the opening was a mere speck of light. After a moment of hesitation, I kept going. The quiet rang in my ears, a damning witness.

Closer inspection revealed a pair of double doors, shimmering with rose-gold tones. They occupied the entire wall, five times my height. Door handles made from hardened pieces of seaweed spiraled from the inner seam of the doors. I paused fifty paces away. The doors would require that much space to move, if opened. They were probably as heavy as mountains.

The entrance sparkled with gaudy opulence. Across the middle, painted in black strokes against the glimmering gold, lay five giant symbols, each as tall as me.

The unknown figures melted, then reappeared as legible letters.

VENTIS

My forehead furrowed. A flood of understanding came next. No doubt this place was the end of the giant tunnel I'd briefly glimpsed from a distance at the *Rostina lu Lune*.

Ventis? I asked Ignis.

Nothing.

Why would Ignis bring me here of all places?

Now would be a good time to leave and pretend I'd never been here, but curiosity locked me into place.

To Ventis' . . . what?

Quarters?

Home?

And to what end?

A breeze stirred my hair, drawing me from my thoughts. I tilted my head to the side as a shiver skidded down my arms. Wind this far into the tunnel? That couldn't be right.

The god magic in me brightened in warning. My body became visible as something peeled the power away. I fought to recover my anonymity, filled with an impending sense of doom. The invisibility returned, but only for a moment. Soon, the appearance of my toes, ankles, and knees mocked my attempts to maintain it.

A gust of wind shoved me away from the doors. I tumbled back, spinning head over heels until I lay on my knees, palms flattened against the floor. Wind pressed into my spine like a heavy boot. My head hit the ground with a *thud* that jarred my thoughts sideways. A roar rose, wild like a hurricane, moments before a cyclone dropped from the swathed shadows overhead.

Sand, wind, and pebbles soared around me in violent ribbons. They scratched the back of my hands, my neck, my face. Blood streamed out of my skin, into the ragged zephyr. Pain erupted after. I screamed, but who could hear? No matter how hard I struggled, the pressure that held me down didn't relent.

No breath. No thoughts.

Nothing but hissing, malevolent annoyance. Sand clumped in my eyelashes, burning my eyes. The whirlwind threatened to tear me to pieces. Amidst the chaos, a deep voice emerged.

This, it whispered, *is my throne.*

The dying current echoed as it faded.

Respect me.

The wind ceased.

A final gust crashed into my side, my body rolling until I slammed into the wall with a final *oomph.* Everything quieted. My mouth felt like cotton, bleeding into a raw throat when I opened my eyes. I blinked through dust and collapsed onto my back with a gasp.

A dull bang rocked through my skull. I closed my eyes, grimacing.

Well, that was unexpected.

"What was the point?" I muttered. I startled when Ignis spoke.

To test your power against a god. A living amulet you may be, but stronger than Ventis you're not. This is important information to have. Consider yourself warned, Lady-witch of Alkarra. Ventis doesn't like trespassers.

"You could have warned me," I snapped.

The silence of the tunnel lay in profound thickness as I stood. A new darkness settled. Wary, I glanced over my shoulder. The golden doors were gone, hidden behind a wall of sandstone.

I swallowed through a gritty throat, then used god magic to leave the tunnel. Moments later, the beach house surrounded me again.

I leaned back against the wall and struggled to regain my bearings.

Chapter Eleven

Baxter lounged against the door the next morning, a contemplative expression on his face.

I set aside my empty breakfast plate—littered with crumbs of wafer-like cookies, dried fruit that dissolved into sweet liquid on my tongue, and a slice of a fruit called *tuapa*—and leaned my elbows on the table. My plate clinked with the edge of his, still half-full. Ava ate at my side, stuffing her mouth with another large chunk of bread. A piece dropped to her lap. She plucked it free, chewed, and swallowed.

A bright smile followed.

I chuckled.

"You have the morning off, presumably?" I asked Baxter.

He spun around with a smile. "Yes, for a few hours. A very welcome few hours, too. It's been fun to see Alaysia and tour Father's *Rostina* again but . . ." he sighed. "The mortal collections have kept me busy. Shara did almost nothing for them. I'm surprised so many mortals survived."

"Will she be punished?"

He shrugged. "One hopes. She lost her amulet, which is punishment enough."

No amulet rendered a demigod completely unable to exert magic. Tough punishment, but hardly equivalent to starving children and half-naked mortals, eeking out a life amongst the weeds and dirty sands.

Baxter stepped away from the wall, a hand held out to me. I offered mine freely and he grasped it, linking our fingers. Anticipation glittered in his light eyes.

"Come with me?" he murmured.

"To where?"

"Somewhere new. A surprise."

"Yes." I shot to my feet. "I'm ready. Doesn't matter where, just show me Alaysia. Take me away, you son of a god."

Laughing, he pulled me close. Ava eyed us, nose slightly scrunched, as if grossed out by the display of affection. Remnants of tension still lingered between the two of them—whether Ava had spoken with Baxter about her reticence, I wasn't sure—but not so boldly as before.

"Do you want to come, Ava?" he asked.

She thought for a moment, then shook her head. "I want to go to my manulele!" She brightened, eyes wide. "They are returning to me. Some of them saw me yesterday. The rest will follow."

Baxter glanced at me in silent question. I shrugged.

"Fine by me. You're her tagata."

With a sigh, Bax relented.

"Fine, as long as you stay on your island. Stay away from Daemon. He's only going to make things worse for you, all right?"

Ava hesitated, then agreed with a half-shrug. After a quick hug—one for each of us—Baxter sent her to her island with a fond smile. He turned to me with a wink and tucked me under his arm.

"Shall we?" he murmured.

I grinned. "We shall."

* * *

An island of black rock glittered in the sunlight.

Pockets of emerald flora populated the crevasses where dirt and rainwater collected. White sand stretched into the shadowy, porous peaks, a lovely antithesis to the strange formation. After all the flat land and open space at Ventis' island, the jagged teeth of black mountains were a welcome sight.

Baxter stuck his hands into his pockets, bemused.

"Most demigods avoid this island," he said. "Which is just why I thought you'd like it."

His white shirt, top buttons undone, revealed a hint of chest hair. Sunlight slanted through clouds, illuminating his tanned skin.

"If demigods avoid this island," I said, "mortals must live here?"

"They do. The real name of the island is *Nonnatusnevillatop-utatazo*. Also known as the Island of the Amulets."

My curiosity piqued.

"Amulets?"

"All the amulets."

"What?" I whispered, riddled with shock.

Enjoyment warmed his smile. "Indeed. One could say it's a library of all the amulets." He motioned ahead with a nod. "Let's go. I want you to see inside."

"This isn't some attempt to distract me from the fact that your father still hasn't made time to speak with me?" I asked as I scuttled along at his side.

"It's definitely that."

I laughed, unable to help myself. So far, Baxter had only been able to give me and Ava pockets of time. A letter here, a basket there, a gift in the morning. Snatches of visits came in brief spans—minutes, at most. Having Baxter to myself for hours infused me with a giddy delight.

Meanwhile, Ignis had been utterly silent all morning. Since he abandoned me at Ventis's throne, he hadn't voiced a word.

I hadn't called for him, either.

Hints of life peeked out of the dark rocks. Unfolding flowers strung together like wisps. A willowy bush, draped over a ledge like a waterfall. Petals shivered when the wind drifted past. The splashes of color against darkness illuminated like fireflies at midnight. Brightly-colored birds twittered here and there, wings fluttering as they hustled by.

Octagonal holes had been chiseled out of the stone, then stuffed with sparkling, thin-paned glass. Cracks spiderwebbed through most of them. Lanky doorways with jagged edges led deeper into the rocks, only hinting into darkness.

"This is where the mortals that keep track of the amulets live," Baxter murmured, tone hushed. "They're kept inside, out of the elements. The *other* reason demigods don't come here is because of sheer spite. Many believe that the less mortals know about amulets, the better. Some demigods try to confuse the record-keepers with false information, though most of us don't care."

"What do you think?"

He shrugged. "If it makes the mortals happy, let them do it."

Something in his dismissive response niggled at me. A dividing line. A clear *us* and *them* in the words. Daemon floated to the top of my mind. Would he have any chance of freedom if he propelled his rebellion forward?

I had my doubts.

Darkness dropped like a cloak when we slipped through an oblong door. Baxter stooped in the low hallway. My fingertips trailed along the smooth stone. Sleek, almost oily, but with no residue. Without vision, we navigated a tight maze of left-and-right.

"Baxter, I have so many questions. Is it safe for mortals to live here?" I whispered. "How do they keep track of the amulets? Are amulets *kept* here?"

He laughed. "One at a time. You'll get your answers, I promise. For now, know that it's safer here than anywhere else. Some demigods may not like that mortals track amulets, but they aren't going to commit time to stopping the mortals, either. Father protects this place, anyway. The only time a demigod might bother with this place is if the mortals attempted a rebellion."

"Does that happen often?"

"Not that we hear of."

My stomach churned. Should I tell Baxter about Daemon? Based on what Baxter said to Ava earlier about leaving Daemon alone, he seemed to know *something*. Daemon hadn't presented the information to me, and I had no evidence outside Ignis' word.

For now, I shuffled it to the side.

"What do the gods do when mortals fight back?" I asked.

The question echoed, lost in unseen chambers. A draft of cooler air brushed my right cheek, but Baxter led me to the left. My fingertips lost their connection with the wall as I followed.

"Depends on the god. Most gods ignore their mortals because mortals are the demigod's responsibility. Gelas, maybe, has a bit more involvement than most. Demigods would be punitive. Most anarchists are drowned without question."

Without question rang in the silence.

Baxter put a hand on the small of my back, nudging me to the right. A distant torch flickered down the way. Instinctively, I drew closer.

"An insurrection is normally a problem for the demigods who attain more powerful amulets. The more allegiant mortals a demigod has, the more magic that a demigod needs to care for them."

"Don't demigods want bigger amulets and more power?"

"Most."

"If mortals rebel . . ."

". . . then they threaten the demigod's power. A demigod could be bumped down to a lesser amulet, or lose their *sangessa* to the mortals."

"So it's all a giant power struggle?"

He sighed in answer.

Light broke through the darkness ahead. The edge of something sharp traced my shoulder as we stepped through a particularly narrow section of rock. Brightness returned, revealing an open space. My chest loosened, grateful to get out of the close shadows.

And this conversation.

"There you have it," Baxter declared. "We've arrived."

* * *

"They call me Bene," said a mortal woman with dark golden eyes, sun-weathered skin, and a jewel in her right nostril. She held up both palms. Startled by the warm reception, I pressed my palms to hers. She recoiled with a sharp intake of breath.

"Demigod?" she murmured.

A shuffle back took her out of my reach. She must have felt my magic when we touched. "No," I said quickly. "Not a demigod. A witch."

"But I feel . . ."

She rubbed her palms together with a low wince.

"My apologies, Bene," Baxter hurried to say. "I forgot to warn you. Bianca is a witch and . . . has her own magical power."

Bene frowned, clearly not convinced. She eyed me more warily, fingers grinding together as if to dissipate my touch. Further suspicion coated her tone.

"A witch that speaks Alaysian?"

I nodded, but warily.

Bene's eyes tapered to slashes. "The amulet-breaker? Is that who you are? It's because of you that we lost Luppentonisa?"

Memories of the lovely crimson amulet and Tipa and the rise of the demigods flashed through my mind. The hair on the back of my neck stood up. Bene's tone wasn't friendly.

I said nothing.

"Enough about Bianca. How have you been, Bene?" Baxter asked, smoothing it over with his usual charm. Clearly unable to help herself, Bene fell to the allure of the demigod. She turned to face him, a little smile on her face.

Mortals cannot tolerate god magic, Ignis said.

Not even a touch?

Only from the demigod to whom they have given allegiance.

Frustrating for them.

With palatial skill, Baxter wooed Bene with kindness and words until her suppressed hostility diffused. One fact at a time, Baxter gave her a vague overview of all that had happened the past several months.

"Because of that, Bianca is a living amulet," he said in summary. "Our only living amulet. Of all mortals, I thought she must meet *you*."

Bene's eyes grew. "Living amulet?" she breathed.

While she gaped, Baxter caught my gaze and winked.

Bene leaned closer. A tantalizing smell wafted with her. Cinnamon, perhaps? Her eyes illuminated with renewed interest. Though I felt no immediate trust for her, Baxter seemed eager to proceed. I'd have to lay my faith in him.

After a deep study of my features, Bene straightened. A long finger curled into her palm in a beckoning gesture.

"Come Lady-witch," she murmured. "You are now of great interest to me. Allow me to show you Ibarbelonbabellasaan. The Room of Great Power."

* * *

We wound through more tenebrous halls, illuminated by a torch, in the wake of Bene's nimble path. Like most mortals, she wore few clothes. An oversized shirt, clasped with a belt at her waist, that brushed the ends of her fingers. A small pair of pants cut off at the thigh lay underneath. Every now and then, she muttered something under her breath.

Finally, we spilled into a cave-like structure. Rounded at the bottom, with sloping walls that jutted several floors up, to a wide sky. Streaks of black decorated the gray rocks, sleek enough to slide down. On the far edge, a stream trickled by. At a cleft in the bottom of the smooth stone sat a squat clay jug, collecting water.

"When it rains," Bene said, following my gaze, "we collect the rainwater to drink. Some days, we are able to even collect dew from the fog. Last night, there was rain." She spread both hands and looked up. "Thank the Lei-li gods."

Lei-li. The *good* gods, as witches would say it. How interesting that we should live on different sides of the same world, yet speak in similar ways.

Bene led us straight across the circular floor. Shelves had been sculpted into the chipped walls, organized into columns. Alaysian books, created by sewn covers from leaves, dotted most of the shelves. What they used for parchment, I couldn't fathom. Nothing like what we had in Alkarra.

Above each column lay a depiction of an amulet. Each rendering was exquisite. Every amulet was slightly, or drastically, different. I could have been convinced that the gem itself had been placed into the wall. If my assumptions about the organization were correct, each shelf held books about a particular amulet.

"Have you closed Luppentonisa's shelf?" Baxter asked. His voice echoed slightly off the empty shelves, wide room.

Bene pressed her lips, then nodded. With a hand, she motioned to a shelf off to the left. A black line crossed the painting at the top, a near-perfect rendering of Luppentonisa.

Like most of the other amulets, four shelves, each as tall as my forearm, lay empty below. Apparently, they didn't have *that* many books on each amulet, but room enough in case the need arose. Ava had given me a book on Luppentonisa that I left in Alkarra.

With a thought, I brought it back.

The temptation to read it, now that god magic helped me understand Alaysian, swept through me.

Instead, I held it out to Bene.

"For you to keep," I murmured. "I think it means more to you."

Bene hesitated. Her gaze slipped to the book, then back to me in astonishment. Questions filled her eyes, but they remained unasked. She touched her chin with her thumb, then accepted the book and tucked it under one arm.

"Thank you."

She continued walking. Baxter sent me an approving nod that I pretended not to see—I hadn't done it for him. We followed until Bene stopped on the far side of the cave, in a pool of sunlight. An overarching cliff prevented sun or rain from touching the shelves, which protected the books. Rolls of thick fabric bunched above each shelf, likely released during bad weather to protect the shelves.

Bene turned to me.

"The amulets are something we are careful to track, and they . . . they grow on us. Though they are often instruments of torture, we form a sort of interest in knowing where they are and what they're doing. The amulets themselves aren't bad."

Her implication lingered.

The demigods are bad.

Monilay mal.

With a wave of her delicate hand, she gestured to a shelf thickly cluttered with books of varying widths and heights. Rocks wedged between several at intervals, leaving five or six to stand on their own. A rudimentary organization. The whole cavern lay in repose.

Quiet and bright, an outdoor library.

"It's a lovely place."

Her chin notched higher. "Thank you. Ventis provides a demigod to see to our needs. We have few requirements, aside from the occasional help with fresh water. Fruit trees and fish supply our food. Once a month, our demigod takes us to other islands to interview other mortals, find the amulets."

"Amorette," Baxter murmured in my ear, "is the demigod here."

"That seems kind of her to do," I said slowly.

"No other god would support us," Bene said ruefully. "Gelas is quiet in the northern kingdom. Ignis and Tontes wouldn't be bothered. Ventis . . . well, I *do* think he cares, though we never hear from him directly. At least a little. As the third god, it's surprising."

"You mean he's the third born?"

She laughed, a light, tinkling sound. "The gods weren't born. They just . . . they are and have always been. Some say that they were created from chaos and silence, but no one knows. Tontes is attributed to be the oldest. Then Ignis, Ventis, and Gelas, the youngest. Their power structure changes. Most of the time, Tontes has the greatest power."

Not an update I wanted to hear.

I considered the shelf where a detailed painting of Nicomedi-anthekus lingered.

"Nicomedianthekus," Bene murmured as she followed my attention. "Our most popular amulet."

"Because it's lost?"

"Yes. Mortals are always hoping to find it and gain the favor of Gelas." She shrugged. "We follow reports for it, write notes, seek it ourselves. Some mortals dedicate their life trying to find it. Legend states that Nicomedianthekus was the first formed amulet after the gods were banished from Alkarra. The oldest of all amulets, and perhaps the most powerful. Gelas seeks it still."

"Are the legends true?"

A smile changed her face from a serious scholar to an amused bystander. "I don't know. Nicomedianthekus has been gone for centuries. For the gods? A blip in time. For mortals? An eternity. Interest begins to wane."

Had I known the extensive history behind Nicomedianthekus, I may never have pretended to find it. Then again, if I hadn't, I wouldn't likely be in Alaysia now.

"As a living amulet," Bene continued, "you have . . . earned a shelf, I suppose."

"Ah, no. Thank you."

Her gaze tapered. "It wasn't a request. We are scholars here. Perhaps not as advanced as witches might be in Alkarra, but we take pride in our work. God magic creating a living amulet? We will absolutely be learning more."

My response faltered, because I didn't know what to say. The promise in her tone led me to wonder what they'd ask of me. Interviews, perhaps. More time answering questions? I shuddered at the thought. Definitely *not* what I'd come to Alaysia for.

Suddenly, my hope of getting rid of god magic seemed so far away.

I liked Bene and her spunk. I could appreciate their desire to learn, yet there was so much I didn't understand about my situation as a living amulet. A week ago, I couldn't wait to get rid of god magic and never hear the word *amulet* again.

Now?

I wasn't so sure.

Of considerable concern was whether the magic *could* be taken away. Memories of Luppentonisa's black, charred surface after I had touched it rippled through my mind.

My greatest concern, Ignis said.

For the first time, I didn't mind him guessing my thoughts.

Mine too, I replied.

"Give her Luppentonisa's shelf," Baxter said, drawing me back.

Bene grunted, then assented with a single nod. "I will obtain a book to start her record. Please, excuse me. You may read, but be very careful with the pages."

Bene disappeared through a different hole, leaving Baxter and me alone in the quiet, mortal library. The twitter of a bird issued from the rocks. A shuffle of wings. I stepped farther into the circle encompassing all the shelves. A quick count affirmed fifty. Fifty amulets, all of them clustered by god, if the similar colors meant anything. Not all of them appeared functional. Several had been crossed out with a black line, like Luppentonisa. Some appeared to be in question with no books and utterly empty shelves.

Leda would love this place, a historical record of god magic.

"I wanted you to see all the amulets," Baxter murmured, "so you could understand god magic and Alaysia better."

I spun around to face him. He had his head tilted back, eyes closed. Sunlight warmed his face, making it impossible to read his expression.

"Thank you."

He smiled, as if sun-drunk. His eyelashes fluttered open, long and dark against his light green eyes. He blinked, caught my gaze. With a lifted hand, I motioned to the shelves.

"Your Father is good to protect this."

Baxter's gaze tapered. "It's not so much goodness as strategy that compels my father to maintain this island."

"What do you mean?"

"The gods always want the upper hand. One way to do that? Control the amulets. If they obtain an amulet from their brother, they have greater control. Bargaining power, if you will. For example, Ignis has lost several amulets now that things went bad in Alkarra. He's in a weaker position than usual. If one of the brothers gained another of his amulets?"

"They'd control him."

"Exactly."

This fact only threw Ignis' motives into far greater question. I tensed, waiting for Ignis to comment.

He gave none.

I dismissed these intrigues as I strolled closer to the shelves, drawn to Ignis' by sheer color palette. Feral crimson, blushing pink, burnt orange, and a burgeoning yellow decorated the black rocks above the shelves with alluring splashes of color. Now that I could read Alaysian, I wanted to sink into the historical facts.

A depiction of a strawberry-colored amulet, heart-shaped, lined with white diamonds, drew me close. White paint indicated its name below it. Handuinolomolokaya. I trailed the tip of my finger along the thick spines of the books. Little hairs sprouted off the tattered edges.

With as much nonchalance as I could muster, I pulled the book off the shelf and asked Baxter, "So your father has Amorette keep track of what the mortals are learning about the amulets?"

"Yes."

"She reports anything interesting to him?"

Baxter nodded, throat bobbing. "Smart, if you think about it. He can care for mortals and keep track of his brothers."

The strangeness of his tone concerned me. Baxter had largely been indifferent, if not fond of, his father. Today, a note of uncertainty colored his tone. My confrontation with Ventis reminded me of the power of the gods.

"Do you think one of the other gods has Nicomedianthekus?" I asked lightly. "Maybe Gelas lives so quietly because he has to."

Baxter tilted his head to the side. "I hadn't thought of that."

The errant thought flittered through my head, and then

back out again. Gelas had no reason to hold much of my consideration, though I couldn't deny curiosity about the quietest of the gods. The book on Handuinolomolokaya drew my attention again.

When I began to read, the letters on the page remained the same—the Alaysian script didn't change to Alkarran. My mind, however, comprehended it the moment I laid eyes on it. Instant translation, something not yet established with goddess magic. So powerful.

As I'd presumed back in Alkarra, the columns and rows in the book dictated basic facts. Mortal name. Island. Where the amulet was seen. Details. Presumed amulet, known demigod caretaker, and more. With meticulous care, I shuffled through the book. Baxters gaze remained on me a few paces away. I pretended not to feel the weight of his stare. In the ensuing quiet, water dripped. The gentle scent of moss and greenery filled the air.

After I shelved it, I stepped back.

"Where do these mortals learn to write?" I asked, eyeing a cluster of shelves that must belong to Gelas. Ice blue. Deepest sapphire. Glittering silver. Staring at the colors brought the Icelands of the Southern Network to mind.

"Amorette," Baxter murmured absentmindedly. He peered at a yellow amulet portrayed in his father's cluster. "She teaches them how to read and write, and how to track facts. She provides the paper, water, travel, those necessary things."

"Sounds like a full-time job."

Baxter frowned. "She is a . . . growing favorite of Fathers. His happiness *is* her job. As Bene said, they aren't so needy here otherwise. The opportunity to learn and grow keeps them appeased."

"Happy mortals, happy demigod?"

Baxter attempted a chuckle. It died on his lips.

"Not exactly."

"If the mortals are content to learn and grow and be useful, why doesn't your father allow more of them to do so? Presumably, you'd have a more stable society."

"He might, but it's more up to the demigods than him. Most demigods don't want to invest as much time as Amorette."

His shifting discomfort led me to change the subject.

"Assuming this is all current, there are fewer amulets than I expected," I murmured, spinning in a slow circle. A quick count of active amulets revealed that Tontes had the most with sixteen. Ventis had thirteen. Gelas eleven. Ignis?

Eight.

During the rise of the demigods, three amulets had been taken from Ignis' children. Jote's, Mordecai's, and Bram's. Bram's amulet waited in the beach house for me to do . . . *something* with it.

The other two?

The North and the East held them hostage. Perhaps they had destroyed them, tossed them in the ocean. I wasn't sure.

Another amulet, so familiar to Luppentonisa, had a white slash next to the painting. The scripted name below was Samthanruadanosa. It hadn't been crossed out . . . yet. The painting perfectly portrayed the amulet that I had back at the house.

"Eight is the least any god has ever had," Baxter murmured, as if reading my thoughts. "If Ignis loses one more amulet, he will be, in a sense, incapacitated. He won't have enough functional magic available for his demigods to support the mortals."

My breath hitched.

Incapacitated?

"He'll be forced to build his power by creating more amulets," he continued. He peered overhead now, oblivious to my frozen state. "Amulets require time, concentration, and magic to create. The gods craft them in the Heart of Alaysia.

Meanwhile, his demigods would be without support, without magic, for up to centuries. His mortals? They'd die."

A fluttery feeling overtook my chest. I couldn't take my eyes off of Samthanruadanosa.

"Or," he said slowly. "He could be the most powerful god here."

"Because of me?"

His silence affirmed the question. Suddenly, our trip to Ibarbelonbabellasaan made a lot more sense.

"You're telling me," I whispered, "that Ignis, his demigods, and all his mortals fates are tied up in my power as an amulet?"

His whisper echoed behind me.

"Yes."

Chapter Twelve

When Ava returned to the beach house a few hours after me, she lay in a dark stupor of thought. Instead of playing with the abundance of toys that littered each floor, she sat on the wet sand and stared at the waves.

Baxter left as soon as he saw me safely back. In the silence, I stewed.

"Do you want to talk about anything?" I asked Ava as she nudged a few pieces of slippery, pink fruit across her plate at dinner that night. Her gaze darted to mine, then back down.

She shook her head.

Despite my desire to like and trust Daemon, I couldn't help but wonder if he'd told Ava about the rebellion. Bringing it up with her seemed foolish. What if he'd stopped his plans? I'd alarm her for no reason. Besides, I had only Ignis' word to go on.

Her depression likely had something to do with her birds, which she'd only said, "hadn't appeared," the whole time she'd been there.

Concerns for Ava—and myself—meant sleep eluded me that night.

I fretted in the hammock, awash with all I had learned at Ibarbelonbabellasaan. Bene's distrust. Baxter's hesitation. I tripped my way through strange dreams, oddly surreal, before a sharp voice woke me.

"Bianca!"

I jolted up, blinking into darkness. "What?"

"Bianca!" Ava jabbed me painfully in the shoulder with her finger. "Wake up!"

Bleary-eyed, I rushed out of the hammock. Ava's silhouette stood next to a broader figure. Gio. Darkness lay thick on the world. The restless waves banged more violently than usual. No moonlight eased the harshness.

"We need help," Gio said.

"What's wrong?"

"Daemon," Ava whispered, voice teary. "He's injured. He needs magic if he's going to survive." Her ice-cold fingers grabbed mine. "Help him?"

Grasping for understanding, I sat up. Sleep dissipated slowly, but still clung to my sluggish brain. Ava's frantic voice, pleading eyes, eliminated time to decide whether this would be a good idea or not.

"Y-yes. Take me to him."

Gio let out a relieved breath. "All must be done in secret. Ava, you must stay here."

Ava's back straightened until I thought she'd snap. Her hasty rebuttal in flowing Alaysian left no question—she did not like his order. Gio listened patiently. At the end of her tirade, he shook his head.

"No."

Ava scowled.

"It's too risky for you and *everything* else," Gio said. "You cannot go."

The drop in his tone snapped Ava out of her rage. Her lips parted, then pressed back together. She swallowed and turned away. With a wave of her hand, she gestured for me to go. Gio grabbed my wrist and tugged me to the doorway.

"No time to waste," he said crisply. "Take us to Daemon's collection with god magic, please. I can tolerate magic."

We arrived within a thought. The quick change of darkness for darkness made the adjustment easy. Gio pressed into the night, undaunted. The waves crashed more closely and the sand wasn't so fine against my bare feet. A metallic, coppery smell lingered in the air. Blood. Suppressed groans rang from not far away, along with quiet murmurs.

"Do anything you can to save him," Gio murmured.

"Even magic?"

"Yes."

"But ..."

My refusal trailed away. *The god of fire told me not to* wouldn't make any sense for a mortal from Ventis' kingdom.

"More lives are at stake than just his," he continued, oblivious to my hesitation. "I can't say more."

"Is it wise for them to know that I can do magic?"

He hesitated. "I don't know."

Questions would arise. Besides, this wasn't my land to save. Could I let a man die, though? Especially one that Ava cared for so deeply. Gio stopped walking. I stalled at his side.

Low torches illuminated a body on the sand, surrounded by frightened mortals. As I approached, one of the torches flared with a swirl of embers, which I ignored. Daemon's low moans filled the air.

I knelt at his side.

Blood oozed into the sand near the right of his ribcage, where a sharp, pointed stick jutted from his chest. Crimson stained the sand that clung to his skin where it leaked down his side into a puddle.

"What happened?"

The words sounded Alaysian to my ears. I'd unintentionally

used god magic to translate the words so the mortals wouldn't be frightened of me. If Gio noticed, he gave no indication.

"Doesn't matter," a nearby mortal said. "Can you help?"

"It does matter," I snapped. "What happened?"

"We don't know. He arrived like this. If you ask me? A demigod likely threw this piece of wood into Daemon's side to kill him, then returned him here to die."

Daemon groaned, head thrashing to the side. Anxiety built within me. They wanted me to save him? I had no idea how. If I pulled the stick out, would he bleed to death? If I didn't, would he anyway?

This time, I spoke in Alkarran so the others wouldn't understand. "I'm not an apothecary," I hissed to Gio. "I can't just save almost-dead mortals!"

Gio peered right into my eyes. "But you can do god magic, with which you can make *anything* happen."

I licked my lips. "I don't know how to do this! What if there are details and layers and . . . I don't know!"

The torches flared. God magic moved through me, racing fast.

You do, Ignis purred.

Frustrated, I turned away. *How? I just* think *this all away?*

It is that easy, as we have discussed.

This is a little more difficult than a few scrapes and a headache, I snapped.

The requirement is the same.

With goddess magic, apothecaries learned how to knit the body back together over years of practice. They rejoined bones, sinew, muscle, skin. Specific incantations had to happen in layers, however. Blood vessels first, then fascia, then skin. An apothecary had to *see* the damage to repair it. What if layers of trauma existed in Daemon's body that I couldn't see?

Or was god magic so wholly different?

The color leached from Daemon's lips, which mumbled

more than groaned now. Panicked chatter issued behind me. Gio grabbed my arm.

"Can you save him or not?"

My next thought wobbled when I asked Ignis, *I just . . . will it so?*

Eager magic prickled to life.

Together, Ignis said firmly, *we will save him. Uncertainty is the death of any magic, Bianca. You must trust me.*

I don't want to.

Then this man dies.

The desperation of the mortals pressed in on me. I only had minutes, and this couldn't go wrong. The urge to talk to someone—anyone but the god of fire—pulsed through me. No, that certainly couldn't happen. Ignis was all that I had.

"Fine," I muttered. "But we do this *my* way."

The control is yours.

I put my hands next to Daemon's wound as my mind spun through a logical approach. Maybe god magic didn't need the same instruction, but a plan anchored me out of my slippery thoughts. Daemon's blood trickled through my fingers, warm and sticky.

"First the blood," I whispered, eyes closed. Intent, hope, god magic, whatever it was, swelled in my chest. I yearned for Daemon's healing, and my love for Ava drove the magic to a greater surge.

The trickle of blood staunched. It slowed to a drip.

It stopped.

I studied Daemon with a wary eye. His ragged breathing eased, but his color remained gray. A deep breath settled my wild thoughts, exacerbated by the slippery magic under my skin.

"Now for pain."

Let him sleep, Ignis said. *It is the most compassionate approach.*

Daemon's features slackened. Someone gasped. A sob

echoed from behind. I ignored them, too focused on the magic to respond.

If I pull the wood out, he won't bleed to death, right? I asked.

Trust yourself.

It's the magic I don't trust, I snapped.

His firm insistence held no reprimand. *Trust yourself with the magic. It obeys your command. You are the master, not the servant. Take control.*

With that command spiraling through my mind, I braced myself in the sand, then looked to Gio.

"Grab the stick with both hands," I said. "You're going to carefully ease it out. I'm going to command the magic to heal him from the inside out as the stick moves. Do you understand?"

Gio nodded, firm and confident.

My face flushed as I pressed my hands on either side of the wound to counter the stick. At my nod, Gio gripped the end and eased it slowly back. The torches issued greater light. My hands circled the injury as I directed the god magic into the severed tissues and fractured bones.

The skin around the stick began to tug. Daemon twitched, nose twisted up as if in pain.

"Easy," I murmured.

Gio slowed. A drop of blood slipped around the stick, staining the sand. Gio moved it another fingers-breadth out. A rush of blood and fluid followed in a wave of clotted red and black.

"A little more."

With a firm tug, the stick released from Daemon's side. More liquid spilled. Daemon gasped in a breath, then coughed. With all my concentration, I willed the magic to heal shattered capillaries and damaged tissue. To fix the bruised remains. To restore whatever had been there—though I couldn't see the injuries.

As the fleshy wound exuded a lighter hue of blood, I closed my fingers over the top. A mere thought knitted the tissues together. They pulled and tugged under my fingertips with a swirl of candescence in my veins.

My fingers dropped away.

A perfect, pink line remained behind.

A quick glance to Daemon's rising and falling chest confirmed that he breathed easier. Color returned to his lips, his cheeks. With his forearm, Gio swiped a lock of hair off his forehead.

"He looks good."

Stunned by the speed of Daemon's physical healing, I leaned back. Another thought removed the blood from my hands, Daemon's side, Gio's palms. The sand. Mortals gasped. Gio watched the mortals, then me, with an unreadable expression.

"We need to check for other injuries."

You don't.

I stopped. *Why not? He might have other wounds.*

Trust yourself with the magic, Ignis said lightly. *Command all to be healed with your intent, your thoughts, your will.* This *is how it is done, and so easily. The gods are not fools, Bianca. You disrespect me.*

It can't be that easy.

It is.

My mouth opened, then closed. Too tired to argue, I did as Ignis directed. Bruising on Daemon's forearm faded. A cut under his chin. A swelling black eye. All disappeared.

Daemon's eyes flew open.

Shock rippled through the island in low cries. Instinctively, I stepped away from him. Mortals surged forward, surrounding Daemon all at once. I walked backwards. Gio straightened, watching me with a wary eye.

I didn't want to be here anymore. All of this magic frightened me. The power at my fingertips. The lack of restraint. Where did this magic end?

What could I *not* do?

I'd just healed the leader of a potential rebellion. Surely, that wouldn't go unnoticed. The mortals would talk about it. The gods would know—arguably already did know. A feeling deep in my gut told me that nothing happened here without a reason.

Why else would Ignis care about Daemon?

He didn't.

Ignis cared about my use of his power.

Sunlight collected near the horizon, turning it to a pale blue. More silhouettes and bodies became apparent by the moment. Mortals shoved out of boats and stumbled up the island. I had to get away from them.

Gio attempted to wade through them, calling my name.

I met his gaze.

Just before I sent him back to the *Rostina*, I mouthed, *sorry.* Once he disappeared, I left as quickly as god magic could take me.

* * *

Ava found me at the beach.

I stood in the surf and stared at the rolling waves. Though my hands were clean, Daemon's hot blood seemed to coat them. The coppery scent was thick enough to taste. All of it flashed back through my mind. Daemon's contorted face. Ignis' voice. Powerful magic in my body.

Ava touched my arm, eyes a soulful question. Pain twisted her full lips into a grimace.

"He's fine," I whispered.

Tears filled her eyes. She said, "I'm sorry."

Wind whistled by, grating and sharp. Granules of sand blasted us from the side. On the horizon, a building storm passed. The inky clouds lent a foreboding to an already tempestuous morning.

"Why?"

She leaned into me. Her face burrowed into my dress. I dropped my arm around her shoulders as a buried sob broke loose. She clung to me, shaking. I slipped my fingertips through her hair in placid lines, like Mama used to. Minutes later, her emotions ebbed.

Ava wiped her eyes with the back of her wrist. "Daemon is my friend. One of the only ones that I have. Here," she added softly, after a moment.

"Are you close to him?"

She shrugged. "He used to frighten me, but not anymore. He cares."

"Were you afraid he would also die?"

Fresh tears glittered in her eyes, but she only gave a stoic nod. Likely, Ava summarized her old life in Daemon. He, the symbol of who she had been. For him to expire would mean something frightening to her, I imagined.

In Alkarra, Ava had created a safe new world. We'd firmly punctured that haven when she arrived back to Alaysia, laid bare against her old life.

Gutting.

"You're stronger than the ghosts, Ava," I whispered.

Her welling tears slid free. She cried against me until her sobs quieted. My thoughts calmed. In the mellow silence that followed, I thought I could hear the whispers of Letum Wood.

Chapter Thirteen

Later that day, Daemon regarded me down his long nose. A note of annoyance colored his expression, as if irritated that he hadn't saved himself. Amidst the frustration, I sensed reluctant gratitude. He lived, at any rate, which created *more* questions about god magic.

And whether I wanted to be rid of god magic. I had an increasingly difficult time saying *no* to that question.

His mouth tugged down, nostrils flared. I started to regret my decision to check on him. Slowly, one of his knees began to bend. Realizing what he meant to do, I rushed forward. My touch sent a physical shock through his thick body.

"No," I said.

He paused. Glared.

"Don't bow to me."

Ava stepped up from behind. "He must. You saved his life, earned his *sangessa*. This is how it's done in Alaysia."

"No *sangessa*." I shook my head. "I'm not a demigod. Not a monilay."

His ridged brow deepened. In a gesture I hoped meant something near equality, I held up both palms, close enough for him to touch. Uncertainty deepened into astonishment. Not a sound came from the other mortals cluttering his island. He turned to Ava, incredulous.

Ava shrugged.

Desperation lay palpable in the air.

"I am not one of them," I said.

"This is the way of things, Lady-witch," Daemon muttered. "My debt of gratitude will be filled with my lifelong service to you. You earned control of my life through your magic."

"It's forbidden for a witch to receive *sangessa.*"

Daemon paused, eyeing me with deep skepticism. He looked to Ava. She shrugged again. After what felt like an eternity, his cheeks puffed out.

"I think this is not true," he muttered.

"Prove it."

He scowled. "I cannot, so I must accept what you say because I cannot prove otherwise."

Relief swept through me. Daemon's gaze darted to Ava. Hesitating, she nodded. Daemon motioned to the beach, not far away, with a wave of his hand. "If I cannot give you service, then I must give you part of me."

Terror struck my mind at the thought. "What does that mean?"

He thumped a fist over his heart. "An *asi fatu.* A truth of my heart. Come." He nodded to the same spot. "It is time."

* * *

Daemon, Ava, and I lowered to the sand.

With a raspberry from his lips and a jerk of his chin, he sent residual mortals scampering back to their islands. With no *sangessa* surrender to witness, they skulked away. We sat in dry sand, my toes buried in the darker, wetter band near the rushing waves. Ava remained on my right. Daemon, on my left. He stared hard at the water before words spilled out.

"I have planned a departure."

The words sent a glacial chill through my blood. I sucked in a sharp breath, but didn't dare look at him.

"I share this with you to satisfy my debt," he continued woodenly, as if afraid he wouldn't finish if he stopped. "You now have power over me, if you wish to have it, to execute your will. My debt is paid for saving my life. Or . . ."

He trailed away.

Monilay mal ran through my head over and over again.

The bitter side of Alaysia was almost impossible to reconcile against the wild, easy beauty. Glimmering beaches. Comforting surf. The easiest, most powerful magic in the world. My curiosity to see every room in the *Rostina lu Lune* meant I could stay here for months. Then new facets of the *real* Alaysia manifested, and I didn't know where I stood at all.

"A departure?" I whispered.

He nodded.

"What does that mean?"

Daemon shook his head, a sharp back-and-forth.

"His obligation is fulfilled," Ava said quietly. "He doesn't have to tell you any more of the details. Unless," she added with a sharp tone, as if reprimanding *him*, "you wanted to help with the escape."

Daemon cast me a sidelong glance, but didn't move his head. I blinked, stunned by her quick understanding.

So, Daemon *had* pulled her into it after all.

"Help?" I said.

"They need wood," Ava said in a rush. She pushed to her knees, fists in the sand, at my side. Eagerness overtook her entire body. "To make boats. That's it! You can conjure all the wood you want with the god magic. My friends have been collecting supplies for months now. Driftwood, fishing lures, offerings for

Prana, whatever might be needed. All they lack is the boats to get across the sea. There is no wood here."

Pieces shifted together. Ava's confusion around Daemon's driftwood house when we first returned. Gio's insistence that Daemon must stay alive if all the others would survive. Ava had spent hours here the past couple of days.

Annoyance at myself flared brighter. I *should* have been concerned. Daemon had clearly involved her. I licked my lips, my mind awhirl. A sickening feeling dropped through my stomach as another thought became clear.

"Where are you going to take these boats?" I asked Daemon.

He didn't meet my gaze. "To the land of the witches. If little Ava could go and survive, then so can we."

The feeling of a punch in the gut followed. Jikes, but they wanted to get to Alkarra. To cross the bloody ocean in tiny boats that would never hold enough supplies for any mortal.

I turned to Ava, but she'd curled in on herself. No longer a ball of energy now, she resembled more of a frightened child. She refused to look at me. What secrets did she hide? Thousands, if I had to guess. Brushing that aside to deal with later, I faced Daemon fully.

"How many of you?"

"Fifty," he muttered.

The number almost made me faint. Providing wood for that many boats wouldn't be difficult with god magic, but did they realize their own suicide? That many mortals across the entire ocean would be a feat of magic, not luck or planning or logic. Not to mention the disaster *if* they arrived on Alkarran shores.

Questions of how Ava had survived such a trek across the ocean and sky renewed again. She'd never had the words to answer when we had asked back in Alkarra. Now that we spoke each other's language, I longed to ask again.

Ava continued to look away, head resting on her knees, as if she wasn't part of this conversation.

The more pertinent point renewed.

"Alkarra isn't safe for mortals, Daemon. Witches will . . . they will be as likely to kill you as any *monilay mal.*"

He gritted his teeth, jaw tense.

"Ava says it's a wealthy land. Plenty of food, forest, water. Life is easier there. The witches are not welcoming, but did not kill her. We don't need much, just our freedom. Just . . . a home that is *ours.* No demigod to serve. No demigod to deny. It is our right. I feel it in *here.*"

Passion thickened his voice. He pressed his fist to his heart while tears brightened his fierce eyes. I opened my mouth to protest, then closed it again.

What to say?

Freedom wasn't mine to give or take away, neither was Alkarra. If they wanted to attempt a trip across the ocean, was it my place to stop them?

Yet, could I in good conscience help them?

"Tell me your plan."

Daemon hesitated. Something in my tone must have convinced him to trust me, because he leaned forward, finger in the sand, and began to draw.

What followed was an explanation through crude pictures. Vessels they wanted to cross the sea with. Small, to save wood to make more. The boats would barely admit one mortal and the supplies necessary to survive for a few days. For fifty mortals, he planned on seventy-five boats. Twenty five to carry additional supplies and offerings for Prana.

He spoke about water pouches made out of leaves. Spare fishing lures. Clothing to protect from the sun. A more sophisticated plan than I'd expected unfurled. They would fish along the way, guided by stars. Wayfinding. Choice. Heading west, like Ava did, to avoid storms in the east.

None of them would survive.

My obligation to talk Daemon out of such a foolish notion

weighed like a heavy stone in my chest. How could I soften real-ity? I couldn't. He would be leading all of his people to a watery grave. Not to mention Prana, who posed a formidable, jealous foe.

Finally, he slowed and stared at me in stony silence. A dare, I imagined, to refute him. Weeks alone on the ocean, under an awful sun, without any magic. The only way to *help* this exodus was to stop it in the first place.

"How many days to get to Alkarra?" I asked.

He shrugged.

"The mermaids took me," Ava piped up. "Then there was . . . I . . ." Darkness clouded her expression. "I think, perhaps, plan for . . . a month?"

Unspoken words lay behind her uncertain, squeaky voice. I put a hand on her shoulder to comfort her. At eleven years old, Daemon should never have involved her. He laid on her a burden of sharing information and experience she shouldn't have to bear.

"Then you should plan for supplies for sixty days. There will be storms and food will be lost and . . . who knows what else? There's no way you can carry enough water for two months, Daemon."

His eyes glinted.

"Unless," he purred, "a magic-holder came with us. Or . . . a magic-holder *took* us to the land of witches."

With a cold feeling in my chest, the real game lay in front of me. Daemon didn't want help, wood for boats, or to ride the waves for a month or two.

He wanted my magic.

I lurched back.

"You want me to take all of you to Alkarra?"

"You can do magic!" he cried, arms spread. "You can do *anything*. If you take us to the land of the witches, all of us will be saved. You said it yourself—you are no *monilay mal!*"

"That doesn't mean I can be manipulated," I snapped.

He glowered. "If you don't help us, we'll go anyway. We are prepared and we will see our freedom through. Yet our blood is on *your* hands if any of us die!"

"There's more to this than just the logistics of crossing the sea, Daemon," I hissed. "I cannot bring you to Alkarra. Mortals are not welcome there. *All* of us would be killed."

"We are not welcome here, either."

"Witches will hurt you. Out of fear, they might hunt you down. Harm you. Your life will not be any safer."

"There is land as far as the eye can see, is there not?"

Reluctantly, I nodded.

"There are spaces and mountains and trees bigger than the *Rostina*?"

"Yes," I whispered.

Ava curled away again, shrinking small at my side. She must have extrapolated with them about Alkarra. Daemon had been dreaming of such a thing for years—planning for it even—now Ava made it seem possible.

He leaned closer. "Then it is already better. For, in the land of the witches, we would have somewhere to *hide*."

A considerable chill swept through me.

"It might be perceived as an act of rebellion against the gods," I quickly said. "An act or declaration of war. Then your gods would descend on my land and kill tens of thousands. The blood of my witches would be on my hands as well."

Daemon's lips drooped as he considered this.

A squeak came from Ava.

"Baxter!"

Daemon's scowl faltered as he gazed beyond my shoulder. I glanced back to find Baxter striding through the sand, a perplexed half-smile on his face.

"Bianca?"

"Later," Daemon growled.

Shaky, I rose to my feet and slid my ankles through the sand where Daemon had drawn the pictures.

"Merry meet!" I called, pasting on a too-tight smile. Baxter paused a few steps away, eyes bouncing between me and Daemon, who stood like a board at my side. God magic came to life with a languorous little yawn inside me. Baxter had hidden his amulet beneath his clothes.

"What are you doing here?" he asked.

"Not much."

Another damning silence followed. The weight of what Daemon had just revealed lay like a stone between us. If I told Baxter, would Daemon be killed to squash the escape?

Undoubtedly.

In truth, I wasn't sure who *this* Baxter would be. The fragmented sections of my friend pieced together in a way I couldn't yet reassemble to a clear picture. Would Baxter always be *my* Baxter when put into a position of pure power?

Baxter cleared his throat. "Daemon, good to see you again."

Daemon bowed all the way at the waist, as if inspecting something in the sand. He straightened, expression sour. He'd returned to the cold-faced leader that laughed a little too loudly. The sight of a mortal giving deference to Baxter flipped my stomach. Observing Daemon in vulnerable obeisance felt like I'd stepped into his own torture.

"Rise," Baxter said in an offhand way.

Memories of Baxter in Papa's office, surrounded by scrolls that he capably plucked from the air and dealt with one at a time, whispered through my mind. The confidence from there remained the same as here, but it felt different. Sharper, perhaps. More pointed.

Baxter clasped his hands behind his back. "I have become the new demigod over your collection, as of this week. I apologize it's taken me so long to let you know—it's been quite difficult to clean up Shara's mess."

Daemon said nothing.

My stomach tightened.

Well, wasn't that the worst. I definitely couldn't tell Baxter *now*.

"Shara will no longer be watching over you," he continued in a light tone. "I plan to stop by each morning to see how you're doing, at least for the first couple of months. For starters, what do you need now?" He tossed a hand toward the hammock stretched between two trees. "You need wood for structures, apparently."

Ava stiffened.

Daemon sucked in a breath.

"A structure to live under would be wonderful," I said with a glare to Daemon. "Great idea, Baxter."

Daemon relaxed. "Freshwater. Wood for structures. Lots of it." He cast me a sidelong glance. "Lots of wood."

Baxter nodded. Underneath his shirt, the amulet glowed a bright argentine, then faded. "Anything else?"

Daemon hesitated, then shook his head.

"Your water barrels are refilled. They will refill each morning. If you need food, let me know." Baxter regarded the trees with a tilted head. "Do you need more fruit? I see no *umu* or *seema* bushes."

Hesitantly, Daemon nodded.

A cry came from behind. Several new trees elongated on different islands. Bushes appeared from the sand, twirling along the ground. Vines filled with dangling fruits, plump and bright orange, hugged existing trunks. They spiraled high, burdened with food. The laughter of a child rang out as one particularly heavy fruit dropped into his father's waiting hands.

"Any babies about to be born?" Baxter asked, ignoring the cries.

"Three."

"The mothers are healthy?"

"Yes."

"Good. I will bring a midwife with me to meet with them."

Daemon's jaw loosened slightly. His nostrils flared as he ground out, "Thank you."

"I'll return tomorrow." *This* Baxter reminded me of Papa's Assistant, but . . . more authoritative. "In the meantime, please gather your collection and ask about any health issues that I can help with at daybreak tomorrow. Bianca, a word?"

Daemon's glittering stare bore into me as I stepped away with Baxter. Ava waited at Daemon's side, eyes wide in silent surprise. Apparently, she hadn't expected Baxter to show up today any more than I had.

In hindsight, it made too much sense.

At the water's edge on the other side of the island, Baxter stopped. He ran a hand through his hair, consulting a paper he pulled out of a pocket. A list of names ran down it, the length of his forearm. The top five had been crossed off. As he stared at it, a line formed through the next one. He folded it back together, accordion style, and tucked it into his pocket.

"Return to the beach house?" he asked. "It's not safe for you to be anywhere else, and I have more islands to care for now. Besides," his eyes cut to Daemon, who stood in stony silence on the beach, "Daemon is . . . difficult company. I'd rather you not be alone with him. Tonight, I'll try to stop by, but Father has finally seen Shara's accountability meetings through. It freed me up to visit and supply all the rest of the islands I haven't seen yet."

"Of course. We'll return now." I studied him, anxious over his thin lips and pale appearance. He was anything but pleased with me. "Are you upset?"

"Concerned." A hand passed over his face. "Exhausted. Can we talk more tomorrow?"

"Yes."

With a weary nod, Baxter left. A hole seemed to remain

where he once stood. I stared at the spot while I gathered my thoughts, then shifted back with a sigh. A small hand appeared, fingers threaded through mine. A glimmer of embers caught my eye, then winked away.

"Shall we go back to the beach house?" I murmured.

Ava nodded.

"Then let's go."

I issued the magic, grateful to leave her collection far behind.

* * *

Chips of fire swirled in a mute sky that night. Ignis's voice rolled through my body, waking my god magic.

You seek me.

Irritated at the unstated truth, I leaned back on my hands. Yes, I did want to talk to him. No, I hadn't asked him to come. Like always, he appeared at his whim. Or maybe he never left.

The surf remained invisible except for the sound. No moonlight tonight. Nothing but darkness, fallible sand beneath my palms, and smattering stars aloft.

"I have a question."

Come with me.

"To where?"

Somewhere more beautiful than this. We can discuss your question there.

"Is there such a place?"

Yes, but I would like your permission to take you there. It is . . . part of my world and would mean a great deal if you would agree to see it.

I straightened. "A god who asks permission before he uses magic? You impress me, sir. Next thing I know, you'll stay out of my head."

His stoic silence held a flair of long-suffering.

I broke into a grin.

"You have my curiosity and my permission."

The magic that bore me away deposited me on the bank of a foggy stream that cut through dark stone, black as pitch. Electric green moss draped over the trees, rocks, and ground. Mist clung to the air, churned by a waterfall only a few paces away. The water, pristinely pure, trickled by my feet.

"Jikes," I murmured, head tilted back.

Trees stretched overhead with leafy fingers. Fronds cluttered the thick, lush earth. Leaves that were flat as paper fanned in circles, like umbrellas, and blocked out the starlight overhead.

"Beautiful."

Amaranthine wings fluttered on a nearby tree. I ducked when dozens of butterfly-esque creatures took to the air. They skimmed close to my shoulders, brushing my cheeks. I smiled as they flew into the humid forest, where water dripped from leaves and raced down trunks.

Lush. Warbling. Sultry with heat. Sweat collected over my spine. The air felt thick enough to chew, but the wild beauty stole all the discomfort. Undoubtedly, he'd brought me somewhere in his kingdom.

A first.

"You're right," I said softly. "It's more beautiful here."

When Ignis said nothing, I continued.

"My question, if you're ready, is about the mortals."

Proceed.

"Could Daemon be successful with an exodus? Could fifty of them actually make it all the way to Alkarra in small boats?"

A pause. In it, I held my breath.

No.

I closed my eyes.

Ventis is already aware of the growing insurrection. It's why he appointed Baxter as the new demigod. When their needs are met, the frenzy will calm.

"What if it doesn't?"

Then they will die.

A bitter taste surfaced in my mouth, even as I felt some relief. Perhaps Ignis was right. Now that Baxter would be present, could it mollify the hunger for Alkarra?

I doubted it.

Daemon sought more than consistent water, food, or health. Hunger burned in him—deep, deep down. He yearned for freedom. Opportunity. Daemon wanted more than an easy life.

"He wants his *own* life," I murmured to myself.

You are correct.

Vexed at the intrusion, I snapped, "So why doesn't Ventis let them go? They don't want this life. Why do you keep them here if no one likes it?"

Do you want them? Ignis asked, amused.

I hesitated.

"Alkarra wouldn't want them, but that doesn't mean I don't."

I didn't ask what Alkarra wanted.

"I'd take them back to Alkarra with me," I whispered, "if it would actually make their life better. I don't think it would."

That, he murmured, *is why. Where would they go? We cannot form new land without Prana's permission.*

"I didn't know that."

Something like sadness stained his tone. *Our sisters seek to punish us for Tontes' deeds millennia ago.*

"Two thousand years isn't enough?"

Time does not exist in the same way for you as it does for us.

Moments passed while I sat with that, attempting to comprehend the impossible.

"Basically, you won't set them free because the mortals can't do magic?"

They are magicless beings in a world run by magic. By nature, they are going to struggle until we have our own true land again.

In a sense, this is the kindest fate we have for them. For the time being.

I tucked my knees into my chest and peered over the water. "I don't think that's true," I whispered. "There must be another way."

In all my eons, Ignis murmured, *I have never observed differently.*

"Then maybe you need to get out more, too."

He laughed, a rolling sound. I set my chin on my bent knees and stared into the darkness. My fingers dug into the soil, expecting to hear voices, but none came. Thoughts of home surfaced. Letum Wood. The comfort of their close branches, mossy vines. Leda's imperious tone, chastising me for something.

Papa.

A rush of homesickness caught me by surprise.

Your sorrow is mine, Lady-witch.

The compassion in his voice startled me. With a dismissive chuckle, I murmured, "I miss Grandfather. He always knew what to do in sticky situations like this."

Tell me about him.

Vulnerability stole over me, arresting my words. Ignis asked for the gift of honesty. He wanted me to willingly tell him about the pieces of my heart that ached so profoundly now, when I felt certain that, because of our connection, he already knew many of my thoughts.

A gift, then.

He'd brought me to this lovely, nighttime forest. I could return favor for favor.

Half-laughing, I first told him about Mildred, then Marten. Their hidden romance, the child they had together, my father. The story unwound, filled with sorrow and giggles and a fondness that rises only in reminiscing. By the time I finished, the tension had loosened in my chest.

"Grandfather loves me," I finished quietly. "I feel it every day."

You question your father's love for you.

"No." My brow drew down. "No, not that. I . . . I question his trust in me. Because of that, I question our closeness and our relationship." Regina, Head of the Masters in the Northern Network surfaced in my mind, followed close at heels by Mama. "I question a lot of things now."

If you ask me? It's not only fair that you question your father— but also necessary. We must always question the motives of others, even those we love. There is no one to take care of us but ourselves.

"I question *you* after what I learned at the Island of the Amulets."

As you should.

"You've lost too many amulets."

Yes. Should I lose one more, I must retreat and rebuild.

"Can't you do that now?"

No. It requires time—a lot of it—and power to build amulets. To harness magic into a small sphere that can then be shared. The process is neither simple, nor easy. Withdrawal is required. Total focus and concentration.

His confirmation darkened an already wretched picture. I considered what would happen should Ignis also lose me. Did he know that I hid one of his amulets in the beach house, uncertain what to do with it?

He might.

Yet, he said nothing.

I considered the astonishing thought that he might not know about the other amulet.

One takes a risk—or one's children take said risk—and it doesn't always work to one's advantage. In eternity, this has never changed.

"When your children attempted to take over Alkarra, you mean?"

Yes.

Another long silence fell between us.

"You want to teach me god magic because you want me to stay with you in Alaysia, don't you? To be the amulet that stops you from losing all your mortals, your demigods. You want me to be the amulet that keeps you from losing everything."

Ignis lay in contemplation for so long I thought he'd left. Only the gentle trickle of the stream, the easy dance of fog, filled the air now.

How long have you lived, Bianca?

The change of topic startled me. "I'm twenty-two in a few months."

I am endless, like the other gods and goddesses. Have you considered what that means?

"No."

I have lived and will *live far beyond you. The way I view death and creation and the cycle of life isn't the same as witches or mortals or demigods.*

"If that's true, then isn't life a giant circle to you? What do mortals and witches matter in the expanse of eternity?"

You are more valuable than that.

"Because I'm a living amulet?"

Yes, and perhaps the greatest weapon the world has ever known. You could change the course of history.

Irritation swept through me.

"I'm more than just a weapon," I muttered.

No one disputes that.

Shame boiled inside me, then faded at my initial surge of frustration. Didn't I want to be a weapon for Alkarra? I'd come to Alaysia to get rid of the god magic, but I *stayed* because maybe god magic offered the bigger answer I sought.

How to protect my witches. My forest.

My home.

Without something different, unexpected, and clever,

witches would never defeat the amassing demigods. I should be grateful, not bothered, that Ignis constantly referred to me as a weapon.

From this, I turned my thoughts.

"What of all the other witches and mortals in the world that aren't so useful to you? Not everyone can be a god magic weapon."

They have their purpose as well. Perhaps not so great, however.

He spoke so mildly I could barely comprehend. Did all gods and goddesses dismiss our lives so easily? My mind skimmed over Prana. She held considerably less regard for the lives of witches and mortals than Ignis. Deasylva? I knew so little of her, the goddess that shifted in the background of my world.

My forest.

To some extent, my heart.

Cloaked from me, Deasylva was a mere shadow. A thriving, vibrant apparition. One who I wanted to thrust into the light, but didn't know how.

"What if Tontes wins?" I asked in a raspy voice. "What if he *is* stronger?"

Then the goddesses will fight, and all of Alaysia and Alkarra will be destroyed.

"All of it?" I whispered.

When the gods and goddesses are at war, all ends. So much magic. So much power. Destruction is the only result. Then, we would have to begin again. A new world. A new Alkarra. Such devastation is . . . wrenching. Horrific.

Images swirled through my mind. Whether born from my own imagination, or given to me by Ignis, I couldn't be sure. Smoke and ash and darkness and a deep sense of mourning pervaded them. My soul shrank from the shadows such images brought.

As brothers, Ventis, Gelas, and myself seek to deal with Tontes before our sisters get involved to stop him. In the end, Lady-witch, all we want is our land. We crave Alkarra. It is our home, long before it was yours.

A cooling sensation rippled through me. I shouldn't have been surprised that the gods wanted Alkarra. They had lived in the land two thousand years ago.

"I see," I murmured. "Is Alkarra really all you want?"

No.

"Then what?"

Attachment.

Startled, I could only blink.

"To what?"

Wrong question.

A rush of intuition prickled up my spine. "To whom?"

Witches think little of the before and after to your life in Alkarra. Deasylva has not asked for your devotions, so you think only of this life, not all the other lives that follow. Eternity is an empty place when one navigates it on one's own.

The air thickened, as if he expected me to understand something right now. I didn't, nor did I want to. Not for a god that invaded my thoughts, my land, and attempted to fashion me into a weapon to be controlled.

Not ever.

"What attachment is it that you seek, Ignis?" I whispered.

That, he murmured, *is no business of yours. Yet.*

The final word resounded like a hidden cry. Could a god feel such depths of pain as I heard in him now?

Rendered mute by the tethers of emotion I felt from him, I watched the lacy tendrils of smoke and fog curl through the air. Water dripped onto my neck, slipped down my temple. Whether my own, or this forest, I couldn't tell.

Could we really be strong enough together to save Alkarra from Tontes? I asked without my voice, because I couldn't bring myself to say the words.

His reply reverberated like a promise.

Yes.

No stirring of branches or birdsongs interrupted the reverie that followed. Only the tumble of water through the hall of rocks.

Are you not obligated to discover the depths of what we could do together? You speak of the value of lives. Are you more important than thousands upon thousands of witches in Alkarra? Is it fair to refuse a life of magical power and privilege when you can also provide safety?

My fingers curled, digging into the skin of my knees. He put into words what I'd been silently spinning around all this time.

Could you live with yourself if Tontes overcame Alkarra because you didn't explore our depths together?

I whispered, "No."

You must choose eventually, Lady-witch of Alkarra, for both magicks will not coexist for long. One of them will take your life, should you try to keep them both.

The revelation stunned me. I straightened, struck mute for moments.

"What?"

Can you not feel the rising intensity of the god magic? The waning power of the goddess? It's already beginning.

"That's . . . I can't . . . it's not fair."

No one said it would be.

"So I have to choose?" A hand pressed over my heart, as if I could keep it locked inside. "You want me to choose between magicks?"

I didn't ask this of you, Lady-witch.

Emotion thickened my voice. "You want me to give up Alkarra in order to save it. That's my home. My family. My witches. You can't ask that, Ignis. You don't get to ask that."

You would be free to live in Alkarra and with me. In doing so, you would have the most powerful magic while you fought for and protected your land, if you wish. Or, if you also desired, you could stay in Alaysia. In my kingdom, whatever you dreamed would be yours.

My head lifted. "If you're not asking me to give up Alkarra, then what *are* you asking?"

I want you to give up Deasylva.

Chapter Fourteen

Returning to Ava's collection the next morning felt like crossing a field of coals.

Necessary to do what was needed, but it wouldn't be pleasant to tell Daemon no, I wouldn't help their exodus.

I came to save Alkarra.

Bleeding heart or not, I couldn't lose sight of that.

A sleepless night left me on edge. Half-dreams of Letum Wood on fire, the trees screaming, and me unable to stop it, woke me repeatedly. Always to the sound of Ignis's voice.

I want you to give up Deasylva.

After declaring such a thing, Ignis had retreated, leaving me to wonder all night long.

Gloomy clouds filled the skyline with frothy depths, where an approaching thunderstorm overtook the dome of the earth— no easy feat in a world of water and sky. The broiling masses swept closer, violet-black and thick as pudding. Wind rushed past, sweeping grains of sand over my arms.

Ava studied the sky with pursed lips.

"Tontes," she muttered.

Electricity filled the air, standing the hair on my arms up on end. I shuddered. "Let's get this over with."

Daemon waited on the beach along with a group of mortals. Fish scales speckled his forearms, glinting despite the lack of sun. Humidity made the air thick and ominous as he closed the space between us, a silent question on his thick features. As promised, Baxter had provided wood, which lay in piles between trees.

"I'm sorry, Daemon, I can't help you."

The deepening scowl didn't frighten me, but Ava shuffled forward. My hand on her shoulder stopped her from putting herself between us. Several moments passed while Daemon took that in. Lightning crackled over the sea.

"The blood of my mortals," he growled, "will stain your hands."

Fury rose in me. "I'm not a pawn, and neither are they. I want to help, but leading you to the land of the witches isn't the answer. It's a death wish. You're not prepared for the seasons or the witches or the magic or—"

"That is for us to know!" he thundered.

A wave swept up the sand. Wind gusted by, shivering the thin dress I'd quickly plucked off the wall at the beach house.

Incoming.

Movement caught my gaze. Four figures strode over the top of the waves, bound for here. The same four demigods that had hunted for me around the beach house.

"Jikes," I muttered.

Ocean churned into a froth under the broiling sky, developing a sickly green tinge. Daemon barked at the mortals behind him. They splintered, scuttling to nearby huts or throwing themselves into the water to swim away. The four demigods closed in, as if swept by the storm.

Thunder exploded.

They came sooner than expected. They are here for you, Ladywitch. Tontes, like all the gods, wants you on his side.

"Tontes can rot at the bottom of the sea."

It doesn't work that way. Regardless, his sons will try to convince you to join their father. Should they be unsuccessful, they plan to take you prisoner.

"How did they know I would be here?"

You're not difficult to track. Also, I may have told them.

"What? Why?"

Let's just say we have greater opportunity to prove our abilities together. That is all.

My fingers tightened into a fist at my side. "Why are you incapable of giving warnings?" I hissed.

One forgets such things.

"Right," I muttered.

The closer the demigods approached, the more the god magic sprang around inside me. My blood agitated to a frenzy, more intense than anything I'd yet felt. A reminder of what he'd revealed last night—that the god magic would grow in power, the goddess magic wane.

Somehow, I perceived that all four of these demigods had amulets.

Yes, this felt different.

The feeling of moving magma sifted through my veins, drawing me more fully into the moment. Ignis murmured, *you will be even more powerful with me at your side. I ask only for your trust.*

"After you told the sons of Tontes to find me here?" I cried. "Not a chance. You have your own plans."

No, he drawled. *I helped them understand they'd find us here. You are correct. I do have plans, but they are only for your own good.*

"Forgive me if I don't trust you. I happen to like making my own decisions, thanks."

Forgiven.

With a growl, I forced my rage aside to focus.

Ava eyed me warily. I snarled into the wind, hair whipping around my face.

"Can we do this confrontation elsewhere? The mortals don't need to be in danger."

No.

"I won't let them harm the mortals."

Clearly, they know that. As I mentioned before, misplaced compassion and a bleeding heart, but we'll discuss that another time. Tontes has leverage against you if they attack near innocents. If you don't do what they ask, they will kill a mortal.

"Not on my watch."

This is our chance, Bianca, to begin your protection of Alkarra. Power magnified his tone. *Show them just what the Lady-witch of Alkarra can do. Establish your power. Prove to them who you are: granddaughter of the lioness of the Central Network. I will be here to guide you.*

Mention of my grandmother shocked me.

Mildred.

A woman of tenacity and spirit and grit. The witch that stood against numberless foes and won. *My* grandmother.

My feet planted more firmly.

"You're right."

As if she sensed a change in me, Ava lifted her chin and straightened her shoulders. "The Sisterhood never leaves a fight," she whispered.

I squeezed her shoulder.

"We are not done here, god of fire," I muttered. "You and I will be talking after this."

He said nothing.

In a blink, the demigods stood on the beach a few paces away. I recognized their basic forms. Only the middle demigod stood out, with reddish hair and bright eyes. Neel. The one that had almost sniffed me out at the beach house. He advanced at the forefront, sparkling eyes narrowed.

Two demigods flanked him, legs braced. The fourth remained back. They moved like trained Guardians, ready to pounce on the next objective. Neel tilted his head back and drew in a deep breath, as if testing the air.

A coy smile wrapped his lips.

"They say you can understand us," he called. "That you speak Alaysian through the power of god magic."

I tightened my grip on Ava's shoulder in a silent command not to say a word. Papa would tell me that confidence was the sharpest weapon and caused the deepest wound. Thinking of him gave me another burst of courage.

"Correct," I called.

"Your name is Bianca?"

"What is yours?"

He grinned and gave a flourishing bow. "Neel."

Distant thunder filled the pause that came next. Neel's studious gaze tapered as he straightened. "How powerful are you, living-amulet-Bianca, the amulet-breaker and Lady-witch of Alkarra?"

"More powerful than you."

Ignis chuckled in my ear.

You do delight me.

Neel shuffled forward, one eye tapered in thought. With every step, my god magic expanded. It pressed against the walls of my veins, held in only by willpower.

In a thought, I sent all the mortals in this collection to the beach house. Ava left with them. Her warm body disappeared beneath my hand. She'd be upset that I didn't keep her at my side, but they needed her help.

And I needed her to be safe.

My body burned in response to the magic, likely from so prodigious an act. Bram's amulet had limits back in Alkarra.

"What limits would a living amulet have?" I whispered.

This, Ignis murmured, *is what we shall test today. Hold nothing back, Lady-witch of mine. You have my trust.*

The four demigods stiffened.

I smiled.

With a subtle shift, I canted my body to the side, my right leg braced back. Viveet appeared in my right hand, brought from Alkarra by sheer instinct. The relief of her in my palm gave me a delicious zing of power.

Only a weak flare of goddess magic illuminated her shaft. No warmth or friendly fire burst to life—but the metal of her hilt in my hands was comfort enough.

I crouched.

Neel's eyes widened.

The two in the back whispered, but I couldn't hear. Their eyes darted around. They made plans.

"What are they saying?" I murmured. Neel tilted his head to the side, a hand on his chin, as if assessing what to do with me next. Removing the mortals would have changed their plan. They didn't know where I sent them, so he'd have to recalculate.

A plan to flank you. The one in the back is watching for Baxter. Neel is to distract you so they can attack and return you to Tontes.

Baxter.

Why would he be here?

"A sword?" Neel finally called, arms spread open. "Are you so ready for a fight, Lady-witch, that you would pull a weapon on those who come in peace? We only wanted to meet you."

"Right. You're showing up with a storm like that for a tea party?"

Neel chuckled.

"We don't drink tea here. That's weak, for mortals."

The demigod on Neel's left disappeared. Instinct more than thought propelled me to spin to my left, sword extended. These were tactical foes. They'd know that my right side was weakest, because of the way I stood.

The demigod appeared, as anticipated, on my right. Propelled with the momentum of my counter-turn, Viveet sank into his fleshy side. He howled, his fine-boned features twisted in agony. Blood spurted from the filleted skin near his ribcage, spraying into the sand.

He disappeared.

His reddish-but-strangely-silver demigod blood stained Viveet's metal as I faced Neel again, back in guard. Ignis laughed, a cackle of pure glee.

Neel frowned.

The demigods blinked out of view at the same time.

Give me speed, I commanded.

It is yours.

Instinct took over.

Only a shift of sand preceded an attack at my back. Propelled by god magic and at an impossible speed, I shoved Viveet behind me. She tucked under my arm, next to the left side of my ribcage, and jabbed at the closest body back there. A grunt followed. I held her stable with my left arm, whirled around using the same momentum, and swung my right hand in a fist.

Bright, green eyes met mine a second before I smashed his nose. The demigod crumpled, unconscious. He disappeared, likely sent away by Neel.

Two demigods remained.

A third attack came on my right. I magicked myself out of reach, landing behind him. My right arm slipped across his throat as Viveet shrank with god magic, no larger than a hand knife. She pressed into the skin along the right side of his throat. My legs wrapped his torso as I snaked my left arm under his armpit, anchoring Viveet. It all happened inexplicably fast. What might take three seconds in Alkarra was only one second here.

The demigod grabbed my arms and ducked, attempting to

flip me on my back. With a surge of magic, I twisted, interrupting his momentum. We toppled to the sand, breaking apart.

I jumped, gaining both feet.

Viveet returned to her natural size as I swept her off the sand and dropped back into a crouch. Blood smeared the neck of the demigod nearest me. He scowled, nostrils flared. Slowly, the blood faded. The cut healed.

Not a gash remained.

Power infused me, enveloping every muscle in my body. This heady feeling. The indomitability of god magic. It buoyed me up, billowing unbelievably hot. No fear of these demigods followed. Why would I be frightened of them? With this power, I could do *anything*.

Neel peered at me, as if he sensed the shift. Finally, I could feel some of what Ignis meant. The extent of our ability to fight together. The force of it swelled within, pushing out thoughts of anything else.

Grinning, I beckoned with a curl of my fingers.

The other demigod disappeared.

Neel lifted both hands. "You prove yourself," he called. "We shall only ask questions, if you insist on violence."

"You surround women to *question* them, do you? Yes, I've heard of your kind of interrogations. Not for this Lady-witch."

A hint of Baxter's arrogance showed in Neel's growing smile. Something dark curled away inside me at the thought.

Demigods.

Monilay mal.

I saw it now.

Not all of them are bad, my heart whispered, Baxter's face coming to mind. *Not all.*

"We have questions." Neel shrugged. "That's all. If we agree to stay on this side of the beach, will you answer them?"

"No."

I edged back. *Where is the other one?* I asked Ignis, glancing to both sides. In the distance, the storm surged. Mountainous waves. Ebony clouds. Near-constant grumblings from the sky.

He is not here anymore, Ignis said.

Can he still attack?

Yes, from elsewhere. They must know I am tracking this area. I will sense him when he appears. Neel may have a plan to position you somehow so the other demigod can return without warning.

"Then what do you desire?" Neel called to my silence.

"That you leave and never come back to this collection."

Neel laughed, doubled over. A maniacal edge colored his forced hilarity. He stopped, face firm as diamond edges now. No amusement lingered, only flinty eyes and a stony press of lips.

"I don't take orders from anyone but my Father."

"Then we are at an impasse."

He lifted his eyebrows. "The deference was a mere formality. We take by force what isn't given willingly."

I smiled.

"Same."

A quick blink preceded a pause. Such hesitation was an opportunity. *Magic,* Papa whispered from the depths of memory in his usual calm way, *is only as good as the surprise in which you create with it.*

Regardless of the confusing emotions I held around Papa these days, I leaned gratefully into his lessons now.

Shallow and thin as a pencil, a trench raced through the sand between me and Neel. The line extended past me, around him. The subtle shifting of grains didn't draw his gaze at first, neither did the bright, red powder that followed, unnoticeable in the dim light. Ground cayenne pepper and yellow hellfire pepper from the West, plus a smidge of a few other ingredients Merrick had once shared with me.

All of it commanded in an instant.

Neel's posture changed. He sank a little into his legs, bracing himself. I lifted Viveet higher.

No sign of the other one, Ignis murmured, anticipating my thought. As a battle companion, he was ideal.

"Alkarra is a very different place, no?" Neel asked, inching closer. His gaze darted over me, assessing. He mapped out a quick attack. I shifted to the left, forcing his plan to change. He sidestepped to the right, eyeing me.

Three steps until he touched the trench.

"Quite different."

"Are you enjoying your stay in Alaysia?"

"Immensely. The hospitality has been delightful."

A crash of thunder broke the sky.

"You are not in Alkarra anymore, Lady-witch," he screamed over the ruckus. "You are in Alaysia, and my Father makes the rules here!"

One step.

The god magic required by my plan ballooned in my chest when Neel's foot stepped on the powder, just the way I intended.

Light exploded.

Neel wheeled through the air, thrown back like a rag doll. Sand sprayed out, sharp and painful against my skin. Heat and granules followed, booming. Neel slammed into the surf with another reverberation of prickly thunder overhead.

I brushed the sand out of my eyes.

Snarling, Neel strode out of the waves. Burns reddened his skin, like the top layer had been peeled off. Blood poured down his body. Grains of sand thickened his hair, swept away from his face.

Two steps out of the water, he collapsed.

Wind gusted by, flapping my dress. The broiling storm slipped overhead, casting the world in darkness. Neel held himself in the surf, arms braced. Salt water against the open skin couldn't feel good. The peals of thunder felt as if the entire world had been grabbed and shaken, like a child's toy.

Rain appeared all at once, like Tontes had poured a bucket. It drenched the world, sluicing in raw sheets. Scattered drops pinged across Viveet's blade.

"Go back to your father," I shouted, "and tell him to leave me alone. He can't have me."

Neel challenged me with glittering eyes.

"Make me."

Step back, Ignis whispered, *and crouch.*

I obeyed.

Two demigods appeared the next instant, hurling themselves at the spot where I stood. One demigod crashed into the other where my head would have been. They groaned, petaling to different sides. One lolled in unconsciousness—again. The other moaned, hand pressed to his head.

I chuckled and stepped back, eyes on Neel. The relentless crash of thunder, streaking lightning, pounding surf issued through the torrential rain. I pointed Viveet at him.

"Next time," I hissed, "you won't finish this fight alive, just like Bram, Jote, and Mordecai. I am not only the amulet-breaker, but the Lady-witch of Alkarra. You should fear me."

A whirlwind of fire swept me away.

Chapter Fifteen

ontes' nefarious storm darkened the sky and agitated the ocean, but a walled garden of what could only be the *Rostina lu Lune* protected me. Busy stacks of turrets, parapets, battlements, and guard houses populated endlessly behind each other. Like a child crowding all its toys together. Greater height, width, size continued to unfold. It sprawled so endlessly.

I pressed my back to the closest wall, slid down, and closed my eyes.

Close call.

My body settled, my thudding heart slowed. Sand had gathered in my mouth during the fight. I struggled to swallow as I wiped the gritty granules off my cheeks and out of the corners of my lips. Viveet lay inert at my side. After several moments of debate over whether I should keep her, or send her back to Alkarra, I sent her back. Safer there. With god magic, she was easy enough to pull to my side when needed.

The momentary isolation was a welcome opportunity to pull myself back together, though I had no idea why I'd brought myself *here* of all places.

I tilted my head back to study the space.

Leaves shivered as wind stirred the world like a giant pot. The towering walls of the garden buffeted the currents into a calm oasis. Lights from the *Rostina* revealed hints of life inside. Bowls of burning sand. A torch in a window. Shadows as someone shifted past. Mats of leaves covered open doorways, tacked at the bottom corners to prevent rain.

Through the doorway to this garden, I could just see an utterly still area, not unlike the baileys back at Chatham Castle. This space lay open to the sea, elevated to afford a view of the surf. Water fountains sparkled as they tossed droplets into the air. Benches, pots of white-and-gray flowers, and fence-like walls surrounded it. Twisting spears of sand adorned every few paces.

Across the way, an open tunnel occupied most of the view. It was wide enough to admit three carriages abreast and soared hundreds of paces overhead, funneling farther into the gigantic castle. Lights flickered down the tunnel, illuminating the darkness with bursts of white. Other doorways branched into unknown places, undoubtedly deeper into the belly of this slumbering giant. The inky depths of the hole swallowed my thoughts.

Given the opportunity to go into that tunnel, I'd wager that a set of glimmering, golden doors could be found.

Why, I asked Ignis, *am I here?*

A whisper scurried by, but it wasn't Ignis.

Approach me.

Ventis.

A weak surge of annoyance rippled through me. The last thing I wanted to do now was speak to another god.

"What?" I whispered.

Approach me.

One truth had become abundantly clear: the gods and goddesses toyed with me, little else.

Ventis invited me to Alaysia, then took his sweet time

meeting with me. No time together had surfaced—nor promise of any. He kept Baxter busy and isolated and buried in obligations. Ignis set me up to fight the sons of Tontes without warning, and Tontes wanted me as his slave. Only Gelas posed no perceived threat, which made me more nervous than all the rest. Why was he so quiet in the northern Icelands?

Meanwhile, demigods threatened my life. One god had become my sort-of-ally and another my enemy, all while mortals looked to me as a savior.

Today, Ventis had undoubtedly observed my ability with god magic at Ava's collection. Now *he* wanted me, too. A dawning realization crept through my mind. Who had the power here? Not the gods. Not the demigods. Not even the witches.

I held the power.

It was time for me to use it.

"No, thank you," I said mildly, clapping the sand off my palms. I stood, yawning. "I'm rather tired today."

All the wind in the garden ceased. A gentle pall, like shock, hung in the air. Thunder crashed over the distant ocean. In the passing moments, my body had relaxed enough for me to feel the pain of battle. A groan issued from me when I remembered Ava and the mortals.

They needed to return to their collection and get settled back on their islands. First, I would apologize for using magic on them without permission. Doing so might have saved them, but still . . .

I stood to leave, then stopped.

Two figures crossed the open area outside the garden. Gio, for certain. Wind ruffled his salt-and-pepper hair as it gusted by. His calm expression gave nothing away, despite the wild gesturing of the demigod next to him.

Flaming red hair, kinky on her shoulders. Pale, freckled skin.

Tipa.

Daughter of Gelas, and the demigod that helped me out of

the sticky situation at the Golden Guinea Hen during the uprising. Gio lifted a lazy eyebrow, then nodded to something she said. Tipa stepped back and tossed her hands in the air.

"Fine!" she cried. "I'll find her myself. This is ridiculous."

"The Lady-witch is here."

Gio turned, gaze piercing right into me. Tipa whirled, peered at me through narrowed eyes, and let out a long sigh. She muttered something, stalked closer, and left Gio without another word.

Amused, Gio faded back, toward a side door.

Grim-faced, Tipa approached. She grabbed my arm. "Come, I shouldn't be here. Let's go somewhere else."

* * *

We didn't speak until the *Rostina* lay far behind us.

The storm tempered into sheets of rain and a slate mat. Drizzle splattered the top of the ocean like falling needles. Halfway to the beach house, Tipa's pace slowed, then stopped. I braced myself.

"What are you doing here?" I asked.

She frowned. Drenched strands of hair lay flat against her head, trailing in wet ropes to her shoulders. Water trickled down the side of her neck. "My father sent me to check on you."

"Because of the storm?"

She eyed overhead, then nodded. Her brow arched as she studied me. "You seem hale enough."

"I managed."

"What happened?"

"Four of Tontes' sons approached me. They wanted to take me back to Tontes."

Her lips pursed in thought. "Did they hurt you?"

"They tried."

"And you stopped them?"

I held out my arms, silently saying *I'm here, aren't I?*

She lifted an eyebrow. "Good. They could use a knockdown from a witch, though Tontes will be surly for days. Expect flooding. Sorry I came too late. I couldn't find you. Your mortal said that—"

"Ava is not my mortal."

Tipa rolled her eyes. "Whatever. The girl. She said you were at her collection. By the time I arrived there, no one remained. Did you send all those mortals over here?"

"Yes."

Astonishment filled her voice. "Why?"

"To protect them."

She studied me like something she couldn't quite figure out. I wanted to like Tipa, but something held me back. I couldn't really understand what she thought, or where she stood, in relation to witches and demigods.

"Thank you for checking on me," I said.

She shrugged.

Like Deasylva, Gelas had always been in the background. A quiet god, hiding in icier planes of the sea. Was he an ally? The thought nearly made me laugh, but reminded me of his shadowy figure in this game. A player I couldn't discount.

The moving pieces tallied a complicated game.

"If Gelas sent you, does that mean your father is also interested in me?"

Tipa's body stiffened. "Don't read into it," she muttered. "The gods don't care about you, Lady-witch of Alkarra. Only what you represent. Good luck."

Her words rang long after she left with magic.

Only what you represent.

Despite myself, I couldn't help but think of Prana. *Remember your forest,* she had said. *Trust no one.*

* * *

Morning opened like a scroll as night wound away, tucked against the far skyline. Stars evaporated. Heat returned. Always, the hiss of the ocean nearby. I stood in the doorway of the beach house, shoulder pressed to the wall, as I watched the darkness escape, the light reclaim the sky. Baxter's quiet breaths, steady and calm in sleep, came from inside. He'd appeared moments after I returned, anchored me in a hug that lasted minutes, then railed against Tontes for an hour.

Ava said nothing all night.

Memories from yesterday buffeted all around. I thought of Merrick, Papa. What would they have thought of such battle-ability? What would Papa say now?

Think it outloud, B, his voice surfaced from distant places in my mind. I closed my eyes, leaned into it with a mental hug. When I disentangled myself from his memories, I opened my eyes to find Alaysia again.

Alaysia.

Storms. Demigods. Power.

Yesterday swirled through my mind with renewed strength. Ignis hadn't spoken a word since I left the collection, and I was grateful. Space. Time. I needed distance to think clearly about how easily we paired together in a battle situation. How swift our work had been.

How simple the magic.

One could almost say that Ignis and I made an absurdly compatible pair. He saw what I couldn't. I acted when he didn't. To fight with god magic? I *had* become a new sort of weapon, the salvation of Alkarra if we couldn't stop the demigods from rising again. What else would stop Tontes?

Not his brothers, apparently. At least, not alone.

My breath increased as I thought of Ignis' offer. Keep Alkarra. Keep my family, my life, my witches. Keep *Ignis*.

Sacrifice a goddess.

Murkiness rose with thoughts of Deasylva. Who was she?

What power did she truly hold? The magic of the forest, obviously. Presumably, even more than that, since Prana feared her. Letum Wood held deep, abiding allegiance to the silent goddess as well.

Did I?

How simple it would be to forsake her, claim all of this. Such power. Dexterity. If I truly wanted to save Alkarra, forsaking god magic would be a mistake. To save my land, I *needed* Ignis.

The tug of loyalty simmered in my thoughts.

You are deep in thought.

Ignis' voice in my mind pulled me out of the spiral of questions. I sighed, not certain I wanted him back yet. With the power of Ignis came . . . well . . . Ignis.

Did I want a god in my head all the time? A moot question. He resided there whether I wanted him or not, and that didn't bode well. My chin tilted back, sending waves of hair out of my eyes.

"I don't want to talk to you yet, if we're being honest."

You're angry.

"No," I snapped. "I'm livid. I deserve a little advance notice when my life is in peril, thank you. You're supposed to be on my side!" I cried. "Yet you invited those buffoons and I could have died."

Danger has always been so orderly and gives advance notice, does it?

Images flashed through my mind. Animals in Letum Wood that attacked without provocation. Demigods in the Golden Guinea Hen. Mabel's hideously twisted smile. The erratic snatches of memory made me scowl.

"Fine," I muttered. "Point made, but I hold my ground. Don't be a jerk. If you want me on your side, can you be a little nicer? I want to like you, Ignis. You make it impossible."

He paused.

You're not the first to say it, he said with some loathing in his tone.

I snorted. "That just makes this even more ridiculous, you realize?"

What burdens your thoughts tonight?

Reluctantly, I allowed the change in topic, but only because I had my *own* questions to ask.

"Tell me about Deasylva," I whispered.

The sound of the surf rolled through the air, the only thing that I could hear for several moments. Just when I thought he'd left, he spoke again.

She is my favorite of the sisters, if I had to choose. Don't tell Sarena. She takes exception to everything.

"Sarena is the goddess of the desert?"

Yes.

I filed that away for later. There was no doubt that goddesses existed anymore. My floundering over that had long since dissipated, even though I didn't necessarily understand it. The details, however, remained elusive.

"Is Deasylva kind?"

He snorted.

Very.

"You say it like it's a bad thing."

Kindness is as much a weapon as rage.

"Then why hasn't she revealed herself to me?"

Who says she hasn't?

Again, my reply stalled. I let out a long breath, more frustrated than ever.

"Does she require blind obedience or something? She's never revealed herself to me."

Would it be blind obedience in your case?

Any reply dissolved in my mouth. How to answer that? Prana's warning surfaced in my mind again, like bubbles from the sea.

Remember your forest, trust no one.

"Is Deasylva the same thing as Letum Wood?"

No. Consider me and fire. I am part of fire, and it is part of me, but we are distinct and separate. Deasylva asks much of those that she imbues with power. Her servants are proven, yet powerful. At least, historically.

"Why are you willing to speak about your sister? Doesn't she stand in direct opposition to what you want the most?"

Ignis chuckled.

Potentially, yes. If you are to give your allegiance to me, then it will be because you desire it. I want your willingness as much as your abilities and power. All options will have been presented to you, and you will have chosen. Deasylva desires the same, I would imagine.

"But we don't *know*, because Deasylva hasn't said as much."

Not in words.

What other way was there to say it? With a growl, I shoved off of the doorframe.

"Fine," I muttered. "I'll continue to think about it."

Think it over carefully. We've only begun to prove the power of our abilities together. Like you, I have no desire to see Alkarra destroyed. It is a beautiful land with more history than a witch could possibly understand. If we can save it together, we should.

A deep affection for Alkarra swept through me. In a trice, I felt the roots he held in the land of Alkarra, understood his fierce pride and longing to return. The sensation ebbed slowly, but lingered in the cavity of my chest.

Also, he added as an afterthought, *stay on guard.*

A shuffle of sound drew my attention back to the beach. Ignis disappeared—I could feel him leave this time. Had I become more sensitive to his presence now, or did he allow me to feel his removal so I knew he gave me the benefit of mental privacy?

I hoped for the latter, yet it seemed most likely that I became more in-tune with the god magic everyday. Gio strode between two trees, headed toward me. Bright eyes met mine with a wide grin.

"Bianca?"

I returned his smile, grateful to think of something else for a while. "Merry meet, Gio. How are you?"

He spread his arms. "Another beautiful day in paradise. Although too hot already," he added with a grimace. Oppressive heat simmered like the air on top of boiling water, hotter than it had been so far.

"You prefer cooler climates?"

A blush crept along his cheeks, as if I'd caught him in an embarrassing admission. He glanced to the north.

"The cooler air of Gelas' kingdom does appeal on these violently hot days, yes."

"Gelas is north of here, correct?"

He nodded, then shivered. "Far north. With glaciers and freezing temperatures and ice, ice, ice. So much ice. All his islands are frozen. No sand. Just ice."

"That *would* feel nice right now," I murmured.

Gio stopped a few paces away, hands in his pockets. Linen pants flapped around his legs. Again, he wore no shirt, revealing muscular arms, though thin. His excitement dimmed.

"I bring welcome news from the *Rostina*. Ventis has officially requested your presence. Today." Gio swallowed. "Ah . . . right now, in fact. Is Baxter here?"

"He's inside, yes. Ventis wants to speak with me now?"

Gio nodded.

Ah, Ventis played the cards of political surprise again. I lacked astonishment or gratitude. Waiting for him felt like an old game, and the temptation to refuse—again—rippled through me. I cast that aside. Not after I had denied him yesterday. Besides, I did want to speak with him. Hadn't I come partly for this?

I lifted a mild eyebrow, though my stomach twisted. My subdued smile was fraught with tension. "Of course he wants to meet unexpectedly and on his own timeframe. Excellent news indeed. Shall I wake Baxter?"

"All will be well, I'm sure." Gio's forced smile hardened. "I will escort you to Ventis now. No need to wake Baxter. He won't be allowed with you."

"I already know where to find Ventis, if you'd rather stay here with Baxter."

Surprise registered on Gio's face. "You do?"

"I've been to his throne before."

Gio swirled his fingers. "In the wind?"

"No."

"Is it so?" he murmured. He leaned forward. "You heard Ventis call to you? And you responded?"

"Sort of," I drawled. "It's a long story."

Understanding flickered through his eyes. He suppressed a smile. "Gods can be . . . sensitive. Allow me to walk you to the *Rostina*? I desire to see the request through, like a good mortal. Amorette will, ah, be upset if I don't."

"You take orders from Amorette?"

"When she comes straight from Ventis, yes."

"I see."

Gio nodded. "Let's be off, then. Gods don't enjoy waiting."

The phrase *like a good mortal* rankled my growing ill-humor, but I shoved that aside as I stepped into the sand, heart in my throat. A swirl of embers followed as we strode into the trees, *Rostina* bound.

Chapter Sixteen

The sparkling gold doors were closed.

Gio shifted next to me, at least twenty paces from their glimmering surface, face averted, hands folded behind his back. He bent at the waist, shoulders hunched. A gentle shine brightened his skin, flickering from shallow, burning bowls of sand on either side of the tunnel.

"May I leave, Bianca?" he whispered, clearly uncomfortable.

"Yes, of course. Thank you, Gio."

He scurried back, quick as legs could carry him. I watched him go, feeling as if my only lifeline scuttled away. With a deep breath, I turned to fully face the doors, then startled.

The right door, previously closed, had pushed open into the tunnel without a sound. Light billowed out, yet not a noise issued when it moved. Ventis must have done it with magic. A breeze stirred my hair, carrying the scent of open sky and coastal seas.

They beckoned me closer.

I could only stare.

Originally, I planned to approach Ventis to ask if god magic could be removed. Now? I floundered. To what end did I speak with the god of wind now? If god magic could be extracted successfully, would I do it?

I didn't know.

A conversation with Ventis afforded more benefits than that. Information, for one. Satisfaction of my insatiable curiosity, for another. Perhaps an opportunity to prove what Ignis had told me about life in Alaysia.

Was it worth it?

Only one way to find out. I cautiously approached, rolling on the balls of my feet. The culmination of the days here built into a strange string of events that, until this moment, had felt extraordinarily unnecessary. Now that my meeting with Ventis had come, I couldn't help but wonder if they'd all been to prepare me for this.

Would I *see* him?

Ignis had been slippery. Sincere one moment, calculating the next. I had a hard time understanding him and his unpredictability. If Ventis was the same, conversation would be difficult to navigate.

I had a feeling it would be different.

Thoughts of Prana's corporeal form—as strange as her eyes appeared—bolstered my wavering courage. God or not, Ventis had to be something like us. He had children. Wives. Endless life. He couldn't be that strange.

If he revealed himself.

I stood close enough to the canted door that I could touch the edge. Infusing as much steadiness into the words as I could, I called, "May I enter?"

The giant door creaked, then opened toward me with a groan. Taking it as permission, I wandered inside.

Sunlight spilled free, revealing a bright room set in a wide cave. The entirety of the far wall had been removed, overlooking the privacy of the sea. Waves slammed into a balcony with rocks as a barrier. White foam frothed between the stones, then retreated with a hiss. A gentle spray drifted into the tunnel. Beyond it glimmered the endless sky.

The room stretched into a smooth floor of rounded rocks that pressed against each other, sealed with a sand-like mixture. The bottom of my feet slipped over their silky tops.

Hundreds of paces of space opened up on either side. A circular cavern. This part of the *Rostina lu Lune* was a gigantic cave set into the side of a sand castle, with half of it left open to the wide sky. The breeze nudged me to the left. I followed the subtle guidance, head tilted back.

Rock formed a half-dome ceiling with a hole in the middle. A waterfall tumbled free, slammed into the floor, then whispered to the ocean. The rocks darkened at the very top, where mist and dried saltwater created strange images in dust and shadows.

Ushered by the wind, I stepped closer to the waterfall. It should have roared, but rustled quiet as silk. Did magic hush it?

The walls of the cavern were filled with holes, jagged edges. Stuff lingered inside with an overabundance of luxury. Silk pillows. Blankets of softest down. Bowls of burning sand lined in pearls, coral. Flat areas held dozens of woven baskets, about the width of my arm.

No, *hundreds* of woven baskets.

Driven by curiosity, I slipped closer.

Food filled each basket. Dried fish with blackened scales. Flaky pink fruit, shredded into a pile as long as my arm. Purple, round things that looked like seeds the size of my thumbnail.

Cups made out of leaves stood behind the baskets, each one graced with a large pearl right in the middle. Golden thread sewed the cups together, forming a water-tight container the size of my hand. Different colored liquids filled each. Most of them appeared to contain water. A sweet smell emanated from those closest to me. Though my mouth hungered at the thought of all the resplendent flavors, I didn't touch them.

My eyes skimmed each basket as I walked along the cavern wall. Sand, scratched away from the damp wall, dribbled beneath my fingertips as they slipped along.

The wind slowed to a trickle, then stopped.

I paused.

On the other side of the cavern, around the waterfall, dangled complicated swings. Seats instead of hammock beds, like the mortals slept on, suspended from lower parts of the ceiling. Thick ropes similar to some I'd seen on Eastern Network ships held them firm. One of them creaked as it shifted in the wind. Pillows piled on top provided a barrier from the rope bottom.

For several moments, I listened to the gentle whine of the sea. The whistle of air in my ear, bright and calm at the same time. The tips of my toes ran over the stone flooring, the smooth, gray rocks a strange difference compared to the reddish-brown cavern walls.

To encompass it in a word?

Elegance.

A dark hole near the floor on the far side of the cavern disappeared into darkness. A hallway, most likely. Perhaps to the *real* throne. This felt like an in-between. A place Ventis brought those he . . . wanted to talk to?

Destroy?

As beautiful and brilliant as this cavern felt, I had a feeling it *wasn't* where Ventis really lived. Why stay in a cave when the wind commanded the sky?

"Hello?" I called.

My voice reverberated off the walls. A playful current of air twirled around my legs, ruffling my skirt. I chuckled.

Welcome.

My heart leapt with surprise. Today, Ventis' voice reminded me of a silk banner flapping in the wind. It came from everywhere and nowhere at the same time.

"Ventis?"

As you seek. Your patience has been exemplary for a witch. Forgive my delay in seeing you.

The placating tones set me on edge, but I forced myself to relax my arms at my side. His delay in seeing me had surely been intentional and strategic, which called for me to reciprocate, however more cleverly. The building question in my mind was, why delay?

"I understand."

How has your time in Alaysia treated you?

"It's been . . . interesting."

A low rumble shook the cavern. A trickle of sand dropped nearby. I shuffled to the side, then realized that Ventis had been laughing. Was he *in* the *Rostina?*

Interesting, he murmured with amusement, *is certainly one way to put it. The differences between this place and the land of my sisters is. . . startling. We don't have the luxury of space. There is less land here and more magical structure and control.*

"So I've been learning."

Ignis has been teaching you, has he not?

"Of a sort."

Ventis chuckled. His affable tone made me want to like him, but I didn't dare.

Baxter speaks very highly of you.

Hearing Baxter's name in Ventis' voice felt strange. All this time, he'd constantly joked about being the *son of a god*. Until this moment, it never seemed fully real.

"Baxter is . . . he's wonderful."

You two have formed a strong friendship.

He spoke with confidence, as if he had somehow sensed this truth himself. "Yes, I think so."

Also with you is my granddaughter, Ava.

"She's full of spirit."

Like her mother, Christa. Ava and I have not formally met.

"So she's mentioned," I said wryly.

She doesn't think highly of me. A note of regret lingered in his voice, woven around threads of something like amusement.

"No," I murmured. "She doesn't. I think she wants to love you, but she'd never admit it."

Also like her mother, who sought refuge from life as a demigod in that small collection, with Ava's Tama. It is not easy to be the child of a god.

"Baxter hasn't had many complaints."

Affection brightened his tone. *Baxter is special. He always has been. His mother, Yamara, was the same way. Saw the goodness in everything.*

"Was?"

Yamara has passed to the next world, where she continues to grow, though she misses our son.

His easily spoken words arrested my thoughts. *The next world, where she continues to grow.* Is that where Mama was now? Did she miss me as desperately as I did her? Undoubtedly. With the questions came a wave of surprise.

"I didn't realize his mother was dead," I murmured. "He never mentioned her, now that I think about it."

The topic is a sensitive one.

"You still see Yamara?"

Always. Those I love are always with me, whether here or there.

The agony of losing Mama rippled through my mind in a wave. Did a god experience grief the same way as witches with each loss? For Ventis, Yamara wasn't gone. Perhaps eternity wasn't so bleak when one could see all.

Ignis provided a stark rebuttal to such a thought.

Mama's eyes remained bright in my mind as I asked, "Do you love them? The women that bear your demigods."

Each one.

"Is it worth it to love so many?"

Always.

The word expanded, rippling over the cavern walls in faint echoes. I tilted my head back, lost to the ringing.

"What is it like over there, on the other side?"

The wind stirred.

Better.

Longing welled up in me, and the sense of being a speck in great vastness. What I wouldn't give to see Mama again. To know the other side, drawn like a dark curtain over this one. Ventis swept these thoughts away, bringing me into the moment again.

I apologize on behalf of my brothers for all that has befallen Alkarra. As soon as I heard the news that demigods may have been there years ago, I have attempted to learn more. Sending Baxter was a way for me to keep eyes on Tontes and his children.

The opening to get answers was a welcome one, though something cautioned me not to fully trust him.

"How did you know about the demigods going to Alkarra?"

My brother, Ignis. All of it originated with Prana.

Her name prickled coldly along my spine. "I've heard. Sounds like Prana is always creating trouble."

A ripple moved through the cavern walls, as if Ventis made an *mmm* sound. I held onto a hammock when the ground shifted.

Indeed. Years ago, Prana came to Alaysia and spoke with Bram about magicless witches in Alkarra. His tone dropped into something like godly disgust. *He eventually stole an amulet and went to Alkarra, which is when I learned of her involvement. You know the rest.*

The puzzle pieces clicked more fully together. Prana's appearance in the gardens at Chatham Castle. Her desperation to fix an error. Her reminder at the ocean. She wanted the demigods out of Alkarra so desperately because *she* had put them there.

A burning rage re-kindled deep in my chest. Though I'd

known or surmised much of this already, Ventis had clarified the details. Until the intricacies were laid out, it had all felt nebulous.

"Prana," I muttered.

The machinations of gods and goddesses, Ventis said, with warning, *are not yours to judge.*

The feeling of being chided, like a small child, set my teeth on edge. Did Ventis defend Prana? Ignis had warned me that life for goddesses and gods was different than witches expected. Their opinions and views are broader. I began to understand that now.

Tontes poses as your greatest obstacle for removing demigods from Alkarra.

"He's not my obstacle," I countered, "as much as he is yours."

Oh? His voice curled in a way that I couldn't possibly fathom. *Do enlighten me.*

"If you allow Tontes to continue attacking Alkarra, then your goddess sisters will get involved. Witches may not know all of Alkarran history, but I know enough to surmise you don't want that to happen again."

A wild bluff, mostly, based off what little Ignis had said. Posturing at its finest. Whether or not Ventis had reason to fear Deasylva, I wasn't sure, but it felt obvious after all Prana had said. Prana feared Deasylva, so it stood to reason her brothers might as well. Not to mention the fact that Ignis actively wanted me to reject any form of allegiance to the goddess.

That meant something.

The only truth I clung to was the one I felt most certain about: *trust no one.*

Tontes has his own ideas of risks and rewards, Ventis mused. *The rest of us don't always follow.*

"I find that hard to believe," I said lightly, "considering that Ignis allowed his children to rise in an attempt to take Alkarra."

And yet, he parried with a sharpness of tone, *you still collude magic with him.*

A crack of water slapping rock startled me. On the patio, a boulder rolled across the ground, water gushing behind it. The sea retreated, and the rock remained. Though I hadn't moved, it felt as if the world flipped around beneath me.

I mentally backed down, duly reminded of my position in Ventis' own *Rostina.*

The gods are touted as selfish, Ventis continued, *but my sisters are equally so. Don't let Deasylva fool you, Bianca. She desires your ability and loyalty as much as Ignis. Your status as a living amulet is not so much a question of magic, but a question of allegiance and power.*

"Ignis has stated as much."

He is wise, if not occasionally reckless.

Silence settled over the cavern while I absorbed what he said, broken by the whispers of water. Could I trust Ventis? Not wholly. Marten would never hail me as an Ambassador because alacrity wasn't my forte, but I knew sincerity when I heard it. In regard to the magicks, I felt what Ventis said was true in my bones.

These two magicks couldn't thrive in close proximity forever.

Although subtle, the god magic grew hotter daily, a gradual expansion and bullying. Goddess magic inched farther and farther away in response. I lifted my hands, peering at my fingers. A symbol of our ability as witches. The harnessing of magic to change our world. My throat dried like hot sand when I noticed that my fingers trembled.

"What happens if I forsake Deasylva?" I whispered.

Then you will be of the gods, he said brightly, *and have all at your feet.*

"I don't want Alaysia."

His tone lowered. *Who said that you must settle for Alaysia?*

I scoffed. "You think the goddesses would allow me to remain in Alkarra with god magic?"

If you are preventing the destruction of the land and another war of gods and goddesses?

The question had been drawled like a lazy yawn. With it, an assumption that the only path to save Alkarra was this one. I frowned at the implications. Living as a god magic amulet amongst witches. Able to do magic but . . . distinctly different.

Untenable.

By the good gods, though, it would be effective. Wouldn't such a special ability make the most powerful Sisterhood in all the world? Matthais' disregard for me doing the work of Protectors would fade into time and disrepute. He'd have no outdated opinion to stand on because I would be far more mighty than him.

The thought of such power used as a force for good through the Sisterhood—and for Alkarra—made me burn with hunger.

"Why would you let me save Alkarra?"

The question rang in the quiet for a moment.

Because it is yours to save. Tontes may desire another enemy and worthy foe, but we do not.

A sense of not having the bigger picture made this conversation feel like grasping at pieces in the dark. Assembling a puzzle by feel instead of sight. Why should I trust Ventis?

Could I afford not to?

The choice of your loyalty is not as simple as which god or goddess to accept, but whom will you save? If you want to save the land of Alkarra, you will remain with Ignis. Tontes will not back down from a fight. Competing god magic is all that stands between his domination of Alkarra and your freedom. Ignis has created an interesting weapon in you. You are, perhaps, the only weapon to stay Tontes.

"Goddess magic isn't strong enough?"

The moment the words escaped me, I felt their foolishness.

Didn't I already know this? Demigods with god magic were stronger, faster, more powerful. God magic was frighteningly easy—how *well* I knew this.

Ventis only chuckled.

His words curled like burning paper in my chest, ashy, hot, smoky. This conversation felt like a declaration of war. A warning. Prudence pushed me closer to caution than posturing.

"Perhaps I should pay more attention to what Ignis says," I murmured lightly, despite the proverbial knife I felt hovering at my neck.

It is all, he whispered, *that we ask.*

* * *

Surreal disbelief fueled the next hour of my life.

Alaysia moved like a dream around me as I contemplated my conversation with Ventis. A vague, distant paradise with sharp teeth. At the conclusion of our conversation, the wind had ushered me out. Baxter had been waiting outside his father's doors, he'd wrapped me in his arms, and brought me . . . here.

His . . . castle within a castle.

With a hand on the small of my back, he ushered me into a broad room, large as the banquet hall. Soaring ceiling. Stained glass windows. Chiseled designs of playful wind curling up the walls, coy and flirtatious. Flecks of broken coral lingered in the sandstone walls, adding a sheen of color to the room.

I stopped, arrested by the swelling size, the daunting beauty. Caverns of rock, magic, and sand.

He paused, his breath a hitch.

"You all right, B?"

"Fine," I whispered, not to disturb the reverence of such a place. He put a hand on my arm. I drew from deeper ruminations with a jerk. Concerned, grassy eyes peered at me. I sighed.

"I'm fine."

He enveloped me in his arms until I felt the thud of our hearts mingling. My eyes closed. I swayed closer to him, breathing deep a musty, sweet smell. His body felt like the only true anchor I had. In mere moments, the rooms didn't exist anymore, just the molding of the two of us. He held me tight, as if he sought the same stabilizing power. I sent aside thoughts of Merrick to focus on Baxter.

Sweet Baxter.

After my heart slowed, my courage returned. I pulled away to gaze into his worried eyes. The tip of his finger brushed a lock of hair away from my cheeks, tucking it behind my ear.

"You survived my father?" A wry smile reassured me that Baxter remained the Baxter I knew from Alkarra. I laughed softly.

"He was surprisingly approachable."

A knock on the door rang into the room. He frowned.

"A moment, please."

I nodded and he left with an irritated breath.

With life back in my body, my heart an easy plod again, I whirled around to contemplate these dauntingly majestic rooms. Hallways bled away from this space like life-giving arteries. Further elegance was hinted at between the interplay of shadow and light. Sheer curtains. Simplistic, plush furniture. Golden edges and murals with subdued, classic color palettes.

My feet itched to explore.

Instead of venturing into unknown territory that wasn't mine, I drew closer to the wild. A balcony larger than the Upper Bailey at Chatham Castle sprawled outside. The wind played with my hair as I crossed to the side to peer at an endless skirt of water. The *Rostina lu Lune* sprawled to either side, impossibly endless. Instead of exulting in the adventure and glory of such a thrilling land, I thought of home.

Letum Wood.

Leda.

Marten.

Had Scarlett announced the new High Priest? And if so, who had she chosen? What topics had Hiddleston attempted to debate with Leda lately, if any? Such thoughts comforted me, as if I could keep my friends close by rumination. No letters had arrived, though I had only sent one myself.

Concerning, on many levels. Did the gods block the magic that brought letters?

Or had my friends forgotten me?

No, I doubted that.

Merrick's intense figure lurked in the recesses, a shadow that I desperately wanted to think about, but held in reserve. Emerald eyes. Sandy hair. Quick smile set in chiseled features. Merrick and I had parted as friends. Yet despite attempts to turn thoughts of him away from my time here, he returned again and again.

A touch on the small of my back, and then a warm body at my side, drew me back to Alaysia. Thoughts of Merrick fractured into a thousand pieces when Baxter stood next to me, smiling wide. Falling daylight highlighted his handsome features, cutting shadows across the hollows of his cheek.

"So," he murmured. "I want to apologize for not being with you when you were called to Father's side. I had no idea that—"

I pressed my fingers to his lips.

"Not your fault," I whispered. "I could have woken you, but you seemed tired. Gio said you wouldn't be admitted, anyway."

Curiosity stole across his features when my hand dropped. Brows lifted, he asked, "Dare I ask what Father said?"

My lips parted, then closed. I sighed. Ventis set out the terms of god magic quite clearly, but none of the words to summarize our conversation flowed. One thought looped around instead.

To whom do I belong?

The thought of Tontes overtaking Alkarra in a storm built in my mind. Lightning setting the forest on fire. Thunder so loud it would drown out reason. I *could* fight for Alkarra better with Ignis as my magic, and that's what I didn't want to admit.

Ventis was right.

Except for one *if* that lingered in the background.

Deasylva.

An unknown goddess, with quiet acclaim and a hidden presence in the land. Apparently, I knew of her. Perhaps through the forest. But I didn't *know* her at all. The gods wanted me to make an impossible decision.

Choose their magic, their life, or a goddess who had never revealed herself. By sheer willpower, I kept my response to Baxter from wobbling like a drunk Guardian.

"I don't know what to think about Ventis, honestly."

"Was he kind?"

The blunt question startled me. I turned to face him. "Of course. Why wouldn't he be?"

Baxter leaned his forearms on the bannister and gazed out. His eyelashes fluttered, busy with thoughts. "My father is a good god," he murmured, "but he's not perfect. I never know what side of him will come out."

Is he a good god? I wanted to ask, but dismissed the thought. My darker side said no, there were no good gods.

"We all have demons," I murmured to be gracious.

Baxter shifted, leaning his palms back on the railing. The effect of sunset on his skin made my breath catch in the back of my throat. The heat of his touch on my spine renewed in a flash of memory, then faded.

"Are you comfortable telling me what you discussed?" he asked. "Your conversation is yours. You have no obligation to me."

But I did. Whether rooted in our friendship or the new, possibly romantic waters, I couldn't be sure. My affection for Baxter was genuine, yet it wasn't breathtaking, the way it had been with Merrick.

Expecting the two experiences to be similar sounded like madness itself, yet . . .

"Of course I'm comfortable with you." I held my arms across my middle as I stared back into his apartment, the ocean behind me. Bowls of burning sand flickered inside. Sand spilled outside one, dropping into narrow lines that raced along the walls and illuminated the entire room with flames. The rock danced with shadows. A sweet fragrance reminiscent of sage floated past.

"I think I expected more arrogance." I chucked Baxter in the ribs with my elbow. "Kind of like his son."

He grinned, his teeth a flash of white against the growing darkness.

"Son of a god," he murmured.

My amusement sobered as I gave him the best summary I could manage with my thoughts cast so far here and there. He listened intently, murmuring a question every so often.

"He basically said that I have a choice," I finished with a heavy breath. "I can save Alkarra from Tontes by giving Ignis my allegiance . . . or I can choose goddess magic, and by extension Deasylva, and allow Tontes to take over Alkarra. Whether I believe it's true that Tontes could defeat his sister so easily . . . I'm not sure."

Baxter frowned. "Likely quite true, unfortunately."

"Are the goddesses so weak?"

"It's not necessarily about weakness, but more their differences. All of them have had two thousand years to prepare for a sort of re-match after the goddesses banished them. To my eye, Deasylva has prepared. The other goddesses? I wouldn't know. Tontes has, certainly. He has the most active amulets, you noticed? Besides, the way the gods have structured their magic makes it faster, more versatile." His brow rose. "You know how true this is, of anyone, right?"

I reluctantly nodded. Oh, how well did I understand.

Consternation filled his features as he fell into a long, vacant stare. A curl dropped on his forehead and I brushed it away. He blinked, peering at me with a little smile. I moved closer.

"But how god magic is used is also inherently weak in different ways," I murmured to the thrum of the waves below. "Ventis can take your amulet at any time, can't he?"

He nodded.

"And you wouldn't have any magical power?"

He shook his head again. "It's the way of the gods," he muttered, straightening. His hands found my hips, pulling me closer. "Magic is exploitable, controllable. Meant to be used against, not always for. The gods, as giving as they might be, always seem to have an angle."

His bitterness made sense, though fraught with depth. A greater source than dependence on his father for magical ability might be found in the folds and layers of his irritation. My hand went to my chest, covering the flat part of my breastbone, above my heart. We all lived on borrowed magic, in some regard.

Somehow, I'd just managed to trap mine.

"Ignis said that he can take the god magic out of me, but he doesn't know if I'd survive the process. Like Luppentonisa."

Baxter's head snapped up. His eyes found mine instantly.

"You're still speaking with Ignis?"

"Yes, of course."

His gaze turned stormy. His head tilted to the side, filled with warning and concern.

"Bianca . . ."

I held up a staying hand. "I know. I know. His magic links us together so I hear him all the time. I haven't seen him," I hastily added, as if that made it better. "He's sarcastic and rough around the edges and protective and sometimes kind and . . . he doesn't strike me as the god of death and destruction that I expected. I haven't forgotten what his children have done to Alkarra. But . . ."

The words failed.

I can't deny that we're powerful together, I thought to myself.

A flare of light out of the corner of my eyes nearly drew my attention, but I ignored it. Was it Ignis? Likely. If I turned to the right, I'd probably see a swirl of embers.

I didn't want to see those embers.

The spying god.

Baxter's light eyes regarded me as he tightened his hold. He relaxed a little, but remained tense through the shoulders. My hands moved to his chest. The linen felt firm, yet soft. A sweet scent issued from his breath, a warm caress against my cheek, when he said, "Be careful. Ignis is cunning and smart and loves a puzzle."

"Could have warned me sooner?"

Baxter reached for my chin. With a gentle hand, he tilted my head back. We studied each other, daylight bright overhead. The roar of the surf crashed in the distance. My heart beat a mellow staccato in my throat as I slipped my hand over his. His skin was so warm.

His gaze darkened, dropped to my lips, so serious when limned in question.

"I want to kiss you, B," he murmured.

My heart snagged.

"I know."

A confident, easy smile appeared. "Will you let me?"

Breathless, I nodded.

My eyes closed as his lips pressed to mine. The heat seared, a question and a beckon. His fingertips slid around my jaw. I grabbed his shoulders and pulled us tight, erasing whatever space remained between us.

Butterflies fluttered through me when he deepened the kiss, an arm tightening around my waist. His amulet pressed against my chest, igniting fire and flame and magic. The tips of my fingers traced his neck, the curls at the back, his shoulders. I gripped his arms as he pulled away with a slow breath in.

An adoring gaze followed. He smiled and pressed his forehead to mine.

"Well," he murmured.

A long, shaky breath escaped me. My knees felt weak. Exhausted. The kiss had been exultant, but subtle. The world tilted for a moment, then righted itself.

"Well," I repeated with a smile of my own.

His palm pressed against my neck, hot. "You and me in Alaysia, B. It wouldn't be the worst thing."

The words felt impossible. Terrifying. Maybe because of the truth that lurked behind them. A servant of Ignis in an equally magical world. Powerful, instant ability at my fingertips. With the gods, I could protect my land, visit my friends in Alkarra, move easily through the world, and ignore the restrictions of incantations.

Could I do it?

Could I *trust* them?

There was as much to leave behind as there would be to gain, yet I couldn't deny the allure. The draw of Alaysia and its wild power. Ventis had been correct: my decision was not a question of desire, but a question of *who to save*.

Myself.

Or Alkarra.

But what, whispered my stirring heart, *about the forest?*

Prana's warning slipped through my mind again, quenching the heat of Baxter's kiss with the cool touch of history.

Remember your forest. Trust no one.

I blinked away the foggy remnants of home to touch his cheek with my fingertips. The heat of the amulet pressed into my chest like a brand, scorching my blood. I lived so hot here, a burning witch.

"Do you really want me in Alaysia with you?" I whispered.

The dance of his fingers across the back of my neck sent a shiver down my skin. He curled his fingers more tightly around the base of my neck, clinging to me.

"I know I want to help Alaysia," he admitted with a wry smile. "And I'm beginning to wonder if it might be the best thing that ever happened to me, should you also stay."

A resounding echo of his words, empty and hollow, followed. My lips burned as I pulled Baxter into another kiss to silence the roiling fears. His hands splayed across my back, yanking me closer. Our lips melted together, fierce with bottled passion.

Memories of Letum Wood, of Alkarra, faded away.

Not now.

For now, I wasn't the Lady-witch of Alkarra, weapon of the gods. I wasn't the servant of the forest goddess, nor the daughter of Derek Black.

For now?

No god, no goddess, no family, no magic could hold me. I spiraled into spirit and power in the world because I belonged to this moment.

To myself, and perhaps . . . to Baxter.

* * *

Baxter's fingers linked through mine, lazy but warm, as we strolled through yet another hallway. A hundredth room.

An additional wing.

With his free hand, Baxter waved into an empty apartment on our left.

"Aaaand . . . this is also a room."

I feigned surprise and delight, drawing a chuckle from him. In truth, this immaculate, barren space looked just like the other twenty-four we passed in the last several hours. Empty, expansive, yet different in minor details. Instead of a stone floor, white tiles. A covered portico instead of a balcony, and two doors outside instead of one.

"When someone stays in a room, we customize it to them through magic." He eyed me. "Sort of like I did for you at the beach house. It's why we keep them empty until they're needed."

"Do you need to conserve magic?" I murmured.

He shrugged. "Perhaps, but my new amulet has so much power, it may not be as necessary as it was in Alkarra."

Early moonlight trailed behind us as he tugged me out of the room. The hall raced endlessly forward, narrow and splintered as it appeared into the other byways that led to more rooms and unopened doors and stairs and grandeur and space.

"All of this," I said into the hushed quiet, "is now yours?"

We passed a gilded mirror, sparkling with golden edges and seashells on the corners. A burning bowl of sand suspended from the ceiling, flickering higher. As we passed out of its range, it extinguished. Ahead of us, another one illuminated. Such magical use was reminiscent of Alkarra, and settled a bristling anxiety in my chest.

Baxter moved through it with an assessing eye. Already, plans seemed to boil through his mind, bubbling to the surface. The political scene in Alaysia would be different from Alkarra. Though I'd sensed some sort of hierarchy and structure amongst demigods, I hadn't been fully able to suss it out.

What would Baxter do if not political work?

"Do you have dances here?" I asked. "Balls? Parties? How does a demigod really gain political power in Alaysia?"

Baxter huffed a laugh as he opened a closet door, gazed around a bunch of linens, and shut it again.

"Demigods have parties, yes. Not often, and it's more about food than dancing. Relationships are vastly different here. In that I mean there are none outside of demigod siblings. Mostly, there is competition amongst demigods. Vying for the position of favorite.

Like Amorette," he added as an easy aside. "She's constantly attempting to build a stronger case for Father's love against mine."

Amorette with her lovely, short hair and bright eyes, equally as wary as they could be conniving. Hardly surprising that she'd have great motivations.

"Are you the favorite?" I asked.

"For now."

The fallibility of such a statement startled me. As a lone child, I couldn't fathom any competition from a sibling. Instead, I had competed with the Network, which tugged at my father's attention far more greatly than any child ever could have.

"And now," I added lightly, wanting to turn my thoughts to happier matters, "you have this big, lovely part of your father's castle all to yourself."

"Hard earned," he muttered, "I tell you, but yes. My father's gift for accomplishing my mission. A rather short mission, really. Three years for all this? The gift is a bit ostentatious, but so are the gods. I don't mind," he added in a murmur, "because I've wanted this part of the *Rostina* since I was a little boy."

"I thought the bigger, more powerful amulet was your gift?"

He scoffed. "No. Consider that a work tool. In order for Father to keep his mortals from rebelling, he needs demigods that actually care for them. The amulet is how I do *his* job, so to speak."

Yet also how Baxter held onto any sort of power.

Ventis held tight strings over Baxter, and the thought made me uneasy. Irrefutable ties, in a sense. Reminders of mortal rebellions drew my thoughts to Daemon, but I pushed them back out. In the morning, I'd get an update from Ava.

Hopefully, Daemon's planned exodus truly had been quelled by Baxter's timely arrival. An arrival that, in hindsight, seemed particularly well-timed.

We wandered farther, passing more rooms. One held a

hearth and chimney—the only place I'd seen such a normal, Alkarran thing—and another entirely comprised of empty shelves carved into the sandstone. Paintings decorated a wall here and there, painted right onto the sand. Whorls to represent wind cluttered much of the art.

Waves.

Sea.

Chaos controlled.

The evening had long since advanced past deepnight while we explored his home together. My eyes felt heavy, but now that I held all of Baxter's attention, I didn't want to let go. We wandered down staircases, past dribbling waterfalls, and through rooms painted silver and gray. The expanse of Baxter's wing of the *Rostina lu Lune* rivaled Chatham Castle. My witchy mind could hardly comprehend such immensity.

Or opulence.

Golden skirts. Pearlescent sheen. Furniture here and there that added a touch of elegance to each hallway. A mug of water appeared in front of me as we walked. Baxter conjured a piece of sweet bread and shared it with me. Peppermint candy. Chunks of fruit.

So lavish.

So . . . easy.

"Is this what you've always wanted?" I asked as we passed underneath a ceiling filled with paintings of demigods wearing amulets, riding waves. Wind twirled through sky with grains of sand that glimmered. A tiled floor stretched out here, blue and gray alternating. It led to a winding staircase that plunged up and down, into darker paths.

"Always," Baxter murmured, a hand in his pocket. "I ran these halls as a child, when my older brother, Waray, lived here. He was Father's favorite for most of my childhood. I was similar enough to Waray that Father sent me on the mission to Alkarra with a promise of this part of the *Rostina lu Lune* should I be successful."

Baxter spread his arms, as if to say *and here we are.*

"Where is Waray now?"

"Died, while I was gone."

"Baxter, I'm sorry."

A melancholy shrug followed.

Not for the first time, I couldn't help but question Baxter's motives in Alkarra. He'd always been genuine, and I sensed the same now, but knowing this prize lingered back at home made me wonder.

"Why did you end up so different?" I asked.

He stopped under a doorway, gilded with etched designs of mermaids, and glanced back at me. His features formed a silent question.

"The other demigods," I said quietly. The sons of Tontes lingered in my mind, rabid on the water. "They don't care about mortals. About . . . anything but power. You're not the same. You're kind."

A smile softened his intense features. He clasped my hand, guiding me into a narrow hallway that spilled into a library filled with books.

"Not all demigods are bad, for one. You just haven't met the good ones. And," he drawled, "there aren't as many of them. Honestly? Alkarra changed me. I saw how things are different, that there's a better way. Plus, I had Ava, whom I genuinely care for. She softens me," he murmured thoughtfully, then added, "while she also exasperates me to no end."

I laughed. "She's wonderful that way."

A ladder lingered a few steps in front of us, cloaked in shadows. Moonlight slanting from a wall of windows on the opposite wall brought several such ladders into view. They led to a second story of books, ringed with shelves, and those at least fifteen paces high. More ladders gave access to further sandy tomes. My fingers itched to open a few. Baxter gazed on it all with an interested but detached air. He pulled us farther along, down a darkened hallway.

Sensing an opportunity, I said, "Ventis mentioned your mother."

The words dropped between us like falling eggshells. Ventis' revelation had opened an unknown aspect of Baxter, one that I wanted to explore. A part that surely grieved and knew heartbreak. One that I could connect to, perhaps find a portion of Baxter that he may have sealed off long ago.

His lips thinned. "That," he muttered, "was not something I asked him to do."

"Yamara was your mother?"

"Yes." He tightened. "And she's not a topic of conversation for tonight."

His stiff tone lay between as we continued down the hall. My thoughts meandered with questions. Though disappointed, I could hardly blame him. Hard topics were hard topics. His rigid hold on my fingers eventually eased. When we stopped in a broad room with furniture, books, and long, flat tablets of sand, he relaxed.

Baxter lifted his arms, encompassing the room.

"This," he said, "is my preferred room for now. It's where I'll deal with my siblings and business for my father."

I ran a finger along the soft grains of sand in a nearby wooden tray. The sand lay as deep as my first knuckle. Next to the tray, a wooden stick, blunt at the edge. In the sand was written a message, then signed by Amorette.

Father would see you in the morning, early dawn.

"Alaysian messages," Baxter quipped with a little smile. "We don't use much parchment here except for the books. Instead, we use magic to write each other messages, or stop by."

"Far more personable," I murmured.

A dark chuckle followed. "That's one word for constantly getting challenged by siblings who think they can do better than you."

My gaze darted around the room. The color scheme was far more like the Baxter I knew back in Alkarra. Masculine, but professional. Dove gray divans with burgundy blankets neatly folded over the back. A driftwood table that hosted a sand tray with wooden stylus, and a jar that sprouted baby white flowers.

Neat, as ever.

"How old are you?"

The question barreled out of me, unexpected by both of us. Until I heard the words, I didn't realize they lingered in such a pressured way. More lay behind such a question than just the answer. The answer *meant* something, and he seemed to sense it.

Words hesitated on half-open lips. Finally, he said, "Fifty-four."

My eyes widened.

"Fifty-four?" I whispered. "That's . . . only slightly younger than Papa."

He stepped closer with a poorly-hidden grimace. His fingers found mine, linking us immediately, as if he sensed my need for grounding.

Shock rippled through me.

Fifty-four.

His tone remained light when he asked, "Does it seem strange?"

Wariness lived in such a question.

Of course it seems strange! I wanted to shout. In terms of lived experience, he'd lived nearly as much *time* as Papa. My nose wrinkled on the thought that Baxter could be my father.

"If you want to put it in witch years," he hastily said, "I'm basically twenty-five. Most demigods live to two hundred, just as a few witches are lucky to make it to a hundred."

A very, very few, I longed to add, but sealed my lips.

"Fifty is a quarter of our life expectancy," he continued. "Not that different from you, really."

His optimistic attitude aside, the math calculated in my head automatically.

"Assume I live to ninety," I murmured, not quite able to meet his gaze. "That gives me seventy more years of life, which puts you at 120. You'd live almost another hundred years after my death."

"And all of those years with you," he whispered, "would be worth it."

My eyes fluttered closed. The day rushed up on me. Meeting with Ventis. Baxter's own castle. The world of Alaysia. A whirling sensation twirled through me with the thoughts.

Suddenly, all of it felt so overwhelming.

"Bianca, we're friends first," he whispered. "Nothing has to be decided today or tonight or this month. I know it's . . . a bit weird . . . which is sort of why I haven't brought it up before. But it's also something we could work through. All right?"

I pulled in a calming breath, met his gaze, and nodded. His warm smile sent reassurance through the bestial panic.

"Thank you," I whispered.

His fingers threaded through my hair, then returned to his side. With a weary hand, he scrubbed his eyes.

"It's late. We need to get some rest. Before you go, however, I wanted to see if you would be willing to help me with something?"

"Anything."

"Gelas has requested an audience with us. Well, not as much with me, but I will be part of this. Apparently, he wants to talk with you."

I blinked several times, startled. Of anything I expected Baxter to have said, *that* was not it.

"The god of ice?"

He nodded warily. "My father gave his permission, as you are technically his guest and under his protection. He said if I go with you, and you're willing, it's safe."

I bobbled the idea in my head for several moments. The urge to go immediately took me by surprise. More of Alaysia to see. More of the gods to understand. More that I could report home to Alkarra. Recalling Marten's caution to prudence, I viewed the offer as the leader of the Sisterhood would.

Diplomatically.

Also with heady caution.

"Is there a reason not to take such an invitation?"

Baxter shrugged. "If Tontes made the request? There would be thousands of reasons not to go. Gelas is mostly harmless, I think. Curious, at most. If nothing else, it will give you a chance to visit the Icelands in the more northern part of Alaysia. Father wouldn't have approved if he felt it wasn't safe for you."

Exhausted or not, a thrill zipped through me. Gelas had been a slippery figure so far, like an icicle sliding out of one's grasp. Little more than rumor, instead of presence. If I couldn't understand Deasylva, at least I could paint a clearer picture of the gods.

"I would love to."

His shoulders eased back. He smiled. "Thank you."

A shuffling sound came in the distance, followed by a low exclamation of pain and a muttered something.

Baxter chortled. "Gio," he called. "In here."

Gio appeared, red-faced and flustered. He limped slightly with his left foot. "Stubbed my toe," he muttered.

Baxter set a hand on the small of my back. "Bianca and I are going to the Icelands tomorrow morning," he said to Gio. "Please, bring her some of the dresses I set out the other day after they're brought back from the laundry first thing. Also, make sure that breakfast is delivered before we go, if you will."

Gio smiled warmly. "For the Lady-witch of Alkarra," he murmured, "it shall be done."

I managed a wooden smile in response.

Gio disappeared down the hall as I turned back to Baxter. With a sigh, he pulled me into his arms. I sank into his chest. The hum of his heart, the warmth of his arms as they encapsulated me, sent reassurance all the way through the cold uncertainty inside.

For now, Baxter's comfort made home feel not so far away.

Chapter Seventeen

The Icelands of the North reminded me of discarded sapphires.

Snowy glaciers dotted a freezing sea thick with fog and bitter air, like bobbing diamonds. Breath billowed in front of me as I clamped my arms around my body to rein in a shiver. Baxter had sent a dress to the beach house that morning. A lovely thing, with capped sleeves, a wide neckline, and blue lace trim against linen. It reminded me of sky and sand, perfectly matching Baxter's loose pants and sky blue shirt with buttons along the middle.

Definitely not warm enough for Gelas' kingdom, however.

A pink-tipped nose greeted me when I turned to the side. Baxter, teeth chattering, stood next to me. His smile was more grimace than anything pleasurable. "Sorry," he murmured. "I forgot how cold it can get up here."

A downy coat appeared on my body from shoulder to ankle. Wide buttons matched the blue stitching of the dress, and the dark brown material felt thick and heavy. The bitter chill that welcomed us ebbed into something less nefarious with the coat as a shield. The dress itched. I hated the slippers he'd sent with it, but gritted my teeth through the experience.

Why he loved matching, I couldn't fathom.

"Let's just say," he chattered, "that Gelas *really* likes the cold. Not all of the Icelands are this bitter, and it's warmer inside. C-c-come on."

He put a hand on my elbow and escorted me up a snowy path that led to an ice mountain at least as tall as Chatham Castle. At the foot of a shimmering blue wall appeared a door made of wood. The tiny entrance was swamped against the unbroken plane of ice.

At the door, Baxter knocked. I tilted my head all the way back. The muscles in my neck pulled when I stopped to study the top of the glittering structure. A glacier, for certain, that ended thousands of paces overhead. Footsteps sounded, then stopped. The door groaned, creaked open.

A pair of familiar eyes peered out.

Seeing me, Tipa opened the door wider. A black coat, tied at the neck and with separate bows all the way to her knees, kept her warm. Thick pants, tucked into a pair of boots, were covered by a skirt which hid her legs from view. Her assessing gaze lingered on me for a moment longer than necessary.

"He's waiting," she said, clipped. She disappeared from view as the door swung open.

Baxter pressed inside. I followed.

* * *

No light brightened the inside of Gelas' glacier home, but the area remained visible all the same. Frozen water fissured into deep crevasses. The buttresses ascended high, stretching almost out of sight. Daunted by the weight and presence of such raw power, I said nothing.

A wide pathway cut straight through the ice. Jagged walls

enclosed either side. Chilling black bands began at the floor, blending upwards in tones of sapphire, then aquamarine, and finally silver. The stratified colors curved and twisted, as if the water had melted, frozen, and melted over and over again.

The glacier clearly split it into sections where hallways slid into different, darker areas. No torch, candle, or bowl of burning sand could be seen. A chunk of ice dribbled down the wall not far away, landing with a crash. It fractured into thousands of splinters on the floor.

Tipa strode over it with a crunch.

Baxter kept an arm around my shoulders as we advanced. His gaze darted around, assessing. Based on his quiet perusal, I doubted that he'd been inside before. In this place of ice, I felt no cold. Our breath wasn't visible, and Baxter's reddened cheeks had softened. Tipa strode like a Guardian into battle, reminding me of our encounter outside the Southern Network market. She'd been a determined force then, too.

Through a dizzying maze of ice walls and blackened stone floors, the glacier opened. Tipa led us into an atrium-like sanctuary of . . . nothing.

Scooped walls of ice curved into a perfect circle. The sparkling sides rose into a thin dome overhead. A frozen glaze so thin I could see the sky that soared above left a distorted view of the clouds. The top lingered ages away—too far for birds to fly. As if Gelas had reached down with a giant hand, taken a scoop out of the earth, and sealed it with glass.

How simple was the world of the gods.

Yet so vast.

Below the sparkling roof lay an immaculate black stone floor. The polished sheen gave an appearance like lacquer, shiny as a mirror. I caught a glimpse of my own astonished face when I peered down. Ice walls met the black stone along the edges of the perfect circle. Everything was symmetrical and immaculate in a simplified way.

Glorious, frozen water.

Tipa stopped a few steps in. She paused, gazed around, then spun. Her eyes met mine. "Good luck," she murmured.

With a flip of her long red hair, she strode away. The gentle tap of shoes on the floor escorted her out until the wooden door that we had entered through closed. Baxter spun in a slow circle, hands in his pockets. Frigid air, cold as an ice bath, filled this room. My ears ached, and I wished for the warmer passageways back.

"Let me speak to Gelas first?" Baxter murmured. "It's better if I handle the conversation."

I conceded with a reluctant nod. Icicles rained down the far side, skittering across the glossy ground. A voice followed, accompanied by crackling ice near the wall at our back. I spun to face it.

Welcome Baxter. Bianca.

The voice seemed low, rippling, and guarded. Tense, I would say, but I didn't know this god at all. The hair on the back of my neck stood up.

"Your invitation is an honor, Gelas." Baxter bowed his head, hands at his back. He returned them to his side a moment later. "Thank you for having us."

I gave no such obeisance.

You are the Lady-witch of Alkarra?

Baxter nodded to me, as if to give me permission, but I ignored him. No demigod could scare me into submission to a god, not even Baxter. Alaysian dangers notwithstanding.

My chin lifted.

"I am."

It is interesting to meet you.

"I feel the same way."

Do you live up to a title such as yours? The Lady-witch of Alkarra.

Judgment colored his tone. Did I imagine something slightly

familiar in the way he spoke, or did the acoustics of such an empty place play with my head?

"That's for you to determine, I would imagine," I said lightly.

Baxter sent me a sharp look, but I ignored that, too. I kept my head tilted back, studying the ceiling when a groan issued from it.

Gelas made a low, musing sound.

Given what I have observed, he murmured, *no, I don't think you live up to your title. Thank you for asking.*

My arms turned rigid. Baxter reached out to touch my sleeve, but it didn't calm the heat in my chest.

Well.

"Is there a reason for your inquiry, Gelas?" Baxter asked with forced mildness. I knew the tone well. I'd heard him use it with Council Member Aldred before, when Aldred was all up-in-arms about something ridiculous.

A witch that would leave her homeland to chase a presumably more powerful magic is a witch to cast into suspicion. My brothers may be enamored with their new trinket, I am not.

My arms clenched to my side. Baxter gave my elbow a reassuring squeeze and spread his hands.

"Ask your questions."

Why are you here, Lady-witch?

The question drove right to my heart of hearts. Vestiges of Gelas' voice echoed in the silent, tomb-like walls, as if the ice wanted to cling to him and never let go.

"I came to see if Ignis would remove the god magic from inside me. Now, I just want to save Alkarra from Tontes."

Do you feel the power of Ignis could provide the opportunity to stop Tontes?

"I am . . . exploring the possibility."

Some of the suspicion that hovered in the air ebbed after a long silence. In the quiet, the hair on the back of my neck stood up. Though I couldn't tell where, I felt that Gelas stood somewhere close. Invisibly so.

How badly I wanted to see him.

Have you already considered giving your allegiance to Ignis?

I nodded.

Silence.

Baxter shuffled at my side, head down.

To Ignis, you are a weapon. You realize this?

"Yes."

I swallowed, pained by the admission, true as it was.

And you accept this?

"I didn't say that."

Gelas stewed in silence.

I sense a deep presence in you.

My stomach clenched, already prepared for what he'd say next.

Deasylva.

The word boomed along the ice. A crack, then an explosion, ripped through the wall to our left. Ice dropped, shattering. Baxter had gone utterly still.

My breath caught.

How long have you been goddess-touched?

I blinked, startled by the question. Suspicions had long raged between Leda, Hiddleston, and myself as to whether or not I *was* goddess-touched, and what it meant. No confirmation had been issued beyond my relationship with the forest, and that was an assumption.

"I . . . I don't know."

Do you have loyalty to the goddess of the forest?

All thoughts emptied from my head. I had nothing certain to say.

Your silence, Gelas finally said, *is interesting.*

Whether it pleased him that I had no immediate response, or

annoyed him, I couldn't tell. Beneath all his questions, I sensed a test. Not a trap, but an attempt at discovery.

"I don't know the goddess of the forest," I finally said.

A lie.

"She's never revealed herself to me."

Do you believe that to be true, or are you another witch that chooses to lack your own self-awareness, as most do?

The acerbic tone was a jab, and I received it with a visible wince. My jaw tightened. There was bullying, and then there was *this.*

"Easy," Baxter murmured to me.

"No," I hissed.

"Bianca—"

"Can we cut to the point?" I advanced several steps, staring hard at the ice across the way. Splinters formed there when he spoke, as if Gelas had an epicenter. I sensed him there. The god magic in my body detected his proximity, like magnets drawing together. Given the chance to choose a spot, I'd wager he stood about three paces away. Cold radiated in flares on my cheeks from there. It vibrated with tension and energy. A thunderous presence lurked.

Poised.

Why do you think I called you here, Bianca?

"You want to know if I'll be loyal to whomever I choose. You don't believe I'll be loyal to Ignis, should I choose to keep the god magic. You think I had already declared loyalty to Deasylva and that I'm about to betray her. Is that correct? You think you can't trust me."

Correct. To embrace god magic would forfeit all in Alkarra.

"Ignis says otherwise."

And Ignis tells you everything?

Silence followed.

If you haven't even asked the right questions of the god of fire, whom you claim you explore possibilities with, then I harbor doubts over your ability to save Alkarra.

My nostrils flared. He had a point. Ignis said I could live in Alkarra, but did he mean it. Gelas continued.

I don't think you have it in you to truly embrace Alaysia, Ignis, and god magic.

The challenge irritated me. His cold judgment was like a wound to my honor, and I didn't appreciate it. A vein of truth lay twisted deep in his question, though. I asked myself the same thing.

Could I choose Ignis?

Could I live in Alaysia?

If choosing Ignis over Deasylva resulted in the ability to save Alkarra, it would undoubtedly upend my entire life. Yes, I might be able to *go* home, but would it really be home anymore? Unlikely that the trees would respond to me. I'd be different from witches.

Distinctly apart.

Other.

My belief is not in your ability to give loyalty to god magic, Gelas continued, *but to give up everything else that you love. Your ties to Alkarra, your family, your friends, are deep. If you truly want to save Alkarra from Tontes, would you do* whatever *it takes?*

"If you have to ask," I snapped, "then you don't know me at all."

I know you better than you think.

His immediate rebuttal unseated me. I shuffled back a step, blinking.

"How?"

All the gods have watched you, Bianca. We all wait for our chance to get what we most want.

"And what is that?"

Alkarra.

I shivered, cut through by an icy knife.

You are that chance for all of us. Why do you think you're really here *in Alaysia, Lady-witch of Alkarra?*

"To clean up your mess," I muttered, "and help you prevent a war between yourself and the goddesses."

Tell yourself that, if it comforts you, but you are at the whim of gods. After our discussion today, I hold no reassurance that you know what you're doing. Alkarra is not safe in your hands, nor is the god magic. You are fickle and misaligned.

Fury bubbled within me.

Gelas drove his point home with one last question. *Do you even know to whom you are loyal?*

Baxter's hand clamped on my shoulder.

"She's not a pawn, Gelas, in the game of the gods," he said firmly. "Not even for my father. He wouldn't appreciate you treating her this way."

Ice broke behind us, skittering onto the shiny black floor in a sea of prickling gems. The crystals slid to a stop past my feet, forming the shape of two footprints not far away—right where I'd suspected him.

Your denial is appreciated, Baxter, but she is little else to the gods. Tell yourself otherwise, if you wish.

I forced a long, slow breath.

Go home, Lady-witch of Alkarra. You toy with powers beyond yourself here.

Infuriated, I spun on my heels.

"Bianca, wait!"

"No. The god commands, and the god receives."

The thud of my feet on the stony floor carried me across the open expanse. Baxter called after me, but I ignored him. Frustration flared in long fissures of heat that had nothing to do with god magic. I shoved through the door, allowed it to slam at my back, and stalked through the halls. With god magic to guide the way, the path opened before me in lines of light, leading to the door out.

Not a soul showed up in the halls, not even Tipa.

I exploded outside.

The door slammed behind me as I stood under a sparkling, but cold, sun. Ocean agitated a frozen beach, sloping as water moved underneath a layer of ice. Baxter appeared at my side, lips pressed.

"That," he muttered, "didn't go well."

"You can thank your god-uncle."

He drove a hand through his hair. "I told you to let me handle it."

"He spoke to me."

"Yes, and then you became disrespectful and arrogant," he countered in a modulated tone, as if he spoke with an angry toddler. "The gods aren't . . . they don't tolerate disrespect, Bianca. You're navigating this world the wrong way."

By sheer willpower, I forced myself to calm.

"I answered his questions with my honest feelings, Baxter. That's all. I wasn't trying to give offense, but he was. On purpose."

Baxter opened his mouth, then closed it.

"This is what I do, Bianca. You need to let me do it."

"No one speaks for me."

He growled. "That's not the way it works with the gods. We're in Alaysia, not Alkarra. You may be the leader of the Sisterhood there, but you're nothing more than a witch here."

"Wrong," I hissed. "I am the Lady-witch of Alkarra, a living amulet, and the most powerful vessel of god magic next to a god. *That* is who I am, and they know it. Do you? Do you realize what they're doing? They're toying with me, Baxter. And *you* don't see it. That's what happened here today."

Shock registered on his features. His jaw slackened, then pressed back together. A pause, then a flutter of memories, arrested my next response. I turned away with a frustrated breath.

"You're right. I can be quick to speak without thinking, but that doesn't mean I'd change anything about my exchange with Gelas. He was being a bully, questioning me in an impertinent way. There was a better way to ask those questions, though I agree that they should have been asked. I'm sorry that put you in an awkward position, but I'm not sorry for standing up to him."

I met his befuddled gaze.

"If they really want the Lady-witch of Alkarra to help them defeat their own brother, they'll get me as I am. Gelas, clearly, wants nothing to do with me and that is fine. I don't want anything to do with him, either."

Baxter processed that with a little sigh. Eventually, he nodded. "Fair," he whispered, looking like a lost puppy.

"I need a break. I'm going to return to the beach house. I'll see you later."

Chapter Eighteen

Despite all the grandeurs of the gods, the empty beach house called. I yearned for simplicity.

For the damp smell of cedar and moss and forest. For space to run and run and *run*.

All of Alaysia's treasures amounted to very little land. Few opportunities to truly escape existed, at least until I knew more of the tributaries and smaller island chains. Kingdom boundaries, demigod territories, it all hid an insidious culture of power and struggle. The only refuge was Alkarra, or the beach house.

For now, I settled here.

Gelas' question bounced through my head.

Do you even know to whom you are loyal?

I didn't want to answer that question, because the answer would land somewhere between *I don't want to know* and *I don't want to say,* and it would be far too close to the *I don't want to leave Alaysia* side of things as well.

The cold of the Icelands warmed out of my body as I stared up at the ceiling, hands stacked behind my head. With Ava at her old collection again, attempting to trap her manulele birds and let them roost in the hedges Baxter had conjured for her out of magic, the only sound I heard was the crash of waves.

An hour later, after I mentally combed through what had happened, put it into neat boxes, and stacked it away to process later, I sat up. A wrapped package bounced next to me on the bed, appearing from nowhere.

Curiosity urged me to open it with god magic. Frivolous use of the powers, perhaps, but Ignis had never protested.

A rolled piece of paper lay inside. When I pulled it open with both hands, my breath caught. A drawn image unfurled over the page in inky, black strokes. A familiar face, feathered with small slash lines.

Papa.

The image showed him crouched down, his back against a wall. He peered out, eyes narrowed in concentration. His forearms were braced on his bent knees. Shadows and lines created the wall behind Papa, tapering to a vague background that gave no clues as to where he was. The slant of his brow, his intense eyes, the steep attention. As if someone had taken Papa in real life and smeared him on the page, line by line. My heart fluttered.

"Papa," I whispered.

My fingertips trailed over his face. When I accidentally touched it, color sprang to the paper. I sucked in a sharp breath, recoiling my hand. Papa's countenance filled with life, as vibrant as if I *could* touch him.

A living painting.

The image moved slightly. In the shift, Papa gazed around, head swinging to the side. He crouched like a coiled jungle cat, face wary, expression focused. I sucked in a breath, eyes watering.

My thumb touched Papa's shoulder. Gray and ebony flowed through the page like spilling ink. It expanded within the drawing of his torso, lightening and darkening to create texture.

He wore a dark shirt. Shadows highlighted the image behind him into tones of early twilight.

Another touch brought life to the background. Red rock walls. Linen pants. Leather shoes. A market in the West, perhaps?

That didn't make any sense.

Why would Papa be in the West?

Color filled the page with untold vibrancy. Tears clogged my throat, but I swallowed them back. Greater pains assaulted me than fear for Alkarra. Being so far from home, out of reach of everything solid, tossed me on a tempestuous sea. Despite my anger toward Papa for leaving without explaining anything to me, I longed for him.

"Do you trust me, Papa?" I whispered, my voice wobbling. "What dangerous thing are you doing now? Or are you running away from everyone, even me? You told me nothing."

The question remained unanswered.

Scripted words appeared on the bottom of the page in fire-red. Ignis whispered with them.

Forgive my brothers.

"A peace offering?" I murmured.

Yes.

A laugh bubbled out of me. Hopeless, this land. Infuriating one moment, endearing and full of wonder the next. The weight of Gelas' interrogation weighed heavily on me as I regarded the picture, but thought of Ignis.

"Papa is all right?" I whispered.

As you see.

"A welcome gift."

I know. For added measure.

Magic lifted my hand from my side. Flames appeared there, dancing along my skin with a warm caress. Streaks of fire elongated into swooping bands that joined together in a high angle, then swept down either side to form a smoldering petal in my palm. The work continued, growing up in lines of glimmering crimson.

"A burning flower?"

We harness fire.

Tears thickened my voice. "Yes," I murmured. "We do."

Gelas is cautious. He has always been tenacious and locked in. He doesn't believe you appreciate the weight of your decision and wants you to prove your loyalty. For the three of us, there is no room for error again.

My eyes lowered. Ignis gave me exactly what I needed. Truth. Clarity. As lovely as Alaysia had become, it still felt murky. Hidden. At least Ignis was straightforward.

"Can you really help me save Alkarra from Tontes?"

Together, yes. Do you trust me, Bianca?

My throat tightened. Unshed tears wavered the view of the glimmering flower in my hand. In the back of my mind, I heard Prana's voice.

Remember your forest, trust no one.

Why was I still here? I'd met with Ventis. Tested god magic. Knew its depths, or at least I thought I did. This moment, I could return home to Alkarra with infinitely more information than we had before. Perhaps even cobble together a plan to defeat rising threats from our island counterparts, but that didn't mean we'd win.

I stayed because I loved Alkarra. Not to mention the definitive problem of god magic in my blood, my body.

In truth?

I had no idea if I did the right thing, or if I trusted Ignis. I pulled in a slow breath through my nose, buying a moment of recovery to answer the question.

"I want to."

Ignis retreated, the embers dropping inert to the ground.

* * *

Ava peered at me as a wave rolled past, swooping warm water over my bent legs. I sighed. The humidity of the day settled as the sun sank toward the far horizon. All day, I'd been lost in swirls of Icelands and demigods and Alkarra. Baxter kept his distance, and so did Ignis.

"What happened with Gelas?" she asked.

"A lot of things."

Ava splashed her toes in the water. I canted my head to look at her, resting my folded arms on top of my knees. Hot sunshine burned into them, and I relished the zing dancing on top of my skin.

"Are you happy being back here, Ava?"

Her forehead ruffled into thick lines. She took several moments to reply, lips pushed to one side of her face.

"Yes, and no."

"What makes you happy?"

A fluttering smile appeared for a moment. "Baxter takes care of my collection now. That makes me happy. They have fresh water all the time. Enough fish. More fruit trees. A few of my manulele birds have returned. Daemon is healed. Still grumpy, but . . ."

She shrugged.

I almost laughed. Demigods couldn't fix everything, I supposed. Rumors of an exodus had quelled, I hoped, from Ava's lack of indication about it. Better not to bring it up, I imagined, and let it fade into history.

"Do you miss Alkarra?" I asked.

Ava's thin hand pressed to her chest. "So much. In here. Alkarra is a place of adventure and friendship and . . . spirit."

My throat felt heavy when I swallowed. "So is Alaysia," I murmured.

She scoffed. "But Alaysia has demigods. The *monilay mal* will never leave. They are always part of the islands."

Her words hung like coats in the air, heavy with truth. Sensing a rare opening of honesty, I pressed my luck.

"Why don't you talk about Christa?"

Water tinkled in the background, rushing by, as Ava frowned.

"Christa?"

"She was your mother, right?"

"She . . ."

Words failed. Several times, she opened and closed her mouth. In the end, she released a raspberry and muttered, "Christa was mean. She didn't like me or Tama very much."

"That can't be entirely true. Didn't she visit you pretty often?"

Ava rolled her eyes. "It *is* true. At least a little."

A wave flattened past, rushing over my heated skin. The cool water slipped away, yanking the warmth with it. The sun-kissed afternoon made me feel drowsy. I let the topic go when Ava shifted, the corners of her mouth pulling low.

"What happened on your trip over to Alkarra?" I asked. "You've never mentioned it before. You had to be on a boat for weeks to go so far."

Darkness overcame her expression. "Scary," she mumbled, then shivered. Goosebumps raced across the open back of her shoulders.

"Do you want to talk about it?"

"Why would I?"

"Talking about scary things feels good sometimes."

"It wasn't good."

"Sharing the bad," I said gently, "helps it leave you forever. Then it won't be bottled up inside."

Ava mulled this over, head cocked to the side. Her variegated hair fell in dark waterfalls to her shoulders. The youth in her voice created a strange disparity to the darkness in her words.

"Tama said that ghosts live inside us. If you don't let them out, they live through you."

Papa and Mama drifted through my mind, followed by a flashing image of Regina. I shoved them aside with mild annoyance.

"Sounds about right," I muttered.

Ava's hand, still on her heart, curled into a fist. "No ghosts here," she murmured. "No ghosts."

Sensing a closing of that topic, I set my chin on my knees. Ava didn't want to talk about the things that haunted her, and that seemed fair.

I didn't either.

The glimmering sea stretched into the horizon, a lovely, sparkling sight. Sunset crawled overhead in whorls of watery orange and yellow. The hues brightened my shadowed mind, illuminating the questions I still hadn't answered. Thoughts of Gelas returned, a reminder that no matter how far we ran away from truth, fear kept a steady stride.

Do you even know to whom you are loyal?

Chapter Nineteen

A thick piece of paper, cut to a perfect diamond, lay in my hand. I regarded the blocky text a third time, with less curiosity and more dread.

The god of wind formally invites you to the Rostina lu Lune for a beelae near sunset.

No embellishments adorned the paper, not even elegant words or a scrolled design. An oddly simple invitation. Abrupt, too. Apparently, I had no opportunity to accept or deny such an invitation, for the *beelae* began in a couple of hours.

Scrawled along the bottom was a note in Baxter's handwriting.

Pick your dress—they will all compliment my colors.

"What's a *beelae*?" I asked Ava, passing her the paper. She tossed it onto the table without looking at it.

"A family dinner."

"A dinner?"

Ava's eyebrows rose. "Yes, and it's very elegant. Quite nice. There will be lots of demigods with fine dresses, and so much food. Christa spoke about beelaes sometimes. She didn't like them." Her nose wrinkled. "Lots of talking. Christa didn't like to speak."

Sounded a bit *too* much like a ball.

"Lots of eating, fancy dress. Great," I mumbled. "Why didn't Baxter tell me about it?"

Ava shrugged. "Ventis probably didn't tell him. The gods do what they want." She threw her hands in the air. "It's Alaysia."

My teeth clenched all the way to my molars. Pop up social engagements, last minute invitations, and lacking explanations weren't my idea of a good time, but I shoved all that aside. No doubt it would mean something to Baxter, and I still wanted to support him. Heated exchange with Gelas aside.

She waved to the wall, where several dresses hung from pegs. They'd appeared with the invitation. A dreamy look crossed her eyes for a moment as she reached out, tracing her fingertips down the lace of the closest one.

"Aren't they nice?"

"Very beautiful."

Baxter and I hadn't spoken since our trip to Gelas' kingdom the day before. The silence weighed on me. Was he frustrated with me for speaking my mind? Maybe he sought to give me space, the way I asked.

Well, I'd find out soon enough, at any rate.

A quick scan of the dresses left me in a quagmire of uncertainty. None of them looked all that comfortable. Or all that . . . *Bianca*. Perhaps that was the point, however. Baxter's function, Baxter's family.

I could align with Alaysian fashion for one night, couldn't I?

Ignoring the clench of my stomach at the thought, I stepped to the other side of the room to study the gowns.

Ava scrutinized the first one, something I pictured a bold

witch like Alina, High Priestess of the Southern Network, wearing. The back dropped halfway down the spine, with a high neckline in the front and straps for shoulders. Pearls sparkled along the edges in a faint blush of yellow and gray. The fabric appeared soft to the touch, like a cross between silk and velvet. Flowers ruffled the waist and neckline, bunched in hints of lemon.

Another dress with fitted sleeves and a tight bodice boasted a full skirt, the color of slate. Rosy tones lay under the skirt, which would stop somewhere before my knee. I tilted my head, startled.

Interesting.

The final dress carried a complicated tapestry of beadwork and glimmering ribbons. Pewter designs swirled with black to create the illusion of a moving wind through the skirt. More beads glimmered in the bodice, as if flung into the air. Sleeveless, but lovely, it wrapped all the way around the back and dropped to the floor. It would be heavy, for certain, and hot.

Witches in Alkarra would be scandalized by any of these choices, which gave me a delightful thrill of rebellion. The excitement quickly winnowed to reality. Whatever I wore had to bear me through an elegant dinner with a likely hostile crowd. Though none of them were to my taste, I chose the first gown with Alina in mind.

Thoughts of her would grant me power.

"Good." Ava nodded. "I liked this one best for you."

With her help, I slipped inside, yanked it down, and settled it. The shoulders were too wide, the bodice too short, and the skirt too long. God magic bundled the back so it crept up from the waist, adjusted the material around my shoulders and skirt, allowed it to settle like a glove.

Ava tilted her head to the neckline, where the gaudy flowers sprinkled. "The flowers are popular, I think. Baxter likes them."

"They're hideous."

She hid her giggle behind a hand. The leaves caught my hair, jerking it painfully. With another thought, the flowers faded into smoke, appearing instead as an embroidered design. Threads stitched into flowers with depth and shadow, highlighting the same canary-and-gray colors. Ridding the awkward flowers removed the bulky feeling of the dress. I sighed.

"Much better."

Her eyes danced as she nodded emphatically.

"The *beelae* is for Baxter." Ava brushed specks of sand off the bottom of the skirt with an approving purse of her lips. "It's a party to welcome him home. To congratulate his work on his mission, so it will be very important to him. He will see sisters that he hasn't spoken to in years."

"Thanks, that context helps."

My loose tongue would be bound, then. I imagined more lay behind this *beelae* than just a celebration of his mission. A reintegration with his siblings. A chance to show his presence amongst the other demigods locked in the land of the gods.

A statement more than a dinner.

The burning question that lingered was this: why give that statement at all?

Ava eyed me with a critical perusal I imagine she inherited from her mother, then stepped back. A drop of her shoulders and a tilt of her head indicated approval. I'd take what I could get. The tips of my fingers nervously smoothed the gown down.

"Don't you want to come?" I asked.

Her nose wrinkled. She recoiled in disgust. "To the *beelae*? No! *Monilay mal* everywhere. I'm happy to stay here. Tama used to leave me alone every night to light the lamps. I like the quiet."

Oh, jealousy. A quiet night on the beach sounded lovely compared to a dinner with demigods. She quirked a smile, as if she could read my mind.

"Will I suffice?" I asked, twirling. The simple skirt, only a few thin layers, fluttered around my legs. The modifications ensured it fit like a dream. Without flowers snagging my hair or scraping my arms, I felt free.

She grinned.

"Very nice."

My hand reached up, touching hair softened by special soap that pulled the salt water out of it. It trailed off my shoulders in satiny strands. A slight curl rolled the bottom, softening the look.

"Is wearing my hair down acceptable for a *beelae*? I have no idea what to expect when I arrive."

Her eyes widened with delight. "Shiny and lovely. You are beautiful, Bianca."

I smiled. "Thanks."

"Which shoes?"

With a critical eye, I regarded my options. Convoluted things, they appeared, made from wood and undoubtedly heavy. A pair of sandals with complicated laces waited, but I didn't want to figure the design out.

"No shoes," I said firmly. "Barefoot is perfect."

"The sisters will all be envious." Ava cackled, both arms wrapped around her stomach as she laughed breathlessly. "So jealous of the Lady-witch of Alkarra! They will hate you for your natural beauty when they have to try so hard with magic."

I attempted to smile, but it felt brittle. That exact thing worried me the most. Baxter had nine sisters. Was I supposed to impress them? Be honest? Hold back? This would be a lot easier if I had a warning.

Ava flounced away, still laughing to herself, as I regarded my reflection in the elegant mirror. Feeling like a fraud, I turned away. My gaze landed right on a trunk, filled with clothes. With a glance over my shoulder to ensure Ava couldn't see, I reached for the hidden amulet. My fingers touched the chain. I tugged it free, staring at the chiseled facets. Red heat stared back.

Samthanruadanosa.

With a noise in my throat, I shoved it into a pocket I created into the dress with magic just as a knock issued on the door.

"Lady-witch of Alkarra?" Gio called brightly. "I am here to escort you to your very first *beelae*."

* * *

My god magic whisked me and Gio to the main portico of the *Rostina lu Lune*. Bright stars smattered across a velvet sky. Ocean danced. Water smashed. Perfectly warm air drifted by, a balm over my skin. I closed my eyes and breathed deep the salty smell of the sea.

The *Rostina* lay in a strange quiet. Gio tugged me toward an interior door while he chattered about sand structures, god magic, and Ventis' deep love for big skies. My fingertips trailed along the edge of a wall. The compressed sand was smooth, like marble.

"You are lovely tonight, Lady-witch of Alkarra." Gio's dashing smile flashed in the glowing bowls of sand that brightened the portico. "Your fashion taste is . . . far greater than most."

He glanced at the stitched flowers, then winked. Gio had seen the dresses before I made the alterations, no doubt. My palm ran along the bodice.

"Think it's all right that I altered it?"

"Baxter is an understanding demigod."

Gio pulled me away from the view. Ahead of us lurked the black hole of the tunnel, but I ignored the entrance to Ventis' personal quarters. With a bent elbow and my arm tucked under his, Gio led me deeper inside. His presence stabilized me as we stepped through a new doorway—this one triangular—and into the castle.

"Baxter wanted to escort you himself," he murmured, low,

"but Ventis called him to last minute duties. Immediately after the *beelae*, he will need to speak again with his father. He wanted me to let you know in advance. His schedule is quite busy for the rest of the week."

A hidden grimace lingered in his words. Disappointment flooded me, but I forced it back with a smile.

"Baxter is a busy demigod."

"He will be engaged in speaking with his sisters tonight. It will be best for you to listen and speak when he indicates for you to do so."

Gio halted when I stopped near a glowing bowl. Wary, he studied my features.

"He wants me to stay quiet?"

One of his shoulders canted up uncertainly. "He wants to understand how his sisters feel about *you* before . . . ah . . ."

"I make a mess of it like I did with Gelas?"

Gio rolled his lips, then swallowed. When he spoke again, amusement thickened the words. "I wouldn't have said that," Gio drawled.

"But Baxter would."

Gio stared at me.

"I understand," I murmured through gritted teeth, though everything inside me rebelled. "Baxter is trying to protect and help me. I'll be a flower on his arm for the night."

"The most beautiful flower," he murmured. "His sisters are competitive. They want to be favored, as he is. Some of them? They will do anything to have his position. This is not a family. It is a battery of barracuda."

Hallways and doors peeled off here and there, plunging into different areas of the castle. Gio pointed out a wall plastered with starfish, each with varying golden tones that matched Gio's honey eyes, or deepened into umber. Strings of pearls wound along walls, leading the way to various parts of the castle. Crimson pearls for the library. Azure for a dining area. Smoldering dishes of sand cast light onto the floor. In the distance, the ocean constantly roared.

Gio moved at a steady clip, chattering happily about artifacts or wings of the castle as he did so. We twisted through the *Rostina lu Lune* in a tour that I never wanted to end. The expansive interiors, built without regard to physics, dazzled me. As a tour, it was lovely. By the time Gio slowed, breathlessness overtook me.

Also, gratitude for nixing the flowers.

Too soon, yet not soon enough, the sound of chattering voices wound down a narrow hallway. Gio motioned me ahead of him, because it was too narrow for two abreast.

The close space opened into an altitudinous room reminiscent of Baxter's personal castle-within-a-castle. Chandeliers suspended from dried seaweed glimmered with flaxen light, shallow carafes of burning sand illuminating them. Four different staircases spiraled to third, fourth, and fifth stories. Divans, couches, and other comfortable furniture scattered here and there. I wanted to sink into the plush of a nearby chair and stay there all night.

"The sisters will be assessing you as the *beelae* progresses," Gio whispered as he motioned me out of the grand area and toward a tight hallway off to the side. "They want to know more about you because, naturally, they don't trust you. May I caution you? If Baxter approves of you speaking, perhaps to Amorette, don't give too much away."

"What does that mean?"

Gio pressed his lips. "Don't make references to how much power you have, or your association with the gods. Answer their questions, but not entirely."

"Shall I eat the dinner, but not taste it?"

Gio burst out laughing, a delightful sound. "Fair, Lady-witch of Alkarra. Fair. All I have for you is advice. *Monilay mal* lurk everywhere."

Double doors thrown open waited ahead. Inside, hints of a sprawling dinner table could be seen. Clay plates. Wine goblets carved from shells. Sparkling silverware. Milling bodies filled the room with women, except for one obvious male standing in the middle. Baxter. Gio paused just outside the door, in the shadows. He stepped back so as not to be seen and left me alone in the doorway.

He retreated with a whisper.

"Trust no one."

All sound ceased.

I held my breath as the attention of each demigod sister in the room locked on me. The intensity of stares, the shift in the air, made me feel naked as I stood before them. My shoulders dropped back, chin notched.

A broad-shouldered body stepped in front of me, breaking the trance. I tilted my head back to see Baxter regarding me with a tense smile that cut through my fears. He looked so frazzled, so pulled-apart. A hand reached out, and I accepted it. He squeezed my fingers.

"You're stunning tonight," he murmured.

"Am I late? I'm sorry if—"

"No." He held up a hand. "Not late. I had Gio get you after everyone arrived. I wanted to . . . prep them."

"For me?"

He shrugged, gaze skating away. A stone gray shirt that perfectly matched my dress, threaded with similar skeins of thread, ran over his shoulders. His light eyes against dark hair caused my stomach to curl, but the whole effect dimmed from his low appearance.

Voices picked back up. Movement returned behind him. I tugged on his hand, drawing his gaze back to me.

"You all right?" I whispered.

His scrunched features relaxed. With a little smile, he

reached up to touch my face, then stopped halfway. His hand lowered back to his side.

"Fine. Just . . . distracted. This is a big deal and Father sprung it on me unexpectedly. I'm sorry, Bianca. I didn't know or I would—"

"Gio told me. It's fine."

Baxter managed a quick smile. His gaze dropped, then lingered on my now-embroidered shoulders, my waist. A frown creased his brow, but just as quickly disappeared. With a step inside, he pulled me next to him.

"Please, come with me. Gio has . . . prepared you?"

"Yes."

"I'm sorry it has to be this way," he murmured, "but I don't know what to expect from my sisters tonight. Let's get this over with. The sooner I can send you back to the beach house, the better for you."

He offered an arm, and I accepted. Baxter's depth of concern left me uneasy as I pasted a smile on my face and gazed around. The Lady-witch of Alkarra feared no demigod. In truth, I had more power than any of them, and likely more than Baxter. Despite time and work with Ignis, the edges of my god magic still eluded me. If anyone in this room should be feared?

It was me.

I had a feeling his sisters knew that already.

That thought kept my courage high as we advanced into a room of bright, malice-filled eyes.

Oh, how revealing tonight would be.

Chapter Twenty

Gaggles of women formed pockets around the rectangular room, illuminated by carafes of burning sand spaced evenly along the walls. Nine of them would be Baxter's sisters, so who were the rest?

Gauzy dresses and fluttering hair ran amok, most of them gilded with obnoxious sprays of flowers on their dresses. I bit back a giggle. No wonder Baxter had frowned. I'd altered the only consistent fashion trend in the entire room.

Stirring air twined through two sets of open doors with a hint of sea spray. Wild places right outside this close-packed room calmed me. A young woman approached with a grand smile, her gaze fixated on Baxter.

"Baxter," she murmured, hands held out. "So good to see you again."

They pressed palms together, then embraced. She bore little resemblance to him, with her pale skin, freckles, and twiggy body. No amulet was apparent. Her eyes remained fixed on Baxter, though I mentally prepared for her to acknowledge me with a greeting

None came.

"Evangeline. It's good to see you again."

With a pointed turn of her back, she gestured across the room with a question I didn't hear. Forced to step away from me because of her angle, Baxter shuffled to the side. My smile tightened.

Another demigod sister approached, this one more boisterous. Her loud laugh carried as she locked Baxter into a hug. She spoke in rapid-fire Alaysian, but managed to say nothing at all. A crock of burning sand brightened when I gazed on it with bored disinterest, now a few steps away from Baxter.

Embers burst into the air in a colorful gush.

My lips twitched in amusement.

Remember, Ignis purred, *what you are.*

From all sides, eyes stared into me. Curiosity, too. I met each stare as it came. Heads turned. Bodies tilted. Whispers populated. A few bolder sisters held my gaze, then glanced away. None were friendly. Some came with a downright challenge. Whether they saw me as an annoyance or competition, I couldn't be sure.

Almost an hour into the conversations, I realized my god magic hadn't brightened. In a room full of demigods, I should have felt their amulets and power. Intrigued by a new mystery, I peered around.

Did no one wear amulets?

A room of demigods wearing amulets should have set me on fire, particularly with so many present. Nothing felt any different.

Odd.

Baxter spoke in animated tones with yet another sister— the seventh, I believed—that had approached. Words like *mortal responsibility* and *new ideas* and *stability* slid through his lips. Her disinterested gaze deadened with each passing sentence.

I slipped closer to the second set of open doors. A wide

balcony waited outside, limned in moonlight. Cool tufts of air beckoned me out of this stuffy room and into openness again.

While I sidled surreptitiously closer to the outdoors, I turned my attention to the other women in the room. Mortals, yet not servants, like Gio. They wore elegant dresses, but lacked the *allure* of the demigod. Each seemed as at home here as anywhere else. They fluidly moved, laughed, and kindly scolded the demigod sisters.

The women of Ventis' harem, I presumed. Clearly, Ventis honored them. It felt like an ungainly display. A morsel of affection and power and attention against a backdrop of slavery. The mothers may be loved, but they were still in chains.

They are more powerful than you think, Ignis murmured.

Power in chains?

If you look at it that way.

I'm a witch who roams free. How else can I see it?

Such an attitude is not something the mothers would understand. It's not the way we do things here. Is that something you can accept? That the world operates in different ways for different persons?

Daemon surfaced in my mind, followed by the mortals at Ava's collection. His hunger for freedom. The desire for choice and power. Did Ignis justify the way he lived through telling himself that his mortals *wouldn't understand*?

Ignorance was no excuse.

No, I said. *I cannot accept that.*

Ignis fell quiet. A firm gust of wind blew past, carrying a different voice with it.

My children, please be seated. Loyal mothers, take your rightful places.

The shuffling of bodies followed and I cursed under my breath, a longing glance cast to the sprawling patio outside.

So close.

Baxter returned to my side, a hand momentarily on the small

of my back before it dropped away. His tension had magnified undeniably in the passing hour, but so had my own. It expanded between us like a growing storm.

Mortal women slipped over to the farthest table, nearest the patio. They chose chairs that faced the room in an elegant spread. At the end a bassinet stood. A young woman, not much older than me, hovered over it in a protective presence. She peeked past a linen blanket draped over the top and smiled.

The newest son, I presumed?

Another long table waited in the middle of the room for the demigod sisters and Baxter. It faced the mothers, who smiled affectionately at the congregated demigods. Baxter nudged me to the middle. "We honor the mothers," he murmured quickly, "at each beelae. Father requires our utmost respect of his wives."

The demigods stood behind scrolled chairs, then dipped to one knee, which hovered above the ground, toward the mothers. A nudge from Baxter and I followed suit. The mothers spoke in unison.

"Rise."

The demigods slid into their seats.

The sparkling, bright ambience belied the omnipresent hostile undertones. They didn't want me here, and who could blame them? This was a family affair. An opportunity for Baxter to speak frankly with his siblings after years of being away. A chance for them to congratulate him on his success.

Which, now that I thought of it, wasn't clearly defined.

The mission had been successful because he relayed information to his father from Alkarra, but that seemed empty. Those uncomfortable thoughts swirled away so I could focus on the moment. For Baxter, the veritable white sheep in a field of black.

He leaned close. "I asked my sisters not to wear their amulets tonight because I know how uncomfortable the amulets make you. If they seem on edge, that's why."

My breath arrested.

"What?" I hissed.

"There would be at least ten amulets present. Could you tolerate that comfortably?"

"Baxter!" I groaned, putting my forehead in my palm. "Now they're going to *hate* me. No wonder they're glaring at me! I would have dealt with the discomfort."

He frowned. "It'll be fine. We're in my Father's house, so he will protect us. They don't need the magic all the time. Things are already going better than I expected."

"Let me go back to the beach house so you can enjoy this night with your siblings," I pleaded. "They can have their amulets, and you can talk to them without constantly checking on me. I wouldn't feel bad, either. Me being here makes it about me, not you. This should be for you."

"I want you with me."

"I know, but it would be better for you if I wasn't here."

He waved a hand, dismissing that. "Father insisted, anyway."

"What? Why?"

Mortal servants in pristine outfits and starched clothes appeared from a doorway in the far wall to the right, drawing his attention. Heavy platters loaded with bright red lobster tails, prawns speckled with sliced green onions, shells packed with what appeared to be minced fish, and sliced fruit, were arranged in bright flashes of color. The mortals' cheeks, reddened from exertion, fixed into smiles as they set the trays down, then they bustled back for more.

When the last tray had been delivered, the mortals scurried back through the doorway.

Eating began.

Spoons and forks served the food magically. Small scoops appeared on my plate in bite-sized delights. Golden-fried scallops topped with a white dollop of sauce. Bread folded into a petaled bowl, then glazed with something sticky and sweet. A white fruit the size of my thumb peeled back to reveal a bright coral interior.

Glimmering silver forks, a tiny spoon, a petite knife, lay in lines above my plate. A drink with bubbles filled a goblet on my left-hand side, then another appeared with a yellow, milk-like substance.

I tried to take it all in.

A demigod sister on Baxter's other side spoke. She wore a fluffy dress that stopped mid-thigh in layers of emerald and fuchsia. To my left sat Amorette.

Unable to help myself, I turned to face her.

"I'm sorry," I said quietly. "I didn't ask Baxter to tell you to leave your amulets behind. I would never have asked such a thing. It must be uncomfortable."

Amorette froze, eyed me, then turned back to her plate. She said nothing. I reached for a fork, fiddled with it, and set it back down. With both wrists leaning against the edge of the table, I turned back to her. When I spoke, I did so quietly, so Baxter wouldn't overhear.

"Why do you hate me?"

Amorette reached for her goblet, had a sip, and set it back down. "It's not hatred," she murmured, "as much as dislike. We have no reason to trust you except for Baxter's word."

"You wouldn't find out for yourself?"

She shrugged. Her lips barely moved. She kept her focus on the plate, gaze fixated. "It's likely you'll die while you're here, so why bother?"

I almost choked.

She continued.

"Demigods aren't close, at least not across gods. We don't know other demigods well. Regardless, we can't—and won't—ignore the fact that witches have lost or destroyed demigod amulets."

"They invaded my land and attempted to take over."

Amorette considered that. With a dainty motion, she sliced through a flaky piece of fish and let it peel off to the side. A scoop of a creamy substance, topped by a crackling, golden layer like sand, appeared from a spoon.

"While that's also true," Amorette murmured, "it doesn't change the fact that amulets are missing, demigods are dead, and Baxter flaunts a witch from Alkarra like a new toy. You are everything we never wanted in Alaysia."

A symbol.

No, a weapon.

Nevermind that the demigods brought this on themselves—Amorette and her sisters didn't seem to care about that. Her words remained with me as she turned her back to close the conversation. Any possible excitement over the delectable food and luscious smells fled. A hollow feeling replaced the hunger.

Across the way, a squalling sound issued. The young mother reached into the bassinet, pulling an infant out. Chubby fists and a reddened face came next. A cooing sound rippled down the entire demigod table. When a breeze tickled by, the infant soothed.

I forced myself to pick the fork back up.

This is impossible, I said to Ignis in a fit of frustration. *They've already decided to hate me and it's not my fault. Why should I try any harder?*

Only, he murmured, *the children of Ventis. Not all of our demigods are so closed off.*

You're trying to tell me it would be better in your kingdom? I sent a firm scoff. *Your children are the ones that died or lost amulets at my hand. I hardly think they'd welcome me with open arms. They'd probably throw Luppentonisa's remains at me.*

You've met all my children, have you? You who are frustrated at Amorette's closed-mindedness and unwillingness to let you prove yourself. You hold your own prejudice.

I sucked in a breath.

Duly chastised, I replied, *You're right. I apologize. Perhaps your children are more open than these.*

No apology required, Lady-witch. In my kingdom, you would hold the highest of honors.

Before I could ask what that meant, ten mortals marched into the dining room. They stood in two lines, one in front of the other, sorted by the tallest in the back. Once assembled, the front row began to sing. Sopranos and altos warbled into the room, joined moments later by deeper baritones in the back. A hush fell.

I picked at a spongy-looking square, but it tasted like ash. The drinks held no flavor. The sea spray no tang anymore.

The glittering grandeur of the *Rostina lu Lune* melted away. Fantastical or not, this place hid a rotten heart. At my side, Baxter chattered happily with his sister. Another rotated through, taking her place. My lips tingled as I thought of the kiss in Baxter's rooms, but it faded quickly this time. An empty place stirred near my heart, a hollow spot.

Trust no one, Prana reminded me from the depths of memory, *and remember your forest.*

* * *

Four hours.

Five courses.

Six shows from mortals.

A stint of wine tasting.

The *beelae* crawled into the early morning hours, well past midnight. I stepped outside, my cheeks flushed with heat. Demigods and mortals lingered with impressive social resilience, though the edge in the air had faded when the wine was passed. I pretended to sip. When Baxter glanced over, I'd smile to reassure him, then wished the time didn't crawl by. His sisters kept him engrossed in conversation for the duration of the *beelae*.

Intentional strategy, I presumed.

Finally on the patio, and all alone, the ocean breeze pressed on my heated skin with a cooling touch. I leaned into it, relieved and refreshed. Waves crashing below heartened my limp courage.

I had no reason to give up all hope. This was one night against many, and everyone had bad days. Wonders existed in Alaysia. Many, in fact. Baxter's sisters were not one of those wonders.

Over the course of the meal, I understood their resentment had little to do with lacking amulets and everything to do with what I represented. The Lady-witch of Alkarra. Weapon of the gods.

Hadn't Tipa warned me?

The milling of mothers and demigods felt far away on the patio. The balcony railing was cool under my hot palms as I leaned against it, wondering if I should leave. How long could this last, anyway?

Baxter's tightening smile, and the sense of disappointment in . . . something . . . that he was less able to hide as the night wore on, disheartened me. Was he irritated with me? His sisters? The situation? I couldn't be sure. His conversations with his sisters fell on deaf ears. His desire for better things, for change in Alaysia.

They didn't listen.

The blending of the two worlds came with a more impressive struggle than I ever expected.

A difficult evening, Ignis said.

"Very."

You don't love conversation for the sake of conversation?

A snarky laugh followed.

"I don't mind conversation," I countered, then sighed. "I just know when I'm not wanted."

Thoughtful silence followed. Unable to help myself, I aired my thoughts. "Baxter loves this life, though. He's driven by politics and dinners and events and working the room in favor of his beliefs and goals. I want to go run through my forest and eat bread in my cottage. This is not me."

Your self-awareness is impressive. Yet, love is about discomfort. We grow into new creatures together.

"Love?" I squeaked.

Lust, then?

Either word felt strange on my emotional palette. I swirled back through that thought, erasing it for now. Tonight wasn't the right time to tackle the way I felt about Baxter. Too many other concerns hung over that question. It wouldn't be fair to answer.

"Regardless, why doesn't Baxter let me go back to the beach house so no one is miserable?"

He cares for you and wants you at his side. Perhaps it's how he shows—or feels—his affection.

"You're right."

How do you show attachment?

My brow wrinkled. "I haven't thought of it before."

Vapor collected in front of me, revealing a familiar scene. Letum Wood. High-stretching trees. It dissipated, and my heart yearned for it again.

"Yes," I whispered. "The forest."

Parting is built into everything.

For some reason, his vague comment struck me as insufferably funny, even when it had no humorous base. I giggled, shoulders shaking. Nearby, a torch brightened.

Reality sobered me quickly.

"Is it enough to care for someone else? Can the basis of a relationship be built on respect and admiration instead of . . ."

I trailed away, unable to complete the thought. Such an act would require me to define my feelings for Baxter, a truth that eluded me.

I believe so.

"Which is more powerful?"

Depends on who you are, I suppose.

I pressed my cooling hands to my cheeks, grateful to be out of the crowd. I tilted my head, closed my eyes, and reveled in the breeze. Though I'd nibbled at food, I felt overstuffed. The too-hot feeling subsided. Long enough in this calm, and I'd fall asleep.

A pressured tone came to Ignis' voice. *Your night is about to get more difficult, Lady-witch.*

My eyes flew open, alerted more by the tension in his voice than what he said. "What is it?"

Visitors are incoming. Don't speak. They're close enough to hear you.

Who?

The children of Tontes. You can't see them, but they approach. Five, I think. If I'm correct, he sent his strongest sons, all with amulets.

Wind fluttered my hair as I spun around, making a show of watching inside. Clouds scudded past a low moon in intermittent shadows, but nothing appeared out of the usual at the *Rostina lu Lune.*

Where?

They approach from below, invisibly. You should feel the amulets in moments.

Heat elevated my blood.I felt hot. Itchy. The power swelled inside all at once, like magma.

Yep, I internally gasped. *Feeling it now.*

Tontes must somehow be aware that the demigods inside are not wearing amulets, and he wants to attempt to take you.

From the Rostina lu Lune?

There is no accounting for taste, he muttered. *Tontes has always been proud and insufferable, but stealing a guest of Ventis from his Rostina is something else altogether.*

Ventis will stop this, I presume?

Not likely.

Why not?

With Ventis? One never knows.

The agitation of god magic affected me more than I liked. Magical ardor swarmed from the inside out, too agonizing to tolerate for long. It had never been this reactive or alive. Not in Papa's office with Bram and his demigod followers, nor on the beach days ago. Why had it become so powerfully hot?

Shall we deal with this together?

Questions, combined with the restlessness of too much god magic, forced me to answer the only way I could.

"You bet we will."

Do as I say and trust your instincts. We want to save the mortals and demigods inside, but also make a statement of your power against Tontes. One that ensures he won't try this again. Tonight will be our greatest challenge yet.

Chapter Twenty-One

A rustle of fabric gave the demigods away.

With god magic frenzied in my blood, I magicked myself to the middle of the expansive patio. The moonlit sea faced me. A lovely night for an approaching bloodbath.

Five, Ignis murmured. *Fanned around you at mostly even paces. All are on the patio right now.*

Despite his report, I saw nothing. Heat continued to build under my skin as they approached, uncomfortably hot.

With the magic, I sent a thought to Baxter.

Get all the mortals out of the beelae now. Tell your sisters to find their amulets and return. The children of Tontes are on the patio. I will distract them while you arm yourselves.

A beat of silence passed. I stepped back when a scuffle came from the right. Inside, a quieting. Time paused.

Now, Baxter!

Scrambling issued from the banquet. Chairs scraping. Over-confident voices calling out orders. The lack of chaos—or gaiety—would also clue in the children of Tontes. Didn't matter anymore. If I kept the attackers busy, the mortals inside would be safe.

"You're back, Neel?" I called.

Neel appeared with a bright smile ten paces away. His pearly teeth flashed in the moonlight, hair ruffled.

"Since you can be hard to convince," he murmured, "we thought we'd give you one last chance to come to the more powerful side of Alaysia."

Two flank him on each side, Ignis murmured.

Same demigods as before?

Different.

Can we take five at the same time, you think? We managed three, but only barely.

From a logistical perspective, doubtful.

Neel advanced a step. When a trickle of wind slipped by, I braced myself. Ventis would say something, surely. Command them to leave.

No such order came.

Plans flashed through my mind. Five demigods. Five amulets. Patio off the sand. No visible weapons to call on. Viveet returned to my hand with a thought, but issued no hint of magic this time. No illumination. No friendly blue fire. That, I'd have to deal with later. I searched my memories for something—anything—to create a solid plan of attack. Papa hadn't trained me to stand against five demigods.

Who needs training, Ignis said with a thrill of delight, *when one has powerful magic?*

"So," Neel drawled. "What'll it be, Lady-witch? Will you come with us now, or are you going to make this bloody?"

I scoffed. "The only blood I remember from last time is yours, Neel. Did your brothers recover?"

He grinned. There was entirely too much confidence and a low-level mania in the gesture. My stomach curled inward like a dying flower. Something wasn't right here. The feeling of missing a step jostled me from the inside out.

What don't we see? I asked Ignis.

Currently attempting to figure that out.

"Beautifully recovered, thanks to god magic," Neel called. "As always. Is that a no, then? You won't be coming with us to meet our father?"

Torches flared to twice their size behind me, roaring with a loud, growling sound. Neel startled, gazing past my shoulder, then back to me. I suppressed a smile.

"That's a no," I murmured.

He held out his hands in a helpless gesture. A tsking sound came from his teeth. "Too bad," he murmured. He tilted to the side, hands cupped around his mouth, and shouted. "Bring them back!"

A choking sensation stole my breath as I glanced over my shoulder, past the patio and back into the banquet room. Baxter, Amorette, the demigod sisters, and all the fleeing mortals shuffled back inside from the hallways that splintered off. More sons of Tontes strolled in behind them, putting our new count at eight.

Ropes bound Ventis' demigods and mortals. Gags filled their mouths. Murderous rage flashed over Baxter's face as other sons of Tontes shoved him to his knees in the doorway to face me.

I forced my breathing to calm.

Right.

No amulets.

Fifty-something hostages.

Intriguing, Ignis murmured.

Where. Is. Ventis?

One never knows.

"Since you insist on doing this the hard way," Neel drawled, "we shall accommodate. You have an obvious weakness for saving others, so we thought we could work that to our advantage. You come with us to meet our father, or all of them die."

"You would do that in Ventis' home?"

Neel scoffed.

Humidity built in the air, broiling overhead. Stars disappeared behind a mat of tenebrous clouds, which bubbled higher, expanded with frightening speed. They blocked the moon in a breath. Thunder growled, distant and low.

Neel's cat-like smile meant he wouldn't hesitate a moment to dispose of any one of these mortals or demigods.

Why is Ventis allowing this? Can't he blow them away in a gale, or something?

A positively wonderful question, he retorted with an edge in his voice. *Until that is discovered, caution is best. Let's test what we can do, but I won't have you hurt. All of his women can die, for all I care, but I won't let you be at risk.*

Whether his concern was born from a sincere desire to keep me safe, or to protect me as a weapon, I couldn't tell. Either way, I took it as a potential advantage in our favor. The four other demigods made themselves known. The good gods, but they were massive, hulking beasts.

Did the sons of Tontes grow to twice the size of other demigods?

"So what is it, Lady-witch?" Neel snapped.

Can't you just take them all out now? I asked. *God of fire, and all that.*

Neither Ventis nor Tontes would look kindly on a mass killing of demigods before attempting to talk them back to their holes, Ignis countered. *If it comes to it, wholesale slaughter is an option, but one I'd rather entertain as a last-moment scenario.*

Right. They look like the kind of demigods that want to talk.

He chuckled.

I rolled my eyes. No matter. I'd deal with Ventis later. For now, I had demigods to handle.

With magic, I moved closer to the *Rostina*. The five of them tightened their formation, fanning more widely behind Neel. Despite their behemoth sizes, I couldn't help but feel that Neel was the true risk. They might have brawn, but I knew his speed. He carried himself like a fighter. Tense, agile, and ready. The others? Distraction. Brute force, if needed.

"What does Tontes want with me?" I shouted over a burst of thunder. It swept closer, born on swift winds.

Neel shook his head. "Not this time," he called. "No stalling, no distractions. We have you right where we want you. You come, or they die."

A cry rippled across the patio. I shifted to the side to find Amorette in the hands of another brute. He cocked an arm around her neck and tightened. Her face bloomed with red. She scratched at his arm with her nails.

I took myself to the demigod with a thought and dug Viveet's sharp blade into the spot where his kidney waited.

"Let her go," I growled.

He released her. Amorette toppled, then scrambled free. Ropes appeared around her stomach, slamming her into the wall. She grunted, her features twisted in a grimace. Next to her, Baxter seethed. A knife pressed to his throat, a thin line of blood already visible from the blade. He regarded me with wild, white-rimmed eyes.

I'm fine, I said to him with a thought. *I've got this handled.*

He tried to shake his head, but the knife dug into the sensitive skin that pulsed. I glowered and the demigod stopped.

Neel appeared inside with a flash. "Thank you," he purred. "You just made our job a lot easier."

Too late, I realized my mistake.

The doors to the balcony slammed shut as rain descended. Thunder clapped. Lightning streaked. Hail the size of my thumbnail slammed into the *Rostina* doors, thrumming. I'd just put myself into a closed room with exits that I didn't control.

Their exact plan.

Whoops, Ignis murmured, with entirely too much glee. *Looks like we'll have to take them down one at a time.*

Why didn't you warn me?

Because you know what you're doing. Trust yourself, Lady-witch, for I trust you completely. Now, let's see what we can make happen here, eh?

His excitement didn't curb my frustration. A bloodlusting god in my head, too much power in my body, and a room full of staring eyes. Not my ideal fight, and certainly not one that Papa had trained me for.

Teeth gritted, I moved to the wall with god magic, placing my back where I knew no one could come from behind. It left the room sprawling in front of me to the left and right. In their haste to escape earlier, chairs had been kicked aside. A few broken clay plates and glass littered the floor as potential hazards for fleeing feet.

I kept Viveet extended out in front of me. No illumination of her ivy glowed near the hilt, then ebbed. Goddess magic absent or not, I felt comforted by her presence all the same.

"Position yourselves amongst the mortals," Neel called as he side-stepped in front of me. His legs braced. "Make it so she can't single you out without harming one of them. I'm sure Ventis wouldn't appreciate you killing one of his wives, Lady-witch?"

A challenge.

Or a test of my precision with the god magic.

I glowered at him.

A cudgel appeared in his right hand. A thick piece of drift-wood embedded with a jagged, black stone at the top, like a morning star. Shards of glass dotted the handle around his grip. Dried blood flaked free as he spun it around at his side, twirling it with an agile wrist. He hefted it toward me with another confident smile.

Time for the Head of the Sisterhood to do what I did best.

Clever surprises.

I disappeared.

Neel shifted his weight to his back leg and tightened, holding himself before I advanced. Instead of attacking straight on, I magicked myself to the side and came at his weapon arm. At the last moment, he spun toward me. I deflected with Viveet. A crack of glass splintering off his cudgel hissed along Viveet's shaft as I shoved it to the side.

I stepped back.

He switched hands.

"I'll stay visible for you," he called in a mocking tone. "The Lady-witch of Alkarra that can't even fight a demigod. Are you the one they sent to save your land? If we kill you, all the better, I say."

With magic, I sent a rope of fire to snag his wrist. Neel deflected it off with a shake, cut the whip in half in a swing, and returned into a fighting stance. The skin around his right wrist sizzled, and the smell of burnt flesh filled the air. He didn't seem to notice. Seconds later, the skin repaired.

How badly do they want me alive? I asked.

Knowing Tontes? Very much so. But god magic can heal almost any wound you sustain, so long as it happens quickly enough. They would be willing to hurt and maim and save over and over again.

"Dark buggers," I muttered.

"Come at me, Lady-witch of Alkarra!" Neel screamed, face flushed to crimson. He tossed the cudgel back and forth and swung it around. A mortal woman ducked with a squeal, a second shy of having her neck cut in half. "Come at me!"

I reappeared to draw his attention away from the screaming hostages. He spun toward me with a wild grin and charged. Burning sand appeared on the ground between us, each granule glowing with fire. He stormed through them, flames licking his feet. A howl of shock bore him out of the fire pit, but I commanded the flames to follow. They greedily consumed his legs.

Water doused the fire. Neel grimaced, teeth clenched as he stepped away from the watery, char residuals. Just as quickly, his smoldering shoes and pants repaired themselves. The scent of burnt flesh disappeared. He growled, teeth bared.

On your left.

I ducked, and swung Viveet high. She missed a demigod as he feinted from that direction. A third demigod barreled from the right, invisible at first. As he leapt over me, I stood, infusing magic into my legs for greater strength. The demigod rolled across the back of my shoulders, then flipped into the wall, head-first. He hit with a sickening crack against the doorframe and fell to the floor, inert.

Ignis pealed with laughter.

The sons of Tontes went into full attack. Neel stood back, barely visible between incoming, massive bodies. I'd injure one, only to have him disappear. Another would charge, sometimes two. The magic—maybe Ignis himself—infused speed into each move of mine. My hits slammed harder than any demigod. My legs spun more quickly, my jumps soared so high. The floor cracked beneath the demigods when I shoved them down.

Yet, the demigods that had been injured returned, an endless cycle. They swapped with demigods guarding the hostages, and fresh bodies followed.

This, I panted to Ignis as I bridged backward onto my hands to dodge another flying fist, *needs to stop. Nothing will ever be accomplished.*

We're tiring their magic. How do you feel?

Magic yanked me to the floor before a flying plate slammed into my temple. I popped back to my feet, whirling away from a side assault.

Magically? Fine.

Time for some creativity.

With a break of two seconds that came in between the next attacks, I scrutinized the room. The children of Tontes remained embedded within the mortals, but that could be worked with. In a single command, I cast burning nets. Lines of vermillion combined into a tangled, hot weave that dropped on each demigod.

They flailed and screamed. The scorching ropes draped around them in a sizzling hug. Mortals peeled back, tripping in their haste to get away from the yowling demigods. Lightning struck somewhere nearby, illuminating the room with a frenzy of light.

"Is your Father displeased?" I called.

Neel's eyes brightened, then dimmed. He snarled, attempting to fight free of the ropes. Demigods all over the room cast water on the nets, quenching them. Others magicked them away.

Keep them using their magic, Ignis said hurriedly. *They'll tire. They'll run out and have to leave.*

How long will that take?

I don't know.

Don't move! I commanded the mortals and demigod sisters through the magic, so the children of Tontes wouldn't hear. *Stay where you are!*

The mortals and demigod sisters froze, eyes wide. They stared at me in terror. Steam and smoke curled through the room, acrid and damp. At my command, the ground turned into squares of fire, like a maze of coals. A mosaic of the way I felt inside. The burning heat, so overwhelming. Too much god power for me.

Too many amulets.

Demigods stumbled onto the squares. Agonized wails followed as they tripped, falling onto the sizzling tiles. One demigod magicked away, face veiled with blisters. Another disappeared, hair on fire. With god magic, I released all the bonds on the mortals and sisters.

"Go!" I commanded. "Get out of here!"

Cooled pathways appeared through the superheated floor. As ropes dropped from wrists and legs, women scuttled free. They dashed into the hall. The distant wail of the baby disappeared as the mothers ran for their lives.

Three of Tontes' sons have left, Ignis said. *Five remain.*

Neel stalked toward me, feet protected by something as he crossed the floor. Water flooded the room from the far corner, sousing the burning ground. Viveet sweated against my palm from the moisture in the air. Outside, the rocketing thunder continued to roll around like marbles in a metal drum.

One second Neel glowered at me, the next he was gone.

Drop to the floor.

The command almost came too late. With god magic to give me speed, I flattened myself. Neel flew overhead in a failed attempt to tackle me. He would have driven me into the glass doors, impaling me with shards. I popped back to my feet, but he whirled around, cudgel swinging wider than it should have.

At the last moment, he released the weapon. I shifted to the side too late.

Pain tore through my thigh.

I gasped. Heat flooded my hand as I reached to my left leg. Blood chugged from an open wound, spilling on the sand floor. I pressed my hand over it. The filleted skin peeled back, glittering with a piece of glass embedded inside.

Ignis!

I see, Lady-witch.

The piece of glass soared out of the wound and into the air, clattering to the ground several paces away. Fire concentrated over it, burning like a wild thing. Two of the mortal women screamed. Near the doors, one of Baxter's sisters attempted to herd them into the twisting hallways of the *Rostina lu Lune.*

In the corner, Baxter had overtaken Neel. Blood smeared Baxter's left cheek as he ducked another punch, and the fist flew into the wall with a crack. Neel grunted, but Baxter uppercut him in the gut. He doubled over, wheezing.

Hold the wound tight, Ignis instructed. *The magic will heal you.*

Blood slowed between my fingers as I clenched my hand around the broken skin. Pain still lanced through me in sharp spikes, all the way to my hip. The skin began to knit together, painfully so, as if someone had taken thousands of needles into the open wound.

Another shrill cry near the door grated in my ears. A mortal woman, accosted by a son of Tontes as she tried to escape. Lightheaded, I sent cages over the tops of the demigods that harassed the remaining demigod sisters. The bars sizzled with heat. One demigod attempted to douse the resulting fire, but only a few droplets of water appeared.

Was his amulet running out of magic?

The constant presence of thunder drove chaos into the room. Healed back together now, but still bright with pain, I leapt to my feet. Sticky blood coated my hands. My hair pasted to my forehead from the humid room. Children of Tontes disappeared one at a time from the cages. Two of them came back. Three didn't.

Three left, Lady-witch.

Baxter gasped on the ground as he attempted to stand. Neel glowered at me from across the room, near Baxter. Yelling at the top of his lungs, his entire body trembling with rage, he held up both arms. The world shifted to the side, rocking the castle as percussive thunder slammed into the *Rostina lu Lune.* The building shuddered. Cracks formed in the ground, climbed walls. Lightning split the sky wide open, hitting bolt after bolt after bolt in unrelenting sequence. Rain lashed the windows, sending floods down the walls.

My ears rang.

I couldn't think.

Sand trickled into my hair. Open mouths indicated that the remaining demigod sisters and mortals were screaming, but I couldn't hear over the thunder. My body clacked together from the force of Tontes' power in Neel's hands.

I brought Viveet higher in guard and braced myself.

Neel advanced.

Who is stronger? I asked Ignis.

You, Lady-witch. Definitely you.

Time slowed.

Neel closed in on me. I felt all the way to the bottom of the god magic and perceived no end. No fatigue. No tiring of power. Instead, a current of something else lived there.

Energy.

Connection.

Sheer glory.

In a moment of clarity, I understood what it meant. Knew exactly what Ignis had been trying to understand all this time. I was more than a living amulet. We didn't just share a magic.

I was a conduit *for* his magic.

With his permission, I could access the direct power of the gods.

You understand, he murmured.

Terror descended with the realization. I stared at Neel, comprehending the horrifying implications. The danger. The torrential harm that this could scourge the land with. A terrible beauty, this magic. A shining beacon of power and death and hope.

I tugged on it.

Magma appeared in the cracks along the walls, the floors. It bubbled to the surface, flowing free. With a thought, I accessed the power more clearly. I sent the mortals out of the room and deposited them safely on the portico. The daughters of Ventis went to different parts of the castle, farther away. Baxter disappeared as cascades of bright red magma spurted into the room, racing toward Neel. It consumed him in a wave, splashing. He screamed, then silenced in a second, dead under the burning, melted rock.

Another demigod attempted to conjure water, but the magma vaporized it with a hiss. The demigod sputtered, disappearing with a scream as magma claimed a leg. The power moved quickly now, bowling over me. Through me. Into the room it charged, a presence unto itself. I stood so powerfully, cradled by the heat and magic. It crackled to life through me.

Was I in control or was Ignis?

Was there a difference?

I lifted above the flowing heat. The air wavered as the last of the demigods disappeared.

With the amulets gone, the pressure in my body wound down. Distress cascaded into relief. The fever ebbed. Breathing hard, I commanded all the magma back to Ignis' kingdom with a wave. It curled away, disappearing in black lines until the pyroclastic force vanished.

The ransacked room remained. Charred floor. Broken walls. Plates, utensils, food tossed around, smearing the chandeliers. Scorched sand littered the floor. Spiderweb lines snaked through the walls, and the world still trembled. Outside, the storm lashed more ferociously than ever.

I collapsed.

Lady-witch?

As the pain ebbed, so did the power. God magic leaked away from me, spilling into ether. The connection closed, like a narrowing flame that snuffed out. A long, black tunnel appeared around my vision. I blinked, trying to make sense of the voice calling my name.

An indomitable presence stood near as Baxter skidded to a

stop in the doorway. I'd sent him away, now he returned. Fear filled his face.

A touch on my shoulder, gentle as a bird wing.

Lady-witch, I have you.

The room grew long. Time ceased. I rocked back, blinking, as the darkness around the edges began to close in. Baxter's terrified expression heightened when I lifted into the air, cradled. Something incandescent embraced me with a warmth that didn't burn.

Baxter shouted my name as he rushed closer.

The *Rostina lu Lune* faded to black.

Chapter Twenty-Two

Softness cradled me.

Gentle linen on my cheek. Bedding underneath my left hip bone, where I slept. My arms curled around a pillow that I held close to my chest. With a sigh, I allowed sleep to drift away. Memory resurfaced.

My eyes shot open.

Sultry heat sprawled around me, manifested by mist in the air, so thick I could bat it aside. A canopy of greenery extended upward, but stopped in firm lines. Blinking, I realized a dome separated the rainforest from where I lay.

I sat up.

I sprawled in a bed in the middle of a circle, covered by glass that extended hundreds of paces wide. It ended on what appeared to be a view of the ocean. Memories of the Saltu Jungle in the Eastern Network flittered through my mind, then back out.

This was the same, but oh, so different.

The bed where I slept was so big I had to crawl across it, then slide down. It stood far above the ground—the top of the mattress reached my shoulder. Quietly, I padded away, down the space.

Water sluiced down the sides of the glass, which peeked into the deepest heart of this forest. Strange flowers. Bugs the size of my hand. Life teemed around the dome, heady and lush.

My fingertips trailed along the side of the glass. Exotic flowers unfurled in a yellow-orange grouping, with black centers. A plant with teeth opened and closed slowly, a trap for water that trickled out of sight down a long, green stalk. A bug with ten eyes, four long arms, and a bright azure body skittered away, sliding down the side of the dome.

My breath caught at the sheer majesty. A density of magic, I could *feel* it.

"What is this place?" I whispered.

Ignis remained nearby, I could sense him now. I couldn't see him, yet he was palpable all the same.

This is the heart of my kingdom.

"The heart?"

No demigod, witch, or mortal has had the honor of gracing my home. You are the first for many things.

"Not even your partners?"

They had their own accommodations, apart from mine.

Ignis had taken me away from the *Rostina lu Lune*. Ignis, who had never revealed himself to anyone that wasn't a partner. My fingers retracted from the glass, daunted by what he shared. I wanted to ask why, but didn't dare.

I slipped closer to the light along the far wall, where fresh air filtered inside. A table structured out of ochre wood stood in the way, filled with an array of food. Round bread the size of my palm, puffy in the middle. A red paste, swirled with light green seeds in a spiral design. What appeared to be jam, or sauce, filled smaller crocks around it like falling petals.

I grabbed a piece of the bread and continued on.

As I walked, I tore a piece free, balling it up before popping it in my mouth. It was soft between my teeth, not at all gritty or floury. It melted, like butter held it together.

I trailed my fingers along a vine that dropped on the other side of the dome. Roseate flowers twirled around the sides in coils as small as my pinky nail. A drop of water landed on one of the ends, pasting it to the glass.

I kept going.

"You're the god of fire," I murmured, "so why such greenery?"

Fire, he replied, *feeds all the beauty in the world.*

A quiet contemplation filled his voice. He spoke less jauntily than usual, though I wondered if he just wanted to give me space. I padded closer to the opening ahead, a broadening light in the overgrown jungle. The canopy gave some comfort, but this forest was unnervingly thick. Letum Wood had room to breathe and run. This? This was magic run amok, tangled in earth, bound together.

Ignis remained quiet as I worked my way to the end. Finally, a seascape unfolded. I stopped at the mouth of the dome, arrested.

A world of volcanoes surrounded me in a ring of fire. Blowing magma gave way to lush green mountainscapes that plunged into the sea. Plumes of smoke belched from distant terrains. Above all, heat opened the world, thickened the air.

"Your kingdom," I whispered.

Mine.

Until I saw his world, Ignis's depth of power remained elusive. Weak by reputation, now. A false rumor, certainly. Standing here made it clear that Ignis was a god. The majesty of his volcanoes dwarfed me. The gray-and-ebony streaks of cooling magma as it seethed, flowing in bright lava arteries to the ocean.

Dotting the landscape were other fiery structures. Those volcanoes were far smaller, speckled in the greenish-blue water like sea freckles. Other islands. Had Bram or Jote been in charge of any of them?

"How much of what I can see is yours?"

Anything not ocean, for as far as you can see, and then some, is my kingdom. The brothers keep our space from each other. Our sisters never leave Alkarra to bother us here, which is how we prefer it. As siblings, we're not that close.

"So I've noticed."

My sisters are not so different.

"Yes," I muttered wryly, "Prana was quite affectionate and loving toward her sisters."

He laughed. A gentle motion slipped behind me, like a hand trailing across the small of my back. When I glanced over my shoulder, nothing could be seen. I turned back to the vista, my heart locked in my throat.

"It's . . . breathtaking."

It can be yours.

An empty space opened inside me, warring with the thrill of such a land. The desire to stay, my longing to go back to Alkarra, were at war with such rampant wildness. Freedom. Power. The quiet plea in his voice only enhanced my confusion, burdened from the memories of last night.

The way we battled together.

The depth of power at my disposal.

All of Alkarra to save, he murmured gently.

The reminder sent my heart into a whirl of imaginings that ended in the same place as all the rest.

"Tontes fears me now, doesn't he?" I whispered.

Yes.

A pause.

He actively seeks to destroy you. He has already sent more of his children into Alaysia to find you, to kill you.

"What was he doing before?" I asked with a morbid spike of

amusement. Neel's rampaging snarl, the promise of death in his gaze, made me shudder.

The raw power from the ring of fire awed me.

Testing you.

The truth of that sank all the way through my toes.

"You have been as well."

Yes, and now we know what you're truly capable of. We could fight Tontes together and win, he said lightly, with a curl of pleasure, *which means I fear for you now more than ever. Yesterday, I realized . . .*

He trailed away, entirely too serious for a god that all but laughed his way through the battle only hours ago.

"Did it surprise you, too?" I asked, recalling the moment I realized my power as a conduit.

He silenced.

Perhaps. I feared for you at the end. That surprised me more.

I sank to the ground and pulled my knees to my chest. My chin rested on top, peering out. My legs felt like a barrier to hold back Alaysia. The edge of my middle finger trailed the scar on my thigh, a burning testament. A memory, always with me. I wrapped my arms around my legs to have something to hold onto, and watched the waves crash into the shore far, far below.

Are you in pain? Did you heal?

"No pain."

A relief.

Frustration tripled through me. I pulled my bottom lip through my teeth, then asked through a heavy breath, "What does this mean, Ignis? Something happened yesterday. I . . . the god magic in me . . . our connection . . . it's bigger than I thought."

Indeed.

Another long pause swelled between us. I leaned back on my palms, stretching my legs into a ribbon of sunshine. If he didn't have the words to define it, I wouldn't either. Instead, I let it loll inside like a ball.

A secret.

Speaking of secrets.

I reached into my pocket, startled to connect with the chain of Samthanruadanosa, still there after all that occurred last night. I still didn't know why I'd taken it, but something about having it close had felt right. Now, maybe I understood.

"I have something for you."

The amulet dropped out of my pocket when I pulled it free. It waved back and forth, dangling over my legs. The bright claret facets, stunning in the sunlight, drew my eye. It wasn't Luppen-tonisa—too different with the size and general shape—but it could have been for the cascading heart fire.

Trapped flames.

Ignis spoke in a whisper. *Samthanruadanosa.*

Carefully, I lowered Samthanruadanosa to a cleft in the ground next to me. It lay back, rolled, and then stilled. The chain clinked as I dropped it into place next to the amulet.

"I took it from Bram during the fight in Papa's office."

You've had it all this time.

"You didn't know?"

No. Despite what you think, I have not always been spying on you.

My heart raced.

A quiet silence followed. I drew in a deep breath, grateful for the chance to think. With Samthanruadanosa, he had enough amulets to keep his mortals and demigods alive and happy. No destruction of his kingdom would happen if I left. Giving the amulet back to Ignis might have been a mistake, the surrender of my only bargaining chip.

But I didn't think so.

Already, I felt lighter. Different. Freed from a silent burden.

Why have you given it to me?

"To protect you. This." My hand waved out. "All of them."

You could have given it to Ventis or Gelas or Tontes.

"I know."

This . . .

The distant sound of waves was the only thing I could hear as I silently finished the thought for him.

This changes everything, I thought.

My children tried to destroy your home. Luppentonisa irrevocably changed your life, and perhaps not in ways you wanted. Yet, you give me this amulet when you could use it to your gain?

"Yes."

The amulet disappeared. For a second, I felt its absence in my chest. A vague stir and disheartened quiver that faded away. As if the god magic recognized the withdrawal of a friend.

Another rolling span of quiet followed.

"I'm sorry about Luppentonisa," I said, when I couldn't stand it any longer. "It was a lovely amulet. When it wasn't, you know, locking up my goddess magic. After all I have learned here, I'm sad to have destroyed it." My fingers curled over my heart. "I'm honored to hold its power inside."

Thank you.

His whisper trailed away, swept on a breeze. The familiar burn of his presence hesitated just behind me. I could sense that if I leaned back, I'd touch the god of fire. Instead, I gripped my knees. A trail of fire graced my shoulder, then faded.

"What now?"

His voice sounded farther away, as if he'd withdrawn. Business lined it, crisp and tight. *Trouble stirs in Tontes' kingdom. The reckoning approaches.*

"What reckoning?"

The reckoning of magic that has built up to this moment. Now that Tontes is properly riled, the three of us will need to make a stand against him. Ventis and Gelas will want to know your decision soon.

"My choice between you and Deasylva?"

Yes.

Pain stirred in my chest at the thought. I wasn't ready. I'd never be ready. The simplification of such a problem made me want to laugh, as if I chose bread at a market instead of the fate of two different, beautiful lands.

I can protect you, my Lady-witch.

"I know."

This could be ours.

The word tangled me up inside. *Ours.* He spoke of something beyond Alkarra now. Life with him. Life *here.* Would it be so terrible? No. With Ignis, I'd be safe. Alkarra would be safe. There was magic and land to explore. Power to share and distribute more fairly to those who had none.

A world to change.

"I see," I whispered.

The choice is yours. I bid you to remember that the magicks cannot coexist forever. You could run back to Alkarra and attempt to forget all of this, forget me, but eventually . . .

He simultaneously squelched any desire I might have to return to Alkarra and hide from this problem, while also reminding me that time wasn't my friend. With Tontes on the prowl, a decision had to be made.

Soon.

"If I stay with you, will Tontes have the power to destroy Alkarra?"

No, because we will save it together.

"If I don't stay with you?"

It would be best for Alkarra, Ignis said gently, *if you didn't delay your decision too long. Tontes seeks Alkarra above all else, even you.*

"I understand."

Do you trust me, Lady-witch?

"Yes."

Something rippled through me at the immediate reply. It was true. Entirely true. Wholly true. I could hardly believe it, but knew that I felt it in my bones.

Affection bled through his tone.

This pleases me greatly. So long as your allegiance becomes mine, your life is yours to do as you wish, Lady-witch of Alkarra and weapon of the gods. I will be with you in all things. Always.

* * *

Ava tackled me.

I landed, back in the sand, with an *oomph*. Her skinny arms encircled my body with a suppressed sob.

"You're alive!"

I pressed a hand to her back. "I'm fine, Ava. I just . . . I needed to recover. I promise."

Tears dropped onto my collarbone as she wept. The flurry of emotion didn't last long before she bounced back to her feet, sniffling. Her wet eyes peered at me with deep concern. I pushed myself to my feet.

"I was scared," she whispered, taking my hand. She pressed it to her face, the tears hot from her skin.

I pulled her into another quick embrace, then spun around when the sound of a throat clearing came from behind. Baxter sat on the steps of the beach house, peering at me with a shadowed expression.

Relieved to see him, my shoulders slumped. "Merry meet," I said around a sigh. "I'm glad you're here. I've been worried about you and your sisters."

He managed a half-hearted smile. "Ava," he said quietly, "let me talk to Bianca, all right?"

She hesitated, then nodded.

"I'll send you to your collection to check on your birds for the day."

Her expression brightened a little, though hesitation lingered in her droopy lips. With one last squeeze around my waist, Ava disappeared. The air felt empty without her. The stolen moments and clinging embrace wouldn't suffice for actual time with her. For now, it would have to do.

I sat on the steps of the beach house next to him. He scooted over to make space, but our shoulders still touched.

For several long minutes, we said nothing.

"Ignis sent a message to me, said you were fine but . . . I didn't know what to expect. Somehow, Ava heard rumors about the beelae and . . . I didn't realize she was that worried. I'm sorry she tackled you."

The sheepishness in his voice made me chuckle.

"It's fine. I'm relieved to see her as well."

He peered over, concern evident in his heavy brow. "You're all right? When you left you looked . . . half dead."

Last night sprinted through my mind in vague spurts. Reservations bubbled up next. The gods, but I'd messed things up for him.

Or had I?

Couldn't that blame go to Tontes? It should, but I had my doubts it *would*.

"Yes, I'm fine. No lingering pains at all, actually, though it didn't feel good at the time. Ignis healed me immediately." I lifted the edge of my skirt, indicating a silvery scar, as long as my hand, across the thigh. Through my eyelashes, I peered at him. "Do you have a huge mess to clean up?"

He scoffed, running a hand over his face. "Definitely."

"I'm sorry, I—"

A lifted hand stopped me. "Not your fault," he said. "You saved the day, for certain. You were correct, I have to admit. I shouldn't have had my sisters remove their amulets. I just . . . it's been hard for you here. I wanted to alleviate some of the strain."

Until he exonerated me, I didn't realize how much tension I

held over his response to the events. I breathed out a little more fully.

"It was very sweet of you, Baxter. I just don't think your sisters appreciated you taking care of me first, and I wouldn't have blamed them. I . . . wish it all happened so differently."

He ran his thumbnail over his lips, a long stare occupying his gaze. Blinking out of that, he put his hands on his thighs.

"Listen, B, I'm not sure how else to say this but . . . things got weird last night. I have a feeling it's only going to get worse." He swallowed, a pained look on his face. "I'm not sure Alaysia is safe for you anymore. I think you should go home."

"But—"

"I know. I know you want to stay. It's better if I deal with everything. You should go back to Alkarra." His voice firmed up. "Now. Take Ava with you. You'll be safer there."

"I won't."

His gaze lifted to mine in silent question.

"Tontes," I continued. "Ignis said he wants me dead now. A lot of things were discovered about me being an amulet yesterday and . . . anyway, Ignis wants to wait. Let this play out a bit more. He said the *reckoning is coming* and things are in disarray for Tontes. I . . . have to choose, Baxter, between the gods and the goddesses."

"Choose the goddesses."

"It's not that easy."

"No," he murmured. "It's not that hard."

Words choked my throat. I turned away. Baxter sighed and ran a hand over his face.

"You trust Ignis?" he asked.

"More than I trust your father."

He blinked several times, startled. Ventis' utter lack of presence last night—in his own home, with his wives and children at stake—had sent my mind into a whirlwind all day.

Why hadn't *he* done something?

"I see," he murmured.

"I'm not sure you do."

Baxter shot to his feet with a growl. He shoved his hands through his hair. "B, I don't know what's going on. I'm confused, frustrated, and I'd feel better if you were safe in Alkarra."

"My safety is not your responsibility."

"It is."

"I've got this, Baxter."

The agony in his tone tore through me. "I don't like you being here," he whispered.

"What do you mean?"

"It's not right. You're not a mortal, not a demigod. You're going to become something you're not if you stay too long. If Ignis has a too-deep hold on you."

The awkwardness we'd been dancing around for days cleared, and I saw everything more clearly. Baxter, my friend. Torn in half, living between two worlds, trying to patch them together and make them work.

A rush of compassion followed. I gave a small smile.

"I can take care of myself, Bax. After last night, I hope that's fairly apparent. Thank you for your concern."

"You shouldn't have to," he growled. "I'm trying, B, but . . . so many things are out of my hands. I don't know what to do anymore. I'm not sure who to trust. My father left us to deal with the attack from Tontes last night and didn't even say a word. After last night, something feels wrong. He's stacked me with duties that, if I don't fulfill, will result in my loss of an amulet."

"He's holding you hostage?"

A stricken expression crossed his face. "I suppose you could say it that way. Without an amulet, I'll have no power, no position. I'd never see Alkarra again, nor would I be able to send *you* back, should you remove the god magic."

I swept to my feet, grabbed his hands, and forced him to look at me. Vulnerability and fear bled through his intense gaze as we stared at each other. Our fingers threaded together, clamped firmly.

"Bax, what do *you* want?"

He paused. Was it the first time anyone here had asked him such a question? Intrigue and competition from his sisters and grand expectations from his father had been drowning him. Baxter was a demigod burdened with ties, responsibilities, and loved ones he sought to care for and satisfy.

Impossible odds.

"I don't know for sure what I want," he admitted with a dark laugh. "Not anymore. It was so clear to me when I came. Go to Alaysia, report on my mission, make life easier in Alaysia. Now? My sisters are pushing back on my ideas. Father let us remain in harms way. Nothing makes sense anymore."

"Do you want to go back to Alkarra?"

A hand reached up, touching my face. "I love Alkarra." Unspoken words lingered in his voice as his fingers dropped back to the side.

"But?"

"But there's so much good I can do here," he murmured. "So much . . . change that could make Alaysia a better place, for the gods, demigods, mortals, everyone. I see it, they don't. I can't help but feel responsible to do something different for everyone. Despite its imperfections, I love Alaysia. Returning home has been more intoxicating than I expected. I missed it."

A heavy cloak of obligation bowed his shoulders. His eyes remained stormy, pained. I squeezed his fingers. So much swirled between us that it should prevent the budding feelings.

Yet . . .

The restless truth inside me finally settled with a little sigh of understanding. Finally, I knew what I felt for Baxter. The line I walked of affection, friendship, or a deeper love.

"Can we agree on one thing and take a burden off you?" I asked.

He lifted an eyebrow.

I smiled to soften what I was about to say. "That we're better friends than lovers? That we have different paths we're meant to take, each one powerful and important? We'd never be happy living in the other one's world, and I don't mean just Alaysia and Alkarra."

His eyes widened, then calmed. The longest exhale escaped him. I held my breath, afraid of what he'd say. Stating the truth settled me—it was right. As glittering and beautiful of a home and affection that he offered, it wasn't mine. I held love for and respected him, but would never settle into diplomacy and events and talking.

I wanted to be free.

The challenges of Alaysia, demigods, gods, and hostile families paled in comparison to the other very real issues. To drive my point home, I stepped closer to him. The air charged between us. We had chemistry, but chemistry wasn't enough.

"Baxter, would you live in a cottage in the middle of Letum Wood for me? Would you be happy in a forest teeming with goddess magic and hostile dragons and running with me in the snow?"

He thought so hard I wondered if he heard. Finally his lips parted as he drew in a breath. "I want to say yes, but after time passed . . ."

"You are made for castles and politics and massive change. I want to thrive in the background, create safety for my Network, and exist amongst my trees. We could make a relationship work, but would we be better for it?"

"Not always."

Sadness swamped me. "I will always care for you, Bax."

"Agreed," he whispered. A tiny smile claimed his lips, awash with relief. He drew in a deep breath. "I wasn't sure . . . I thought that maybe it was me or . . . I didn't want to disappoint you, all the way over here. I wasn't going to say anything."

Affection swept through me. I tightened my hold on his hand, grateful that we found the same conclusion. That amidst all that had—and would—happen, Baxter and I stood on firm ground.

He pressed our foreheads together, eyes closed. I drew in a deep breath, comforted by the scent of ink and something more wild that carried him around.

"Always friends," I murmured.

Chapter Twenty-Three

A jagged storm tore the horizon in half.

Winds whipped by, scattering sand. The grumpy, overcast weather of the day gave way to a murky sky. Ava remained at her collection, while I lay in the hammock, letting it creak while my thoughts ran.

The quiet time set me back on steady ground. With more alacrity, I reviewed all the significant events of the past several days. Frequently, my thoughts touched home, then spun away. No, I couldn't let those distractions enter the equation. My answer to Ignis's challenge of loyalty had to focus on all of Alkarra.

No letters from Leda, Marten, or Scarlett had come in the last two weeks. Unlikely that they'd forgotten me, which meant goddess magic didn't deliver this far away. My friends couldn't send things with god magic, the way I summoned Viveet. Too far, or did something else block it? It seemed entirely plausible that the gods might somehow prevent letters from reaching me.

The thought made my stomach queasy.

Memories of Letum Wood overpowered me. The smell of moss and growing things drifted up from deepest recollections.

Soft dirt in between my toes. Snow thick as frosting. The stages of life that the forest moved through played out around me. When I opened my eyes, sand had turned to trees.

My hammock lay between two trees taken right from Letum Wood. Behind them waited ancient giants thicker than entire houses. Their empowering presence loomed out of sight. I sucked in a breath, waited for the voices. The sound of their rustling, naive concerns.

None came.

I reached out to touch a vine as thick as my wrist, and the illusion disintegrated. The beach house returned.

Of course.

Somehow, I'd created the vision through god magic, like Baxter once did. A dream, that was all. The vibrancy didn't sing deep in my blood. It felt hollow as bird bones and just as fragile. Not real.

Was Alaysia the same way?

A voice called from outside, breathless. I sat upright, slipped out of the hammock, and rushed to the door. Gio appeared from the trees, doubled over.

"Baxter?" he cried. "Is he here?"

"No. He left hours ago."

Gio frowned. "Where?"

"I don't know. He said something about business for Ventis."

"The *Rostina lu Lune* is empty. I can't find anyone."

"Is something wrong?"

Lost, Gio shrugged.

Ignis spoke next. *Trouble stirs.*

The growing line of storm clouds on the far horizon drew my gaze, hovering right over the spot where I imagined Ava's collection. Everything about today made me uneasy, which further heightened the restlessness. I blinked, startled when a smudge of charcoal clouds expanded near the horizon in a sky-shattering explosion of power. Thunder followed, audible from here.

I straightened, a new gust of wind surging by.

"Tontes?"

The reckoning, Ignis said solemnly, *has come.*

His dark tone sent a shiver through me.

Ava needs you.

Without a word of explanation, I used god magic and left Gio alone at the beach house, my heart in my throat.

* * *

The sea churned around Daemon's island, frothy and white with foam. The bruising storm percussed with approaching thunder and lightning as I arrived, baleful welcoming notes. I jogged through the sand, toward a group of bodies gathered between the two trees that once held Daemon's house.

No house stood there now.

Nothing remained.

Everything had been dismantled. Trees hacked away at the top. Fruit stripped from new bushes Baxter had produced. Remnants of leaves—and not many—littered the sand with rocks, but nothing more. The entire beach had been denuded of resources.

"Ava?" I called. "Ava?"

Twenty mortals scuttled back at the sound of my voice. As they moved, my jaw dropped. Boats filled the beach beyond them. Seven of them, to be correct, all lashed together. They were crude, but not horrible, with enough strength to stand a thin chance of crossing the ocean. Immediately, I recognized the wood that Baxter had given them as the source.

Jikes, this wouldn't end well.

Supplies filled each dinghy. Ropes. Baskets. Clothing. Fishing nets, bunches of line. What appeared to be jugs of water, tied closed. All of it was lashed down with braided seaweed, anchored to the sea crafts. Four men scurried around, moving quickly between boats. Their uneasy gazes darted to the sky, then back. Urgency compelled their final preparations.

On the beach, women quietly wept, sobs lost to the noisy thunder. Understanding dawned all at once. I sucked in a breath, terrified when I saw Ava amongst those in the boats.

Ava.

They hadn't let the idea of leaving go. Daemon had been silently preparing this entire time, using Baxter to his advantage. Ava looked at me, wide-eyed and pale from where she sat in the middle boat. Her lips soundlessly formed my name with fear.

Enraged, I shouted at Daemon over the wind.

"You can't do this!"

He paused. Rain pelted his arms and thick shoulders. The worst of the gauntness had left his face the last several days. He'd eaten well. Pinkish scars showed on his body where I'd healed him with the magic.

"We have to leave now," he called.

"Do you not see the storm?" I pointed over the water. "You're going to your death!"

"It will distract the god of wind," he shouted. "We must go before we're found out. They'll find the dinghies now. We can't stay. The time has come."

"The gods know!" I thundered.

Daemon ignored me. His hair pasted to his head, already slick with rain. With magic, I appeared at Ava's side in the boat. It pitched up and down with sickening lurches that twisted my stomach.

"You cannot go with them," I growled. "You'll die on the water."

"I must plead to the goddess of the sea on their behalf!" she cried. "It's the only way they'll make it. It is my duty. Daemon has told me so."

"Prana will break you in half," I snapped, "right after she half-drowns you, then feeds you to her mermaids. Daemon is a monster if that's what he told you. You have nothing to do with this."

"She didn't kill me the first time!"

Her savage cry shocked me to silence. I stepped back to keep my knees underneath me. What could she possibly mean? Ava's eyes scrunched through the pounding rain, a guilty expression on her face.

"The first time?"

Ava closed her eyes and shook her head. "There's no time to explain. I must go with them, Daemon is correct. There is no Tama to stop me. I *will* go with them! They deserve to be free, too. I will see you in Alkarra!"

She clung to that hope as desperately as she held onto the side of the tilting boat.

"Ava, the gods know. You're not going to make it. They're going to stop you all before you can even leave. Tontes is conjuring this storm. It's *not* a sign to go!"

"This is my fault," she cried, eyes wide. "I told them they could do it. I told them it was possible."

"You're eleven!" I snapped. "They are grown men. This is their responsibility, not yours."

"We willingly take our chances in a new land," Daemon shouted with a thump of his fist on his chest. He stood at the front of the boats, glowering at me. "If we die on the way, we have chosen our life path. If life is hard there, it's harder here. We will be better with the witches than living off a pittance in Alaysia!"

With a ragged breath in, I quelled my rising frustration. I had to think like Marten. Questions of fairness and justice and hope stirred in my chest, but it was too late for that discussion. Didn't I secretly want this for them? Freedom.

Choice.

Yet, it wasn't mine to give. As Baxter had cautioned me before, this was a world I was unfamiliar with. Not only did a far worse fate wait in Alkarra—whose witches were practically primed to destroy mortals in their fear of what mortals could do to their magic—but me bringing mortals to Alkarra could be seen as a battle cry. A reason to stir the gods to war against Alkarra.

"And Ava?" I snapped at Daemon, shoving wet ropes of hair out of my face. "Will you let a child die, too?"

He hesitated, eyeing Ava. Two of the mortals shoved the boats into the water. Ava gripped the sides, face white as snow. A woman cried out, then silenced when a boom of thunder landed. Wind swept by with building power. Daemon grabbed my arm and hauled me out of the boat. He stalked to the other side.

"Get out. The time has come."

"Don't do this," I pleaded, following. "Don't go out there."

He snarled and shoved my hand away. With a grunt, he and another mortal male pushed the dinghy into the battering waves. Once far enough in the water, Daemon deftly jumped inside. Each mortal male had a boat, the rest brimmed with supplies. Ava rode with Daemon. The five of them began to frantically row.

"Ava!" I screamed.

A bolt of lightning slammed into the water, exploding not far away. Ava cried, dropping into the vessel. Waves crested higher, rushing toward the tiny island. Mortals scrambled away as panic sprinted like fire across the place.

"Ava!"

This was my fault. I should have watched her more closely. I should have asked, checked in. If I had just—

The wind grabbed the boats, yanking them out to sea. Water collapsed over the crafts, threatening to drown them. With powerful arms and quick movements, the four mortal males fought the waves. Their greatest effort was entirely futile.

Ava glanced back, terror in her face. She scrambled to dive overboard and swim back, but I used the magic to pull her to me. She dropped into the water, then appeared at my side, soaking wet.

A voice thundered through the storm.

Tontes.

You wanted a rebellion, mortals?

Based on the pale-faced horror on Ava's expression, I reckoned she heard him this time as well. Embers appeared in the air, but immediately blew west under the influence of the wind. The thundercloud and the wind struggled, each pressing against the other. The wind conspired to push the tempest back, but the storm billowed high and fast. Nefarious darkness covered the world. Not a single light could be seen while the gods battled in the sky.

Wind lashed painfully against my face, driving the sand into my skin. Ava cried out, huddled against me. I held her tight and stared into the fray. Beyond the crashing waves, two mermaids surfaced with a flash of hair and a sliver of fins.

They disappeared.

Have your rebellion, Tontes growled, *you worthless fools.*

Daemon paused his frantic paddling, jaw slant, head tilted back. Had he heard Tontes? For a moment, the waves slowed.

The world stilled.

A crack of thunder, then a bolt of lightning followed. Daemon collapsed. The vessels burst into flame, consumed on the water. Wind shoved them farther away from land, where it would be impossible for us to help. The remaining three men disappeared into black waves. A hand flailed above the caps, then sank.

High-pitched squeals replaced gurgling screams. Flashes of bright mermaid fins appeared on top of the water, flapping around. They sank, then a spread of blood darkened the churning ocean.

I almost vomited.

Ava screamed, face white. I held her shoulders so tight my hands ached. I turned her into me so she couldn't see the pink, foamy water. Rain slanted in my eyes, pelting hard, making it difficult to see. I scrubbed it away, but more came.

A greater swirl of fire surged against the wind again, attempting to twirl around me. Their blooming lights remained unbothered by the torrential rain. In the chaos, voices barked at each other.

Ignis.

Tontes.

Ventis.

Leave her! Ignis boomed. *The Lady-witch of Alkarra is mine.*

She has conspired to incite mortal rebellion, Tontes hissed. *You see the evidence before you. Did she not work god magic in their favor without authorization? Was she not here when they departed?*

Ventis's deep reverberation followed. *The Lady-witch of Alkarra is my visitor by invitation, and under the protection of Ignis and myself.*

Despite the violence between brothers, the embers continued to fight against the surging winds. Their bright crimson forms were no match for the gale. Finally giving in, the embers whisked away, out to the sea. The surging clouds stalled in their distant progress.

At my side, Baxter appeared.

He held an arm up against the blowing sands that scoured his face. I could barely hear his shout over the gale. His curls flounced around his temples, streaming rain. He squinted, water glistening on his eyelashes. He grabbed Ava's other arm.

"Go back to Alkarra!"

"No!"

"Now, Bianca!" he commanded. "You will not survive this time."

Vengeance, Tontes cried, *will be mine. I call the Lady-witch of Alkarra to the Council of the Gods to face her punishment for inciting rebellion.*

His voice boomed through the sky. Ava tilted her head back, then screamed into the wind. A feral, wild thing.

"I hate you!" she shouted, sobbing. She swung at the wind, kicking. Baxter lost his grip on her slippery arms. She grabbed sand, chucking it into the wind. "I hate you! Everything bad that happened is because of you. Monilay mal! I hate you, god of wind! Grandfather," she finished on a choking sob.

Two demigods appeared on top of Ava, tackling her to the ground. Her wild eyes met mine a second before she vanished. I lunged too late.

"Ava! No!"

Six demigods ringed me and Baxter. I stared into their cold eyes, helpless against the brewing violence I saw there. Baxter, Ignis, and I could fight all six, but what about Ava? Where had they taken her?

Baxter growled.

Three demigods swarmed him. They ripped his amulet free and dragged him into the water. Enraged, he kicked one in the chest. Two others appeared and shoved him under the incoming waves. His shoulders thrashed, but they held strong. His amulet lay discarded in the sand, glimmering in the low light.

"Let them go!" I shouted into the thunder. I tilted my head back to the sky and spread my hands. "I'll cooperate if you let them go."

Baxter surfaced with a gasp. The demigods held him with one at each arm, a third by his hair. The other two remained back, upper lips curled. They forced Baxter to look at me. He sputtered, face contorted in rage.

"Look at that," one of them sneered in my direction, with a lecherous smile. "The witch can be persuaded."

"Trust none of them!" Baxter shouted. "They're—"

His cry burbled in the water.

"Baxter and Ava will be with us," the closest one growled to me. "Should you try to escape your appearance at the Council of the Gods, their deaths will be slow and sweet. God magic heals as much as it destroys. Such torture can be a vicious cycle."

The rest of them cackled like desert dogs in the Western Network. Lightning streaked across the sky, slamming into the sea. Wind stirred.

Is that true? I demanded Ignis. *Can they torture and heal and torture again? Would Tontes do that to Baxter and Ava?*

Ignis' reply echoed in a somber way.

Yes.

Bring the Lady-witch to me, Tontes bellowed.

The gentle cadence of Ventis' voice replied. *So it must be. The Council will begin in an hour.*

Chapter Twenty-Four

Sea water sloshed around my waist when the demigod deposited me . . . somewhere. He left with a jaunty smirk and a flippant smile.

"Don't forget who awaits torture," he sang, then added with a mutter, "Should have done this on the first day."

Head canted back, I surveyed my new prison. An open marshland without walls. Spikes carved from stone leered out of watery shadows. Fog lingered, hiding the roar of waves in the far distance. A boggy, rotten stench entered my nostrils. My nose wrinkled. The good gods, but Tontes stunk.

Water rippled around my waist. In the shifting fog, I could just make out a narrow channel of reeds, leading farther away. To the ocean beyond? Water rushed around me, frothing and smelly, with bits of dead fish and chum.

"A swamp," I muttered. "Lovely, Tontes. Points for smelly creativity, you mongrel dog."

The words rang hollow across my new confines, but venting frustration loosened my chest a bit.

I licked my lips, detesting the salty taste. Too long down here and my skin would peel away from my body, thanks to this acrid sludge. With god magic, I created a raised ledge, then climbed onto it and out of the crepuscular waters. Green muck churned like tea grounds.

Ignis?

No answer.

Baxter's cries flared back to remembrance. *Trust none of them!*

Surely, he meant the demigods, though there hadn't been time for clarification. My heart withered at the thought of Ignis betraying me. Would he? I didn't want it to be true, not after all we'd been through.

Yet . . .

Intentionally, I put my mind back on what happened. Papa returned in my moment of floundering with his steady advice.

Process it, he always said, a hand firm on my shoulder. *Think it through, B. You can't hide from shock or emotions. You face them, they go away. Simple as that.*

One moment at a time, I replayed the events starting with Gio's arrival and ending at Ava's collection. Methodically, I analyzed each piece. Gio. Daemon. Ava. The storm. The demigods' arrival. The paralyzing fear. Every now and then, I murmured facts aloud, just to keep myself on track. The rhythm and process soothed me until I felt that I saw things as clearly as I ever would.

Ignis?

No response.

As my shock faded, so did light. Sunset lolled through the foggy marsh in faraway, blunted hues. The fetid fog lingered in the air, clinging to my clothes, my hair. My thoughts unwound, wild, like a freed whip.

Full darkness descended.

With it, a chilly breeze. If I was truly in Tontes' kingdom, where was that? Closer to the north, presumably, based on the cooler water and nip in the air. My wet clothes made me shiver, so I dried them with magic.

I closed my eyes.

Thinking had kept the chasm of hopelessness at bay for a while, but now the utter terror of my position struck with full force. Would the gods give me a chance to give allegiance? Unlikely, if Tontes had too much sway. Only the three brothers' who planned to stand against Tontes—with me as their power of stopping him—stood between me and death.

The power of my connection with Ignis resurrected with a little shiver. Such wild ability, uncontrolled power. A yearning for home swept through me. Until now, I'd mostly staved it off. Shoved it back to make room for what lay in front of me.

No more.

Marten and Leda rushed into my mind. Papa. Scarlett. Merrick. Memories with them twined around, fluttering in and out of focus, until they landed on the one place I *couldn't* bear to think about.

My forest.

Letum Wood.

Unable to stomach the pangs, I closed my eyes. Moments before I had to face a Council of the Gods—whatever that could mean—the last thing I should think about was home. The place I might have to forsake in order to save it.

If the gods killed me, what hope did Alkarra have in standing against the demigods?

Papa?

My heart floated in a vast sea of agony. An empty chasm, like a wide pocket of space waiting for something to make it small again.

No, I should plan.

Think of strategy, a way out of this. Cleverness. Tricks. Confident plays that would boggle even the gods. That's what the Sisterhood was supposed to be, right? Unconventional. Outside the box.

No plans surfaced.

Clever tactics failed me.

Only Letum Wood rose through the noise, standing stolid and tall.

Rage followed. All of this was Deasylva's fault. She who revealed herself with a sentence on a tree, then withdrew. She who demanded, but didn't manifest. Ignis had, at least, been with me. Carried everywhere, part of my spirit, my mind.

To what claim did Deasylva hold?

Tears clogged my eyes. I tilted my head back. If Deayslva was a true goddess, and if I was her servant, then she'd be listening. Now, of all moments, she *must* listen. This was her only chance.

Otherwise, I swore all to Ignis.

The Lady-witch of Alkarra, weapon of the gods.

"Tell me why I shouldn't give you up for the greater power that Ignis offers?" I pled. "Give me a reason to believe you can save Alkarra."

Silence.

Utter stillness.

The cold feeling of a razor in my heart followed. The thunderous noise of the gods interplayed against such a hush. Ignis held presence and power in my thoughts.

"Nothing?" I whispered.

A tickling sensation wrapped around my foot, twining and lazy. With a gasp, I jerked back. A vine spiraled up my ankle with familiar, triangular leaves sprouting from a skinny stem.

Letum Ivy.

It curled up my leg, breaking free at my knee to extend to my hand. The strand wrapped around my wrist, and stopped into a curlicue on my palm. With it came a humming sensation.

Thrumming power. Familiar and mighty. It looped around,

unhurried and placid at the same time. Unlike god magic, this was far more illusive.

I held my breath.

A voice swelled from depths deeper than I knew possible. Halcyon and mellow. While the gods thundered and raged, this little thing came in a gentle approach.

You, it whispered, *are no weapon.*

The bog changed.

Instead of black walls and darkness, a small child shimmered into sight. Restless black hair, wispy around tiny ears. Stormy eyes. She toddled, alone near a tree, barely old enough to keep her feet under her.

Me.

I remembered the uneven ground at my small feet, the smell of greenery thick in the air. Then I fell. My palms scraped a root and pain lashed through my palm again, in the bog. I sucked in a sharp breath. On instinct, I jerked forward to catch the little girl, but it was all illusion. Gauzy smoke dissipated under my touch.

Little Bianca toppled, hands planted on a tree trunk.

Blue light warmed beneath her touch, a meek shimmer of aquamarine that wound up the tree, then faded back into roots. Unaware of the magical signature, little Bianca grunted. She suppressed a frustrated cry, balled a chubby fist, and pushed back to her feet, unaware. Her fingers grasped for purchase along the trunk as she navigated her journey over roots, blue lines trailing each tiny touch. Her fingers dug into the soil when she fell again. Grubby hands grabbed branches, scratched over the grass.

Blue light followed her.

A slightly older Bianca appeared, black hair in a braid. A panoramic view of Papa wrestling with her beneath the soaring trees stretched out. Grandmother in the house, calling out for dinner. Warm candlelight filled the windows, even as night crept in. Mama weeded in the garden, hat bobbing over the wooden fence.

The images changed again. Four-year-old Bianca held a sword, a thick braid on her shoulders. Her confident feet touched roots, dancing over the top of the forest. When she swung too hard and over-spun, her shoulder hit a tree trunk. Light exploded through the tree, shimmering in blue lines like a starburst.

She giggled, pushed back off, and charged Papa. He collapsed under her with a dramatic cry, and they fell to the ground together.

The scene blurred.

You are, the voice asserted, *no weapon.*

I reached out, longed to touch Papa. To connect with little Bianca. To draw this young version back into me and harbor her there, safe from all the storms that awaited. In the memory, Mama's head lifted from the other side of the garden fence yet again. Her bright smile illuminated my chest, setting my heart to fire.

She was so young, her face so pure.

"Bianca!" she called, laughing. The perfect melody of her voice took my breath away, filling me with light and heat and tender affection. I caught a sob. "You are so brave," Mama called. "You're so strong! You can do anything."

Tears blurred the memory.

Papa let out a fake cry of outrage, and the illusion of my childhood bled away with a happy shriek.

The scene dissolved into five-year-old Bianca as she climbed on top of roots, then slid down the other side. A wash of blue trailed at her back. Six-year-old Bianca scrambling up her first vine and into the forest ceiling. Spiraling sapphire light rippled down the vine with every hand hold.

Seven-year-old Bianca rolled in the grass, laughing.

Eight-year-old Bianca, shivering in a rain storm as she tried to pretend she wasn't lost. Blue light raced through the ground ahead of her, guiding her with bent branches. Raindrops large as candle flames splashed on her shoulders. The chilly memory rippled back through me with a shiver.

Callbacks happened at top-speed now, flying past with wild abandon. Darting down trails at ten—blue footprints bright behind me. Splashing in the creek at eleven. Digging in the ground at twelve. Falling asleep in the sunshine at thirteen, tucked into the juncture of a tree and a branch. Cyanic light cloaked me.

You are no weapon.

The recollections whirled in a dizzying spiral. Reminders. Through it all appeared the same guiding light, echoes I hadn't seen at the time. Branches reached for me in the memories. Grasses gave way. Trails appeared.

The forest—no, Deasylva—had always called to me.

I had always answered.

Dormant power swelled beneath the journey. Magic. Tenacity. The potency welled up like a bubbling fountain, a mountain about to break open.

Such power.

Bated ferocity.

My breath caught.

"I remember," I whispered. "I remember it all. I remember *you.*"

Letum Wood. Deasylva. The trees might be sentient apart from Deasylva, but her power thrived from—no, because of— her trees. Understanding flooded me. Different, but one and the same.

You are no weapon.

"I am no weapon. I am the Lady-witch of Alkarra," I whispered, hand on my face, "and the goddess-touched servant of Deasylva."

The memories disintegrated. Mossy branches faded into black tendrils of wretched fog. The sound of the sea overtook my whispering forest, like a drawn blanket. The sweet smells faded. Water droplets slapped my cheek, a cool push back to reality.

Light spilled into my brackish prison. A demigod held a torch out, face scrunched as he glowered.

"Let's go," he called. "Time to face the Council of the Gods."

Chapter Twenty-Five

Everything disappeared.

A breath later, I stood somewhere new. The demigod was at my side, hand on my shoulder. The heavy weight anchored me. I kept my eyes closed, taking in the sounds first.

Thunder.

Crackling . . . something.

Bursts of heat.

"Welcome," he called jauntily, "to the heart of Alaysia, the meeting place of the Council of the Gods."

Finally, I opened my eyes. A captured gasp stalled in my throat. Thready breath escaped my lungs as I stood there, unable to comprehend the sight that surrounded me.

The gods.

We stood in what could only be the Heart of Alaysia, a circle thirty paces wide. Black stone, slick beneath my feet, reminded me of Gelas' home. My toes stumbled on the smooth structure, a round center in the middle of primitive chaos.

A storm circled overhead with fuchsia clouds. They glittered with lightning. Wind hurried by, sweeping in an arc that twirled the storm like a top. Pebbles scoured my cheeks as the breeze brushed through the circle, whipping like a chastisement.

Below the churning nebula, much farther out from the black circle where I stood, lay a ring of volcanoes. Smoke belched from their giant tops. Magma cascaded free in glowing crimson rivers, crusted on top with a layer of dark gray. Sprays of lava erupted every now and then, arcing into the air like thrown glitter. Heat rippled through the air in luxuriant waves.

At the base of the volcanoes, lay a field of ice tens of thousands of paces across. Twisted, contorted sculptures marched in hues of deepest blue, filling the space from the base of the volcanoes to the black circle. The tops of the amassed glaciers sparkled white and silver, reflecting flashes of lightning. Thick chunks of the ice had fissured, leading to deep grooves in a maze. They formed a wall, hundreds of paces overhead, that stopped just before the circle.

I swallowed hard.

Jikes.

The Heart of Alaysia.

The place where all the gods merged into one terrifying interior. The god magic inside me soared. Bright. Heady. Too powerful. It would incinerate me from the inside out at this rate.

I panted from the heat.

The demigod released me with a shove. "Good luck, Ladywitch of Alkarra," he cried, then laughed. A portion of the hellfire agony faded when he stepped farther away. He grinned, a challenge in his gaze as he shuffled back. "Dare you to run."

With a rangy laugh, he winked out of sight.

Attempts to take in the towering volcanoes were in vain. There was no comprehending such rampant calamity. The heat. The agony of the magic. All components of my current situation led to nothing but despair. How could I possibly get Baxter, Ava, and myself out of this alive?

I'd been pinned down, all right.

Heat spiraled through my veins. I longed to throw myself against the ice and melt into the wintry floes. My fingers trembled when I held them higher, staring at them in wide-eyed fear. Smoke curled off the top of my skin.

Let the Council of the Gods begin, came Tontes' thunderous voice. *The accused has arrived, in all her guilty glory.*

The wind calmed, opening my ears to hear better. An unnerving silence resumed. Is this what Baxter had faced all day when he returned from his mission?

Ignis? I tried, my inner voice trembling.

No response.

My breathing came faster now. Too fast. When my head swam, I forced myself to slow. Was Gelas here? For all I knew, he hadn't been present for the attempted exodus. At least, he hadn't demonstrated himself there. Not that he'd be likely to help. Of all the gods, he held me in the greatest contempt.

Tontes aside.

As my guest, Ventis began, *and as god of the escaping mortals, I will speak for her innocence. The mortals have long planned the exodus, which I have monitored from the beginning. Her presence had no effect on moving it forward more quickly.*

A rumble broke across the sky, as if Tontes chortled.

She is mine, Ignis murmured quietly. Relief spread through me at the sound of his voice. *I will also speak for her.*

You claim her? Tontes asked. His voice turned up, which seemed to mean something I couldn't figure out.

Ignis hesitated.

All the world quieted.

I do.

As I claim Alkarra, Tontes snapped. *It doesn't mean anything. Have you gained her allegiance? With no formal agreement, you have no bedrock beneath you, brother.*

The acerbic reply sent the volcanoes into a red-hot frenzy. Ear-splitting thunder followed. The ground trembled. Fire flared to life at the edge of the black circle where I stood. I shuffled back, putting myself in the dead center to avoid their inferno. The flames grew to walls. They emitted no heat, but ribboned overhead, encasing me in flickering color. I tilted my head back, spinning on the spot.

Surrounded.

The rumble of Tontes, and murmur of Ventis, continued in the background. A figure appeared in the flames. I paused, arrested. The god magic truly whirled now, as if it would take flight. The allure of the demigod was a pittance against *this* force. My feet stumbled, longing to bridge the gap.

Out of the light, features materialized. Stormy eyes peered at me. Dark hair cut in thick locks on his head tossed around in the wind. Ignis. He had a strong jaw, chiseled features, firm chin. Broad shoulders led to long arms, hanging at his side. Given a chance to guess, I would have assumed he was fifty, with wisdom and experience in hardened eyes.

The intensity in which he studied me made my heart stutter. Trouble and concern brewed there.

I breathed.

"Ignis."

His head tilted back.

Lady-witch, he murmured in my mind, and his voice matched the intensity in his gaze. The soft edge of concern startled me. *You're all right?*

"Can I speak out loud?"

He nodded. *They can't hear through the flames.*

I drew in a breath. "I'm fine."

How can you be?

The question was metaphorical, at best. Agony filled his expression, which had become more sonorous with every passing moment. The Heart of Alaysia melted, I was lost in fire. Belching volcanoes ceased. The churning sky with peals of crackling thunder silenced. The only thing that existed was this moment.

Me.

Ignis.

His magic filled me with potent power, expanding like steam.

Ignis studied me for a long time. Through his intense perusal, I felt a moment of knowing. Of . . . *understanding.* Whoever he was, I knew him. Connection existed between us, thriving and hot.

By force of will, I dragged my gaze away. No, I had to stay present. Had to choose what was best for Alkarra, not myself, though the temptation to throw my allegiance at his feet and stay with him forever nearly tore me apart. Baxter's warning rang through my head, as bright as the flashes of electricity.

Trust none of them.

Prana had said the same, hadn't she?

Trust no one, and remember your forest.

The time has come to choose. His hushed voice spread like a spike of heat over my heart. *Will you give me your allegiance? In doing so, you save yourself and Alkarra. Or will you . . . try to go back to the land of the witches?* He stepped closer. *I can stop all of this right now if you say the words.*

I blinked. "*Try* to go back to Alkarra?"

His nostrils flared. *Tontes intends to prove that you aided a rebellion and should be executed. Our sisters would be unable to save you.*

I frowned. "But I didn't. I tried to stop them."

I know.

"The demigods came to Alkarra and killed *us,*" I hissed. "Doesn't it work both ways?"

And we won't seek justice against our sisters for those lost demigods, he countered gently.

"Since when does Tontes care about mortals?"

Since you've given him reason to be concerned.

Unable to tear my gaze away, I studied him now. His fists clenched in balls at his sides. The knuckles blanched. Why so tense?

You trusted me this morning, he murmured. *Has that faded so quickly?*

The question lay heavy in my heart. To whom did I give my allegiance? Where did my trust *truly* reside? Memories of Alaysia spun through my mind. The infinite beauty. The power.

Yet no matter how lovely Alaysia could be, Alkarra would always be home. The newness of Alaysia would fade, but my love for Alkarra would be a stalwart beacon. I closed my eyes, breaking the trance Ignis held over me.

Deasylva's voice resurrected, the quiet, powerful reassurance. *You are no weapon.*

Ignis didn't remind me that he offered everything he had. He didn't mention that he gave me the ability to save Alkarra, to work with a most powerful partner to keep the gods at bay. He just stared at me. If I had known any better, I'd say he was . . .

Frustrated.

My fingers curled into a fist. Something ground beneath them. I glanced down to find crushed Letum Ivy in my hand. The leaves were tattered, the vine snapped in three places, but they filled me with reminders all the same.

I sucked in a breath.

The allure faded. My connection with Ignis ebbed in the background for a moment as I stared at the battered symbol of my heart.

I am no weapon, I thought.

The memories returned all at once, dizzy in their speed. With them came more. Leda. Camille. Chatham Castle. Mildred. Papa. Marten.

Merrick.

My head snapped up.

Merrick.

Running through the forest. Laughing under the trees. A touch on my cheek. Hazel eyes. Flashing swords. Moments of sheer frustration, deepest love. A double whomp landed my heart back in my chest, where it belonged. The thought of Merrick reminded me of what was real.

You are no weapon.

Doubt faded away, fizzling. My affinity for Ignis wavered. The attachment we'd forged through magic and near-death and time settled into a corner of my soul I'd never be rid of. Ignis had driven all the way to my heart center. The idea of spending more time with him, at his side in Alaysia, filled me with a deep longing.

I couldn't trust it.

Because I wasn't his weapon. Nor Ventis, Tontes, Gelas, or Deasylva's. Not even Alkarra's weapon.

I was Bianca Monroe.

Lady-witch of Letum Wood.

"Jikes," I whispered.

This wouldn't be easy. Tears filled my eyes, blurring Ignis' profile when I found the courage to face him again. I swallowed, throat bobbing painfully, as I lifted my chin.

"Thank you, but no. I will not grant you my allegiance."

Shock rendered him utterly still for three seconds.

He blinked.

"No?"

The fact that he'd physically spoken arrested me for a moment, pulling me back into his draw. Tears blurred as I doubled my resolve.

"I am no weapon. I am the Lady-witch of Letum Wood and servant of Deasylva. My allegiance rests with my goddess."

Astonishment flooded his face. "You don't know her."

"I do."

"But Alkarra—"

"We'll figure it out."

"How?" he snapped. "How could you possibly—"

"I don't know. I don't know the details, I don't have a plan. I only know what's real and steady and strong and true and that's me. I am not your weapon. I am Bianca Monroe, Lady-witch of Letum Wood."

Annoyance filled his expression. He turned away, his jaw so strained it threatened to break. A flash of red caught my eyes in his fisted hand. Crimson. Burnt orange. Rotating yellow. Samthanruadanosa. He wore the amulet that I had returned around his neck. But why? Why would a god wear an amulet?

Ignis sucked in a breath, then let it out. *I can't save you this way,* he said with a note of fear. *You will die. You will die by my brothers, or by the removal of my magic. Either way, I don't desire to lose you.*

"Then I die," I whispered the wobbly words with Daemon in mind, "by my choice."

His eyes closed. My heart beat an unsteady rhythm. Moments later, they opened again. Disgust, then frustration, finally something infinitely softer appeared there.

He shook his head.

Indeed, he murmured. *And a powerful choice you have made. Perhaps it is the right one, but a difficult one for me to accept.*

A tear dropped down my cheek. "My allegiance has already been given, long ago, and I will honor it to my dying day. Forgive me, Ignis. My forest requires me."

A stricken expression crossed his face. *I can feel your sorrow, Lady-witch. I can feel your truth and know your pain. I sense your loyalty. You have saved me.* The hand holding Samthanruadanosa lifted slightly. *And I will extend the same to you, consequences be damned.*

A premonitory shiver ripped through me.

Ignis glanced overhead, then back to me. His shoulders expanded as he drew himself taller.

In a few minutes, you will have no reason to trust me. I ask you to do so anyway, no matter what you hear. You need to know what Ventis and Tontes will say next if Alkarra is to survive. At the right moment, I will attempt to remove my magic from you. It's the only way to save you from being a slave at Tontes' hand. Like Luppentonisa, I don't think you'll survive the withdrawal, but I will do my best.

His lips tightened. Clearly, it pained him to say as much.

I could only nod.

One last, long stare stretched between us. The magic inside me curled toward him, as if it understood. Ignis nodded slightly, rigid through the neck and shoulders. He held his arms at his side like he braced for a blow. Ignis and all the flames disappeared at once.

Sound returned.

Clouds of smoke billowed in sooty bellows above the volcanoes, feeding the dark storm overhead. Rivers of magma flowed to the twisted crevasses of the icy ocean, where fire met water. The lava hissed in cooling steam.

Tontes boomed again and again, wordless now, like frustrated drums. The angry bursts thickened my head, making it almost impossible to think. Wind twirled in restless agitation. Lightning struck the ground not far away. The force threw me off my feet. I skidded across the ground, rolling, until my spine collided with the edge of the circle.

For several moments, my chest locked. By the time it gave way and I could suck in a breath, my head swam. Arms bent, I shoved off the ground. My shoulder ached from ramming into the ice wall. My hip protested a rock on the ground.

Tontes' livid voice rippled in the air. *Bring the demigod and mortal. Let them all face judgment together.*

Baxter appeared on the other side of the circle, bound in cords. A bruise purpled his left eye, and a gag was stuffed in his mouth. He knelt, hands tied to his ankles behind his back. Blood stained his wrists. He wore no amulet now.

I stumbled closer.

"Baxter."

A quick, panicked jerk of his head stopped me. I paused. Ava appeared next to him, bound the same way. Her eyes were so wide they ringed in white. The temptation to send her to Alkarra with Ignis' magic nearly overcame me, but I held back. My presence close to her might only make it more dangerous.

Would they kill Baxter?

Baxter leaned forward, as if he could express something through his eyes, but another burst of thunder broke through the air. The reverberation shook the ground. Baxter tightened to brace himself.

My entire body stiffened out of my control. Magic dragged me to the middle of the circle, then spun me around. Baxter and Ava were at my back, out of sight. Nearby, ice groaned.

A burst of wind scattered ice shards into the air. Ventis' voice came with it, barreling past in a boom that made it clear he spoke to everyone present.

State your claim, Ignis. Has allegiance been granted from the Lady-witch of Alkarra?

Baxter's head whipped to mine, wide-eyed with fear.

A soft reply came next.

No. The witch is a servant of Deasylva and claims loyalty to her goddess.

Relief melted Baxter so quickly he hung his head.

You will not relinquish your goddess? Ventis asked with a curl of surprise.

"No."

Wind built. An electric charge blossomed through the air, expanding with ferocity.

That, Ventis murmured, *is disappointing to hear.*

Then she shall be compelled to be our servant, Tontes declared, *as we have planned. What are we waiting for?*

My blood turned to slush.

"What?"

I will not make an enemy of Deasylva, Ignis said. *If you compel her servant to be a slave to your magic, you do so at the risk of inciting war with the goddesses. And you do so without my support.*

A clap of thunder, very much like a snarl, echoed through the Heart of Alaysia. *Know your place, little brother. My business is my own. If I want a war with the sisters then I shall instigate a war. Alkarra belongs to the gods.*

It does not, Ignis replied.

The witch is mine to control, as we agreed, Tontes thundered. *With her, we shall finally take back Alkarra.*

Her power is too extensive to allow her to go back to Deasylva, Ventis said through a gust of wind. *You know this, Ignis. We will not change course now, no matter what you think is wise. No matter how fond of her you may have become.*

Rage rushed through me.

All the sordid pieces laid out in a confusing array. Ventis invited me to test my abilities. Ignis used me to understand the extent of the powers. Tontes tested me at every hand. The entire visit to Alaysia was a planned expedition to give *them* more information, more ability to dominate Alkarra.

Yet, in this grand design, what had changed for Ignis?

Clearly, each confrontation I had faced was part of a greater plan. Had Ignis and Ventis and Gelas not planned to go against Tontes all along?

A sinking feeling told me it was true. All of them lied to me. All of them planned to work together this entire time—they just wanted to see what a living amulet could do. Tontes wanted me as his living amulet slave.

Jikes, even Daemon's exodus must have been allowed to set

me up, all this time. A manipulation. A way to suss out exactly what I could do—for them. It explained why Ventis allowed his *Rostina* to be invaded instead of stopping Tontes. My heart cracked right down the middle.

Then Ventis and myself will use her in the invasion of Alkarra, Tontes said. *The sisters will not be able to defeat us then. As most powerful, the claim is mine. If she will not give us her allegiance to make this easy, we will force her into it.*

My breath notched higher, trapped in a spiral of disbelief. Tontes' words replayed through my mind.

Alkarra. Invasion.

The gods, but I'd almost played right into their hands. Had I given Ignis my allegiance, he would have turned it to his own purposes. Instead of saving Alkarra, they would have, somehow, forced me to destroy it. If I'd learned anything over the past two weeks, it was the intricate depths of god magic, its flexibility, its power.

Somehow, it must be possible.

Wounded, I couldn't help myself. *A lie?* I asked in a plaintive whisper. *All of this?*

Yes.

This whole time?

Until two days ago.

Two days ago. Frantic, I thought back, but too much cluttered my mind. With a growl, I snapped, *What happened two days ago? You deceived me for weeks and changed your mind on a whim?*

His whisper resounded in a quiet song.

You saved me.

I attempted to form a reply, but none came. The quiet around him when I returned Samthanruadanosa played back through my mind.

Silence.

You bastard, I snarled.

I warned you about trusting me, he continued with forced placidness. *The only way to save your land now is for me to remove the magic, make it so you cannot be used as a weapon, and hope you don't get torn in half. Unless your goddess intervenes, which she is unlikely to do so far away from her own home, you will not survive.*

Deepening darkness settled in the bowl of ice. Ventis and Tontes voices continued in the background, as if bickering.

I claim the right to use her in the Alkarran invasion, Ventis growled. *She is here as my visitor.*

Your son might be complicit in supporting a mortal exodus, yet you fight for the witch? Tontes bellowed. *This was agreed before we brought her here!*

My stomach knotted. The only reason I wouldn't die was my status as a weapon. Tipa had been right. They wanted what I represented, not me. The ground trembled when Tontes snapped another response to Ventis, nearly knocking me off my feet. Somewhere in the sea, islands must be struck with tidal waves by now.

Clever, I had to admit. In all the scenarios I ran through my head for how the gods could trick me, I hadn't expected them to be working together. For Ignis to test my ability and gain closeness through genuine friendship.

All of it made sense . . . except for one thing.

Gelas.

The witch might have the magic of Ignis, Tontes continued, *but perhaps we can change it. I give her mine, Ignis takes his back. The witch will be in my full control then.*

Can it? Ignis asked mildly, as if yawning. *You think a mere witch would survive an exchange of magic?*

I clenched my fists.

What was he *waiting* for?

Or did all his promises ring with dishonor?

If she dies while we attempt it, Ventis said, *then she dies. What have we lost?*

Deasylva will not be pleased if she dies, Ignis said. *You will have also lost your weapon against the sisters, if the witch dies.*

Thunder clapped again, an oddly dark, amused sound. It continued to roll and roll, until the consistent noise made it clear that it was laughter. Tontes enjoyed himself.

Deasylva poses no threat to the gods. She will soon be stripped of power and left to rot in the ocean, as we were. She doesn't frighten me. I will destroy her forest, and gladly. As the most powerful god, the witch is mine. This Council has finished.

The sickening green color of the sky formed a funnel overhead and dropped toward me. Clouds surged in the tight spiral. Wind whipped my hair into my face. Sand, ice, dust, skittered everywhere, scratching my cheeks. I dropped into a ball on the ground, but the wind tugged me back to my knees.

Clawing for purchase on the shiny black floor was useless, and thunder made it impossible to think. Arm held up to protect my face, I turned my shoulder to the dropping tornado. Fire exploded out of the corner of my eye, but rain dumped on it, calming the flames.

Leave her. Ignis cried. *She will be returned to Deasylva.*

You stand against us, Ignis? Ventis called. *You, the weakest of all? Without her, you are bound, are you not? If you lose her, you won't have enough power to maintain your kingdom. Your mortals will die, as will your demigods. You start over now, brother, and you may never catch back up.*

Not true, Ignis sang pleasantly.

My fingers scrambled for purchase as the tornado descended. My legs blew behind me, ripped off the ground. I screamed, airborne.

Ice crackled, growing to greater heights in front of me. Towers of blue and silver and white raced across the black circle, snaking around the edges. Clear ice formed a glass dome overhead just before I flew out of it. In moments, crisp ice surrounded me in a bubble, staving off the wind. The tornado fizzled away, swept into torrents of rain and wind. I dropped to the ground, crashing with an *oomph.*

The witch, Gelas boomed, *is not yours to toy with, brothers.*

The ground shook as I righted myself. I pressed my hands to the ice walls, grateful for the cool kiss against my burning hands.

Silence followed Gelas' statement.

Gelas, Ventis finally demanded. *What is the meaning of this?*

My breath fogged out in front of me. Startled, I whirled around. The ice protected me, Baxter, and Ava. Baxter and Ava regarded the ice wall in shock, eyes wide.

Cease your attack, Gelas commanded, *and I shall explain.*

Wind and thunder paused. A heartbeat passed. Calm issued in the following silence. The gods waited.

"By the gods," I muttered, agape. "I know that voice."

* * *

Baxter's wide-eyed stare indicated he realized the same thing.

"Gio?" I cried.

Pale, Baxter could only nod.

"Did you know?"

He shook his head.

Gio's voice, so pristinely clear, broke through the Heart of Alaysia. He sounded like a mixture of the god of ice, and my friend. The fast, clipping tones of Gelas, with the gentle purr of Gio. Gelas must have disguised his voice when we visited him in the North.

No wonder he sounded familiar.

Power resonated through each word.

I desire Alkarra as much as the three of you. My former home, the Icelands of the South, call to me. I shall return, but not as a fool. Deasylva and I have an agreement that I fulfill today by protecting her servant.

My heart sped up.

Deasylva?

You betray us by going behind our back to the sisters? Tontes asked.

I fight for my land. No longer will I live on an abomination of a glacier island. The land is mine. The Southern Network will be mine again, with agreement of the sisters, in exchange for protecting her servant. Unlike others in present company.

The not-so-subtle jab sent another fissure of rage through the sky in bursts of sprouting electricity. Hurricane-like winds soared by, scouring the dome. Baxter and Ava's astonished gaze met mine.

"Gio," I muttered helplessly.

Baxter shrugged. Gio pretended to be a mortal to keep an eye on me? Instances of meeting him clicked together. My arrival. The careful way he worded each mention of gods and demigods and allegiance. The moment with Tipa, after Tontes attacked Ava's collection. His frantic search for Baxter only moments before everything fell apart.

Most of all, Gelas' acerbic annoyance when I met him at his glacier. He hadn't been mistrusting—he'd been reminding me.

My belief is not in your ability to give loyalty to god magic, but to give up all you love. If you truly want to save Alkarra from Tontes, would you do whatever it takes?

Tipa had been correct. Gelas didn't care about me either. To him, I was the means to an end.

Namely, the Southern Network.

All the gods have watched you, Bianca, he had said. *We all wait for our opportunity to get what we most want. You are that chance for all of us.*

Gio had been a god all along.

An onslaught of wind and thunder followed, breaking apart

my shock. Hail. Wind. Rage unleashed. The ice globe over my head held firm, shielding the three of us.

He delays for us, Ignis said, frantic. *We must take the magic now, before Tontes suspects.*

"All right." My shoulders jerked back. "I'm ready."

You're not, he muttered, *but you never shall be. Are you certain of this? This will begin the war of the gods. Gelas and myself against Ventis and Tontes. Tontes and Ventis will still come for Alkarra, and you will be forced to defeat Tontes solely with the power of your goddess and whatever interference we can run from here.*

"I'm certain. Do it. Wait!"

Baxter and Ava remained back there, bound. With god magic, I unbound their ties. The ropes disappeared. I healed Baxter's swollen face, willed anything else to repair itself.

"Go back to Alkarra," I cried. "Tell them everything that happened."

"I have no amulet!"

Samthanruadanosa appeared before us, and now everything made sense. Ignis had known this would be a possibility, and brought the amulet in case. Emotion rose in my throat, choking my voice, as I sent it to Baxter with god magic.

Ignis owed me this much.

"Go directly to Scarlett," I told him, past the lump in my throat. "Tell her everything. Ignis is going to remove the god magic so Tontes can't use me against Alkarra. Take Ava. They have to know what to prepare for."

Wind gusted by. An aggressive attempt meant to shatter the glass.

"Not without you!" he cried.

Tears filled my eyes.

"You must or we lose all of Alkarra. Now!"

A landslide of falling ice punctuated the command, skittering across the dark ground between us. Gelas created a wall that rose, separating me from Baxter and Ava. As they disappeared behind the ice, Baxter stared at me, soul in his eyes. He took one glance at Ava, her wide eyes staring around, shoulders trembling, then back to me.

"Survive this!" he yelled.

Gelas's voice echoed in command as they disappeared.

Go!

"Tell Papa I'm sorry." My voice cracked. "I'm so sorry."

A stricken, horrified expression crossed Baxter's face, but Ava let out a scream when hurricane-force winds knocked a floe of ice onto the ground. Half a glacier plunged toward them. The two of them left. Relief and terror flowed through me at the same time. If I truly faced my death, at least I did it by my choice, on behalf of loyalty to my goddess, my forest.

My *self*.

I stood before death knowing exactly who I was.

"Take it, Ignis," I whispered. "I'm ready."

Power built up in my body. Heat. Flame. Burning. I drew in a deep breath, but the intensity grew hotter than it had ever been. The pains of hellfire assaulted me.

Lady-witch of Alkarra, Ignis murmured in a fading whisper, *I will mourn the loss of you.*

The heat overcame me in the next breath. Magic bled free, gushing like a severed artery. I smoldered from the inside out.

Air escaped, wouldn't return.

Ignis! Ventis cried. *Don't!*

My mouth became ash. I breathed heat. A torrid fever ripped through my soul, as if all the sinews in my body had been uprooted.

I gasped for air.

Flames came instead.

Fire, fire, fire.

I choked on the pain. My knees slammed into the ground. My shoulders bowed under the ferocious agony. The air thickened with smoke in my lungs. The scent of char filled my nostrils. The goddess magic reared up, whirling.

Frightened?

God magic left, draining away.

Taking my life with it.

With the last gasp of air, I looked up. Ignis peered at me from the other side of the dome, face twisted in anguish. A shimmering cloud, like millions of miniature embers, flowed between us in glittering whorls. It moved to him, escaping me.

Unable to hold myself up, I collapsed. A spray of embers swirled around me. The world blurred. Screams rang in the hollows of ice.

Pain followed, tearing, wreaking, churning. Magic separated itself from my being. My chest. My body. Everything rebelled as god magic dissipated. Embers swirled out of my nose, my mouth, whisked away with my breath. They danced into the night, billowing away in sparkling fire plumes.

The last of the magic ripped out of me.

I fell into cold darkness.

The sound of someone shouting my name followed. Baxter. Arms wrapped around my shoulders. My body went limp, airborne. A sharp bark from Gelas faded in the back of my mind.

Take her back to Alkarra. Now! If she dies, all is lost.

The world turned to black.

Too cold.

Encroaching, encompassing frigidity.

All heat had been taken, extracted mercilessly. I couldn't stand the pain. My lungs emptied. Thick waves dragged me down.

Into the cold.

Frozen.

Darkness.

Chapter Twenty-Six

Quiet.

A thick gauziness.

There was no pain, no fire. Only a sense of firm ground beneath my feet, and warmth. No ice. No agony.

Sensing light ahead, I turned. A vague glow filled the space, ethereal. I reached out to nothing at first. Then my fingers touched something thick. A curtain of silky material, a firmer barrier than it should be. It separated me from the light on the other side. A shiver extended into the void depths of my soul.

No pain, but no wholeness either.

The light grew, strengthening. It moved, shifted. The pain of god magic being extracted from my body had bled away. No breath or beating heart remained. I pressed my hands to my chest, but nothing lingered inside.

Instead of panic, peace.

Though I couldn't see her, I sensed Mama. The smell of cloves, a comforting fragrance, spun by. Such otherworldly calm. Such quiet. A bright fissure of light, like a peal of laughter. Camille, it had to be. My best friend who had died in the battle of Chatham Castle. I stood in an in-between, somewhere else. The passage of life into death.

Not here, not there.

"Mama?"

Whispers. So many voices at a distance. Giddiness. Depth. Joy and hope.

Growing luminescence.

Shadows behind me and light ahead, a bright disparity between the worlds. In the darkness beyond my shoulder, faint rumblings. Stirrings. I heard voices at my back, too far away to distinguish. There, I sensed panic. Fear. Desperation. Movement.

Ahead, peace. Calm.

Mama.

Grandmother Hazel.

Mildred.

Camille.

A mild voice pierced the silence in a way that seeped into my soul. Like the forest, it infused me, different and familiar at the same time.

A witch in her power is a magical thing. You have done well, Bianca Monroe. Your loyalty is noted.

Emotion welled inside of me like a gauzy vapor. Gentle. Clement, yet powerful. I wanted to lean into the words, the sensation. In the aftermath of swelling gods, violent betrayal, impending death, the tranquility lay like a balm on my puckered, burned soul.

"Deasylva."

You gave your life to save Alkarra, Deasylva murmured. I sensed that the light behind the curtain was her. *You gave your life in allegiance to me.*

"And myself."

A smile filled her voice. *A powerful truth. Are you ready for the next step? You are in the in-between. You may move ahead to the lands and lives that await, or you may return to that life which awaits. In honor of loyalty and love and our unbroken connection, I give the choice to you.*

Could I leave Papa, Leda, Merrick, and Marten? Gain Mama. Mildred. Grandmother Hazel. *Camille.* Oh, Camille. The thought of her brought a half-sob, half-laugh to my lips. The conversations we'd have!

The things that waited compelled me closer to the light. Answers to those undying questions that resounded in my deepest soul. My heart drew out with the thought of seeing my loved ones again.

The lands and lives ahead . . .

. . . would still be there later.

Much later.

When I returned for good.

"Alkarra," I whispered. "I want to go back."

Pain awaits you in Alkarra, she said gently. *Struggle. The difficulty of survival, trust, and heartbreak.*

"I know."

Affection flooded her voice, bathing me in it. I felt embraced, buoyed.

And oh, what a beautiful fight it is, she breathed. *Go to your witches, Bianca. There are battles yet to face, and lives yet to live, waiting for you there. You know where to look, should you need me. Trust yourself.*

I hesitated, reaching for the veil between us. The light had dimmed. The whispers behind me grown more loud, more frantic. Panic returned to my chest. My lungs tingled, burning in the recesses. Life pulled me back, a morsel of agony at a time.

My fingers skimmed the gauzy, ethereal fabric.

"Mama," I whispered.

Her voice flooded me with love. *What a beautiful life,* Mama whispered, *you still have, my darling. You are brave. You're so strong. You can do anything.*

Tears filled my eyes, and they hurt. The light faded. Darkness ebbed back into torment. Sounds strengthened. Sensations. Hands on my arms. Liquid in my mouth. I no longer stood, but lay down. Everything had gone black, or I lacked the power to open my eyes.

Now, all I knew was the pain.

My seared throat felt like grating sandpaper on an open wound. Each raspy breath sent agony through me. Renewed affliction activated with each attempt to breathe. The world smelled like smoke. My heart beat frantically. I wanted to scream. Speak. Beg someone to make it stop.

Tears trickled out of my eyes.

"Give her something for pain," someone demanded. The voice drifted through my ears, burrowing into the back of my mind.

Leda, was it? Why was Leda here?

Where was I?

Marten's gentle voice replied, "She won't swallow if she's not awake. We'll have to wait until we know if she can. She's burned from the inside out. Her throat may not be working. We don't know the extent of damage to her lungs. Or . . . "

He trailed away.

Weakness pervaded me. I wanted to speak. To reach for them, but I could no more communicate than make the pain stop. My eyes wouldn't open. My breath wouldn't come. I didn't know how to live again.

My chest bucked with each desperate attempt to breathe. Emptiness filled me. Cold. The warmth of god magic that had been part of me for months now ceased to exist. In its place, ruin.

Razed destruction.

"Where's the apothecary?" Leda barked.

Baxter replied, his voice a low growl. "They won't be able to save her. I'm . . . trying. The god magic isn't working. It won't heal her. I don't think . . . I don't think it works on her now."

He grunted, as if strained.

"Do your best, Baxter," Marten said quietly. "Counter whatever withdrawal of magic you can, if such a thing is possible."

A pause.

"Ignis says she needs goddess magic," Baxter replied. "I cannot fix this with his magic."

"You want me to just summon a goddess?" Leda snapped, her voice equally harsh and shrill. "You brought her back like this because of *your* gods, *you* fix it with god magic or tell Ignis to get it together!"

"I'm trying!" Baxter snapped. "It's not working. We don't . . . we don't know what this means or how to fix it. This has never happened before."

Another voice piped up from somewhere farther away, as if they stood apart from me.

"Where is Derek? If she's not going to make it, he needs to be here."

Scarlett.

A low burr replied. Merrick. My heart raced at the sound of his voice. "I know where he is."

The denizen of voices speaking back and forth became a confusing blur. The only anchor was the pain. I lived for the space between breaths, when misery didn't flare with such white-hot ferocity. When the agony, for a moment, suspended enough to keep me from succumbing back to the darkness.

Like a looming chasm, the darkness waited. It held me close, beckoning me, trying to pull me into its fathomless depths yet again. A hand pressed on my forehead. Warm. Heavy. Marten's voice followed, speaking a gentle healing blessing. I felt nothing. It didn't work.

Amidst the darkness came a tendril.

Light.

Life.

A reprieve.

Whispers soothed me, coming from back. Far back. So quiet at first I couldn't hear them. When I turned my mind to their sound, I knew them right away. The moment I acknowledged them, they expanded and brightened.

She always comes back.

You belong to us.

The darkness will not win.

We save ours.

Something tugged on me. A gentle feeling near my wrist, like a ribbon drawing around it. The touch felt cool, countering the charred depth. Like a soothing balm, drawn along my aching veins. Another tug, near my other arm.

The edge of the agony receded. The dark pain paused its hungry attempt to consume me. Light burst into my body, easing the burn. I leaned into it. The voices strengthened.

She always comes back.

You belong to us.

The darkness abates.

We save ours.

The song of the trees hummed through my blood, slipping through and around. I thrilled to their voices, my heart a bright staccato leaping again. My throat calmed. Magic pushed against the edges of my skin, as if it would burst out given the opportunity.

The ribbon-like sensation wound up my arm, sliding around my shoulders. It headed toward my chest, slipped underneath my back. Another ribbon slipped up my other arm, closing the embrace on top of my heart.

The burn eased. My breath slipped freely by, without pain. Healing light filled me from the inside.

She always comes back.

You belong to us.

The darkness has fallen.
We save ours.
"Silence!"

The command came from Marten. The room quieted at once. In the following calm, the chant of the trees strengthened. It braced me, healing the broken parts. The pain dissipated. The wretched horror turned to a simmering discomfort. Thoughts formed more easily, less fragmented. All the hurting places settled.

I belong to you, I whispered in my mind.

A thrill of joy ran through their voices, brightening them.

She has returned.

She always comes back.

We save ours.

My heart slowed. I stared back at death, the dark chasm, and turned my back to it with relief. Gratitude.

Not today.

Not now.

I, I whispered to the trees, *am yours. I always come back. You are mine. We save each other.*

The last tendrils of pain slipped away. My hearing sharpened, my fingertips tingled, my body hummed.

I opened my eyes.

$$The\ Returning$$

As I wrote THE FORGOTTEN GODS, I also wrote the final book, WAR OF THE GODS, because I wanted as seamless and steady a transition between the two books as possible.

Welp, turns out *a lot* happens in THE FORGOTTEN GODS.

Within weeks, I realized that I needed to have a *different* book that bridged the gap between book seven and eight. Tying all of these things together dominated the plot of WAR OF THE GODS.

That didn't work either.

To that end, I have a surprise.

THE RETURNING is a novella that takes place immediately after THE FORGOTTEN GODS. It is the desired wrap-up for this story. I haven't publicized it or told anyone about it (except that I have a secret novella in the works) because I didn't want to create any potential spoilers with the titles.

THE RETURNING goes day-by-day as Bianca heals and returns from Alaysia. As you know, *lots happened over there*, but *lots also happened in Alkarra*. This novella bridges that gap and weaves it all together.

Also . . . Merrick.

#Imjustsayin.

AND . . . it's available to read right now.

The only place to purchase THE RETURNING is from my website. **Please visit www.katiecrossbooks.com** to grab your copy in ebook, paperback, or audiobook.

Get the dish on what Bianca's recovery looks like, her reunion with her forest, with Merrick, with Leda, with Papa, and #alltheothers in THE RETURNING.

Trust me.

You *don't* want to miss this.

—Katie Cross

Acknowledgments

I've attempted to write this several times, and every time, found that I had no words to explain what it was like to write this book.

Good grief.

Whatta ride.

First of all THE FORGOTTEN GODS really pushed my limits. It taught me that I can, in fact, write for six hours with only a few breaks for sanity. That I can dream up 10,000 words every day because, frankly, the ideas wouldn't stop. That I can break through barriers and find my own newly honed abilities and depth of power and purpose.

And isn't that just perfect?

Without my team, this book would never have hit your hands. Sam, Mike, Kaley, Kelsey, Kerri, Gemma, Evan, Brandy, Darcee, Louise, and Jenn-ay, you help me do epic things in fantasy literature, and I can't imagine what life would be like without you.

Thank you.

My family, who inspires me to greater magic and passion every day. I love and adore all of you to my utmost being. Thank you for the power you give to me.

Finally, to the most important of all, my readers. This wild ride is nothing without you. Seeing you on our weekly Coffee With Katie calls, imbuing the amazing vibes that you put into the world, keeps me on my toes. I adore you all and love the family we've created.

Now, who is ready for WAR OF THE GODS?!

—Katie

Join Other Witches

Merry meet!

There is more epic magic and wild places waiting for you.

If you want to stay in-the-know about new releases, get awesome discounts (IE—more books, less money), and have free novels and short stories land in your lap, I've got your back.

Go to www.katiecrossbooks.com to join the other witches on my email list, where you get exclusive, can't-find-anywhere-else kind of stuff.

(In fact, I'll send you some free stories right away—first email!)

Or you can go to The Witchery, which is my Facebook group of other readers just like you. Please visit www.facebook.com/groups/thenetworkseries to learn more!

There, you'll see more images of Alkarra, join all your witchy friends, and go to lunch with me on my weekly Coffee With Katie calls.

(No, seriously. I will Uber-Eats you lunch!)

Can't wait to see you there!

—Katie

Also by Katie Cross

The Dragonmaster Trilogy

FLAME

Chronicles of the Dragonmasters (short story collection)

FLIGHT

The Ronan Scrolls (novella)

FREEDOM

The Dragonmaster Trilogy Collection

The Network Series

Mildred's Resistance (prequel)

Miss Mabel's School for Girls

Alkarra Awakening

The High Priest's Daughter

War of the Networks

The Network Series Complete Collection

The Isadora Interviews (novella)

Short Stories from Miss Mabel's

Short Stories from the Network Series

Hazel (short story)

The Network Saga Suggested Reading Order

1. The Parting (novella #1)

Katie Cross is ALL ABOUT writing epic magic and wild places. Creating new fantasy worlds is her jam.

When she's not hiking or chasing her two littles through the Montana mountains, you can find her curled up reading a book or arguing with her husband over the best kind of sushi.

Visit her at www.katiecrossbooks.com for free short stories, extra savings on all her books (and some you can't buy on the retailers), and so much more.